Praise for E

"...Haviaras handles it all with smooth skill. The world of third-century Rome—both the city and its African outposts—is colorfully vivid here, and Haviaras manages to invest even his secondary and tertiary characters with believable, three-dimensional humanity." *Historic Novel Society*

"I would add this author to some of the great historical writers such as Conn Iggulden, Simon Scarrow and David Gemmell. The characters were described in such a way that it was easy to picture them as if they were real and have lived in the past, the book flowed with an ease that any reader, novice to advanced can enjoy and become fully immersed..." *Amazon reader*

"... a very entertaining read; Haviaras has both a fluid writing style, and a good eye for historical detail, and explores in far more detail the faith of the average Roman than do most authors." *Goodreads*

"Historical fiction at its best! ... if you like your historical fiction to be an education as well as a fun read, this is the book for you!" *Amazon reader*

"An outstanding and compelling novel!" *Amazon reader*

A Dragon among the Eagles

A Novel of the Roman Empire

Adam Alexander Haviaras

Join the Legions!

Sign-up for the Eagles and Dragons Publishing
Newsletter and get a FREE BOOK today.

Subscribers get first access to new releases,
special offers, and much more.

Go to:
www.eaglesanddragonspublishing.com

This book is dedicated to the troops of various countries,
Those who have risked, and are risking their lives
To keep our world safe and civilized against the odds.

Part I

Rome

A.D. 197

I

Martis Populus

'The People of Mars'

A.D. 197

They came from all over Italy to join Rome's legions. War was in the air again, and so was opportunity for every young man willing to wear the red cloak of Mars. The hopeful, the bankrupt, the disinherited and destitute - all of them wanted the opportunity to make something of themselves.

When the call went out that Emperor Septimius Severus, fresh from his victories in the recent civil war, was heading east to take on the Parthian Empire, young men began to flow down the roads leading to Rome like spring runoff out of the mountains.

All of these now stood in clusters on the sands of the Stadium of Domitian on the Campus Martius, watching, taking the measure of the men around them as they added their name to the rolls and took up wooden gladii so that the recruiting centurions could judge who was fit for fighting.

Lucius Metellus Anguis, a local nineteen year old, approached the table where a burly centurion and his optio manned one of the many tables.

They eyed him as he approached, the centurion's horizontal crest waving stiffly like an angry boar's bristles.

"Name?" the centurion barked.

"Lucius Metellus Anguis, of Rome."

There was a snigger from somewhere, which stopped when Lucius turned to look at the man who had mocked his name.

"I didn't know anyone from that decrepit old family still lived," the thick muscled, blond northerner said. Some men about him laughed. "Wasn't Caecilia Metella the dictator Sulla's whore hound?"

Lucius turned to stare at the man who stared back without hesitation. Because of his height, handsome profile and size, Lucius was always a target for ruffians who wanted to prove themselves. He was used to it, but still hated it.

"Shut-up back there!" the centurion ordered, standing up.

"Argus, no!" Lucius said to his foster-brother who was in line behind him, and who was about to break the line to take care of the commenter. "Let him be."

Argus returned to the line, the centurion's gaze washing over him in a challenge.

"Sign here!" the optio said, giving Lucius a stylus and indicating the papyrus scroll where he had added Lucius' name.

Lucius bent over the table and signed. *There, it's done.*

Of course, the army would never turn anyone away, especially after so many had died in the civil war, but Lucius knew that he had to show what he was made of next. He looked out at the area where pairs of new recruits were thrusting and slashing clumsily at each other like gladiator clowns in a tavern brawl.

"Pick up a rudus and stand over there!" the centurion ordered as Argus came up beside Lucius, having just signed his own name.

The two young men went to a rack and each picked up a heavy practice gladius.

"Remember what we practiced," Lucius said. "Let's give them a good show, but it still has to look real."

"I won't hit you too hard," Argus laughed. "Just enough to bruise your Equestrian pride."

They waited for the current bout to finish, one of the men being picked up off the ground and led to a bench where the losers sat in shame.

"Metellus!" another centurion called out. "Get out here!"

Lucius stepped forward, shrugging his shoulders and twirling the wooden gladius to get a feel for it's weight.

"Argus!" the centurion called out next.

"Wait!" the centurion at the table interrupted. "Not him. That one!" he said, pointing to the big northerner who had made fun of Lucius in the lineup.

The northerner grinned as he stomped over to get his rudus from the rack and strode out to face Lucius. "I'm going to hit you so hard, Metellus, you won't even remember today. You're going to end up in the kitchens."

"Shut up, Bona!" the centurion said. "Show us what each of you have."

Lucius glanced at Argus who nodded, and then turned to face Bona. The man was about the same height as himself, more thickly muscled, perhaps a former smith. He knew that if he got in the way of one of his full-force swings, he would be in trouble. Lucius stepped to one side, then the other, feeling light on his feet, ready to move quickly.

"Begin!" Bona launched himself at Lucius with a roar that was echoed by the men in the line-up. He sped by Lucius with a cutting blow that would have snapped Lucius' neck, but the younger man stepped beneath the blade and behind the larger one, kicking him in the back so that he fell forward into the dirt.

"Don't let him take a breath!" Argus yelled, but Lucius stood still, calming himself, allowing the other man to get up.

"Come on coward! After this, I'm going to fuck your corpse!" Bona hissed, coming at Lucius a second time with a thrust that caught Lucius' ribs. Lucius held his side where he had felt a crack and pain run through him. His short dark hair was now drenched in sweat. Bona laughed and turned to the line to rally his friends into acclamations, then turned back to Lucius for a third attack. However before he got two steps, Lucius' blade had numbed his left forearm, and swept his knee so that he went down. The laughter stopped as Bona stood again.

Lucius focussed on his opponent, struggling to ignore the burning in his side. He feinted a couple times to see how Bona would react. Quickly enough.

"What are you waiting for, puppy? If you want to be a man of the legions, that thin purple stripe on your tunic isn't going to save you!" Even as he finished taunting, he was rushing Lucius, swatting the wooden blade aside with a hammy fist and wrapping his arms around Lucius from behind as though he were rustling a bull from his herd.

Lucius felt pain lascerating his side, and smelled the stink of raw garlic from behind his ear. He could hear Argus cursing on the sideline, and feel the mocking expressions of those watching.

Then he went limp for a moment. Bona eased his grip a little, and then Lucius slammed his head backward to crush the man's nose.

Bona howled in pain, and released Lucius. The latter rolled away to grab his rudus and limped back to where the northerner was busy catching blood in his cupped hands.

"Who will be assigned to the kitchens now, pig?" Lucius said as he brought up his rudus to slam into the side of Bona's head.

Dazed, the big man swung his red fist, but Lucius dodged it, then landed his own fist into the man's nose once more, sending him unconscious to the sand of the stadium.

Lucius wavered there for a moment, and stared at the men in the line-up.

"Anyone else want to mock my name?"

No one answered except the centurion who had signed him in.

"Come here, Metellus!" the centurion ordered.

"He didn't do anything the bastard didn't deserve!" Argus protested.

The centurion ignored him and looked Lucius up and down as he approached. His arms were crossed, roped with muscles and painted with scars. On his chest harness were at least a dozen decorations for bravery on campaigns Lucius could only imagine.

The young Roman knew this would not be a man to cross, and from the way he held his vinerod, and the marks along its length, it would not be a good idea.

"Yes, centurion..."

"Never mind my name. What was that?"

"Sir?"

"You let him rile you. You dropped your sword and let him get close enough to pick you up." The centurion shook his head as he glanced at Argus pommelling his opponent into the dirt.

"But I beat him, didn't I?" Lucius protested.

"Yes, but you near became useless yourself. If one of that bastard's fists had connected with you, you'd have been done for."

"Yes, sir." Lucius hated it, the humiliation, the blame, as if he had lost the bout.

"But you handled yourself well enough. You have speed, and patience. That's good." The centurion did not smile, but his voice did change. "I'm going to be wanting you in my century when we march east, Metellus. I don't give a damn about your name, or your Equestrian status. The fact that you're not pulling family strings to get a higher rank tells me enough. I'll take him too." The centurion nodded his head backward as Argus' man fell once more with a thud in the clotted sand.

"Yes, sir." Lucius smiled slightly.

"Don't be smiling yet, boy. You won't thank me for it when we're facing down a Parthian cavalry charge in the desert in high summer. For now, get yourself to the medicus at the other end of the stadium. He'll patch you up and tell you how to care for those ribs. I want you fit for training."

"When do we report, sir?" Lucius asked as Argus joined them, barely breathing heavily.

"I want you here in two weeks. We'll be drilling, marching, and learning to fight like Romans. So rest up and I'll see you back here, rain or shine."

"Who do we ask for then, sir?" Lucius asked.

"Decimus. That's me. Centurion in the new III Parthica Legion. From this day on, I own you boys." He looked directly at Argus then and said, "I'll be watching you closely, Argus. I see you can fight, but there's more than bloodying your fists on someone's face that makes you a soldier."

"Yes...sir," Argus said slowly. "Got it."

"Good. Now, get out of here before that northerner wakes up."

Decimus turned and walked away without another word, as Lucius and Argus watched Bona being roused on the bench of wounded men.

The northerner's eyes searched for Lucius and when he saw him, he spat in Lucius' direction.

Lucius ignored him, smiled, and walked out of the stadium with Argus, forgetting to visit the medicus on his way.

The two young men were wrapped in cloaks of elation as they walked from the Stadium of Domitian, past the Baths of Nero and Agrippa.

"I think we made an impression," Argus laughed. "Did you see what I did to that other guy? I don't think they'll accept him now."

"I'm not sure crippling the other recruits was what they had in mind," Lucius said a bit sheepishly. He knew what he had done to Bona.

"Don't start feeling guilty for what you did to that bastard! Everytime someone messes with you in the baths or in the ring at the palaestra, you torture yourself over right and wrong." Argus stopped and held Lucius fast. "He deserved it! Get over yourself."

"Did your guy deserve what you gave him?"

"Yes, as a matter of fact. He did. He was Bona's friend from the pig fields up north, and he was muttering curses at you while you were fighting. I showed him the way of it."

Lucius stared at Argus a moment, trying to figure out his foster brother. They had been the best of friends for years, their families close. Ever since Argus' parents had been murdered, he had lived with the Metelli. He and Lucius had done everything together, drinking, gambling, going to the Circus for the chariot races and the Colosseum for the games. They'd even headed to the brothels for the first time together.

The two young men were close, but still there were times when Lucius could not quite understand Argus' reasoning. Still, when he was in the thick of a brawl, he did not want anyone else but Argus at his back.

Lucius smiled broadly and slapped Argus upside the head.

"You're a real bastard, you know that?" Lucius laughed.

Argus did not smile, but pushed Lucius playfully into a fruitseller's stall, making him topple a display of blood oranges before he ran off.

Lucius followed, laughing as he chased Argus down, with the fruitseller's curses echoing in the narrow stone-flagged street. They ran fast, dodging in and out of the milling crowds in the street of the cloth merchants until Argus stopped abruptly in front of The Nymph and Satyr taberna.

"Come on, I'll buy you a victory drink." Argus beamed. "We did it, Lucius! We fucking did it! Let's celebrate. I'll buy the drinks, you buy the whores."

Lucius paused a moment, looking into the tavern where several people, including some off-duty Praetorians, were sitting at wooden tables with clay pitchers of watered wine.

"I can't right now," Lucius said.

"Why not? We've been waiting for this day for years, Lucius. If not now, when?" Argus crossed his thick arms, his black hair sticking to his sweaty brow, his dark eyes staring at Lucius. "Your gods can wait for once."

"No, Argus. It's because of them that we have succeeded in this."

"No, it's because of all our hard work and training that we succeeded."

"Listen, I'll see you at home, ok? I'm going to the temple to make an offering and think for a while."

"Fine." Argus turned and went down another street. "I'll be in the Subura drinking shit!" he called over his shoulder.

Lucius sighed and watched Argus go. He knew he would cool off after a few pitchers of the vinegar they served in the seedier taverns of the Subura. Argus would come home after visiting another brothel, vomit, and fall asleep in his cubiculum until midday.

Lucius looked up at the blue sky where the sun shone above Rome. The weather had been mild and bright for days now. His spirits were high. When he spotted a blackbird flying in the direction of the Palatine Hill, he took it as a sign that he had made the right decision.

"I'm coming," he said, and set off around the base of the Capitoline Hill to cut through the Forum Romanum. It always did help him to focus, seeing the monuments that his ancestors had erected at the heart of the Empire. The Metelli had helped to build the Empire, and he longed to put his name alongside theirs in the records of the Roman people.

Lucius had often been told stories of his great ancestors, and all that they had accomplished in the days of the Republic. His father never let him forget those long ago days of Republican honour.

The Metelli were one of the oldest families in Rome. They had lived, not in the neighbourhood where his family lived now, near the stink of the Forum Boarium, but atop the Palatine Hill, where only the greatest of Rome's citizens had kept their households.

Metelli had thrived in the Senate, and on the battlefield. They had been victorious in the wars against mighty Carthage, and subsequently held the post of Pontifex Maximus and Dictator. In fact, many of Lucius' ancestors had been great warriors, and it had fallen to them often to lead Rome in war. There was Dalmaticus who conquered Dalmatia, and Macedonicus who put an end to the rebellion in the former lands of Alexander the Great. Another was Numidicus, a politician and general who waged a successful campaign against Jugurtha of Numidia. And then there was Creticus, a praetor, who had defeated and pacified the pirates plaguing the island of Crete.

The Imagines of so many great men lined the current halls of the Metellus domus that Lucius found it hard to ever forget they were there, watching from the other side of the black

10

river, waiting to see what he would do. Lucius saw the day he had joined the Legions as his first act in showing his ancestors that he was in fact worthy of their name.

Then there was the other name, Anguis, the cognomen of his branch of the Metelli. It had always been mysterious to him, unnerving. His father hated the name and had abondoned it himself, opting for Caecilius through some thinly veiled connection. It was only because of Lucius' grandfather that he had been given the family name of Anguis, or Dragon. Legend had it that the name had been given to one of the Metelli on the eve before the battle of Zama in which Lucius' ancestor had fought alongside Scipio Africanus against Hannibal.

The reach and expectation of those long-ago ancestors still had a grip on his family, and guided Lucius' decisions, almost as much as the guidance of the Gods.

Lucius' father however, Quintus Caecilus Metellus, had different ideas to Lucius, different wants for his son's future and the path he would take to get there. Lucius knew that he would have to face down his father about what he achieved that day.

As he stepped into the familiar square before the Temple of Palatine Apollo, he set those thoughts aside. This was where his heart truly lay. As he mounted the white marble steps beneath the towering columns and temple pediment, he took a deep breath of the familiar scents of jasmine and orange blossoms. Peacocks wailed in the nearby gardens of the Palace of Augustus, carried on the breeze that wrapped itself about the Palatine.

Lucius stared a moment at the great bronze doors of the temple, through which he had passed many times. Then he

11

went inside, disappearing into the welcoming smoke of incense and offering.

The temple was dark with just a few rays of light angling their way in through the small upper windows of the temple, lighting a path down the aisle to the statue of Apollo surrounded by the Muses. As ever, the statue seemed to beckon to Lucius who walked toward the altar that was flanked by two tall, flaming bronze braziers.

Lucius reached into the small satchel he had over his shoulder and pulled out a fresh branch of rosemary and laurel which he laid on the altar. He felt his ribs pulsing and wished for a moment that he had seen the medicus before leaving the stadium, but he dismissed the thought and raised his palms up to Apollo, the patron god of the Anguis branch of the Metelli.

"Far-shooting Apollo, I thank you for giving me the strength to achieve success today, for lighting the path before me as you always have done." Lucius paused a moment as he heard one of the priests' footsteps come to a halt nearby. The flames of the brazier flickered and smoked as the priest threw three handfulls of incense on them, filling the air with the strong tang of frankincense and cedar. Lucius continued.

"Apollo, now that I have achieved this first step, I feel fear creeping into my veins like a poison. Please continue to watch over me, to guide me. Let me do honour to my family and my ancestors who have worshipped you since the beginning of our line. Help me to serve Rome and the Empire to the best of my ability, to excel above all others in war, and skill, and wisdom, and to be a man of honour, always." Lucius looked up, his eyes burning with the threat of tears, just as if he were a boy once again, scared of the threat of his father's fist for defying him. He took a deep breath and exhaled slowly, calm again.

The god and his muses seemed to stare down at Lucius, encouraging him, sympathetic to him. So many times, Lucius remembered Apollo appearing to him over the years, in omens and apparitions, those things he did not dare speak of in front of any but his sister, Alene.

"I will not fail you, mighty Apollo. Your favour will not be misplaced as I step into the world beyond the walls of Rome." He raised his palms higher and closed his eyes. "Accept my humble offering..."

When Lucius opened his eyes, the light from the high windows had moved several feet and the priest of Apollo stood nearby, smiling at the young man he had welcomed into the temple for many years.

"You are bleeding, young Metellus," the priest said, pointing at Lucius side where his tunic was purple and red.

Lucius looked down and felt his ribs. "An injury from the Field of Mars."

"Apollo is also a god of healing. You should heal yourself that you may better fulfill the vows you make." The old man smiled kindly, his white beard waving as the temple doors opened and a cool breeze wafted up the aisle.

"I'll go now," Lucius answered, bowing to the priest. "Before the legions march, I'll be back with a small goat and scented oil in offering."

"Apollo will be pleased," the priest said as he joined Lucius in walking to the main doors and sunlight outside. "I expected to see you today."

"Oh?"

"Your eagles have been circling in the sky above the temple all day, glorying in Apollo's light." The priest stopped at the top of the stairs and pointed into the sky. "See?"

Lucius looked up and saw the two shapes outlined against the sun, their cries falling over the city as though from the heights of Olympus. He smiled and felt for the eagle feather wrapped in linen beneath his tunic. He remembered the day the eagle had landed beside him, early one morning when he had left the domus without permission, drawn to the temple square. The eagle had left the token for him and Lucius had kept it ever since, a reminder of Apollo's favour.

"Today is propitious," the priest said, his hand on Lucius' shoulder. "As your old tutor, Diodorus, would say, 'Be mindful of the world about you, for the Gods speak to the fortunate through the world around them.'"

"Yes," Lucius laughed. "I do believe Diodorus said that. In fact he did, many a time."

"Go now. Get yourself to the baths and a medicus before going home." The priest's face grew serious. "Your father will need to know your plans."

Lucius nodded and descended the steps slowly, making his way back down to the Forum Romanum and the Baths of Agrippa. He needed to think. He needed to plan what he would say to his father before he could return to the Metellus domus.

II

Provocatio

'Defiance'

In the dusk light, Rome was yet alive, her arteries flowing with life. Crowds poured out of the Circus Maximus, and the Colosseum to head to the various baths to clean the day's grime from their pores. After that, the tabernae and theatres of the city would come to life.

Lucius stepped into the street from the main entrance of the Baths of Agrippa and scanned the line of theatre goers outside of the Theatre of Pompey. Vendors and beggars walked along the line of Romans who waited, pushing their wares or thrusting grubby hands into people's faces, only to be pushed away by burly slaves and angry senators. Lucius wondered whether any city in the world was as vibrant and lively as Rome.

"Excuse me!" someone said as they bumped Lucius going into the baths.

Lucius immediately checked his satchel to make sure all was still there and winced at the pain. The medicus in the baths had checked him over, assuring him that the break was very small, that his muscles had protected him from the brunt of the impact. He had bandaged Lucius' ribs tightly and told him to not strain himself for several days in order to allow the fracture to begin mending.

"And make an offering to Asclepius too," the medicus had said as Lucius dropped a sestertius into his hand.

Lucius now thought about trying to find Argus and have that drink, but he knew he was only trying to delay the inevitable. Besides, Argus would be impossible to find in the Suburan whorehouses among the groaning and grunting press of dirty flesh. So, Lucius decided to head for the Forum Boarium and home.

As he walked, he reviewed the points he wanted to cover when he defended his decision to his father, speaking under his breath as he went.

"Father, I've enlisted in the legions, I've been accepted." Lucius walked slowly as he practiced, the smell of the cattle markets of the Forum Boarium wafting into his nostrils. He had known that smell all his life, and soon would be experiencing new ones. "I want to see the world, Father. I want to serve the Empire the best way I can. Following the Cursus Honorem is not as important anymore. This is a new world, and I have no wish to be involved in politics. There are new opportunities for Equestrians that there never were before. I can do this, I know I can," the latter more to himself as he stopped before the round temple of Hercules in the Forum Boarium.

"Hercules, grant me the strength to stand up to him." Lucius dropped a coin in the cup a priest at the door was holding out to passers by. Lucius thought of Hercules, travelling the world for his twelve labours, the things he must have seen and experienced...

He could delay no longer. He walked away from the Forum Boarium, up the street that led to the Circus Maximus, and came to a stop outside the crimson door of the Metellus domus with the dragon-shaped knocker on the outside. He knocked and waited for their slave, Junius to answer.

After a minute the bolt slid back and Junius' grey hair peeped through the crack in the door.

"Master Lucius!" The old man bowed and opened the door. "You've been gone so long. Your parents have been worried.

"I've been taking care of some important business. Is Argus back yet?"

"No, master. He has not returned."

"No, I don't expect he will for some time yet," Lucius said, relieved that he was not there to interrupt him in his task. "And my father?"

"He is engaged in the ironing out of a great deal with one of the olive merchants from Gaul in the tablinum. He said he is not to be disturbed."

"No, of course not. I'll wait," Lucius said. He knew that when it came to trading the precious olives and grapes from their Etrurian estate, his father was just as serious as if he were defending the right of the Republic in the Senate house.

"Mistress Antonia is reading to young master Quintus and Mistress Clarinda in their cubiculum if you would like to see her. And Mistress Alene has gone to the lady Claudia's house to see her daughter who is visiting from Aquileia."

"Thank you, Junius. Is there food?"

"They have already eaten, but I have placed some wine, bread, and meat in your cubiculum for you."

"You needn't do that, Junius. I'm quite capable of getting myself to the kitchen for my own food." Lucius had never liked having slaves wait on him, and now that Junius was so old, he was finding it even harder when the old man laboured for him.

"It's no bother, Master Lucius. Besides, the master wanted me to bring him and his guest some food as well, to help their negotiations."

"Olives, cheese and oil from the estate no doubt?"

"What else?" the old man chuckled.

"Please let me know when the merchant leaves, will you?"

"Yes, master."

Lucius left the atrium where he had come in, and walked past the mosaic pool there, still and reflecting the last light of day that came in through the open roof. He noticed the paint peeling on the plaster along the walls as he went, but his eyes were drawn, as ever, to the marble busts of the Metelli ancestors that lined the corridor that led past his father's tablinum, and on to the peristyle garden and the stairs that went to the second level.

The garden birds had grown quiet and the first of the crickets had started to chirrup among the trimmed shrubs and trees surrounding the mosaic seating area where two couches were set out with blankets to ward off the evening chill. Before going upstairs, Lucius glanced into the triclinium to see that the dinner had already been cleared and the braziers had been put out.

I've been gone longer than I thought. He mounted the staircase, trying to get used to the new pain in his side, his body sore, but his spirits so high, despite the nervous energy that was pooling in his gut.

Lucius turned right at the top of the stairs and followed a gentle voice that emanated from the cubiculum of his younger brother and sister.

"...and so the greedy raven took the jewels, and because he had so many in his mouth, he dropped them all and was left with nothing."

From the doorway, Lucius watched as his mother finished telling the story to young Quintus and Clarinda, who were both curled up asleep in their beds, their mother sitting on a backless chair between them, a single oil lamp burning on a pedestal table nearby.

Antonia Metella stroked her children's hair slowly, lulling them to sleep, humming sofly and whispering to them that she loved them.

Lucius realized then how very little they were, and how little he had paid attention to them since they were born, Clarinda having come just two years before.

"I remember you telling me the fables of Aesop. Do they like them?" Lucius asked in a low voice from the doorway.

"They love them, as you did so long ago," Antonia said, rising from the chair and kissing each of the children. She walked over to Lucius, and turned to look about the room, as if to reassure herself that all was safe and secure.

Antonia Metella was younger than her husband, her hair still long and dark, though in recent years grey had started to infiltrate her tresses which she habitually wore up with a minimal amount of decoration. She was a true matron of Rome, not given to overindulgence and gaudy decoration. Her family was everything to her. She grasped Lucius' arm and cast a last look about the walls decorated with fading frescoes of images of Etrurian landscapes, forested hills and vineyards.

"We missed you at the evening meal," she said as Lucius walked with her out of the room. "Your father was demanding where you were. I think he wanted you to join him in his negotiations with the merchant."

"He didn't say anything to me," Lucius answered. "How was I supposed to know?"

"I think he believes you should always be checking with him on things, staying close to him so that you can learn how things work."

"I don't want to know, Mother."

Antonia stopped and turned Lucius to face her, but the latter winced at the sudden movement, however gently it was done.

"What's wrong? Are you hurt?"

"It's nothing, really. I was..."

"Where? What happened?" she asked, her face suddenly piqued and worried.

"I went... I wasn't going to say anything until I spoke with father, but...oh all right. Argus and I went to the Stadium of Domitian to enlist today. I had to go a round with practice gladii with one of the other recruits. I won, but did get hit once or twice. It's nothing really."

Antonia felt the heat rush up her neck and moved to a marble bench where it overlooked the garden.

"Lucius, don't you know what this is going to do to your father? He's been planning things out for you. All those years of tutoring with Diodorus were not meant to take you into the army. They were meant to give you a better, more peaceful life, a life of service to the Empire in the Curia, not on the battlefield.

"I never wanted to sit in the Curia like father. That was his dream, not mine."

"He is paterfamilias, Lucius. He decides for all of us."

"Well, times have changed," Lucius answered stubbornly, trying not to raise his voice. *She's only worried about me,* he reminded himself.

Lucius' mother looked at him then, her eyes glossy and wide, and he thought that he had never seen her look so afraid in all his life. He took her hand and squeezed.

"It'll be fine, I promise. He'll understand. I'm going to eat the food Junius put out for me before I speak with him." Lucius stood and looked down at his mother, her hands wringing the material of her blue stola just enough for him to notice. He smiled and went to his room, leaving her there.

Antonia watched Lucius disappear inside his room and closed her eyes for a moment, her mind spinning. She knew her husband would be furious, unbelievably-so. She also knew that her son was stubborn and unlikely to yield. Times were indeed different in Rome. It was a new age of opportunity for young men. The problem was that her husband was an older man who longed for the past, while her son looked only to the future. Diodorus was no longer with them to balance out the conversation and emotion.

Antonia Metella took a deep breath and stood, looking down into the peristyle garden. It looked so peaceful. It may not have been the gardens of the Palatine, but it had been their familia's home for many happy years. Now, with this one day, she feared that it would all turn to ash.

21

Lucius sat at the table in his cubiculum, tearing hungrily at a piece of meat and a hunk of bread, the red clay plate before him emptying quickly. He had not realized how famished he was.

He was also nervous, and drank his wine more quickly that he should have. When he finished, he went to the window and opened it to allow in the cool evening air. The sky was clear, the moon full and bright, its light shining in through Lucius' window. He stared at the silver orb - it seemed larger than he had ever seen it before.

The moon held his gaze for several minutes, and it seemed to Lucius that a sort of humming emmanated from it, like the plucking of a single note on a lyre string.

Metellus... Anguis... The words seemed to come on the very air, and Lucius wheeled round to look behind him, but all he could see was his bed and the bronze pedestal table beside it, the dragon-clawed brazier in the corner, and his desk, where his empty plate lay beside the flickering oil lamp, beyond which was the small statue of Olympian Apollo, and a dish where the remains of offered insence had turned to ash.

Lucius' eyes remained fixed on the statue as he approached it, his heart racing. He opened a small cedar box and removed a fresh chunk of frankincense, lit it in the lamp's flame, and placed it in the dish.

The statue seemed to move its arm before Lucius' eyes, and the young man blinked, felt his ribs ache. The sound of voices from the artium roused him then. His father's client was leaving.

"Guide me, my Lord..." Lucius whispered to the statue, before going out the door and down to the peristylium.

Quintus Metellus sat at the large, paper-strewn desk in his tablinum, his head in his hands, a headache forming at the back of his brain.

The merchants are getting bolder, he thought to himself. He searched through the scattering of papers and accounts before him, found those pertaining to the deal he had just made, and rolled them neatly. Then he stood, his toga's usually meticullous folds in disarray now, and went to the wall of pigeon holes where he found the one pertaining to his recent visitor. He filed the rolled papyrus scrolls carefully and turned around to fill his wine cup again.

The knock at the door was not welcome. To Quintus, it felt like Vulcan's hammer in his increasingly pained skull.

"Father? May I come in? I need to speak with you about something."

Quintus strode to the door, his anger welling in him. He knew it would have been a good deal for Lucius to listen to, to learn from.

"Where were you, boy?" he snapped as he flung open the door and went back to his desk, barely looking at Lucius.

"I...well, that's what I wanted to talk to you about, actually." Lucius entered, closed the door, and sat in the chair opposite his father's desk. Then he stood again, not wanting to be seated for what he had to say.

"I thought I told you to be here for this deal."

Lucius looked at his father, the clawing wrinkles about his mouth and brow, the increasing whiteness of his shortly-shorn hair. He looked tired, and as ever, his patience was thin.

There will never be a good time to tell him, Lucius thought.

He stopped pacing before the desk and looked at his father directly.

"Father..." he took a breath. "I wasn't here today because I was at the Stadium of Domitian. I've enlisted in the army. I've been accepted."

The silence that hung in the air between them was painful, the anger in his father's face building like water coming to a boil.

Quintus Metellus' lip pursed and then began to tremble, his fists clenching as they reached up to rub his pulsating temples.

"How could you do this?" he said, slowly, evenly. "Are you stupid? What - were - you - thinking? Quintus shot up, out of his chair and leaned against the wall of scrolls and accounts, his heaving back to Lucius.

"Let me explain, Father -"

"Explain?" Quintus whirled around, his eyes wild. "What are you going to explain? How you've defied me? How you've destroyed your only real chances of giving our family the honour it deserves? What about the Cursus Honorem? Our ancestors have followed its path to greatness for generations, and in one fell, miscreant deed, you destroy everything for us!"

"I've done no such thing. The Cursus was always your dream, not mine."

"It is the way of things, you ignorant boy! It is the only honourable way to make a name for yourself in the world."

"Times have changed, Father. A man can make himself in the army if he has a will. Besides, you did your service in the legions. Why is that different?"

"I only served the minimum time required by the Cursus Honorem, a few years. And I was an officer, as was appropriate for a man of the Equestrian class. I could have made introductions for you, Lucius. Instead, you've gone and enlisted with no thought for social rank or standing, no references."

"I was accepted on my merits alone!" Lucius protested. "I don't want favours, nor to be beholden to some other senator."

"That's how things work, damn you!" Quintus Metellus sat down heavily in his chair and leaned on his desk. Then, as if to himself, "I should have known this would happen, two years ago, when he donned his toga and thought he was being a man telling me he was going to go into the army and join the legions. I should have known!"

"Father, I'm right here," Lucius said, exasperated. "There will be plenty of opportunities for me to make a name for myself in the legions. Under Severus, there are a lot of changes being made. I will bring our family name out of the ashes."

"You're a fool, and so is the emperor who thinks he's going to conquer Parthia where so many other, far greater Romans have failed." Quintus slowed himself then, and faced Lucius. "It's time to begin doing something with your life. You've wasted two years on training, and books, and time at the baths, waiting around for some fantasy career in the army."

"There is a long tradition among the men of Rome to join the legions that made her great," Lucius put in.

"Yes, for the minimum amount of time. You've enlisted at the bottom for what, twenty-five years? Is that what the commitment still is?"

"Something like that." Lucius thought that sounded like an awfully long time, but there was no way he was going to say so.

"Do you know how hard life in the army really is? You won't last a month!"

"You did it!" Lucius snapped, looking with disdain on his father's form.

"Careful," Quintus said. "Do you know how many men make it to high-ranking positions in the legions?" Lucius crossed his thick arms, wincing a little at the pressure on his ribs. "Maybe one in a thousand, and those are exceptional men. Lucky men who are Fortuna-blessed."

"I am blessed," Lucius said with certainty, his head higher now.

"Yes, your eagles. I remember." Quintus sat back down, a look of mock pity on his face as he gazed at his son across the broad wooden table. "Two eagles feathers that you fancy given to you by the Gods will not protect you when you march into battle, or when the barbarians come howling out of the moutains with a million arrows raining down on your head." He sighed. *Maybe I'm getting through to him now.* "Listen... Our family has been around since the Republic, but the imperial age is far different. We were great once, and if you follow my lead, our family will be great again. I promise you."

Lucius was silent for a few moments. His face burned and he had to turn away from his smirking father to look at the rusty, unused gladius that hung in the corner. The image of Apollo's statue on the table in his cubiculum flashed in his mind. He turned back to his father, his fists unclenched now.

"I don't believe that my future is determined by the name I bear, but by the person I am and make myself, the actions I carry out. Father, I'm old enough to decide for myself now." Lucius took a deep breath and forced himself to look his father in the eyes. "I choose to make myself in the army, not in the Senate. You don't have to agree with me. I'm telling you, that's my decision."

Quintus Metellus seemed to deflate at the sight of his son standing up to him. After so many years of trying to guide Lucius, of telling him what to do for his own good and the good of their family, he had grown tired of what he saw as Lucius' petulance. *Serves me right for getting him that Greek tutor!*

"I suppose I have indulged you too much. Very well," Quintus said brusquely. "If you disgrace yourself, or get killed, it's your head. But if you disgrace me, or this family, you'll be no son of mine!"

The two of them stared at each other, lacking the words to stop the rift that was growing wider and wider between them, more irreparable the more they spoke.

"I won't disgrace the family, Father. I won't." Lucius stepped toward the table, his fists resting heavily on the rolled scrolls.

Quintus made to reach for Lucius' hands, but instead he took hold of the scrolls and pulled to get them out from under his son's fists.

"I really don't care anymore. You and Argus can do as you please. Quintus is my only son at this point, gods help me."

Lucius backed away, nodding his understanding, unwilling to show the hurt that the words caused.

"I'm here for a few more weeks. I think we'll be leaving before the dances of the Salii, in the month of Februarius."

Quintus did not look up or answer. He was already scribbling notes as to the accounts of the estate, and the next trade deal he was to undertake.

Lucius went to the door of the tablinum, opened it, stepped into the corridor, and shut it gently as he stared at the ground. He looked up when he heard a sniffle.

"Couldn't you make it easier for him?" Antonia Metella said, wiping away the tears that were rimming her eyes. "This will break our family, Lucius."

"No it won't," Lucius answered. "He's got Quintus. The tyrant wants all other inconveniences swept out of sight."

"Lucius-" she said, but he was already storming away past the vacant eyes of their Metelli ancestors.

III

Amor Filialis

'Filial Love'

Lucius paced around the garden, hidden by the greenery. He wanted to scream for all the anger and frustration he felt.

As he gazed about his childhood home, the stained columns, the cracking roof tiles that peered over the edges of the second floor above him, he felt out of place. What had been his home for so long now felt foreign and uncomfortable. He wished the campaign season would arrive sooner.

Lucius sat down on one of the two couches, his face in his hands, a feeling of numbness washing over him. He wanted to feel alive, to feel free. Lucius Metellus Anguis wanted to be the master of his own person, and not enslaved to some ancient ideal of how things were meant to be.

When he heard footsteps echoing from the atrium, he looked up, relief taking hold of him. He stood just in time to see his older sister Alene coming around the corner and into the garden, her eyes searching for him.

"Lucius?" she said, rushing toward him, her long blonde hair falling in thick curls down her back. "What's happened? Junius said you and Father had an argument again." She threw her arms around him and he winced more loudly than he would have liked. "What's wrong? Are you hurt?" She stood back, her eyes concerned, searching his.

"I'm fine, just a broken rib from the stadium." He smiled. "You should see the other guy."

"Don't tell me you and Argus got into another brawl."

"No." How could he tell her? Alene had always been his comfort, his strongest ally in the familia. How could he tell her that he was leaving for who knew how long? "Let's sit."

"Junius!" Alene called.

"Yes, mistress?"

"Some wine please."

"At once," the old man's voice replied. He was always happy to serve Alene.

Lucius looked at his sister, sitting there watching him, refined as ever, despite the worry he knew was churning inside her. She straighted her green stola and waited. He smiled.

All his life, Lucius had managed to stay out of serious trouble, and it was mostly due to the love and watchful eye of Alene Metella. She was his older sister, but she did act like a second mother much of the time. He loved and cherished her for it. As Lucius had grown older, it happened that it was he who began to watch over her, especially when some leacherous creature in the Forum was staring at her. One time, when he was younger, Lucius had pelted one man with pebbles, almost receiving a thrashing for it. But Alene had stopped the man and called others around to help. Ever since then, she had referred to Lucius as her 'little hero'.

As he looked at her, Lucius wondered if she would be all right when he was away. Would she feel betrayed? How about when another suitor came along? He would not be there to ascertain the man with a separate view to the businessman's eye of their father.

"I..." he began. "Argus and I were at the Stadium of Domitian today. We enlisted in the legions. We're in."

Alene stared at her brother for a few heartbeats, her face unreadable. Then, she looked down at her hands and back up again.

"I knew you would do it someday. I just hadn't imagined that the years would fly so quickly." She remembered his decision on the day he had worn his toga for the first time. She had been the first person he had told of his intentions. Now it was here, the day her little brother would head out into the world. She tried to think of a excerpt from Ovid's poems that she could quote, something to match her mood in that moment, but she could not think of anything except Lucius sitting before her, and the thought of him going off to war. "I can't believe it."

"I'm sorry," he said. If he was sorry for anything, it ws for the pain his leaving would cause her.

"Don't feel sorry for following your dreams. Never, you hear me?" she said, her blue eyes flashing in the light of the brazier nearby where Junius had just placed pitchers of wine, and water, and two cups. She picked up a cup and handed it to Lucius, then picked one up for herself. She raised it to him. "May Apollo guide you..." she said, before tipping some onto the mosaic floor and then drinking, Lucius following suit.

When they had taken a few sips in silence, Alene spoke again.

"So that's what you and Father argued about."

"Yes," Lucius replied, his mind back in the stuffy tablinum with his father's face staring at him with loathing. "It has never been my intention to anger or oppose him outright. It just so happens that anytime I make up my mind to do something, something I believe to be right, it's always the opposite of what he believes to be proper."

"You are both different, Lucius. There is no way around it. Ever since his service in the army, he has been a hard, overly-virtuous man concerned more with the public face of the family. He's always sought to raise the Metelli name again."

Lucius looked around to make sure they were still alone before speaking again. "Mother always said that it was Father who brought the family to prominence again, and that he worked hard to do so, to make a good life for us."

"And he is always worried about something ruining that," Alene added.

"Ruining what? We live in this run-down house that smells of Forum Boarium cattle shit when we walk out the door, and the only thing I ever hear told about our great family name beyond this house is how Caecilia Metella was a whore of Sulla's." Lucius stood and pointed down the corridor to the busts of the Metellus ancestors. "Most people these days don't even know who those men were!"

Alene stood and took Lucius' hand, squeezing it with both of hers. "I know. I think greatness means something different to both you and Father."

"That's putting it mildly."

Alene sat down again, this time beside her brother. "When do you leave?"

"Probably toward the end of Februarius. We're to wait for word of training in Rome."

"And Argus? Where is he, dare I ask?"

"He went to the Subura, of course."

Alene looked Lucius in the eye then, put her hand on his cheek. "Don't turn into him, Lucius. I know he is our foster brother, but you are not the same."

"I know. But I also know he has my back. I'll be safer with Argus nearby."

"I know. I just shudder to think of what he'll get up to. You watch, when he stumbles in here drunk, the first thing he'll tell you is something about the flaps of his whore's genetalia, or something about her nipples."

"I think Ovid suits you more than Catullus, Alene!" Lucius nudged her and she blushed.

"Maybe," she laughed half-heartedly. "But I would rather think of that right now than of you going away for years. The more I think about it, the more painful I think it is going to be..."

Brother and sister sat for a while, sipping their wine, each lost in their own myriad thoughts and fears, hopes and dreams. They had spent their youth playing in that garden, hiding behind the columns, hiding from each other, surprising the slaves, laughing...so much laughter, especially when their father was not around.

"Do you remember a time when our father was not so grim and determined?" Lucius asked after a while.

"I think so," Alene answered, and looked around to make sure Metellus Pater was not around. "At least I would hope so. I don't know. I think that he must have been kind to attract mother to him. No?"

"Grandfather was kind, or so I've heard. Mother tells me that he loved her very much and that he doted on you, and that he insisted I receive the proper cognomen of Anguis."

"As you should have." Alene sat up and looked at Lucius, brushing some strands of her hair out of her face. "Listen. Father may be a hard man, but he is the only father we have. You need to make amends with him before you leave."

"I don't think it's possible," Lucius insisted. "In his mind, I've already gone."

"Not in mine!" she snapped suddenly.

Lucius noticed his sister's hands shaking, and when she closed her eyes, her lashes were drapped in tears. Though it pained him to do so, he knelt down on the floor in front of her and took her hands, kissing them softly.

"Please don't cry," he pleaded. "I'm still here."

"Not for long. After Saturnalia, you'll be gone. What if I never see you again? I'm so afraid... I..."

"You of all people should have faith, Alene. You've always understood the Gods and their ways. You remember the day I put on my toga. The Gods are watching me, arent't they?"

"Of course, and I'll make offerings for your safe return every day you're away. It's just that, there has been so much death in the civil war. The emperor is a determined man. He doesn't seem to stop."

"No, he doesn't," Lucius answered. "But he's the strongest emperor we've had since Marcus Aurelius."

"I've lost so many friends to Severus' wars already," she said as if she had not heard what he said. "I don't want your shade wandering the Afterlife so soon. So many dead... and the lady Claudia's son-in-law was one of them. You should see how sad her daughter looks, how frail. She's crippled with grief. The poor girl tried so hard to enjoy herself, but she was unable to." Alene dried her tears and kissed her brother's head. "You'll be marching to the other side of the Empire. Do you have any idea what you'll be going into?"

"No," he answered honestly. "But that's part of the adventure. When Alexander marched to the Indus, he didn't know what he would find, but he wanted to discover the world, to see all its wonders."

"Severus is not Alexander the Great."

"Well, no. But I have the chance to walk, as least partly, in Alexander's footsteps, Alene. I'm so excited!"

As he stared at his sister's face, he knew he was being selfish. If anything, he would fight to stay alive and see her again. He relished the adventure ahead, and the chance to make a name for himself, to prove his father wrong.

"Just make sure that if some suitor comes along while I'm away, that he would meet my expectations."

Alene tried to smile. "I doubt that. Father's turned a few away already. The deals were not good enough." She looked down.

Lucius rubbed his jaw roughly. *Damn the man!* As difficult as it would be to see Alene wed, he knew that it was someting she wanted, especially if it was a love match, rare as those were. But she deserved it. She was one of the kindest, most intelligent, and brilliant young women of Rome. She would have had her pick of quality suitors, were it not for their father's inscessant need for family gains.

"Don't worry about me. I'll be fine. Just try to mend things with Father." She held his face tighly in her hands. "Most of all, just stay alive." She gazed at him for a moment, and he saw how very serious she was.

He nodded slowly.

There was a sudden raucous noise from the atrium then, and the sound of someone falling over, cursing.

"Cunts and violets!"

Lucius and Alene looked at each other.

"Seems Argus is back," Lucius said. They both sat up on the same couch and watched as Argus' tall, thick form came stumbling out from behind one of the columns and into the garden.

"Ahh, there you are!" he slurred, the odour of stale wine wafting toward them. "Ohhhh, Lucius," he paused and looked at Alene. "Sister..." Argus lay down with a thump on the vacant couch, smiling like a satyr at the moon above.

"Good time in the Subura, Argus?" Alene asked.

"Yes. A VERY good time." He laughed uncontrollably for a minute before turning on his side and looking at Lucius. "Not that you care."

"I'm going to bed," Alene said suddenly, rising from the couch and patting Argus' head as if she were patting a pathetic stray dog in the Forum. "You'll feel this in the morning."

"Yes. I will. But it was worth it." He grinned broadly, his eyes rolling. "Lucius...Lucius... There was this whore. She made me bigger than Priapus! I'm telling you, the most amazing tits... Nipples the size of fresh figs!"

Alene looked at Lucius, one eyebrow raised. *I told you so.* "Good night, troops," she said, kissing Lucius' cheek one more time before going up to the second floor.

"She's jealous," Argus mumbled.

Lucius looked at his friend and shook his head. He wondered what indeed Argus would get up to once he was out of Rome.

"Let me guess," Lucius said. "Three pitchers of wine?"

"Nope. Five! They had a special if you paid for one of the girls too."

"Did you blow all of your sestercii?"

"Yesss. But who cares? We're men of the... of the... legions... now..." Argus' voice faded into snoring as he lay there, and Lucius shook his head.

"You are going to feel it in the morning. I just hope I don't have to babysit you across the Empire."

Lucius drapped Argus' cloak over him and stood to go upstairs to his cubiculum. When he turned, his father was standing there staring at the two of them.

Quintus Metellus said nothing. He only stared angrily at Lucius, and then turned to go upstairs himself.

Lucius sat back down on the couch and poured himself another cup of wine.

"You're better company than him," he said to Argus' inebriated form, before draining his cup and pouring more.

IV

Disciplina

'Discipline'

Rome took on a new air for Lucius over the coming weeks. Every time he looked about, he thought of how it would be many months, years even, before he would walk the city's streets again. He would miss cheering for his favourite teams in the Circus Maximus, or reading a new scroll as he sat in the square before the Temple of Apollo, drenched in sunlight, blinded by white marble.

The celebrations for Saturnalia were not as festive as he would have liked, due to the shadow cast over their family by Lucius' silent battle with his father.

More than once, Lucius tried to speak with his father, to mend the space between them with reassurances, promises of future family glories that he could build upon. However, Quintus Metellus pater was beyond listening; he shut his ears to his son, and Lucius in turn decided not to waste his last weeks at home in constant discord. As a result, the usually joyous, raucous affair of Saturnalia was strained and silent.

Lucius could see that this greatly upset Alene and his mother, but he did not know what else to do. His celebratory mood came to the fore when his father went out, which was more frequent than usual.

Once Saturnalia finished, Lucius decided that he would spend much of his time at the gymnasium training and strenghtening himself prior to receiving his orders to report for duty.

When Januarius came, cold and wet as it was, an optio came to the Metellus domus with a scroll for both Lucius and Argus, the latter still sleeping off his evening's carousing.

Junius came to get Lucius, who was talking in the garden with Alene.

"A messenger for you, master Lucius," Junius said. "Looks like a legionary."

Lucius looked quickly at Alene and stood. She nodded and he went away to the atrium. When he arrived, he saw the optio who had helped sign him in at the Stadium of Domitian.

The man wore his armour, but had no weapons besides a pugio at his waist. Hanging from his cingulum was a thick wax tablet which he clutched as he looked about the Metellus domus.

"Lucius Metellus Anguis?" the optio said, looking at Lucius' blue tunic with its silver bordering with dismay.

"That's me, sir. Yes," Lucius answered respectfully, recognizing the man's face from before.

"I'm your optio, Gallus. Centurion Decimus ordered me to notify you and..." he opened the wax tablet and read the name, "...Argus... that you are to report for training tomorrow at the Stadium of Domitian before the first hour of light."

"So, we're beginning then?" Lucius said excitedly.

"Yes," Gallus answered. He was beady-eyed and blonde. A Gaul with short cropped hair. "I hope you don't think this is going to be a holiday, Metellus." He looked around some more. "I see you are used to fine surroundings."

"I'm ready, sir," Lucius said with certainty.

"Good. Because Centurion Decimus seems to think you have the makings of a great legionary."

Lucius said nothing, tried not to smile. Something in his gut told him the man before him would not make things easy.

"Here." Gallus handed Lucius his commission. "And take this for Argus too. I can't wait around for both of you. I have other commissions to deliver."

"Do I need to know anything else, Optio?"

"No. Just show up on time. The centurion will tell you everything you need to know tomorrow. I'd get some rest if I were you."

"Yes, sir!" Lucius said, trying out a sloppy salute.

Gallus shook his head slightly, sighed, and turned to leave. When Junius closed the door behind him, Lucius broke the seal on the small papyrus roll and read it over, silently mouthing the words before looking up at Alene who was now walking toward him from the garden.

"So?" she asked. "What does it say?"

"It just says I've been accepted into the imperial legions...that I am committed to fighting for Rome, and that I agree to be executed if I should desert or show cowardice." He read on. "It also says I'm to be a part of the III Parthica Legion... It's a new legion that has been formed for this campaign."

Alene looked at her brother for moment, about to say something, but then turned slowly and walked back to the garden where she had laid her scroll of Sappho down on the bench. The rain was starting again.

40

Lucius felt a tightness in his chest then, the excitement of the moment far from this thoughts. He rolled the scroll back up and went to Argus' cubiculum.

"Argus, wake up!" Lucius said loudly, making the other young man groan and grab hold of his head.

"Go way," he said

"Wake up! There was a messenger at the door, the optio from the legions, the one who signed us up. He's brought our orders. We start training tomorrow!"

"Tomorrow?" Argus said, rolling over and sitting on the edge of his bed. He swayed a little and Lucius could tell that he was trying not to throw up. "Fuck it..."

Lucius jumped back as Argus heaved onto the black and white floor mosaic, a rancid smell of vinegar filling the room.

"You'd better get that out of your system today," Lucius warned. "I have a feeling they're going to work us pretty hard tomorrow. Here..." Lucius tossed Argus his commission and it landed on the edge of the bed. "Read it over. If you're up for it, I'm heading to the gymnasium again in an hour."

"No thanks..." Argus said weekly. "I'll just sleep some more." He then collapsed onto the bed again, and rolled over onto his other side so that his back was to Lucius.

Lucius shook his head and went back down to see Alene. He could leave things ill with his father, but never with her. He needed to be sure she was all right.

The next day, when the moon was still visible in the sky, Lucius and Argus walked through the streets to the Stadium of Domitian wearing woolen tunics and bracae beneath black woolen cloaks.

The streets were only just beginning to rouse, most of the activity coming from the carts that were allowed to travel to the various fora only in the early hours of the day before being barred from the streets.

They came to the southern end of the stadium where they walked through one of the big arches flanked by legionary troops.

An optio with a horsehair crest and feathers on his helmet blocked their way with his long hastile staff, on the end of which was a brass ball.

"Only training for new recruits today. The army is using the Field of Mars," he said.

"Yes, sir," Lucius said. "We're here to report to Centurion Decimus." Lucius handed him his paper, and Argus did the same.

"Lucius Metellus Anguis, and, Argus..." The optio raised his eyebrows at Argus.

"That's my name," the latter said.

"Fine by me," the optio answered. "Pleb, Equestrian, or Patrician... everyone smells the same when on latrine duty." He handed their papers back to them. "You're just in time. Your centurion and optio are over there." he pointed to a table where Gallus sat. "Hurry up, or you'll feel Decimus vinerod across your backs."

"Yes, sir," Lucius said and strode onto the sands, Argus following behind, glancing back at the optio.

"Arrogant cock," he muttered.

"Shh. None of that. We have to follow orders now."

Lucius strode up to the table where Gallus sat, and saluted.

"Lucius Metellus Anguis, reporting for duty, Optio!" he said, a little too loudly.

Before the table, on the sand, there were about eighty men lined up, Centurion Decimus standing before them in his full armour, his horizontal crest bristling like the hair on an angry boar. Several of the recruits turned when Lucius spoke so loudly, some laughing.

"Shut up, you sons-of-whores!" Decimus yelled, his vinerod cracking against the shin of the man who was laughing the loudest.

Gallus wrote Lucius and Argus' names down as if nothing had happened, and pointed to the rows of men.

"Well, soldier. Go join your century," he said.

Lucius and Argus lined up next to two young men who appeared to be twins from the North. Both had shaggy blonde hair and stared straight ahead, nodding to Argus to do the same as he looked about.

"Now!" Decimus called out so that his voice echoed around the stadium. "You are now my men, your lives are mine to do with as I please. I can yell at you, I can curse you, I can beat you senseless with this." He held up the vinerod that allowed him to strike Roman citizens. "This, my young puppies, is your deliverer...from stupidity, and from death. If you heed this rod, you'll grow to be great soldiers, you'll live longer. Never question my orders, or those of my optio, Gallus, here," he said as the other man came and stood beside him. "We are your new fucking gods, though you should always respect the Gods of our fathers, especially in my century. If you work hard, and fight hard, and do everything I ask you, both the Gods, and me, will be pleased."

Decimus walked back and forth now, slowly, his feet making deep impressions in the sand about them.

"I also have the power to decorate you and reward you." He stared at all the faces before him, mostly young men under twenty-four. He spotted Lucius and stared at him for a moment.

"Some of you come from soft backgrounds where everything was likely done for you. Well, that life is gone. You're going to be cooking your own food, pitching your own tent, carrying your own kit across the world and back again. You're going to be digging your own holes to shit in! And you'll be building Rome's roads across the Empire."

"Maybe we were hasty," Argus muttered to Lucius.

"Who's fucking speaking while I'm speaking?" Decimus said.

The blonde twins looked sidelong at Argus and then quickly straight ahead as if they thought they would be associated with him.

"You?" Decimus said, leaning to Gallus who whispered to him. "Argus, is it?" He pointed his vinerod at Argus. "Come here."

Argus smirked a little, and then walked around from the back row and stood to attention before the centurion.

"You're a big bastard, aren't you? Strong, muscular..." Decimus walked around Argus a couple of times and stopped behind him. The centurion's arms were laced with scars, some old, some newly-healed. "You having second thoughts, Argus? This isn't the life you wanted?"

"No, sir," Argus said with more respect than he had had before. "This is what I want."

The centurion looked at the rest of the men for a second before turning and slamming his vinerod into Argus' back, sending him flying face first into the sand like a child's linen doll.

Lucius took one hesitant step and then stopped when Gallus' eyes met his. Lucius stood still at attention, watching Argus writhe on the ground, trying desperately to get up. He managed to stand, his back muscles spasming and looked straight ahead.

Decimus came around front of him and got in his face. "Anything else to say, Argus? Do you want to leave?"

Argus stared back at the centurion. "No, sir. I'm staying right here."

Decimus looked surprised, his eyebrows up, his head titled. "Very well then. Get back into line."

Argus turned and went back to his place beside Lucius, his eyes challenging anyone who dared to stare at him with mockery, or pity. No one there looked his way.

Lucius wanted to speak to him but held his tongue. There would be time enough later, but he did worry. It had been a hard hit.

"Now, as I said," Decimus continued. "You are never to question me or my orders. NEVER! But, just this one time, I will allow you to ask me questions. This is your only chance, so do it now, or shut up from here on in."

The recruits looked hesitantly from one side to the next, then a youth about Lucius' age with golden eyes and black hair spoke up.

"Name?" the centurion asked.

"Alerio Cornelius Kasen, sir."

"What's your question?"

"Sir, I wanted to know... are we the only recruits? I thought the emperor was raising three new legions."

"Good question, Alerio. The answer is no, you are not the only recruits for the new legions. But you are the only ones in Rome. Most of the recruiting for the new legions will be done in Macedonia and Thrace."

"Sir?" said a thick-muscled, blonde youth.

"Name?"

"Antanelis, sir."

"What do you want to know?"

"What legion are we a part of?"

"The emperor has decided to create three entirely new legions for the coming war with Parthia." There were some gasps among the men, and then confused looks. Decimus shook his head. "I guess some of you have not been listening to the announcements in the Forum, or that you have no idea where Parthia is. Well, I'll tell you. It's practically the other side of the bloody world, Parthia is, and many great Romans have failed to take it. But this time, we're going to do it. So, once the I, II, and III Parthica legions are raised, we will meet the rest of the army at Antioch."

"Which legion are we a part of, sir?" the young man named Antanelis asked again.

"We are the first recruits of the III Parthica Legion, as it said on your commissions. Our job is to train this next few weeks before we set off for Greece to recruit in Athens, Macedonia, and Thrace. Once the legions are complete, we sail from Amphipolis to Antioch."

Lucius looked about, smiling to himself. He had always wanted to see Athenae, ever since Diodorus had told him about it. However, he somehow doubted there would be much time for leisure on the way to Parthia. What really took up his thoughts in that moment were all the possibilities, of proving himself, of winning glory for his family name. Before he knew it, his hand was up.

"What is it, Metellus?" Decimus said.

"Sir, will there be opportunity for advancement in the ranks? I've heard the emperor has made it easier for men to climb."

"Sure, Metellus. You can rise through the ranks if you have what it takes."

Lucius smiled and nodded.

"But," Decimus continued. "There's just one problem with that."

"Yes, sir?" Lucius said.

"For you to climb the ranks, me and Gallus here would have to be FUCKING DEAD!"

No one said anything. All that could be heard then was the winter wind ripping through the stadium seats, and the call of the street vendors outside the Baths of Nero.

Decimus came striding around the edge of the square of men and came to a stop behind Lucius and Argus.

"So, you have a bit of a problem, don't you Metellus? Cause your centurion and optio don't kill so fucking easily! Got it?"

Lucius continued to stare straight ahead. "Understood, Centurion!" he said loudly.

"You won't be so keen once the blood sprays across your face, and you smell the piss and shit of frightened men and horses all around you." Decimus muttered as he strode away. "That's enough questions. You're all to shut up now so that we can start training. Everyone line up by the table over there with Optio Gallus who will give you each your legionary tunic, caligae, and cingulum. Once you've changed into those from your fancy city clothes, we're going to learn the most important thing for an efficient army - marching!"

No one dared sigh, though many felt like it as they all lined up to receive the first of their standard issue kit.

Lucius and Argus looked around at all the other recruits. Most were tradesmen's sons, short, and thick-muscled, though some appeared leaner, having decided that the only way they could eat or send money back to their families was to join the legions.

They were made to change in the open air, every muscle, flab, cut, bruise and birthmark forcibly bared to their fellows. As Lucius looked around, he realized that they would be through much together in the coming months or years. Some would die, some would do great things. Others would show the worst in them. He had no illusions about what a life in the legions was like, but he hoped that those men would be strong allies. He looked forward to the bonds that they might strike up. He was also relieved to see that Bona and none of his friends had been accepted into the III Parthica.

As soon as everyone was dressed, their caligae tightly cinched, Decimus put them all into four long rows side by side. Then, the centurion started to march around the edge of the stadium, with the recruits following, urged by Gallus.

They marched and marched, each man trying to keep time with the centurion, each man receiving his own measure of harsh criticism and correction from the optio who marched alongside them as they went.

When the sky began to darken, and they were all thirstier and hungrier than they had ever been, Decimus called a halt and had them line up in orderly rows.

"That was terrible! You can't even walk properly! How are you going to get across the world to Parthia when you can't even walk around the stadium in an orderly fashion?" He shook his head. "Back here tomorrow for more marching. I don't want to see anyone late!" he said. "Until we get the discipline of orderly marching down, not one of you is going to receive a gladius, or scutum. No armour or cloaks, nothing to try and impress your girlfriends or boyfriends with." He stopped and stared at them all, tired, and sweaty, and starving.

"Dismissed!" Gallus yelled, and many of the men turned and walked away, unable to bear the thought of doing it all again tomorrow.

"Come on," Argus said to Lucius who was talking with the two men, Alerio and Antanelis, as well as the twins whose names were Eligius and Garai.

"I think we should all hit the taberna, don't you?" Lucius said to Argus, smiling.

The latter could not really believe it, but said yes.

"Can we join you?" the twin named Garai asked as Lucius and Argus turned to go.

Argus looked at him and then shrugged his shoulders. "Why not? Seems we're all going to get beaten together anyway," he said. "How about you two?" he asked Alerio and Antanelis.

"I can come for one drink," Alerio said. "But then I have to get back to my home for a dinner my family is putting on."

"I'll come," added Antanelis, the younger, but very strong-looking youth. He walked up to Lucius. "You really a Metellus?"

"Um, yes. You've heard of the family name?"

"Who hasn't?" the younger man replied. "A lot of warriors among your ancestors."

"Well don't hold it against him!" Argus barked, leading the way out of the stadium.

From the way Argus was walking, Lucius could tell that the centurion's vinerod had hurt more than he let on. When they came outside, there was a crowd gathered around a scuffle near one of the arcades of the stadium.

"Those are some of our fellow recruits!" Antanelis yelled, and without another word he ran into the fray.

Lucius strained to see over the crowd, and could hear punches and cries of pain.

They ran after Antanelis and pushed their way through the onlookers to see four of the other recruits from their group facing off against five knife-wielding thugs.

One of the recruits, a tall dark-haired, dark-eyed man named Maren was bleeding, but he still stood in front, challenging the thugs.

"Come here! That was a lucky hit! Try again!"

Before the attacker could move in Antanelis had thrown himself into the mass of men, knocking them to the ground, their own daggers cutting each other.

"You attack one of us, you attack all of us!" he said.

"Well, that was impressive," Lucius said to Argus, before running in to help.

"I've got this!" the one named Maren said.

Beside him, the other three troops who had been attacked, Gaius, Tertius, and Corvus, all rushed in to grab hold of their assailants.

"Try to steal from us, will you?" Corvus yelled, as he landed his fist across the jaw of one with a sickening crack.

It was a full-scale brawl now, and the crowd that had grown around it was like a swarm of flies. Romans yelled and spat, placed bets and cursed.

Lucius narrowly missed beings stabbed in the neck by one thrust, and quickly moved in to twist the man's wrist so that the dagger fell to the ground. He kicked it away and then elbowed his opponent in the face. He then heard Argus cry out in rage as he was hit in the back, and ran to his aid, his fist hammering into the side of the attacker's head.

"I've got it!" Argus raged, pushing Lucius away and kicking into his man's face with his sandalled foot until blood started to spray out.

"Urban cohorts!" one of the nearby merchants yelled from the crowd. "Stop this madness! It's bad for business!"

"Stop this!" came a loud, gruff voice.

Lucius felt himself pulled back violently and turned to see one of the urban guards, a centurion, pointing a gladius at him. Lucius held his hands up and stood beside Alerio who had a bloody nose.

The others were rounded up and pushed against the wall with urban guardsmen standing before them. Everyone was bleeding, but they were alive. The same could not be said of two of the attackers on the ground, lying in pools of blood. One stood gasping, holding his wrist, and two others had run for it, disappearing into the crowd of dirty tunics and togas when the guards had arrived.

"Who's responsible for this?" the centurion stared at Lucius and the others.

Maren stepped forward with Corvus, Tertius and Gaius. "We were just coming out of the stadium after training when these bastards attacked us, and tried to steal my coin pouch!"

"That's not true!" said the man holding his wrist. "They spat on us when they came out. Army bastards think they can do whatever the hell they want!"

"Liar!" Corvus yelled, lunging for the man, but he was thrown back by one of the guards.

"Enough!" the centurion yelled, a great vein pulsing on the side of his head. "I'll have you all in the prison, soldiers or not! You hear me!"

"What's going on here?" Centurion Decimus' voice came down over the entire crowd which parted before him as he and Gallus walked slowly toward the recruits and the men of the Urban Cohort. "These are my men. Why are they being detained?"

Decimus came to stand in the face of the other centurion of the Urban Guard and stared at the man.

The latter was not to be cowed immediately. "They've been brawling, and now two men are dead," he said, nodding to the two bodies.

Decimus looked at the bodies and shrugged. "Suburan gutter filth, is all. These are men of the legions now."

"I don't care if we came out of the same mother's twat, Centurion. They can't do whatever they like in my city!"

"Your city?" Decimus said. "This is the emperor's city, the people's city. And these," he turned to look at Lucius and the others, " are the emperor's men."

"They need to be punished."

"Oh, they'll be punished," Decimus said evenly,"but I'll be dead before you're the one to do it." Decimus' hand went casually to the pommel of his gladius, his chest harness of decorations rising and falling with his slow breathing. "These recruits are going to Parthia with the emperor's army. I don't think you want to be the one to slow the campaign down, as it means so much to the emperor. Do you?"

The guardsman was silent, his eyes raking over the recruits and resting on Maren, who stared right back at him with his dark, angry eyes.

"Just make sure you keep your troops in line, Centurion. We don't need any more problems in the city streets." The guardsman looked around at the crowd and then to his own men. "Pick up the bodies and bring that other one!" he ordered, then turned to the crowd. "The rest of you clear out!"

Slowly, the crowd dispersed and the bodies were dragged away, leaving the ten recruits facing their red-faced centurion and optio.

"I would recommend you skip the drinking tonight," he said to all of them. "Go straight home and rest. I was going to work you hard tomorrow, but now...I'm going to fucking kill you. Dismissed!" he barked, standing there until each one of them had gone. Then Decimus turned to Gallus.

"Make a note. I want that group in the same contuburnium."

"You sure that's wise?"

"Yes. They're brawling fools for now, but once I'm through with them, they'll be fucking unstoppable. Where we're going, we need to stick together, Gallus."

The optio wrote the orders down on his wax tablet and clapped it shut. "Done, sir."

"Gods help me, but sometimes I feel fucking old," the centurion grumbled.

Some of the men still went to the tavern, Lucius and Argus among them. They had had their first engagement as a group and the feeling of exhilaration running through the ten young men was palpable.

They found themselves in a crowded taberna called the Nymph and Faun, in the shadow of the Capitoline Hill's north face. It was growing dark outside, and the group was hungry after their first day of training. Each young man realized things were not going to be anywhere near as easy as he had thought or imagined. However, they focussed on their fight with the cut-purses outside the stadium.

"Centurion Decimus wasn't too impressed," Antanelis said, draining his rough clay wine cup and pouring some more. "I think we're in for a heavy few days."

Lucius looked at the burly youth and smiled. Antanelis seemed affable enough, ready with a smile and conversation, but as he looked around, Lucius noticed some of the others ignoring him. He smiled and nodded at Antanelis, but turned to Argus who was talking with Maren about the fight.

"I just didn't like the look of them," Maren said. "They were looking at us funny, for my money pouch, so, I hit him before he hit us."

"You attacked them?" Lucius said, his anger showing on his face. "Don't you think it might have been easier to just watch them, let them know you knew what they were up to? You could have landed in the prison."

"Pah!" Maren waved it away. He did not seem to care that he was spattered with blood. "They won't be back. Besides, I think we showed our centurion what we're capable of."

Lucius said nothing; a street brawl was not the same as a pitched battle with weapons. He eyed Argus who went silent again at the mention of Decimus.

"You all right?" he asked, touching Argus' shoulder, making him flinch.

"Don't do that!" Argus burst out. The pain was radiating up his back from where the vinerod had hit him, making his whole body tender. He drained his cup, filled it, and then drained another.

"We'll go to the medicus on they way home," Lucius said.

"Fuck the medicus. I'm fine. I just need some more wine."

Alerio, the one with the golden eyes and black hair leaned across Antanelis to speak to Lucius. "I suspect that we'll be moving out soon. Did you hear anything else about the campaign?"

"Only what you heard," Lucius said, turning to talk to Antanelis and Alerio. "I guess we'll be recruiting in Greece soon, and then taking ship to Antioch. You two ever been outside of Italy?"

"Nope," Antanelis said. "Farthest I've been is Rome. My parents own an inn on the Via Flaminia where I've lived all my life. I got tired of handling drunk customers, so decided to enlist. My father was furious at first, but he came around to the idea. I think he's actually proud of me. What about yours, Alerio?"

"Mine? Well, we've been in the legions for generations, so it was kind of expected. Always in the ranks though. What about you, Lucius? As one of the Metelli, you must be doing exactly as was expected."

"Actually no. My father and I don't see eye-to-eye on anything really, especially my joining the legions."

"Really?" Antanelis said.

"Not at all." Lucius looked about the table at the nine young men about him. "I don't care really, cause we're in for the adventure of a lifetime." He stood up and raised his cup to the others.

Eligius and Garai, the twins, shot up and swayed, each having tried to outdo the other in their drinking. They cheered. "Adventure! Women! A life in the legions!"

Tertius, Gaius, and Corvus all laughed and raised their own cups.

"To the first recruits of III Parthica!" Lucius said out loud so that several other patrons turned in their seats to look at the group.

"To III Parthica!" they all drank together, and laughed, all except Argus who could not rise from his seat without wincing.

Just then the tavern keeper brought two trays of bread, cheese, and grilled sausages that they had ordered when they came in. The owner eyed them warily for a moment. "I hope you lads can pay for this," he said.

"Of course we can," Lucius answered, pulling a couple brass semis from his scrip. The others followed suit. "Maren, good thing the thieves didn't get your purse," he said.

Maren's dark eyes looked across the table at Lucius who smiled back at him. "Yeah. Good thing," he said, tossing the coins to the inn keeper.

They fell back into broken conversation as they ate and drank some more, about where they had all come from, the girls in their villages and neighbourhoods, and who they would, or would not miss when they were away. They speculated about the amount of time they would be gone, about the action they would see, and about the rumours they had heard about the Parthians.

Lucius told them about what he knew about Crassus and Mark Antony's experiences in Parthia, how they had not been able to defeat the Parthians. This cast a shadow over the gathering, but he lightened things up, pointing out how Severus was a smarter leader who had the sympathy of many cities in the East because of the empress and her influence.

"I thought you weren't interested in polities?" Argus said under his breath, angry at the pain that kept building in his body.

"I'm not, but the more we know, the better we'll be able to deal with things and make decisions."

"We're at the bottom wrung, Lucius. It won't make a difference what Diodorus or anyone else taught you."

Lucius shook his head. He could see Argus' eyes closing and knew he had to get him home.

"Come!" he slapped the table. "Argus and I need to go," he said. "The night is pressing on, and I don't know about all of you, but I need some sleep for tomorrow." As he rose, he could feel how tired his legs were, and wondered what other parts of him would be hurting in the weeks to come. "Come on," he said to Argus.

The latter stood, holding his breath as he did so, and finished his cup.

"See you all tomorrow," Lucius said.

The seated men waved and turned to each other to talk some more while Lucius and Argus went out of the taberna.

When they were outside, Argus leaned against the wall and groaned.

"Fuck that centurion!" he said. "If he ever hits me like that again, I'll have a dagger in his gut."

"Shh!" Lucius hissed. "Watch what you say. There are probably spies everywhere."

"Shut up, Lucius."

"Let's get to the baths before they close. If you soak your muscles for a while, you won't be so sore tomorrow."

Without saying anything, in agreement or otherwise, Argus followed Lucius in the direction of the Baths of Agrippa. Sleep would have to wait.

Over the next two weeks, every one of the new recruits experienced pain for which they had not been prepared. Training in the gymnasium was one thing, but training on the parade ground, all day, everyday, was quite another.

Lucius, Argus and the others had grown accustomed to the fiery pain that was ever-present in their limbs and lungs, the blisters on their hands and feet, and the bruises on their bodies. Their only respite was a daily visit to the baths, to soak sore muscles, wash away dirt and sweat, and massage knotted shoulders.

Many complained of the ordeal, though among the men of Lucius' contubernium, few ever complained outright. It had become a sort of competition to see who would break first, but none did, including Argus, who had been in the most pain since day one.

Disciplina. Lucius would forever remember that word, for as they all discovered, it was the backbone of Rome's military might, and the very first concept to which they were introduced at the beginning of their training. Disciplina, that wonderful, terrible goddess watched over them every moment, hissed in their ears that she would punish them for the slightest lapse in concentration.

Some of the men claimed to have seen Disciplina herself watching them from a far corner of the stadium with fire in her eyes. Others that she haunted their dreams.

Lucius wondered at this, but who was he to question. He had had his own encounters with the Gods, though he never spoke of such things openly. What Disciplina taught him was that training was an integral part of becoming a legionary, and its importance never dwindled from the basest auxiliary to the highest ranking general.

"The purpose of this training," Decimus would say to them, over and over, "is to provide you with physical as well as mental superiority. A Roman has to be stronger, and tougher than any barbarian to be able to live through any engagement.

Some of those barbarians are seven feet tall, and thick as trees!"

Soon, the men realized that every word that came from their centurion's mouth had purpose, just like his every action. They were leaving soon, and he wanted them to be ready, for all the short, quick training time they had had.

"Training also helps a man to cope with wounds, and also to suppress any fear or panic in battle. Remember!" he would always remind them. "A soldier's first duty is to obey his superiors. His second, is to die in combat if need be."

They had no illusions after two weeks of training with Decimus, but Lucius continued to train hard alongside Argus and the others, ever hopeful of realizing the adventures he dreamed of, and enjoying the hardening and building of their young bodies that had become more solid with each painful day.

Often, Decimus and Gallus would use Lucius and Argus to illustrate various techniques to the group, and they never held back, in demonstration, drills, marches, or other exercises. Everything was repeated, every task received full dedication. The physical scars they all received would last a lifetime, but the skills they gained increased their chances of survival.

Gymnastics, strength-building, running, jumping, swimming, it all helped to make them tougher. When they began weapons training with wooden gladii, and pila, slings, bows, and scuta, they were then made deadly.

Every man found the skill at which he excelled, noted by Gallus on his wax tablets, but it was Lucius who enjoyed success in almost everything, including riding a horse at breakneck speed around the stadium, steering the beast with naught but the four saddle horns hugging his thighs.

"I'm surprised you don't have four legs yourself, Metellus!" Decimus remarked one day.

"Sir!" Lucius saluted sharply as he dismounted.

"We won't be using cavalry in our century, but the skill will come in handy some day," Decimus said. "Keep it up." The gruff centurion nodded and went to discuss things with Gallus who was compiling final lists of contubernia, the groupings of men who would share tents on the long march east.

"Show off!" Argus said to Lucius as he approached. "You're making us look bad."

"I'm just doing my best here," Lucius answered. "If I want to climb through the ranks, I need to excel."

"You're setting yourself up for disappointment, don't you think?" Argus said.

"He's right," Maren added as he came up to join them with a cup of water in his hand. "You heard him on the first day. You won't go anywhere unless either of them dies in the field." He shook his head. "Somehow, I don't think we're that lucky."

"Watch it!" Lucius said. "I don't want that. But, there's got to be other ways for men to rise in the ranks. You hear about it all the time."

"You don't hear the whole story," Maren said. "I've heard of men killing their centurions to move up. It happens all the time."

Lucius shook his head. "Not with me. Besides, that talk is mutinous."

"Suit yourself." Maren shrugged and walked away.

"He's right," Argus said.

"No. He's not."

"Fall in!" Decimus yelled suddenly and every man lined up in perfect rows within a matter of seconds. "Good. Today we're assigning you final contubernia. The men in your contubernium are the men you will eat, sleep, dig, march, fight, and shit with. They will be your brothers...whether you like it or not. First contubernium..."

Decimus went through the lists as they stood there, waiting to hear.

Most were pleased, some not. The century was to be their house, but the contubernium was to be their home.

"Last one!" Decimus said. "Lucius, Argus, Garai, Eligius, Maren, Antanelis, Alerio, Gaius, Tertius, and Corvus."

The ten young men nodded and smiled.

"Don't get too excited," Decimus added, "These lists can change if I see discipline crumbling. If you can't handle it, you'll be replaced by one of the thousands of recruits we're going to pick up in Athenae, Macedonia, and Thrace. Got it?"

"Yes, sir!" they all replied, loud and strong.

"Good. Now, line up to get your kit! One table for your lorica, another for your helmets, one for your scutum, and that last one over there for your cingulum and gladius."

The men stared at the ordered rows of arms and armour, the items they would be wearing across half the world and into battle.

"So? What are you waiting for? Get to it!"

Instead of rushing in pell mell, the first row approached and lined up with all the others following suit in orderly rows.

Decimus leaned over to Gallus, smiling. "I think they're ready now."

"We'll be setting out soon," Argus said to Lucius as they walked through the Forum Boarium, back to the Metellus domus. He was quiet on their way, unlike his usual self. "You sure we're up for this?"

Lucius stopped and looked at Argus, shock splattered across his face. Argus was usually so cocky and full of himself. Lucius could not remember a time when he had not thought he could do whatever he wanted.

"It's a bit late for second thoughts, don't you think?" Lucius answered, his own heart rate increasing. "We've signed up for more than twenty years!"

"I know! I know!" Argus walked over to the steps of the round temple of Hercules and sat down heavily, his lorica, helmet, and covered scutum dropped carelessly beside him.

"Decimus is right, Lucius. Much as I hate the man, or to admit that he has a point. The battlefield is not like the gymnasium, or the training campus. I've heard men talking about the fucking Parthian cavalry. They're covered from head to hoof in plate and scale armour, and their konti lances are fourteen feet long!"

"But that's why we train so hard," Lucius said, standing in front of his friend. "So that we can stand up to that sort of thing. You'll see, it will all kick in when the moment is right."

"You seem pretty fucking sure of yourself!" Argus muttered.

"I have faith that the Gods will look after me. You should too."

"The Gods..." Argus shook his head. "I don't think so, Lucius."

"I know you don't believe much, that you feel they abandoned you long ago when your parents were...." he stopped himself.

"What? Murdered? Yes, they fucking abandoned me."

"And yet they brought you into our home. They ensured that we were placed together in the same contubernium. We'll get through this."

Argus stood, and picked up his things. "I don't know where you get it."

"Get what?"

"Your blind faith."

"It comes from inside." Lucius nodded to the temple before him. "Do you think Hercules didn't question the Gods when he was travelling the world on his twelve labours? Do you think that when he killed the monster Cacus on the steps of the Palatine Hill, he knew that this temple would be raised to him in the heart of the greatest city the world has ever seen?" He waited for Argus to say something, but he only stared at the round temple and its tiled roof. "No. Hercules did what he had to do, day-to-day, whatever the Gods demanded of him. And now he sits among them."

"We're not heroes."

"But we can strive to be," Lucius returned.

"Apollo has played with your mind, Lucius. You live in a world of dreams and omens all the time. I live in the real world." He paused, hefting his things onto his shoulders. "The real world is not full of gods, goddesses, and heroes. It's full of pain, and suffering, and those who survive are those who only deal in such things."

Lucius watched Argus leave through the crowd, pushing a few people out of the way.

"What about Disciplina?" he shouted, but Argus was already far gone.

V

Sanguis et Dei

'Blood and the Gods'

With only five days before the recruits of III Parthica were ready to set out, they were told that there would be no more training until they arrived in Greece. They were to use the time to set their affairs in order, see to final family commitments, and rest their bodies for the long journey east.

It was early morning in Februarius, and the first songs of the spring birds were beginning to come in through the windows of the Metellus domus.

In the upper storey of the house, Lucius sat on a folding chair by the window. He had been up early that morning and decided to go through the many scrolls he had, to decide which ones he would take with him. He had to be careful how many, for he would have to carry everything himself. There were no mules to carry supplies for regular troops.

He held a copy of Arrian's work on the campaigns of Alexander the Great, and of Xenophon's Anabasis which he thought might come in handy as they were going to be fighting in that part of the world. He had a scroll of Gaius Julius Caesar's account of his campaign in Gaul, as well as a few others. If he could have brought them all, he would have, but it was impossible. His old tutor, Diodorus had left all of them to Lucius in his will, and when the old man passed a few years previously, he had given a veritable library of scrolls to Lucius in a thick wooden chest.

"If only you could see me now, Diodorus," Lucius said to himself, smiling at the memory of the kind, old Greek with his long white beard and playful smile. Their days of learning in the Forum Romanum had been some of the happiest Lucius had ever experienced. He could hear the old man reminding him, as he often did, to 'look around at the world, Lucius, for the Gods reveal themselves and their will at every turn...'

"I'm going to see the world now."

Lucius looked out of the window again, and then about his cubiculum. It would be a long time before he saw those faded red and white walls again. The air smelled damp, despite the incense he burned. Lucius ran his finger along the bubbling plaster surrounding the window frame, and it crumbled to powder beneath his touch. He thought that if he ever inherited the house, he would restore its faded beauty, if only for the few happy memories it held.

There was a light knock on the door and Alene peeked her head around the door.

"Lucius?"

He looked up and smiled. He was relieved to see her. He felt guilty for having been away from the house so much in the last weeks, especially as he was going to be leaving for the East so soon and might not see her for several years.

"Come in. I'm just deciding on some things to bring with me on campaign."

Alene entered his cubiculum wearing a long white tunica with a deep green cloak around her shoulders to ward off the morning chill.

"I don't want to disturb you," she said, as she sat down on the edge of his bed.

"Oh, please. I want to spend every moment with you before I go. I'm sorry I haven't been around so much."

She didn't smile. He could see that she had been crying a little. "It's as the Gods will it."

"I'm going to miss you, Sister. So much..."

"And I you. I feel like everything is changing. You leaving - this house, our home, and our familia will never be the same."

"You've never been one for change, have you?"

"Of a sort, yes. But not everything." She sighed, her eyes looking him up and down. "You know you look awful."

"You and mother have been trading notes, I guess." Lucius felt the swollen part of his cheek, just beneath his right eye, where he had been slammed by a heavy wicker practice scutum. "I suppose I've looked better," he laughed, "but I certainly feel better than I look. I've never felt so strong. I feel like I could do anything." He got up and stood to lean on the window sill and stare out in the direction of the Palatine Hill.

Alene had noticed the difference in Lucius' bearing, the far-off look on his features when he stared blankly, his mind churning over the myriad thoughts, dreams, and worries that she knew spun around in his mind.

"The least you can let me do is help you to pack your things," she said, picking up his white tunic with the thin purple stripe around the hem of the sleeves and neck that marked him as one of the Equestrian class. "I don't think you'll have much opportunity to wear this on campaign," she pointed out. "It's legionary red for you from now on."

"Not for long." Lucius stopped packing the scrolls and stood straight to smile are her. "I don't care what our father says. I'm going to climb through the ranks, and the next time I walk through our door, I'll be an officer."

"As long as you're alive and walk through that door at all, I'll thank the Gods..." Alene spun to look away.

"Alene, please..." He walked over to her and held her tightly. "I'll be fine."

"Just keep your new friends close, all right? I'll feel better knowing that you have allies watching your back."

"Of course. We're stuck together, the lot of us. Eating, sleeping and shitting together, as our centurion says."

"That's disgusting. I can't imagine the smell inside one of those leather tents." She smiled and wiped her eyes, then held his face in her hands. "I just want you to stay alive. Whatever it takes."

"I will," he said, staring right back at her. "I will."

Over the next couple of days, Lucius spent time with Alene and his mother as much as he could. They walked through the imperial fora, and went to the baths and the theatre. When their mother grew tired and returned home, Lucius and Alene went out again, to stroll about the quieter streets, and visit the temples where Alene seemed determined to make offerings for Lucius' safety at each one.

Early in the morning on the day before his departure, Lucius rose before everyone else and made his way to the Palatine Hill for a final visit to the Temple of Apollo. The square was quiet when he reached the top of the stairs. The marble was damp from the light rain of the previous night, and a few pigeons shuffled about the base of a great tripod where the priests had lit the fire to honour the god.

Lucius paused to take it all in. Much of his youth had been spent in that place, and the sight of it, the mingled smells of offerings, fire, and water, would anchor him in Rome when he was far away. Two voices echoed from the other side of the square where the vendor of offerings was setting up his table along with his son, Numonius, who was only a couple of years younger than Lucius. He walked over to greet them.

"Salve!" Lucius said.

"Salve to you, Lucius Metellus!" the seller returned, smiling broadly. "I see you're early to make your offering to Apollo."

"I leave with the legions for the East tomorrow, and wanted to spend some time in the temple before anyone else showed up."

"I heard that you had joined. Your sister mentioned it."

"Yes. I'm sure she'll keep you in business while I'm away," Lucius said.

"I'm sure!" the man laughed. "But, let me give you something this day, as a farewell gift." He reached into a crate and pulled out a bouquet of fresh herbs bound in red ribbon, criss-crossed about the stems to look like the fascies, the reed bundles carried by the lictors who followed the emperor about.

"Your wife has outdone herself," Lucius said, taking the bundle. "But I insist on paying you for it."

"But we intended it for you. The Gods have marked you out, young Metellus, as I witnessed on the day you put on your toga. I'm sure this gift will be smiled upon. Save your coin for the march. It's a long way to Parthia." The man smiled beneath his beard and crossed his thick arms over his solid belly.

"You'd better take it, Lucius," said the man's son. "He'll not be swayed. Besides, my mother will harangue him to no end if she finds out he took money when she told him to give it to you."

Lucius accepted the bundle and turned to go into the temple.

"May Apollo guide you and keep you, young Metellus," the vendor said.

"And you also, my friends," Lucius said over his shoulder as he mounted the steps.

The great bronze doors had been left slightly ajar and fragrant smoke wafted through the crack of the temple, wrapping itself about Lucius and pulling him inside.

Later that day, Lucius sat in the peristylium, wrapped in his black cloak, holding the new gladius he had been issued. He and Argus had just returned from the gymnasium, and the latter had gone off to drink with Maren, and the twins, Eligius and Garai, along with Corvus and Gaius.

Argus had wanted Lucius to come, but Lucius had not wanted to. He waited for Alene to return from a visit to the lady Claudia's with their mother. There would be plenty of time for drinking and whoring in the months to follow, but being at home was going to be something of a rarity.

Lucius could just see the hint of light from beneath the door of his father's tablinum; it seemed he was determined to see as little of Lucius as possible before he set out. Lucius wondered whether his father would even bother to attend the

71

meal that his mother had been arranging to wish Lucius and Argus well on their journey.

He gripped the wooden pommel of his gladius and ran his fingers along the ivory handle, watching as the moonlight glinted off of the blade. *Such a simple weapon, but so effective.*

"We'll see how effective soon enough..." he said to himself.

"What's that you're saying?" Alene said, coming into the garden.

"I didn't hear you come home," Lucius said, standing and setting the blade down on the couch.

"What are you doing outside? The night is cold," she said. "Can you believe the fulness of Selene tonight?"

Lucius looked up. "Yes, she's almost as bright as the sun."

Together they both looked up at the great silver orb in the sky above Rome. It seemed to hush the entire city. Then a door slammed and they both looked toward their father's tablinum.

"What's going on?" Lucius asked.

"Mother said there was something she wanted to speak to Father about. Apparently it is urgent and can't wait. She wanted to leave lady Claudia's rather early."

"I wonder what it is?"

"She didn't say."

Both siblings looked toward the door where they could hear their parents' voices getting louder and louder.

"I hope they don't wake up little Quintus and Clarinda," Alene said.

"You can't lock yourself away in here, Quintus!" Antonia Metella said, still wearing her green cloak from outside, and standing before her husband's desk with her arms by her sides.

"Why not? What does it matter?" he answered. "The boy doesn't give a damn what I think. Let him go off to war, and a life of misery with the scum of the legions. He'll have nothing when it's all over."

"You don't mean that."

"Oh, don't I?" Quintus Metellus looked up from his papers and threw his stylus down, colour rushing up his neck into his face and balding head. "I most certainly do. He has no respect for me, though I have given him everything, done everything for him. Has he ever wanted for anything, Antonia? Has he?"

Antonia Metella approached her husband calmly, removing her cloak and hanging it on the folding chair before the desk.

"Only your approval."

"Pfff!" He waved his hand dismissively. "Approval? Does he need his young ego stroked in order to feel he is a man? If that is the way of things with him, then the legions will break him."

Antonia stopped, her hand to her mouth for a moment. For weeks she had been dreading Lucius' leaving, facing her own fears about what he would face, and whether she would ever see him again. She was the matron of her family, and she knew that as a Roman, it was her duty to be strong, especially when it came time to send her son off to war, but that did not make it any easier.

"Then give him strength, Quintus," she said. "Your father saw something in Lucius. He knew he was meant to go by

'Anguis'. The Dragon is in him, as it has been in your ancestors."

"Don't speak of so ludicrous a thing. The words and visions of one mad ancestor do not determine the future of the entire line."

"No. But they can inspire. Perhaps not yourself, as you have made your life your own way. Your father, however, he felt the pull of that symbol, and the ancient dragon was a source of great inspiration to him. He did not insist just before his death that Lucius be named 'Anguis' for no reason."

"My father was mad in the end. That's all he inherited from the Metellus at Zama."

"You know as much as I that that is not true. Your father was as sane as any man, and he loved Lucius as he loved you, though you pushed him away. I beg you, Quintus, for the sake of our family, do not push your own son away. Lucius will make you proud, I promise you."

Quintus jerked at the touch of his wife's hand on his cheek. She had come upon him without him noticing, and he began to shrink away, but stopped. Her eyes held his gaze and he felt himself deflate of the anger that had been building for weeks. She had always had that power over him, and part of him hated it.

"Eat with us tomorrow, Quintus. You are the head of the familia, Lucius' father, and Argus' foster-father. Show the boys that you are behind them as they set off, and..."

"And what?" Quintus asked, pulling away now. "Antonia, what?"

"Perhaps it is time to give Lucius the family armour and weapons?"

Quintus Metellus looked across the room to the large cedar chest to his left, covered with scrolls and accounts, lost beneath the detritus of his business dealings.

"You have served in the legions. Now it is his turn. Those weapons and armour are his by rights. Your father would have wanted him to have them too. It is your duty as his father to arm him when he goes to war."

"Duty? What of his duty to this familia? To me?"

Antonia said nothing. She knew not what more to say at this point.

Quintus had not thought of the armour for years, not even looked at the trunk, for all the items on top of it. Now that he had been reminded, the images of dragons flashed through his mind, and he scoffed, though a chill breath seemed to lick the back of his neck as he did so, as though the ghost of his father urged him to listen to his wife's words.

They are no longer yours... the sickly voice said in his head. Give them to my grandson!

"Leave me," Quintus pulled Antonia's hand off of his arm. "I want to be alone."

She looked at him and knew he was mulling it over. Without saying anything, Antonia picked up her cloak and left the tablinum, leaving Quintus Metellus standing in the dusty lamplight, staring at the trunk.

When she was gone, Quintus Metellus breathed deeply and moved toward the trunk.

"You're all mad," he said, to his father, and to all of his ancestors who had worn the symbol of the dragon. He had refused, but others had not. And yet, he could never bring himself to destroy the objects in that trunk, nor paint over the images of dragons on the walls of the triclinium or in other parts of the house.

Before he knew it, he was kneeling on the ground before the trunk, removing the scrolls and other items from the top, dirtying his white tunic as he did so. His clearing became more urgent, his mood angrier as he moved everything, and then, the lid was open and he was staring into the dark depth of that box, wondering what despair doing so would unleash upon his family. Antonia believed giving the items to Lucius would inspire and empower him, but Quintus believed that they were more likely to drive him mad with arrogance and fantasy.

He pulled aside the black linen coverings and held a lamp over it to see inside.

His eyes alighted on the bulk of the black, hardened bull's hide cuirass and the overbearing image of the dragon in the centre, silver with outspread wings, its hideous maw open to devour its enemies. Quintus Metellus reached out to touch it with a fingertip but recoiled as if it burned him. He cursed himself for a fool and then grabbed hold of the armour's edges and lifted it out.

The armour seemed not to have aged at all; it had remained safe in its well-oiled state.

Quintus vaguely remembered his father wearing the armour, but only as a passing shadow of memory. He had never liked his father, and the feeling had been mutual. He placed the cuirass on the floor and bent over to retrieve the helmet with dragons embossed on the cheek-pieces, and a deep crimson horse-hair crest that leaned slightly to one side because of the way it had lain in trunk. Despite that, it shone.

Quintus imagined Lucius wearing these items over his thin-stripped tunic and black pteruges, the leather skirt and arm straps that also lay at the bottom of the trunk along with the dragon-embossed greaves.

"Fool!" The thought only angered him. Unwanted, the thought of Lucius and the eagle on the Palatine Hill came to him. That time, when the eagle had stood between him and his son before the Temple of Apollo, if he was honest, the moment haunted him. "Gods, why did you take my son from me?"

He placed the helmet down beside the cuirass and reached in to take out the gold-hilted gladius with images of Pegasus, and a silver eagle on the pommel. The ancient pugio of Greek design with the head of Jupiter on the pommel and an ancient hunting scene etched on the blade lay beside it, safely sheathed and unbloodied for years.

The gladius and pugio felt foreign in his soft hands, and he scowled as he stared at them. He knew he was no Cincinnatus, nor a Scipio, he had never grown to be a match for any of his Republican heroes. Quintus Metellus had been left to clean up the mess left by his Metelli ancestors, and the wreck of two hundred years of imperial rule.

"How can a true Roman shine through in this world?" he said to himself, shaking his head. "Let him have the armour. I don't want it." A minute later, the items were put back in the darkness of the cedar chest, the lid slammed shut upon them and all the bitter memories they evoked.

The following night, Rome was uneasy. Terrible winds lashed the city, and three fires broke out on the Aventine, on the Quirinal, and in the Subura. The cloudy sky above the city reflected orange in several directions. The Vigiles, Rome's fire fighting force, were kept very busy.

Lucius had spent the day with Alene and at the gymnasium for training before returning home exhausted, his mind spinning for all the final preparations that had to be made prior to his departure.

Argus had been seen intermittently, coming and going. When Lucius had asked him if he had made all his preparations he answered, 'What's to prepare? As long as I have coin in my purse, and a sword at my hip, I'm ready.'

Lucius admired his frugality, but knew he could not match it. Still, he had mused for a while before sleeping over which items he should really leave behind. Until he had climbed the ranks, he would have to carry everything on his own back.

The lamp burned slowly on the table in Lucius' cubiculum, the flames wavering every so often from the breeze that penetrated his window. Lucius' eyes shut tightly as he slept, turning himself to one side, and then another, unable to find peaceful slumber. His mind had been racing when he lay down, but his body cried out for quiet rest.

On the table, beside the fiery lamp stood the statue of Apollo, his muscled arm outstretched as if to point at Lucius.

If the young Metellus had been awake or aware, he would have seen that the statue began to glow in an otherworldly blue light, that the limbs of Apollo's image pulsed with the fire in his godly veins.

But the Gods are rarely meant to be seen, and then, only by a select few, one of those being Lucius Metellus Anguis.

In his dreaming mind, Lucius saw himself beside the Tiber, long ago, playing in the grass with his wooden gladius.

He saw the tall forms of the man and woman approach him then, their smiles, their severity.

Do you remember? Apollo whispered, the sounds of the outside world having completely died away. *It is time to awaken, Metellus... Anguis.*

Lucius tossed at the utterance of the word, as the images in his mind turned from the shores of the Tiber to a faraway desert where the sky was choked with dust, and the cries of dead and dying men screeched in his ears.

Cavalry, brilliant and shining, shook the earth, and fear ran through him only to be drowned out by the most hideous sound he had ever heard or felt, something to chill the blood through all his limbs. Great wings flapped, razors at their edges, and jaws with teeth half the height of a man roared and gnashed, tearing horse and rider apart in every direction, soaking the sand with lakes of blood as the sun rose and set with the moon, over and over again.

"No..." Lucius mumbled in his sweaty sleep. "Anguis..."

Yes, Apollo approached from the corner of the room. *It is time to fly, to become who you are meant to be, Metellus.*

"Ahhh!" Lucius fell back onto the desert sand, blood all about him, his eyes staring at a star-pocked sky where the full moon shone down on him to cool the heat of battle. Waves of peace replaced the tension racking his body, and he settled back down.

Apollo watched for a moment longer, his timeless eyes looking on the Roman, the heavens reflected in them, whirling stars and fire. He would watch over this one, protect him for as long as he proved worthy.

A better man than your father, Metellus.

Apollo nodded and an instant later, was gone.

Lucius sat up, sweat pouring down his face where the sun shone onto it through the window.

He rubbed his eyes and swung his feet over the bed, head in his hands. A moment later, he turned slowly to look at the statue of Apollo where it pointed at him from the table.

"One more day," Lucius said to himself.

Lucius spent his last full day in Rome as if in a daze. In a way, his mind was already marching east. In reality, it would be many months before they arrived in Antioch, for Decimus and his century, Lucius' century, were to lead the recruitment of troops in Athenae, and then in Macedonia and Thrace.

It was going to be a long haul.

First thing that morning, after waking from his disturbing sleep, he headed straight to the Temple of Apollo to seek some peace of mind, and perhaps some answers to the dreams he had had that night. The god was, however, silent for the time being, though a sense of peace did wash over Lucius after his offerings had been made.

"May the God of the Silver Bow protect you, Lucius Metellus Anguis," the priest said as Lucius descended the marble steps for the last time.

"I will see you again," Lucius answered, taking one last look at the white columns and ornamented pediment high above.

When he arrived back at the Metellus domus, after cutting his way through the thick crowds that were flowing toward the

Circus Maximus for the day's chariot races, he found the house in a frenzy.

"What's happening?" he asked Alene when she came running up to him in the atrium, holding little Quintus and Clarinda's hands.

"Why, we're having a fabulous banquet tonight, for you and Argus. Mother has spared no expense on the food."

Lucius could already detect the rich smell of roast Etrurian boar in plum and wine sauce emanating from the kitchens to his right, as well as freshly baked breads.

"Is Argus up yet?"

"He went to the Circus," little Quintus piped up. "He said he wanted to place a last bet on the Blues."

"I wonder if we'll see him at all today," Lucius said.

"Does it matter for now?" Alene answered. "I'm happy to just sit with you for the day, if you don't have other plans. I mean...tomorrow-"

Alene stopped herself, but Lucius could see that she was on the verge of tears. She'd held in her emotion for many days, but he could see it building to the day of his departure and it pained him to see it.

"Quintus, Clarinda," Lucius spoke to his younger siblings. "Why don't you go and find your play balls so that I can throw them with you in the peristylium for a while."

"Really?" the two of them said, their little faces bright and strange to Lucius in that moment.

He nodded and they ran off. He then took Alene's hand and they began to walk around the perimeter of the garden which was turning greener by the day.

"I want you to do something for me," he said to his sister.

"What?"

"Be happy. I won't be able to bear it if I know you're constantly depressed while I'm on the other side of the world. You're the most important person in my life, Alene, and I need to know that you're happy. Knowing that, will give me strength."

She stopped walking and nodded. "Very well. I'll be happy. I'll read lots of Catullus and Ovid, and write you many letters when I know where to send them to."

"Just send them to me at III Parthica Legion. The army messengers are good, I hear."

"I'll tell you about all the parties I've gone to, and the lacivious men I've turned away." Alene laughed, clearly herself again.

"Hmmm," Lucius grumbled. "No man will ever be good enough for my sister."

"Maybe I'll even find you a wife for when you come back?" she teased.

Now Lucius blushed. "There's a thought!" he said.

"Troops are allowed to marry now, aren't they?"

"Well, I think so, yes. But I wouldn't want to drag a wife and children around the world on campaign."

At that moment, Lucius felt something hard smack him in the back of the head. "Ouch!"

"Got you!" Clarinda and little Quintus jumped up and down, their arms holding several colourful balls. "Get him!"

"I'll never surrender!" Lucius roared and rushed the two screaming children, chasing them around the peristylium, their laughter and cries echoing up through the roof to be swept away on the wind and rush of sound from the Roman crowds without.

The evening meal was set early, for there were many courses to get through, including salads, a variety of olives and cheeses, breads and cooked vegetables, fish, poultry, and the roast boar that was brought out steaming on a large platter carried by two of the slaves.

Lucius felt his mouth water and took a sip of the wine from their Etrurian estate. He shared a couch with Alene, with Quintus Metellus and Antonia Metella to his right, the younger children across, and Argus, already drunk from his betting at the Circus, on a couch to himself.

A single brazier heated the frescoed triclinium where images of mythological beasts, including dragons, danced on walls painted like a forest.

Lucius had grown up with those dragons.

Throughout the sumptuous meal, a slave girl, whom Antonia had hired from a friend, played the lyre for them. The black-haired girl plucked soft notes all evening, her fingers never tiring as she did so, her voice sometimes jumping in to match the melody she played so skillfully.

As Lucius finished chewing his first delicious bite of wild boar, he turned to his parents.

"Thank you for this, Father, Mother." He did not know what to say, but felt that something was needed. "We'll leave tomorrow with happy thoughts and full bellies. I'm sure they won't always be full while on campaign."

"You'll likely starve in the desert," Quintus Metellus mumbled.

"Let's hope not, Foster Father!" Argus said a bit too loudly.

"Somehow, Argus, I think you shall never starve."

It was not a compliment.

Argus smiled and drained his cup again before ripping a large piece of bread from the loaf in front of him, and shoving it into his mouth. He had won at the Circus that day, and had evidently developed a large appetite.

"I'm sure there will be lean days," Lucius said. "But it won't always be so."

"No," his father said. "Most days you will still have your daily ration of rotting garlic to keep you going."

"Quintus," Antonia nudged him, plucking a grape from the vine she held.

Conversation was intermittent after that, partly due to the music played by the slave girl. Her fingers moved quickly and the lilt in her voice seemed to change as she played a rustic song of love lost, and of punishment by the Gods. When she finished, Lucius, Alene, and Antonia clapped.

"That was lovely," Antonia said. "Junius," she called to the slave who stood by the triclinium door. "Take her to the kitchen and make sure she is well-fed."

"Yes, mistress," the old slave answered, motioning to the girl to follow him.

"Now," Antonia said, turning to her husband. "I believe we have other business to take care of?"

Quintus Metellus looked at her and then to Lucius.

"Yes. Now is as good a time as any," he said dully, clapping his hands.

Junius came back to the triclinium, a little breathless, and leading two other slaves who carried a large wooden chest into the entrance of the room, just beside the brazier.

Lucius looked at the chest, and then to his father. "What's this?"

Quintus Metellus's jaw worked itself back and forth a couple of times before he spoke. "Open it. It's yours now."

Antonia smiled at her husband, knowing the effort he put into this moment, but he did not look back at her.

"Thank you, Father," Lucius said, flipping the latch open and opening the lid slowly. "I can't believe-" Lucius' words caught in his throat as he pulled back the linen to reveal the dragon upon the black cuirass, as well as the items beneath it.

"What is it, Lucius?" Alene asked, coming to stand beside him, little Quintus and Clarinda crowding around them too. Argus peered between them from his couch, and then looked at Quintus Metellus pater. "Oh, Father!" Alene said. "Did it belong to Grandfather?"

"Yes," he said, drinking his wine. "I pass it to Lucius now. He'll need it where he is going, that is, if he attains the rank he aspires to."

Lucius put the cuirass down and stood. He walked into the centre of the couches, around the table laden with food, and stood before his father and mother.

"Father, thank you for this magnificent gift. I'll wear it proudly. I swear I'll honour our family with my every action." Lucius knelt then, his head bowed to their paterfamilias, hoping in his heart that this was the peace offering for which he had been hoping.

Quintus Metellus looked down at his son's bowed head. Part of him wished to place his hand gently in blessing upon the short dark hair, to believe that Lucius was capable of the greatness he claimed he could achieve.

Then he remembered his own failed dreams, the fighting, the humiliation, the loss and deception of his life. The loss of his youth, all the fresh opportunities he had had, and missed, rankled him. The thought of his son wasting those same opportunities opened the wounds of resentment anew.

Quintus Metellus withdrew his hand. "I never wanted or wore those old things, but your grandfather did, mad as he was. Maybe once you've gotten your twenty-five years of service out of your system, you'll be able to come back and make a real life for yourself."

Antonia recoiled as Lucius looked up, his face hurt, changed as though the final lamp in a room had been blown out.

Even Argus sat up at that, staring at Quintus Metellus with fire in his eyes, wishing Lucius to slam his fist into the old man's face once and for all.

But Lucius stood, his chin up, his eyes watery but their lids holding back the bitter tears he might have shed were he a boy.

"I thank you for passing the family arms and armour into my keeping, Father." He took a deep breath and straightened his tunic where it had bunched beneath his belt. Then, looking directly at Quintus Metellus, "By the Gods, Father. I will surprise you." Lucius looked at his mother a moment before turning and making his way back to the trunk.

He bent down to grab the leather handles on either end and lifted it up. Lucius cast a glance at Alene who had been standing with her arms crossed beside the triclinium door, and then went up to his cubiculum.

He ignored the sounds of argument and complaint that erupted in his wake, the crying of the children, and the raging of a bitter, resentful old coward.

Lucius paced about his room, staring at the armour, helmet, gladius, pugio, pteruges, and greaves which he had spread out on his bed.

They were beautiful, strong, and mysterious to him, and yet he fought to control the anger he felt toward his father.

"You know you can't bring those with you, right?"

Lucius looked up to see Argus leaning against the door frame, with Alene coming up behind him.

"Lucius, don't listen to father," she said. "He's not right. He's just upset that you're leaving is all."

"I'm sure that's it, Alene," Argus laughed. "The old man was never brave enough to put on the flashy armour. He's jealous that Lucius is." He walked over to the bed and picked up the gladius, nodding at its exceptional balance and keen, oiled edge as he slid it out of the sheath.

"That 'old man' has kept you safe since you were a boy, Argus. Or does it not matter anymore now that you are off on your own?"

"Oh, it matters," Argus said evenly. "Still doesn't change the fact," he turned to Lucius again, "that you can't bring that with you. We have to carry everything on our backs. Only centurions and other officers get pack animals and space on the wagons."

Lucius stared at the items and then looked at Argus. "Then I'll bloody carry them myself."

Argus laughed. "I thought *I* had too much wine. You'll carry those all the way to Parthia? You must be pretty sure of your future promotion."

"Yes, I'll carry them. And yes, I know I'll get to where I want to go."

"Well, don't ask me to help you carry them. They're not mine." Argus walked to the door and turned. "You'd better start repacking. I'm going to the Subura."

Lucius let him go. It was no use. In a way, he knew Argus was right; carrying these extra items was going to be tough, but he knew he wanted to have them with him.

"Are you all right?" Alene asked, standing beside her brother now.

"No. Though I don't know what I was expecting. Should he have smiled, praised me, and forgotten all my harsh words in one evening? I don't think *I* could have done that."

"This isn't how I wanted your farewell banquet to go," Alene said. "The music, the food, the wine...now it's all for naught."

"It's fine," Lucius said, sighing. "The time for me to go is really here now. The Gods have shown us that."

She had nothing to say. Alene put her long arms about her younger brother and hugged him tightly, wishing she could protect him in the months ahead just as easily as she always had when he had nightmares as a child.

As he held her, Lucius inhaled the familiar smell of her hair, the care and warmth of her touch. He hoped he would not forget.

It was still dark when they had gathered in the atrium of the domus. All the slaves were lined up, two of them holding little Quintus and Clarinda upright where they swayed sleepily on their feet. Braziers lit everyone's faces where they stood, waiting for Lucius who was making an offering to Apollo, Janus, and their ancestors in the family shrine.

Quintus Metellus stood still in his toga beside his wife. They were still not speaking to each other.

Alene was surprised to see her father there.

Argus stood in his legionary armour beside the main door, his helmet dangling from one hand and his satchel slung over his shoulder. He chewed an apple noisily as he shifted with impatience, waiting for Lucius so that they could be gone from the Metellus domus.

When Lucius emerged from the shrine, he went straight to the busts of his ancestors, the Metelli in whose footsteps he now followed. His satchel and another bundle containing his new cuirass, helmet and other items were laid on the marble floor before the images of Macedonicus, Dalmaticus, Creticus and the others.

"Ancestors, I honour you. I know that I defy my father by choosing this path... Help me to show that it is the right path. Help me to bring honour and glory to our family. Guide me in decision, and in battle. Know that I remember you, and I remember our gods." He looked at each face in turn, the broad, wrinkled brows, the blank staring eyes, and felt a chill run the length of his spine.

"Apollo, shine your light upon the path ahead of me."

Lucius then bent to pick up his two big bundles, the gladii and pugionis at his sides catching on his cloak. He would have to get used to them.

He hefted everything and made his way to the atrium where everyone was waiting for him.

"Finally!" Argus said.

Lucius shot him an annoyed look and put his things down again so as to bid everyone farewell. He had been expecting the day for some weeks, but now that the time had come to leave, to see his familia lined up to see him off, he was not quite ready.

Lucius walked over to where little Quintus and Clarinda stood, and knelt down to face them. "I don't know how long it will be before I see you both again, but I do know you'll be much bigger. Will you be good?"

Clarinda nodded her head absently, yawning in Lucius' face before he kissed her on the forehead.

"And you, Quintus? You'll be all right, won't you?"

"Why do you have to go, Lucius?" the boy said in a squeaky voice. "Just stay in Rome like father says."

Lucius looked at his younger brother sternly, but did not chide him. "I'll miss you and your antics, Brother. Be good and when you are able, begin reading some of those scrolls I left you. Especially the Argonautica. I know you'll love that one. Alene will read it to you if you like."

Quintus looked at Alene and she smiled back. "All right."

"Good." Lucius stood and turned to face his father.

Quintus Metellus stood there, dressed for an early session at the Curia, the building in the Forum Romanum where the Senate met. He was stern, lips pursed, his thin arms crossed.

Lucius looked at him, willing himself not to stare at the floor. He searched his father's features for some trace of emotion at this parting of ways. Like it or not, it was possible that Lucius would never return.

"Father, I..."

"So this is it," Quintus Metellus finally said. "I hope you'll listen to your centurion better than you've listened to me."

"Hmmph," Argus burst out, cutting himself off at a look from the elder Metellus.

"I'll make you proud," Lucius said, biting back the retorts he would like to have heaped upon his father.

"Just don't embarrass me." Quintus Metellus turned to walk slowly down the corridor toward his tablinum, subtly shaking off his wife's hand as it reached out toward him. Then, he stopped, his back still to everyone in the atrium. "And try not to get killed." With those final words, he closed the door to his room, leaving Lucius staring after him.

"I guess I shouldn't have expected anything else," Lucius said as he turned to his mother. He could see that a stray tear had run down her cheek, but she wiped it away, and pushed her dark hair back over her shoulders.

"Just know that we will be praying for your safe return, Lucius." Antonia Metella stepped up to her son, took him by the shoulders and hugged him tightly, her head resting on his chest. "Please be careful. And yes," she said, holding him at arms' length again, "I know you will make us proud. I've never doubted it."

"Thank you, Mother," Lucius half-smiled and stared at her a moment, for there was something else behind her eyes. "What?"

She gripped his shoulders tightly and stared intently into his eyes. "Remember, Lucius... We are, all of us, Apollo's children. He will watch over you. Remember Him, for He has watched over the dragons of this family for generations."

Lucius nodded. "I won't forget."

"Good. Now you had better get going," Antonia said, stepping back so that Alene could come forward.

Alene Metella stood before her brother and hugged him tightly, her hair falling about his face, her cheeks wet upon his neck as she held him.

"I'll be fine," Lucius whispered. "You'll always be in my thoughts."

With fresh tears in her eyes, Alene kissed Lucius on both cheeks, and reached into the sleeve of her tunic to retrieve the two eagles' feathers that had been given to him the day he became a man. She had wrapped these symbols of the Gods' favour in white silk, and now placed them in the scrip at his waist.

"Apollo guide and protect you, little brother," she managed to say through a shaking voice.

"Why's Alene crying?" Clarinda said, shushed immediately by her mother.

Lucius smiled as best he could and laid his hand on her cheek for a moment, taking in the comforting look of the person who had always looked out for him. He felt his throat tighten, and gave her a final hug before bending down to pick up his two big bundles.

"I'll write," Lucius said as he stood in front of the door.

"Come on, Lucius!" Argus called from outside in the street. "We still need to march to Brundisium with the others."

Lucius nodded. He turned and looked one last time at the only domus he had ever known - the familiar mosaic floors, and the fading colours of the walls. He took in the site of the atrium's impluvium where he used to splash in the water with his wooden ships, and smiled to himself.

"Goodbye," he said at last to Alene, his mother, and the others who were still there.

Unable to say anything else, or find other reasons to delay, Lucius turned and went out into the early dawn light to join Argus.

The two of them walked, laden with their belongings toward the Forum Boarium and the Stadium of Domitian, to find the men of their century and begin their long journey to war on the front lines of the Empire.

Part II

PARTHIA

A.D. 198

VI

Corpus Firmus

'Body of Strength'

The seas were not kind to ships at the end of Februarius, still less so to young men who had rarely, if ever, set a foot off of land.

From the time the first century of III Parthica sailed out of Brundisium, several days after marching out of Rome along the Via Appia, the seas punished them. Young men who in training had been fierce, and strong, and arrogant on the sands of the circus, now huddled in the holds of the three merchant corbitae hired by Decimus to take them to Piraeus outside of Athenae for their first round of recruiting.

It was a long journey across the Adriaticus, and around the peninsulae of the Peloponnesus. Lucius, Argus, and the rest of the recruits in the first ship took turns bending over various buckets to purge their guts between the swells that Neptune sent rolling their way.

Lucius began to wonder if Hades was not a ship, rather than a realm of the Underworld. The stench and sounds were enough to drive a man to madness and regret. When the seas began to calm near the coast, Lucius decided to brave the upper deck with Antanelis and Alerio to get some fresh air.

"Pah! Fresh air at last!" Lucius gasped as he climbed out of the square hole in the deck of the merchant ship.

"Gods help us!" Antanelis affirmed, helping Alerio up and out.

"You ladies all right?" Decimus said from the upper deck where the trierarchus, Captain Chioticus, steered the ship. The centurion smiled at them and Chioticus laughed.

"I hope you Romans will fight better than you sail!" the Greek seafarer roared as spray splashed over the rail to shower the three young men.

"I'd yell back at him if it wouldn't make me vomit again," Alerio said, gripping the central mast beneath the large square canvas sail.

"Just leave it," Lucius said. "I'm sure we make quite a sight."

Antanelis laughed, looking out at the distant land to his left as Lucius climbed up the ladder to speak with his centurion.

"Permission to speak, sir?"

"Approach, Metellus," Decimus said, not attempting to help Lucius who swayed on his feet.

"It's horrid down there, sir."

"You boys better not destroy my ship, you hear!" Chioticus said. "After I take you to Antioch, I go back to transporting grain, wine, and oil. I don't want a ship stinking of piss, shit, and vomit. You hear?"

"Don't worry yourself, Trierarchus," Decimus said. "My boys will scrub the hold clean once we arrive in Piraeus."

Lucius tried not to think about it. Instead he gazed out at an island to the left.

"You know what that is?" Chioticus said. Lucius shook his head. "Ithaka. The island where Odysseus lived."

"Really?" Lucius walked immediately toward the side and gazed out. The story of Odysseus' travels had been one of his favourites as a child. He had also studied it at length with his old tutor Diodorus. "Are we stopping?"

Decimus shook his head. "No time to explore ancient stories, Metellus. We're on a tight schedule."

"Sir, will we have leave time in Athenae while we're there? I've always wanted to go."

Decimus fixed Lucius with a stern look, and crossed his scarred arms. "We're not on holiday. You need to remember that, Metellus. We're in Greece to raise three legions and then march to war with another thirty legions at our side."

Lucius looked down, angry with himself. He knew he had let his childlike enthusiasm get the better of him.

"You're right, sir. There'll be plenty of time to see the world after the battle is won." Lucius stood taller and sucked up his dissapointment.

"Good man. You've got it right." Decimus uncrossed his arms and pointed with his vinerod to some distant clouds to the south. "You'd better get below now, Metellus, and tell the men to hunker down. We're in for some more chop."

Lucius looked ahead to the grey and black clouds that gathered along the coast in thick tendrils like some monstrous Scylla out of legend. He saluted and went back down the ladder to follow Alerio and Antanelis into the hold.

"He seems like a good boy," Chioticus said.

"One of my best," Decimus acknowledged. "But a little too idealistic still."

"Hmm. My father used to say, idealism comes from contact with the Gods."

Decimus looked at the grizzled captain from beneath his helmet's brim, but said nothing.

The storm did not last as long as they feared, and once they rounded the peninsula where Pylos stood as an ancient sentry over the sea, the weather calmed. The way was smooth to Piraeus.

When Chioticus' three merchant ships came into port, the men that poured out of the holds were a far cry from the elite soldiers they were meant to be. Cloaks had been stained with puke, leather gone mouldy, and armour spotted with rust from constant sea spray.

Their weakened state did not extract any measure of pity from Decimus who gave them one hour to unload their gear and find their land legs, before he forced them back onto the ships to scrub them clean. After that, the century was forced to make camp outside the port and then ensure that every buckle and piece of armour was polished, every sword sharp, every piece of clothing clean and free of spots.

Inspection the following morning, they were told, was going to be stringent and unforgivable.

"I'll not have the only Romans in the new legions looking like drunken, sheep-shagging barbarians!" Decimus yelled. "When new recruits step up to the table to sign-up, I want them to yearn to be one of you! It's an honour to serve in the legions!"

No Roman officials from Athenae itself came to meet the first century of III Parthica at Piraeus. After all, there were no tribunes present, the highest ranking officer being Decimus himself. However, a plot of land to the northwest of the ruins of the ancient long walls running from the port to the great city had been marked for the tent rows, training ground and makeshift command tent.

When Decimus saw that they were to sleep exposed on the first night, he set half the century to keep a watch while the other slept. The two halves took it in turns to rest. In the morning, they were told they needed to dig fortifications.

"Might as well get the bloody practice in now!" the centurion barked as the men grabbed their picks and shovels and got to breaking the damp ground.

Lucius and some of the others actually enjoyed the digging as anything was better than puking on board the corbita of Chioticus. The digging took longer with fewer men, but they worked all the harder, managing along the lines that the duplicarius had set out using his groma to align the streets and tent rows in perfect Roman order.

When a crowd of local sailors and shepherds gathered to watch the Romans' toil, Argus turned to a group of them.

"Bugger off, or come here and I'll show you what this pick is really for!"

Before he knew it, he was lying on the ground, grabbing the back of his knee where Decimus' vinerod had slammed into him.

"Anything else to say, soldier?"

"No... ah."

"What?"

"No, sir!" Argus stood, a little too close to Decimus.

"Back up, Argus!" Gallus barked.

Argus stepped back, his knee throbbing.

"Latrine duty for you tonight," Decimus said.

Argus stood there, breathing heavily, but kept his mouth shut.

"Back to work," the centurion growled.

From the corner of his eye, Lucius watched Argus bite his lip and lay into the earth as though he were killing it.

The shepherds and sailors continued to gawk until Decimus approached them.

"By all means, stay, if you want to join the legions. But if you don't intend to join, GET OUT OF HERE!"

The bystanders tripped over each other to leave the field and get back to their own work.

Not many recruits were to be had in Piraeus, but they did come from Athenae itself, as well as some of the distant demes of Attica. Groups arrived from Boeotia, Brauron, Sounion and others, partly because word of mouth had spread that the Romans were there to recruit, and partly because Decimus had sent paid messengers to every town in the region to say that the emperor had raised the pay for standard legionary troops from three hundred to five hundred denarii. Those with extra skills such as metal working, carpentry, or medical experience were able to earn double the usual legionary pay.

The groups of youths who came out of the distant hills and fields were eager to join, to get away from the doldrums of their rural existence, sensing adventure in the opportunity to march into the lands of the old Persian Empire, where the likes of Xenophon and Alexander had campaigned long before.

The Roman troops of III Parthica took especial pride in showing the Greek recruits how to do things, not without humiliation to the latter which Decimus put a stop to.

"You bastards are going to be on the same side. You don't want to piss them off so much as to get a pugio in your back in the thick of things, do you?" This after a particularly rough scuffle between Maren, Corvus and three Greeks.

All of them received five lashes each, and that was lenient.

Lucius and the ten men of his contubernium became accustomed to the close quarters of their leather campaign tent, and the rhythm of their new military life. Granted, they were not yet marching, but they were up before the first hour of daylight, training hard with Decimus while Gallus oversaw the influx of potential recruits, most of whom were admitted to the ranks.

After two weeks, Decimus decided to give those men who had been showing the greatest potential leave to go into Athenae for a full day and a night, so long as they were up early for inspection the following morning.

Lucius, Alerio, Antanelis, Eligius and Garai were given leave to go along with some of the men from other contubernia. The rest of their tent mates, however, were not happy about it.

"I can't believe you're going to fucking go," Argus said to Lucius. "What happened to sticking together?"

"I'm with you, you know that," Lucius answered, his hands out, "but I've always wanted to see Athenae. It's one of the most civilized cities in the world."

"Sounds boring. If I was you, I'd hit the whorehouses in the Piraeus. Now that would be a good time!"

Lucius shook his head. Diodorus had always told him about Athenae, and now he was finally going to see it.

"I'll see you tonight," Lucius said as he flipped the end of his cloak over his shoulder and followed the others, led by Gallus, northeast along the road to the ancient city.

"Form up for inspection!" Decimus shouted when the cornu blared among the tent rows.

Argus picked up his scutum and pilum and went to take his position between Maren and Corvus.

Excitement ran through the men who were walking along the road to Athens as each imagined what he would do with the rare day off from duty. Some would head straight to the agora to eat something other than the usual army rations, while others would head straight for the tabernae and brothels.

Most of the men, including Alerio and Antanelis, did not know much of the famed city of the Greeks, but Lucius did.

From his tutor, Diodorus, Lucius had learned of the great city where Democracy was born, and where the men of the greatest sea power in the world walked among the ancient stones of the agora.

Diodorus told Lucius about the philosophers, of course - of Socrates, Plato, and Aristotle, the latter the tutor of Alexander the Great himself - but Diodorus had also taught Lucius of the men who had defeated the Persians at Marathon, and at the great sea battle of Salamis. This was the city favoured by the Roman emperor, Hadrian, whose monuments Lucius yearned to see. Most of all, he wanted to walk in the shadow of the famed Temple of Athena Parthenos.

Even as the thought came to him, the temple to the goddess came into view as Gallus led all of them around the base of the hill called the Pnyx.

Lucius stopped in his tracks and stared up at the white marble where sacrificial smoke rose into the sky.

"It is as close to Olympus as we mortals can get," Diodorus used to say.

It was true. The temple sat atop the ancient acropolis where Theseus, so the stories went, defended the city against an army of Amazon warriors who had come to reclaim their queen.

"Metellus? You coming?" Gallus said, waiting for Lucius to catch up as the others walked ahead.

"Oh, a... yes, sir!" Lucius continued beside the optio. "You ever been here before, Optio?"

"Me? No. I prefer Rome to this place. Too many people here who think they're smarter than you. Makes me want to hit someone."

"Rome has learned a lot from this city," Lucius ventured. He realized it had been a long while since he had had a genuine conversation involving anything but weapons or exhaustion.

Gallus shrugged. "I don't have time to think of things like that. We have three legions to recruit, and a centurion who will break his stick over my back as easily as he would over yours." Gallus shoved a group of Syrian merchants out of the way as he pressed through a crowd on their way to the agora.

"Emperor Hadrian loved this place, sir."

"So I hear. Soldier!" Gallus suddenly yelled, walking toward two of their group who were already scuffling with three Athenian youths.

Lucius sighed, but did not run to help. Gallus and Antanelis had it well under control. He stood beneath one of the many olive trees that lined the path. Down the hill, he could see that the agora was already swimming with people, He glanced up the hill to his right where he could also see the long file of people waiting to enter the sanctuary of Athena at the top. Some of the citizens held chickens, or bunches of fresh flowers which they would offer to the patron goddess and protector of the city.

He longed to join them, but he worried that it would take all day before his turn came to make an offering. Besides, there were other things that he wanted to do.

As he continued down the path, past the Areopagus to the great agora, Lucius thought about the role that his own ancestors had played in the downfall of this once-great civilization. Metellus Macedonicus, and Metellus Creticus had both left their mark on the lives of the Hellenes, not to mention the horrors that Rome had visited upon the city state of Corinth.

As Lucius walked along the front of the Stoa of Attalus, in the shadow of the Acropolis, he wondered if, so many years later, the faces staring at him from the rows of columns hid any resentment of generations past that would manifest itself on a lone Roman walking among Greeks.

He was not sure that the generosity and benevolence of Hadrian had been enough to repair the damage to the Greeks' psyche.

However, no one waylaid him, or offered him offence as he stood looking up at the Temple of Hephaestus. Amid the milling crowds of men, young and old, Lucius stopped and looked around. The smells of roasted meat and incense surrounded him, and the sun broke from the clouds to light up the world.

In Rome, the Forum Romanum was, to him, a place of business, of enterprise and entertainment. It was where the world was now managed, its fate decided. It was not always pleasant, but it was home to Lucius. He realized, however, as he stood there, that the Athenian agora was a place of history, of time, and of thought. He could sense it all about him, as if the ghosts of a thousand dead thinkers walked up to whisper in his ear of the greatness of the place.

"Roman?"

Lucius was vaguely aware of laughter, but his mind had not yet made the switch to Greek.

"Roman!"

Lucius's turned to see a group of young men in chitons standing a ways off from where he was.

"You sleeping standing up?" one of them asked, chuckling.

"Just admiring," Lucius said, in a not unfriendly tone.

"Why don't you go and see the Roman agora," another man pointed.

They stared at Lucius mockingly now, but he decided not to engage them. He knew he could take them easily, for they were the soft, thinking sort, arrogant, such as Diodorus had once expressed displeasure with as 'an embarrassment to Greek culture'.

He began to move in the direction of the Roman agora when he spotted the red cloaks of his brothers cutting through the crowds.

"Lucius!" Alerio waived and pointed to a sign that displayed a wine amphora where they were all sitting down beneath an rush awning. "Have a drink!"

Lucius approached and sat with Alerio and Antanelis who were joined, surprisingly by Gallus. "Where are the others?"

"They wanted to dip their little pricks before the drinking," Gallus answered, taking the first cup the tavern keeper set down and throwing it back.

"Are the women nice here?" Antanelis asked shyly.

"Pah!" Gallus barked. "Better than in Piraeus, to be sure. Cleaner than the Subura. But I'll be damned if you can get them to understand what you want. You need to point at pictures and paintings to get it right!" he laughed.

Lucius chuckled at the optio's relaxed manner. He'd seen such menus in brothels before, the sort that displayed sexual positions in relief or frescoes on the walls; all one had to do was point and pay, and you got what you wanted.

"Argus won't be happy to have missed that!" Lucius laughed.

Gallus slammed his cup down. "Hmm. Your friend, Metellus, strikes me as a whoremonger."

"Well..." Lucius did not quite know what to say. "I suppose he does like the frequent the lupanars more often than others, sir."

"Ha! Frequent the lupanars!" Gallus shook his head. "I'll bet. Who doesn't? But why pay for it? When we get to Parthia, there'll be plenty for the taking."

Lucius looked into his cup and did not meet the optio's eye. He had always hated the thought of rapine, no matter how normal anyone said it was. Alexander, he had read, had forbidden the rape of girls and women in his army, and punished perpetrators severely. Somehow, sadly, he thought that Argus would not mind so much.

Gallus stared at the three young men. "You three aren't normal, you see. Most of the troops would be in the brothels thrusting away right now, yet you boys sit here sipping wine in the sun with me. Listen, I don't care if you boys bugger each other left, right, and centre in your tent, so long as your equipment is shiny and your swords sharp."

Lucius flushed an angry red and Alerio and Antanelis looked at him, urged him to sit down with raised eyebrows.

"I'm afraid you've got us wrong, sir. We like women as much as the next man, but I don't think you need to reach such conclusions just because we decided to enjoy some wine and the sights of this ancient city."

"No?" Gallus raised his own eyebrows. He had not expected Lucius to speak to him in that way. "As we're off duty, I won't punish you, soldier."

"For speaking truth, sir?" Lucius took a breath. "I wanted to come into the Athenae to see the city itself, to see the monuments my old tutor told me about, to see the embellishments made to it by Emperor Hadrian."

"Hadrian," Gallus. "You know what they say about him?"

Lucius fell back against the wall, exasperated, arms crossed, as Gallus began to roar with laughter.

"I'm only joking, Metellus!" he said, slapping Lucius on the arm. "You take yourself too seriously sometimes, I've noticed. We're going to be seeing enough serious things in the months ahead, so I would actually recommend you let loose and enjoy while you can. Get it out of your system, lads," he said to all of them.

After a few more cups of wine, Gallus left Lucius and the other two men to find his own brothel near the Dypilon gate of the city.

"I don't know what to make of that man," Alerio said. "He can't really handle his wine, I think."

"Not a bad idea though," Antanelis said.

"What?" Lucius asked.

"Hitting the brothel!" Antanelis stood up. "There's one just over there," he said, pointing down the street that faced them. "I can hear the sing-song of some lovely birds in there!"

Alerio looked at Lucius and laughed. Antanelis, as big as he was, could not seem to hold his wine either.

"Ah, you go on, then!" Lucius said. "Get it out of your system. I'm going to look around a bit first. Alerio, you coming?"

"Ahh, well... I know this is a great city and all, but I would happily part with a few denarii to have a clean woman here, then go on the cheap in Piraeus, or in Thrace when we get there. You go look around and then join us. All right?"

Lucius looked at his two smiling friends where they swayed on their feet. He knew they did not share his love of culture and history. He also knew that he would likely never get back to Athenae, that he would regret not seeing the things he wanted to see. There would be other women, but would he have the chance to roam the ancient city again? Likely not.

"I'll join you later," Lucius said.

"Suit yourself, Lucius!" Antanelis swayed in the direction of the brothel he had spotted.

"Stay out of trouble," Alerio said to Lucius, before following Antanelis.

Lucius watched them go, marked the place in his mind, and then turned to go into the Roman agora.

He was immediately drawn to an octagonal structure that towered above the other buildings around it in the marketplace. A weather vane on the top of the white-marble temple twisted as the wind shifted, turning in the direction of Boreas, the north wind. He remembered Diodorus telling him about it, that it was built before the rest of the Roman agora.

Lucius stood looking up at the structure, its simple beauty, and the reliefs of all the winds, including Boreas, Kaikias, Apeliotes, Eurus, Notus, Livas, Zephyrus, and Skiron. Below the reliefs were a series of sundials, and then inside was a clepsydra, a water clock. He went up the few steps to peer into the structure. He heard the drip dropping of the water and tried to remember the lessons Diodorus had given him on the workings of a clepsydra.

He was about to take a closer look when a hand grabbed the hem of his cloak.

Lucius spun, his hand on his pugio.

He was pushed suddenly and stumbled on the stairs to fall back against the white marble of the temple.

"Look! The Roman soldier can't even stand on his feet!" It was one of the youths from the other agora, his friends behind him, snarling. "You think you can just come here and roam about our beautiful city? Eh, Roman? You're not welcome here. Why don't you just leave, stupid ingrate!"

Lucius felt his heart pounding, and fought for self-control. Several bystanders watched and waited, including many of the vendors from their stalls only a few feet away.

"I suggest you leave," Lucius said. "Before you get hurt." He stood up and faced the five young men who began to form in a semi-circle before him.

"Definitely stupid, no?" the youth asked his friends. "What say we teach this Roman a lesson?"

Lucius scanned all of them quickly, their countenances, their lack of weapons, that he could see at least. Most were thin, a couple lean and muscular. He could tell they were not used to heavy labour, but rather spent their time carefully shaping themselves in the gymnasium. Still, they could be wrestlers...

The first lunged with a raised fist which Lucius parried as though his arm were a sword, sending the attacker face-first with a bloody crunch into the temple's wall where he collapsed screaming.

Two more came at Lucius with sloppy kicks that sent him to his knees for a moment. Someone's fist glanced off the side of his head, but he punched out and felt contact while he wrapped his forearm about the neck of another and twisted so that he sent the body into the nearest market stall.

"Leave him alone!" one of the merchants yelled. "You're going to get us all in trouble!"

Lucius turned to see the last two coming at him, only these more confidently, more slowly, crouched.

Wrestlers.

Lucius tried to keep them in front of him, but they were too fast, and before he knew it, one of the men had him from behind, his arms locked painfully, to the point of breaking.

Lucius cried out, and tightened his frame forward so as to not give any more but the hold was solid and unrelenting. Just when he thought his shoulders would snap in the joints, there was a howl and the pressure released.

Lucius dropped and rolled, spinning to see Alerio pounding the face of the man who had just been holding Lucius.

The final youth jumped to his friend's aid by attacking Alerio's back, but Lucius grabbed hold of him before, pulled him back and squeezed his muscular arm about his neck, tight like a great mountain python's coils.

"Enough! Metellus and Kasen! Stand to!"

Instinctively, Lucius and Alerio both let go of their attackers and stood to attention at the parade ground voice of their optio. No matter how drunk Gallus was, his voice still commanded.

"What in Hades is going on here?"

"Sir," one merchant came forward. "Those five men attacked the Roman for no reason. I saw it! He was minding his own business."

"This true, Metellus?"

"Lucius took them on by himself, sir," Alerio said, garnering him an angry stare from Gallus.

"I asked if that's true!" Gallus yelled.

"Yes, sir," Lucius said.

"Well, I'll have to send word to the city administrator that one of the emperor's men was attacked, won't I?"

There were murmurs about the crowd, angry words in Greek cursed at the five young men who were dragging themselves to their feet. They knew that an increase in the number of troops in the agora would be bad for business.

Gallus looked the young Greeks up and down and then scoffed. "No wonder you people couldn't hold your own against us! Ha! Five against one, or two rather, sorry Kasen," he nodded to Alerio who was holding his bloody fist. "You there!" Gallus pointed to the merchant who had spoken up. "You know their names?" He then pointed at the five men.

"Ye...yes...yes, sir," the merchant said reluctantly.

"Good. Then tell me who they are so I can put them in my report." He turned to the five men. "You buggers want to fight so badly, why don't you come and join our legions. You'll get your fill, and learn how to fight like a real soldier, not some pussy parade of little greeklings!"

The five young men, supporting the one with the smashed face, slinked away down a side street. When they had gone, and the agora's noise of buying and selling resumed, Gallus turned to Lucius and Alerio.

"Good fight. But I don't want you getting into any more trouble, eh Metellus? You'd be better off having a good fuck in the brothel. It's safer than sightseeing, ha!" Without another word, Gallus turned and went back to wherever he had come from.

"The man is everywhere," Alerio said.

"I'm just glad it wasn't Centurion Decimus."

"Glad I came?" Alerio asked. "You all right?"

"Yes." Lucius rolled his shoulders. He had had worse, but his urge to see the sights of Athenae was a little dampened.

"Come on," Alerio said. "I actually came to bring you back to the brothel. There's this one Thracian girl. I swear, made like an Amazon queen. She actually turned me down! So, I thought maybe she would go for you."

"We have to pay, right?"

"Well, yes! Of course! She's just choosy is all!" Alerio laughed. "Let's go. After relaxing in there, you, me, and Antanelis can go and see those temples you wanted to see so bad. Sound good?"

It sounded great to Lucius, who followed Alerio out of the agora and down the street to the brothel where the sounds of squeals and giggles emanated from the upper windows.

They walked through a front room where there were several benches covered in blankets and furs. No one waited, and Alerio nodded to the woman who stood with a burly eunuch behind the counter.

"This is my friend," Alerio said. "The one I think Hippolyta will like."

The woman looked Lucius up and down and nodded a little. "Maybe. You can try. She's in a mood today."

"What are you getting me into, Alerio?" Lucius said as they went up the flight of wooden stairs, the smells of spices, oil, and sweat covering the walls.

"Shhh." Alerio stopped before a curtain and motioned for Lucius to go inside. "Go in. If she doesn't like you, you'll be out on your ass in a second like me and Antanelis." At that moment, Antanelis' head poked out from another cubiculum down the hall, his face flushed and smiling.

"And if she does like me?"

"Have fun." With that, Alerio disappeared into a pair of creamy arms that reached out of the cubiculum directly opposite.

Lucius stepped inside and looked about the dim room which was quite spartan but for a small table with a lamp and water jug with cups, and a bed in the centre that was covered in furs.

"So you're the one they were talking of." The deep, voice came from the darker corner in the room, to his right. Into the lamplight stepped a tall woman who was covered only by a pair of leather breeches. Her body was muscular and lean, her breasts pert and pointed. Her red hair ran in a thick braid down to the small of her back to firm buttocks.

Lucius gulped, thinking he had just met a someone out of legend itself. Then he met her eyes, wild and blue as a winter sea. Her lips bunched as she examined him.

"You're not afraid of me, are you?" she asked.

"Of course not. You are...um...well..." he searched for a word, "amazing..."

She did not look surprised. "What have you been doing just now?" she asked.

"I was attacked in the agora." Self-consciously he reached for a cut on his forehead.

"You against who?" she asked, curious, coming a little closer.

"Five Greeks."

"Old men?"

"Young. About my age." He felt like he was going to fail her test and find himself on the corridor floor, but she came closer and her lips curved into a beautiful and hungry smile.

"Take off your tunic so I might see you," she ordered.

Lucius removed his tunic to reveal his torso and she bit her lip.

"You stay," she said, her arms wrapping themselves around his neck and her mouth meeting his.

Lucius felt himself pushed back onto the fur bed and allowed himself to be lost in blissful oblivion, in darkness, and heat, and sweat as he forgot all but the space in which he found himself, and the Amazon queen who caressed every inch of his sore body.

A couple of hours later, the three young men walked lazily along a narrow street, sighing and wishing the day would drag more slowly. They knew there would be no such leisure for some time.

"I think he had a good time," Antanelis nudged Alerio with his elbow, and they both looked sidelong at Lucius who grinned uncontrollably.

"So.... Had a good time then?" Alerio said. "Seems you passed her test."

"We waited for a minute to see if you would be thrown out, but..." Antanelis burst out laughing. "Seems you conquered the Amazon queen!"

"Oh, I don't know..." Lucius mused, still happy and lightheaded from his experience. "I think she is the one that conquered me, and I would happily let her do it again."

"Don't go falling in love with a lupa, Lucius. You know you'll end up depressed and extremely jealous."

Lucius did not say anything more.

"How much did she charge you?" Antanelis asked.

"Nothing." Lucius answered casually.

Both the other men stopped dead in their tracks. "Nothing?" they said together.

"Nothing."

"Come now, Lucius. You don't need to lie," Alerio said.

"I'm not," he answered, his thoughts filled with flashes of the woman's long hair and thighs, the smooth hips gripped in his hands. "I offered to pay...a lot. But she refused. She told me that she was grateful to Aphrodite that she enjoyed herself more than she has in a long time. She thanked me. Kissed me on the lips, and sent me on my way."

"Gods, you're a terrible liar!" Antanelis laughed. "Nice try, Lucius."

"I told you. I didn't pay a thing. She was lovely." He knew of course that they still doubted him, and he did not blame them one bit. The memory of that wonderful woman would keep him warm for many a cold night in the months to come.

The three of them rounded a corner and came to the gate erected by Emperor Hadrian. The wind picked up in that more open space but they pressed on to the temple that Lucius had wanted to see.

Passing beneath the gate, they came into the shadow of the biggest temple any of them had ever seen: the Olympeion.

The massive temple of Olympian Zeus, finally completed by Hadrian, was surrounded by a forest of columns that seemed to uphold the heavens themselves. The people who milled around the base of it were dwarfed by the sheer size.

"It's bigger than I ever imagined," Lucius whispered.

"Did your tutor tell you about it?" Alerio asked.

"Yes." Lucius could hear the awe in Diodorus' voice still, as he tried to convey the size of this monument, second only to the great Temple of Artemis on the other side of the Aegean. "I'm going in. I want to make an offering to Zeus, Protector of Travellers."

"Me too," Alerio said, following Lucius.

"I'll come too. But really, Lucius, you should also thank the king of the gods for what just happened to you at the brothel. No charge! Ha!"

With that the three young men made their way to the far end of the temple where a few vendors sold offerings to Zeus' suppliants.

Lucius purchased a pigeon which he grasped by the legs as it squawked and fluttered, and went up the steps and into the temple, heedless of his two friends who had fallen behind. Inside his footsteps echoed loudly and a novice priest in white robes approached him.

"You wish to make an offering to Almighty Zeus?"

"Yes." Lucius handed over a couple of sestertii and the pigeon.

"Follow me." The priest took the coins and the bird, and turned to go to one of the altars that stood below the large statue of Zeus. Off to the right, Lucius noticed a statue of Hadrian himself, almost as big as the king of the Gods.

"The emperor was a great philhellene, and patron of this city. This temple will be an eternal monument to him, as well as to the god for whom it is built," the priest said, as if he knew what Lucius was thinking.

They arrived at the altar and the priest turned to Lucius. "You may speak your words to Father Zeus, and then I shall perform the sacrifice."

Lucius nodded and stepped forward, his eyes gazing up at the face of Zeus, his arms outstretched.

Father Zeus, Protector of Travellers... Guard us as we march across the world and into danger. Give me strength and nerve in the battles ahead that I may bring honour and glory to my family.

Great Father of the Heavens, let your far-shooting son watch over me always and light my way in the darkness. With your blessing, may Apollo guide me. I honour you, Zeus.

Lucius bowed his head for a moment, allowing his senses to tingle, to smell the strong incense that wafted about the place, to hear the flicker of the flames in the tall bronze tripods that stood to either side of the god. When he looked up, he nodded to the priest.

The dagger plunged swiftly, allowing but a single shriek as the bird's body was sliced open and its innards be exposed.

There was a lot of blood, and it would not stop.

The priest shook his head as he tried to see the minute organs of the pigeon, but the blood kept pouring out of the carcass.

"I don't understand..." the priest muttered.

"What's wrong?" Lucius asked, his heart beating faster, panic fluttering in his gut.

"By the Gods!" the priest shrieked and jumped back as the pigeon wiggled and popped up onto its feet.

Lucius stared alongside the man, struck dumb by the wonder. A moment ago the bird had been dead, as far as he could see, but now, it stood, turned its head and blinked its beady eyes at the two men. Then, as if nothing had happened, it took flight, and soared the length of the temple out into the grey light of day.

Lucius gazed at the trail of fresh blood that the bird had let fall as it flew, staining the marble floor of the temple.

"What does it mean?" Lucius asked, not really hearing himself speak.

"Uh..." the priest muttered, sweat beading all over his brow. "Please, I can't..."

"What does this mean, priest?" Lucius demanded a little too strongly, the fear of what he had seen taking hold of him.

"It means...it...means that...you will see lots of blood in the times ahead, more than you can ever imagine. But you will survive, despite the fall of those all around you." The priest looked up at the statue of Zeus now, his voice trancelike. "You will travel far, and wade through rivers of blood, across deserts and into terror."

"Will I ever make it home again?" Lucius asked.

The priest said nothing. He only mumbled incoherently and then, as if struck, he slipped on the blood about the altar, and lay upon the marble floor, his body wracked by spasms.

Two more priests came running up to help, their eyes looking fearfully at Lucius.

"Leave here now, Roman," the older of the two said as he cradled the head of his fallen colleague.

"He just fell," Lucius said. "My offering, it...it flew away."

"Get out!" the priest yelled again.

"Lucius, come on. Let's go!" Alerio said as he and Antanelis arrived.

They pulled Lucius along the centre of the temple, away from Zeus, to the doors and outside.

"I don't understand!" Lucius said as the cool air licked at his sweaty skin.

"Don't try," Alerio said. "I saw what happened. Don't even try to understand, you hear me?"

Lucius looked down and saw the trail of blood turn right. He broke away from his friends and followed it to the edge of the retaining wall surrounding the temple. Down below, he spotted a few more temples beside a river. It seemed that the blood crossed over the temple and then stopped.

"I need to go down there!" he said.

"No. What we need to do is get to the baths before returning to camp, Lucius," Antanelis said. "There's no time for more sightseeing!"

"He's right, Lucius," Alerio agreed. We don't want to head back to Piraeus in the dark.

Lucius stared at the temple, feeling its pull. He wanted to go there, but he also knew that they had a point. The day was wearing on and this might be his last chance to cleanse himself properly for a while.

"Fine. Let's go. There were some baths in the agora."

"Good," Alerio said. "We'll get some more food too."

The three of them turned around and left the temples beside the Illissos river alone. Little did Lucius know that the temple below was dedicated to Apollo.

The omen at the temple continued to trouble Lucius' mind, so much so that he wished he had not gone there in the first place.

Lying in the Amazon's arms for the remainder of the day would have been much more worthwhile than sightseeing, he thought.

However, there was little time for fretting. Over the following week, as messengers fulfilled their purpose across the Attic landscape and beyond, more and more men showed up to join Rome's legions.

Many did not pass the initial physical tests which, though still not over-demanding, caused some of the malnourished, weak, or dumb applicants to be turned away.

"We've still got to head north to recruit in Macedonia and Thrace," Decimus said to Gallus who was speaking with Lucius and Alerio about some of the new recruits. The centurion was, it was obvious, growing impatient and eager to get underway. "I've just come from the harbour," Decimus said. "Chioticus will be ready in two days to sail north to Amphipolis. If the messengers I've sent ahead by ship don't run into foul weather, there should be a whole city of eager young bastards who want to join the ranks, waiting for us." He turned to Lucius and Alerio.

"I don't want any trouble. I want the first century, the Roman century of III Parthica to be the best, to set the standard for discipline. You got it?"

"Yes, sir," Lucius said. "We'll spread the word."

"Good. Now, get back to your drills, and try to teach these peasants a thing or two, all right?"

"Yes, sir!" the two of them answered, saluted and walked away.

"I think he likes us, old Decimus," Alerio whispered to Lucius as they went.

Two days later, a legion and a half of men set out from Piraeus, around the Attic headland, and north along the Euboean coast for the military port of Amphipolis in the North Aegean.

They were blessed with fine spring weather the entire way, and Lucius and the others actually enjoyed being at sea again. When they had leisure, they stood on the deck of Chioticus' ship, feeling the sea spray on their faces, and breathing deeply of the fresh open air.

Lucius watched the coast glide by, the plains of Thessaly, the hills rising up to the peak of distant Olympus.

"What are you looking at?" Argus came alongside Lucius, his anger and jealousy at the latter's trip into Athens having finally dissipated.

Lucius pointed to the snow-capped mountains. "Look."

"What? Mountains?" Argus shrugged.

"Not just mountains. Olympus, Argus. It's the home of the Gods themselves."

Even Argus did not mock. Though his devotion was little to none, he knew that when confronted with such a place, the feeling that suddenly beset one so was out of the ordinary.

Lucius looked up, his eyes straining to see Zeus' eagles flying about the peaks, their eyries neighbour to their master's throne, to the places where Juno and Minerva walked, where Venus lounged, and to the halls where Apollo's music echoed through eternal corridors.

Lucius bowed his head and, with his palms upward, said a silent prayer to all of them. When he finished, he looked to the rear of the ship where captain Chioticus prayed, eyes closed, above a fiery brazier that had been fastened to the deck where he stood. His lips moved silently, and when he had finished, he poured libations of wine, oil, and milk into the sea.

When Lucius turned around, Argus had gone below deck to game with the others who had not had the opportunity to spend their coin in the agora and brothels of Athenea.

When the fleet made berth at Amphipolis, on the docks lining the river Strymon, the legionary recruits disembarked to find a city of tents and shelters to the north of the settlement, on the other side of the river.

"Looks like the messengers succeeded," Gallus said to Decimus.

"Mars' hairy balls, and I thought we would have a tough time recruiting enough for three legions," Decimus answered, putting his horizontally-crested centurion's helmet on his head, and tucking his vinerod under his arm. "They'd better be worthy."

"I think they may be, sir. These northerners are not soft and learned like the Athenians. They live a more rugged existence."

"Let's hope so." Decimus turned to his optio. "I don't want any trouble. Send word round to all the new centurions and optios that brawling and lack of discipline are to be punished with thirty lashes. Let's show'em we're serious."

"What about camps? We should have the engineers plot them out."

Decimus looked out across the island on which the main settlement was located at the mouth of the river. Sea birds winged about the masts of the ships, cawing and diving for fish and garbage tossed overboard.

"III Parthica to be stationed to the south, between the city and the lion tomb, with I and II east of the river, where the ground rises. Separating them should reduce the number of confrontations."

"You're really worried about these men being unfit for Parthia, aren't you, sir?"

Decimus looked sternly at his optio, surprised and perturbed by his assumption, but admitting to himself that Gallus was correct.

"The emperor has great expectations for this campaign, Gallus. And the Parthica legions that we raise, which bear the name of the campaign already, are expected to perform above and beyond. I'm not nervous, but I would like to get a promotion out of this and, as I'm sure, you would too, no?"

"Yes, sir!" Gallus smiled and saluted.

"Then let's get to work and sift through the turds to find the jewels."

With that, Decimus and Gallus walked down the gang plank to inspect the orderly rows of legionaries who were ready and waiting for their orders.

"That's what I like to see!" the centurion howled in his parade ground voice. "Time to make camp!"

Once the orders for positioning were given out, it was only a matter of a couple of hours before orderly rows of tents were up and the men were busy digging ditches and erecting stockades.

Lucius, Argus, Antanelis, Alerio, Eligius, Garai, Maren, Gaius, Tertius, and Corvus all got stuck in and were one of the first contubernia to finish their stretch of defences, ditch, and palisade. When all was done, each contubernia went to their usual position to set up their hide tent and get the cookfire burning.

During this time, Decimus and Gallus walked among the sea of potential recruits with a body guard of legionaries before and aft. There were men and boys, obviously underage, who had come from gods knew how far away. Some were learned and brought skills, others were peasants; goatherds, shepherds, farmers, tinkers, a few blacksmiths, bakers, foresters and more. They all stood alongside muscled nobodies just looking for some adventure or a way out of their Macedonian and Thracian mountain holes.

There were thousands, but the good news was that many were strong and keen, and desperate to succeed.

"There's a lot of motivation to get out of their little shit holes, from the looks of it, wouldn't you say, Gallus?"

"Seems that way, sir," Gallus was taking quick notes on his second wax tablet as they finished. "Who would you like to start with in the morning, sir?"

"Start with the Thracians, the big ones. I want mass and strength in the ranks. We'll be glad of it when the Parthian cataphracts ride down on us!"

"Yes, sir." Gallus made a note. They would start seeing people at the first hour of light.

The days from then on were filled with gruelling routines for Lucius and his brothers in arms. They trained, and paraded, and sparred with the newer recruits who were brought into the ranks with each new day. Thousands of young men stepped up to sign away the next twenty five years of their lives.

Lucius wondered that so many Thracians and Hellenes seemed so eager to fight for Rome, but the more he thought about it, and the more conversations he overheard, he realized that he had indeed been naive to think Rome had won over the hearts and minds of so many.

"Steady pay, a full belly, and Parthian gold is what I'm here for," Lucius heard one man from Thessaloniki say.

And he could not blame them. From the appearances of most of the recruits stepping up to Gallus' table as he once did, many had known nothing but squalor.

"The legions represent order in chaos," Lucius said to himself, and he fully believed it. Disciplina was the goddess of the legions, and the thousands he watched wielding wooden gladii and wicker scuta on the training grounds were falling quietly into step behind her.

Decimus set a gruelling pace for every day; a march before first light, drills, and inspection, more drills, digging ditches and raising stockades, and then guard duty around each camp.

One would have thought that the centurion believed they were deep in enemy territory, about to be attacked at any moment by howling Parthians, but Lucius knew, even if his tent mates did not, that Decimus was preparing them for what was to come.

When the young Metellus lay down on his mat at the end of the day, or after his shift on guard duty, he always made sure to honour his gods with his prayers to ensure that they still watched over him, though he was only one among the fifteen thousand who now made up the three Parthica legions.

Once the flow of new recruits died down and Decimus met his quota, more ships arrived, procured by Chioticus who could no longer accommodate their numbers.

All six cohorts of each of the three legions were set to drilling on the plains about Amphipolis, their discipline and unity tested, beneath the crack of their centurions' vinerods. In wind, and rain, and sun, and heat, and fog, the legions trained until the men were stronger, more disciplined, more used to any hardship they had experienced in any mine, market, mountain peak, or rock-strewn country farm.

The inhabitants of Amphipolis watched from behind their walls as the legions' ranks swelled and men poured out of the various gates of the camps every day, like an invading army readying itself to lay siege to the ancient acropolis. Daughters and wives were locked away, safe from the sight of prowling legionaries who were permitted to visit the gymnasium and baths within the city walls. Most of the time, however, the troops were told to bathe in the frigid waters of the river, yet something more to harden their senses.

Often, in the late evenings, or early mornings when Lucius was posted to sentry duty atop the ramparts of III Parthica's camp, he would look to the south to see the the great stone lion where is sat upon an ancient tomb looking out to sea. Or he would look north, across the flat Thracian plains to the mountains in the north. The world seemed so big to him now, and he so small. Among thousands of strong, well-trained men, many with ambition to match their skill, how was he, a lone soldier, supposed to mark himself out as great? How was he, Lucius Metellus Anguis, any better than the rest of the men around him?

In his contubernium alone were men who were his equal, so how could he make good on the promises he had so rashly made to his father?

"Just fight your way to the emperor's fucking feet," Argus had said when Lucius informed him of his thoughts."

"That's not very helpful," Lucius answered.

"Maybe not," Argus said. "But I'm sure there will be ways for us to make ourselves stand out once we get in the fight. We're leaving soon, aren't we?"

"Shut up!" Maren hissed from his mat. "I'm trying to sleep!"

"You shut it, Maren," Argus answered, hitting his friend's leg with his fist so that they could hear Maren's angry breathing. "Just give us a minute."

"Yes, we're leaving," Lucius whispered. "I heard Gallus talking to one of the duplicarii about provisions and accounts. The supplies arrived a few days late but today they finished loading them onto all the ships. "We should be sailing for Antioch in two days."

"Good. We've done nothing but train and drill here. There's nothing to do!" Argus protested anew, as he had done for the last few weeks. "They've got to give us some leave in Antioch when we get there."

"Don't get your hopes up," Lucius warned. "The emperor might want to set out right away. Who knows..."

"I hope I get some leave soon," Argus said. "Not all of us got to go and fuck an Amazon in Athenae."

"No. Just me." Lucius smiled in the dark and prodded Argus who hit him back. "We'd better get some sleep. More drills tomorrow. Testudo formations."

"Not again," Argus groaned, feeling the weight of his scutum pressing down on his head and shoulders already.

Two days later, hundreds of ships set out from Amphipolis, just as Alexander's fleet had sailed hundreds of years before. This time, however, the holds were filled with expertly trained Roman legionaries, the men who had brought Alexander's successors to their knees.

The North Aegean was tough on the fleet, as if the Gods were eager to speed the men of the Parthica legions on their way. When Boreas howled out of the North to chill their backs and fill their sails, the fleet sped south over the deep blue swells that lapped at the islands dotting the sea about them.

After many gruelling days at sea, with the men green-faced, the gem of Antioch came into view beneath a midday sun that lightened their hearts, bringing cheers from the stinking innards of the fleet as the men praised their gods for a safe, if not painless, journey.

"Now it begins," Centurion Decimus said to Gallus and his fellow centurions on the deck where he stood gazing at the city. "Get your men cleaned up right away!" he ordered. I don't think it will be long before we're under the imperial gaze and knee deep in Parthian blood!"

VII

Concilium Aquilarum

'A Gathering of Eagles'

Antioch. The 'Rome of the East', they called it. For over two hundred years, the Caesars of Rome had enriched the city that opened the Empire to eastern trade. It was a magnificent polis of close to half a million inhabitants, and countless cultures.

Except, Antioch as it stood downriver from the Mare Internum, was more like a massive army camp now. The legions of Rome and Septimius Severus had descended on the city to muster for war, and the three Parthica legions were the last to arrive.

The coast was choked as if it were the siege of Troy itself, the thousand ships coming to take Helen and the riches of the East.

Parthia was bigger than Troy, and no amount of tricks would work to tear down her many and scattered walls.

"My gods," Lucius muttered to his friends as they all stood on the deck of Chioticus' ship, at attention beneath the gaze of Decimus, Gallus, and some of the other centurions and optios.

"I heard that the emperor has amassed thirty three legions," Alerio said.

"Thirty three?" Eligius blurted from his spot along the rail.

They all stared out at the plains beyond the sea, green and rocky, with the river Orontes cutting through the landscape until it reached the city. It seemed the land was filled with legionary encampments, dozens of perfect squares stretching up to engulf the city.

"I'll bet the Antiochenes don't like this."

"I'm sure they don't mind, Metellus," Gallus appeared beside the group of young men who stiffened their posture at his presence. "This city has gained much from the Caesars' favour - a circus, baths, that aqueduct you see to your right, marble-lined streets, a forum, and a Temple to Jupiter Capitolinus on that hill they call Mount Silpius. The Antiochenes do all right by Rome, don't you worry."

"How do you know all that, sir?" Antanelis asked.

"My father was a trader. He made made trips to this city in his day. Used to tell me stories about it, about how they wanted it to outdo Alexandria in Aegyptus."

Lucius stared ahead as Chioticus steered in to a spot on the beach.

"This is going to take a long time," Gallus muttered, as he looked back at all the ships carrying the Parthica legions.

"Optio!" Decimus called from the upper deck of the corbita.

"Yes, Centurion?" Gallus stood to attention.

"Chioticus says it's going to take all night to disembark three legions. I want III Parthica off first. You take them to the north of the city and set up camp on the plain. I'll follow later, after I report to Caesar!"

"Yes, sir!" Gallus saluted. "What about the vexillaria, sir? Are we marching under our banners yet?"

"No! Not until each legion has an aquila. They're being made here, for some reason."

132

Each Roman legion marched with an aquila, the golden eagle that went before each army, along with the vexillum, the standard bearing the emblem of the individual legions.

Lucius was eager to see their legion's emblem and march beneath the eagle at last, but it seemed he would have to wait longer still.

"Don't just stand there!" Gallus belllowed. "Onto the beach, III Parthica! We're here!"

With that Gallus leeped over the railing himself and landed in the sand, the waves splashing about his ankles as he barked orders.

Argus went next, and down the line until Lucius jumped too. Then all others on the ship followed, including Decimus who had given Chioticus his papers so that he might claim his fee which was a vast fortune in and of itself. It was no easy thing to sail three legions from Greece to Antioch without losing a single ship. Chioticus knew his business well.

The century waited on the beach for some time, until all other centuries in III Parthica were disembarked. When the last, green-faced recruit had fallen to the sand beneath the weight of his full kit, the legion set out along the banks of the Orontes toward Antioch.

Until then, Lucius had been able to store his family armour in Chioticus' ship, under lock and key with the captain's personal possessions, but now, he had to carry his extra load, and already, the extra weight was easily felt. He pressed on, though, for it was up to him to carry it, or lose it, and the latter was not an option.

As the new legion marched along, weaving its way between the avenues separating the various legions, Lucius could see veterans and others staring at them from behind their palisades, wondering at the new recruits, and laughing at the younger men as they passed.

"Welcome to Parthia, lads!" one bulky veteran called, "They eat boys like you for breakfast here!"

"Oi, you with the extra bundle?" another called to Lucius. "Your mommy send you some sweets? Come here and I'll take them off you."

"Look at these little boys!" Yet another called, staring at Eligius and Garai. "I bet their asses are nice and tight! Hey, little virgins! Come here so I can get you ready for battle and the camp!"

Roars of laughter followed III Parthica all the way to the walls of Antioch, as Lucius, Argus and the others all marched, red-faced and staring straight ahead.

Lucius sweat profusely as he marched, catching glimpses of Gallus looking back at him, ascertaining if he could carry the extra load he had so stubbornly insisted on bringing.

Lucius focussed on the sights and smells ahead, the blueness of the spring sky over Antioch, and the low, ragged hills and distant mountains about the city. He knew they were setting off on something incredible, and despite the remarks that met them all along the way from the men of the legions, he knew he was on the right path.

It took them over two hours to get to their assigned terrain north of the city. It was an area of scrub and rock which did not make it easy to plot out. After twice the amount of time it should have taken, III Parthica's camp was laid out and palisaded. Avenues of tents sprang up around the central command tent where Decimus, as Primus Pilus, or head centurion, would sit with the tribunes of the legion, the upper class men who would each command one of the six cohorts of the legion.

Lucius and the others did not recognize most of the men of their own legion, though they had trained together as a cohesive unit since Thrace.

"There are so many of us," Garai mused as the eight of them gathered around the cook fire before their tent where an iron pot of beans and barley bubbled.

Eligius, the latter's brother, dipped a chunk of black bread in the broth to test it. "It's good," he said.

Lucius looked up from where he sat on a stool, polishing his lorica which had already begun to rust because of the sea spray. "And this is just the one camp," he said to Garai.

"How can we possibly lose with over thirty legions on the march!" Argus slapped his thighs and smiled. "We'll be home in no time!"

"I thought you didn't like home?" Lucius said in a low voice to his friend.

Argus shrugged. "There are things I like about it, like being able to do my own thing."

"You'd better get used to following orders then," Maren blurted. "I think Decimus has taken to hating you pretty good."

"Fuck'em," Argus spat.

"Will you shut up!" Lucius hissed. "He's our primus pilus! He's practically the general of this legion."

"Careful lads," Corvus warned. "We're among the only Romans in this legion. Best not give any of the Greeks, Macedonians, or Thracians an excuse to have us scourged."

"Bit paranoid, aren't you?" Antanelis said.

"I wouldn't test it, if I were you," Corvus added.

"He's right," Lucius said. "We need to set the example. If we do, we'll get promoted."

"Not everyone wants a promotion, Lucius," Argus said, running a whetstone along the edge of his gladius.

"Maybe not, but it's better than latrine duty and lashes."

"I have to agree with Lucius on that," Eligius chuckled.

Alerio dished out the soup to his tent mates and they all sat in silence to eat, weariness settling on their limbs.

Lucius thought it felt strange to sit silent for a moment, especially as they were about to jump over the precipice of war at any moment. Still, he remembered Diodorus' advice about noticing the world about him. He looked to the west, over the tops of thousands of black and brown leather tents and banners, to the sea where the sun was setting in a firestorm of orange and purple, the stars chasing after it from the East.

The distant sounds of mumbling men, horns, and horses faded away and it seemed as though a hush fell over the plain about Antioch. He knew that within the city, the tabernae would be full, the theatres packed, and the markets noisy. It seemed an odd contrast that among the tent rows of thousands of soldiers, it was quiet enough to think and fall asleep.

"Stand up!" the peace was shattered by Gallus' voice as he approached their fire, a hazard of being so close to the command tent at the centre of camp.

Lucius and the others put down their bowls and stood to attention neatly.

"I've just had word from our centurion that he's to appear before the emperor in the morning to brief him on the new legions." Gallus cleared his throat. "I want you all up before the first hour, fully kitted out, and in perfect form. We'll be meeting our new tribune and legate commander prior to going to the emperor, so I want you on your best behaviour. Understand?"

"Yes, sir!" they all said in perfect concert.

"Good. You're excused from sentry duty tonight, so polish every strap and buckle, and get some sleep." Gallus turned abruptly and went back to the command tent where he was finishing up his reports.

"We're meeting the emperor?" Antanelis said.

"No, you idiot," Argus answered. "Decimus, the tribune, and legate will be meeting the emperor. We're their escort."

"Either way, we'd better get some sleep," Lucius said, standing and putting the last piece of his armour aside. He had already finished.

Later, as they all bedded down on their mats, each man stared at the tent ceiling in thought. After about ten minutes, Garai spoke.

"Anyone actually know anything about the Parthians or Parthia?"

"Ask Lucius," Argus said. "He's been studying them since we joined."

"Really? Lucius, what do you know?" Garai asked and the others rose on their elbows to listen.

Lucius thought for a moment. He was not sure what he should tell them. Should he say that he prayed to the Gods every night for protection and guidance, and they had better be doing the same? That he wondered if the Gods would hear their prayers? No. He decided that that would not help them.

He needed to give them courage, but also truth, so that they did not fall into complacency.

"I don't know much. About two hundred and fifty years ago, Marcus Licinius Crassus led seven legions to Parthia in order to annex it to Rome. At that time, it was an unprecedented force, seven legions, and yet, at Carrhae, the land was soaked with Roman blood. Crassus suffered a crushing defeat on the tips of Parthian lances, picking Romans off as they retreated."

"The legions retreated?" Antanelis said, shocked, for it was not something that legions did.

"Well, that time they did, and Crassus himself was struck down. Imagine that, the richest man in Rome lying in the Parthian dust." Lucius paused, he could hear their breathing and realized he might have said too much. Diodorus' habit of lending flowery elaborations to details had rubbed off. "I read about it in Plutarch."

"Who?" Garai said.

"Some Greek," Alerio said. "What else, Lucius?"

"Crassus wasn't the only general to fall to the Parthians. Almost twenty years later, Marcus Antonius suffered a huge defeat to that same enemy. According to the histories, the Parthians numbered eleven thousand troops, and the Romans under Antonius had thirty-two thousand auxiliaries."

"*The* Marcus Antonius lost with those odds?" Maren said, his voice revealing some uncharacteristic awe.

"Yes," Lucius said. "And only two thousand Romans escaped.

"I guess we should pick up the pace of whoring before we all die, eh?" Argus laughed, but no one else said anything.

138

"It's not all doom," Lucius added. "During the reigns of Trajan, Marcus Aurelius, and Lucius Verus, Rome finally managed to conquer large swathes of Parthian territory, including the capital of Ctesiphon on the Tigris river."

"We don't have that any more, from what I gather," Corvus said from his dark corner.

"No. But now, they are weakened by internal strife. That's why the emperor is taking us there now. He went once before to punish them for supporting Niger against him in the civil war. Now, it's time to finish the job."

"If they don't finish us first!" Garai said.

"But what makes these bastards so hard to beat?" Argus said.

"Their cavalry," Lucius replied immediately. "Unlike the legions which rely on the strength and skill of every one of its troops for a solid plan of battle, the Parthians rely mainly on two types of soldiers: their heavy cataphracts, and their horse archers. The heavy cavalry are their greatest weapon. They crushed their enemies on the grassy plains far to the east. They have scale armour that covers both horse and rider, and their mounts are of a very strong breed with thick necks, powerful shoulders, and short, thick legs that can carry a massive amount of weight."

"How many of these horsemen do they have?" Argus asked, his jokes at an end now.

"No one knows for sure, but they will number in the thousands at any given time. They wear bronze and iron helmets with neck guards and coloured plumes. They will look tall and imposing to a man on foot."

"What kinds of weapons do they have?" Antanelis asked.

139

"Apart from their full body armour, I read that they carry long, straight swords for slashing from horseback, battle axes, daggers, and heavy maces or clubs. But their main weapon is a sort of lance or spear about twelve feet in length called a kontos. They attack at full gallop and thrust downward with this from the top of their horses."

Lucius paused, and wondered why he was saying all of this. Then he realized he was enjoying the fear that this was putting into them. The group had become more competitive of late. He felt some shame at this, but they still pressed him, as one cannot help but look closely at a dying man in the arena or on the rougher streets of the Subura.

"More. Come on, Lucius. We need to hear it," Argus pressed.

"You need to keep in mind that Crassus only had seven legions, and Antonius had fewer than that in auxiliaries. We are going in with over thirty legions. Our chances are much better."

"How do they fight?" Alerio asked.

"From what I've read of accounts of the battles, the Parthian cataphracts make charges at the enemy and then, on either side, the horse archers provide support by riding in while raining arrows into the tightly packed ranks of the enemy. They have compact recurve bows. There are more horse archers than heavy cataphracts. They fire from full gallop and then continue to fire backward over their shoulders as they ride away from you and wheel for another pass. They'll attempt to break our flanks, I imagine, by firing the entire length of our ranks."

"What armour do the archers have?" Corvus asked.

"Don't know. Not the heavy armour, but I think I read something about linen or felt tunics."

"Ha. Nothing a pilum couldn't take care of!" Argus laughed. "Felt?"

"I hope our generals have a good fucking plan," said Garai as he laid himself back down.

"Thanks for the bedtime story, Metellus," Corvus said, shaking his head in the dark.

One by one, the others all laid themselves down and fell asleep. Lucius stayed awake, listening to the breathing of each man change to show that they were indeed sleeping. As he lay there, watching the shadowed roof of the dark tent flap in the breeze that blew in off the sea, he thought of the dream he had had in Rome, of the desert, and of blood.

I hope the generals do have a good plan, he thought.

The next morning, before sunrise, Lucius, Argus and the others were standing to attention outside the flaps of the command tent, waiting for Decimus to come out and usher them in so that they could meet their tribune prior to going into the city for the imperial audience.

Gallus stood nearby too, watching the tent flaps carefully. He had inspected the eight men and was pleased with the turnout. His only piece of advice for them had been to stop yawning. "You don't want the legate or emperor thinking they're fucking boring you, do you?"

It was harder than it looked, stifling yawns in the pre-dawn light before any of them had eaten, and yet they stood stalk-still, waiting.

Then the tent flap was pulled aside by two guards and Decimus' thick form appeared in the entrance. "The tribune wants to see you lot before we go. Come in."

Gallus led the way in followed by Lucius, Argus and the others in twos.

The command tent was large, and had separate rooms for the various tribunes' offices. In a permanent camp, each tribune would have had his own domus, but in this campaign tent, they shared the administrative space. The legate commander would want them close.

The other five tribunes of the legion were already awake and working, looking over dispatches and plans. They ignored the legionaries as they walked past on their way to the office of the patrician tribune who held command of the first cohort, which was a double strength cohort.

Gaius Livius Thapsus was a Patrician, through and through. He was taller than anyone there, and it leant him an imposing air, but he was also lanky and thin, more the type who would make a show on the Senate floor rather than the battlefield.

Lucius stood to attention with the others, staring straight ahead, his eye wandering cautiously to take in their tribune. The other tribunes were equestrians, like himself, but this man was an aristocrat, with the tidy blonde hair, and long aquiline nose to match. Livius' grey eyes glanced over the contubernium of well-turned-out men before him and he nodded silent approval. Lucius expected the man to dismiss them at first, but then he spoke.

"Good to have a Roman backbone in the new legions, Decimus. I'm glad you pushed to recruit in Rome first." The tribune stood and the men saluted. "At ease, men. There will be time enough for saluting, though I'm glad to see you know when to do so. Well, I don't usually know my troops' names, but I would have your optio tell me, Decimus, seeing as we are about to meet with Caesar."

"Very good, sir," Decimus said, turning to the men, and beginning with Corvus and moving down the line slowly, allowing the tribune to acknowledge each of the eight men. "Last we have Lucius Metellus Anguis, sir."

Lucius saluted again and stood straight. He was sweating beneath his lorica and tried not to shift.

"Metellus?" the tribune said. "What are you doing in the ranks, soldier? Is not your father Senator Quintus Metellus?"

"Yes, sir. He is." Lucius said, finally looking the man in the eye."

The tribune crossed his thin arms over his ornate breastplate with winged victories. "You should be an optio or tribune, young man. Equestrians don't really belong in the ranks these days. What of your political career? I imagine your father would have had different ideas than this. He is...quite..."

"Opinionated, sir," Lucius blurted.

"That's enough, Metellus! Or you'll feel my stick on your back!" Decimus stepped forward, his face shaded with anger.

Tribune Livius laughed. "It's all right, Decimus. The boy has the measure of his father, with whom my own father has crossed swords on the Senate floor many a time." He turned back to Lucius. "I imagine your father was not happy about your enlistment, hmm?"

"Sir. We were not in agreement on the matter, no," Lucius said. "He wanted me to do the minimum time in the army and then follow the Cursus Honorem."

"As well you should have," Livius said. "The ranks are not the place for you."

Lucius felt himself deflate, and could feel the others looking his way. "With respect sir, I believe my place is in the ranks, fighting alongside my brothers."

Decimus stepped closer, but then anger had gone from him. For the first time, a small measure of pride showed on the centurion's face.

"Hmm." Livius turned, his hand behind his back, his red cloak swirling about him. "Normally, I would take that as an insult, but, in truth, I'm relieved to have some true Roman blood in my command." He turned to Decimus. "I'm still not convinced about the Macedonians and Thracians."

"They'll show their worth," Decimus answered. "And our Roman boys have been showing them a thing or two."

"Good. Well, Metellus," Livius said. "It's good you want a fight, because I dare say you'll get one. We're marching into Hades soon."

"Sir!" Lucius saluted, and the tribune nodded.

"Well Decimus, we should not keep the legate and emperor waiting. The first hour of light has begun and we are expected within the city walls. Shall we?"

"Yes, sir!" Decimus snapped a salute and Lucius and the others fell in behind him, the tribune leading the way out onto the Via Decumana, south toward the city.

The legionary camps were all fully awake now, the cook fires burning, livestock moaning, and the centurions barking orders at the ranks beneath them.

They made their way toward the bridge over the Orontes river, just behind the palace complexes near the hippodrome. The sun had risen behind mount Silpius, the golden morning light surrounding the pediment of the Temple of Capitoline Jupiter which rose on the slopes of the hill beyond the city.

Birds flitted along the banks of the river where traders' tents had been set up to take advantage of the legions' presence.

Livius ignored the pleas of the merchants who harangued him as they passed, regardless of rank or interest.

However, Lucius and the others tried to catch glimpses of the wares as they passed; spices, dyes, gaming pieces, wine, Egyptian beer, rugs, cheap weapons, bread, dried fish, everything was available. On the other side of the river, to the south of the palaces, Lucius could see the main agora of Antioch where the early morning sounds of merchants and their haggling customers were already rising into the sky in a chorus of dealings.

Lucius wondered if he would have a chance to go there, but he did not want to get his hopes up. If they were marching soon, there would be no time for going into the city.

They had arrived at the gate house that guarded the bridge to the palace complex on the other side of the river, and Livius spoke with the Praetorian centurion on duty.

The man was enormous, and not cowed by the Patrician tribune. He questioned Livius closely and then checked his wax tablet to see if he was on the list of imperial visitors for that hour.

"Proceed, Tribune," the centurion said. "Legate Tertullius is already with the emperor in the main audience chamber. Go to the northeast building and inform the guards there you have arrived."

Without a word, Livius strode past the Praetorian and crossed the bridge.

The northwest precinct of Antioch, Lucius noticed, was crawling with Praetorians. This was, of course, to be expected with the emperor in attendance, along with all the commanders of this massive gathering. Lucius wondered if the empress, Julia Domna, might also be in attendance.

He had never seen the empress up close, only from a distance during public feast days when she led processions to the Capitoline Hill, or the Temple of Vesta in the Forum.

The streets were quiet in this precinct of the city, but for the guards who stood watchful and imposing. The Praetorians had been cleansed when Severus had taken power, the previous ones having become too powerful, enough so that they took it upon themselves to kill previous emperors.

This had not been something Severus was willing to tolerate, and so he replaced the entirety of the Praetorian ranks with troops from his own legions in Germania, and gave them a pay rise, as he had to the men of the legions.

Severus knew how to treat his troops, and how to preserve their loyalty. Anyone who tried to get at the emperor would not get very far, their guts spilled on the marble floor before they went even two steps with a weapon in hand.

They walked beneath the two and three storey palace buildings that were interspersed with gardens, until they arrived at another thickly-guarded gate that led onto the courtyard of the north east palace building.

The crack of whips and the cry of horses echoed from the hippodrome just to the right, and a squawk of peacocks from the gardens to the left where they stalked the groves of orange and lemon.

"Attention!" Decimus ordered them to stop once they were admitted to the courtyard and Livius spoke with the Praetorians there.

"Your men will have to wait out here, Tribune," the Praetorian said as he scanned the group.

"Of course," Livius answered. "They are but an escort to get here, in case of trouble from the locals."

"Of course," the Praetorian answered. "But I wouldn't expect trouble from the locals in Antioch. The emperor is well-loved, as is the empress."

"The empress is here as well?" Livius asked.

"Yes. Now, you and your centurion may enter, while your men remain with your optio out here."

Decimus walked over to Gallus and gave instructions, before disappearing into the palace behind the tribune.

"You and your men may stand over there, Optio," the Praetorian said to Gallus, pointing to an open space partly shaded by a few olive trees.

"At ease, lads," Gallus said when they arrived there. "Looks like you won't be meeting Caesar today."

Most of the men were relieved at that. Meeting your commanders was one thing, but meeting the emperor was quite something else.

"I'm so hungry," Antanelis said as they leaned against a wooden fence.

"Me too," Argus stretched. "What do you make of our tribune?" he asked Lucius. "Bit of a cunt, isn't he."

"Shh. Watch it," Lucius said. "He's all right. Typical patrician, but I'll admit he surprised me by talking to each of us. That's not normal."

"Livius is as nice a Patrician as you'll see," Gallus said, overhearing. "I'd watch it, Argus. I know these aristocrats can get on one's nerves, but they can flay you in a second while sipping their wine in dainty cups. Keep the stupid comments to yourself."

"Yes, sir," Argus said, smiling, turning back to Lucius. "Bet you're upset not to kiss the emperors foot, eh?"

"I was curious to see Caesar, but I'm not surprised. He's got over thirty legates with him, plus tribunes, centurions and his advisors. He probably wouldn't have noticed us anyway."

"Well, you never know, Antanelis said. "Maybe some day, you'll be up in front of Caesar having praise heaped upon you?"

The others laughed at that.

"Don't get your hopes up," Gallus said, chuckling. "Most of the time, the emperor doesn't know we exist." Gallus stood in front of them and looked at each of them. "Just remember that there are another thirty-odd legions with a lot more Romans in them than you lot. You'll have to prove yourselves in Parthia."

They wondered for a moment if the optio was joking, for his face was in deadly earnest, even though they had be kidding with each other.

"You show Decimus that his faith in you lot isn't misplaced, and he'll make sure you come to the attention of those higher up."

"What happens if we disappoint the centurion?" Maren asked, smirking.

"Then you'll be building muscle while shoveling shit on latrine duty. Got it?"

They all nodded, and were about to resume their banter when Decimus came striding out, followed by Livius, and an officer with a high-crested helmet and flowing red and gold cloak to whom Livius spoke with deference.

"Attention, first cohort!" Gallus barked, and all of them snapped to attention.

The officers approached, and stood before the men, Livius and the legate still talking in whispers. Decimus stood to attention himself, waiting for his two superiors to turn their attention to the men.

There was no introduction, but Lucius suspected that the officer was indeed their legate, Tertullius, the name he had heard earlier.

"Now, Livius," the legate commander spoke up. "Am I to understand that these are the best new recruits of the first cohort?"

"Yes, sir. Or so Centurion Decimus tells me, Legate. I've not seen them in action yet."

"Nobody in the Parthica legions has seen any action yet, as far as I know. Soon enough." The legate turned to the contubernium of young men, assessing them as he might a stallion in the market which he was choosing to carry him into battle. "I am Octavius Tertullius Varo, your legate and commander of the Parthica legions. I report only to the emperor, and I will be the one to command you in all things through Tribune Livius here."

An aide came running up and spoke into the legate's ear for a moment, drawing his attention away. Everyone stayed silent.

Octavius Tertullius Varo was short, compared with Tribune Livius. Every inch of him spoke of wealth and authority, from the line of his solid jaw, to the rich ornamentation upon his brown leather cuirass, pteruges, and the thick purple stripe on the hem of his perfectly white tunic beneath. Even his boots were stunning, made of red leather and ornamented with gold to match his flowing cloak and the sash of command that was tied about his midsection.

The legate turned back to the men. "Your tribune and centurion will inform you in more detail, but I might as well tell you now so you don't think of carousing within the walls of Antioch. The legions are moving out the day after tomorrow. That means, today, you are to make sure that all weapons, scuta, all supplies are well-stocked and cared for. Everything is to be in perfect fighting condition, including yourselves. The auxiliary scouts are already on the move toward Mesopotamia, and we will soon follow on their heels. I expect you Romans among my legions, to set the example. Can you do that?"

He had actually addressed the question to the men, and not to Livius or Decimus. The legate stood there, waiting for an answer.

"Yes, sir!" Lucius and the others finally said loudly, saluting the legate.

"Good. Livius will keep me informed."

With that, the legate nodded to the tribune and together they both went back to the palace where, apparently, there was to be a reception for the command staff, the high-ranking officials of Antioch, and neighbouring allies who had all prepared for the emperor's arrival.

"You heard the legate, men. Back to camp to prepare for the march." Decimus began to walk and Gallus and the men fell in behind him to march out of the palace complex beneath the watchful eyes of the Praetorians.

It was with some longing and regret that Lucius and the others turned away from the inner walls of Antioch, the markets, tabernae, brothels, and baths where they could have enjoyed some measure of civilization before marching into the desert. It seemed now that it was not meant to be.

As they marched back across the bridge over the Orontes river, Lucius chanced a backward look at the rich city, backed by the green, temple-clad mountain behind it. He looked askance at Argus and could see the anger and disappointment etched clearly on his face.

From then on, they were marching into the truly unknown.

VIII

Catinus

'Crucible'

The final day outside the walls of Antioch was spent in drills and final preparations. Rations for the march were distributed and bathing was done by sponge and bucket at the side of every tent in the legion. The luxuries of Antioch's baths would escape the legions, though the rank and file knew that the officers would be soaking themselves before getting dirty.

When the cornu sounded within III Parthica's camp on the day of departure, the long line of march was already snaking its way into the East, thousands of marching men, and beasts of burden carrying the needs of the legions.

The link back to Antioch would be of utmost importance to maintain the supply lines and ensure that the Romans would not starve, cut off from the rest of the Empire.

III Parthica was assembled on the plain when the tribunes arrived with the legate commander to inspect the legion.

Lucius and the others could hear the cornu sounding every so often, and the sound of neighing horses getting closer and closer as the inspection neared the front of the column. Then, he saw them.

As the commander and his staff drew even with Lucius, they saw for the first time the new legion's aquila standard, the golden eagle held aloft by the aquilifer, and the legion's vexillum with the emblem of a centaur on it.

"What is that?" Argus whispered as he saw the red and gold standard.

"Our legion's standard. It's a centaur, half man, half horse, from Greece. Must be because most of the legions are from Greece, Thessaly, Macedonia and Thrace. Looks fantastic."

"Pff. Looks stupid," Argus said.

Lucius ignored him. Argus had woken in a foul mood that morning and nothing could go right for him. Instead, he gazed at the aquila, the vexillum, and the imago, the image of the emperor carried by the imaginifer at the front of the column. All of them hung loftily above the brilliant red crests of the legate, Tribune Livius, and Decimus who rode at the front as primus pilus, head centurion of the legion.

The centaur standards of the I and II Parthica legions passed them on their way to those legions which were assembled a short distance away.

The men of III Parthica expected to wait for the other two legions to be inspected, but the cornu sounded loud and clear and the command was given to move forward and join the march.

"Forward, III Parthica!" Decimus yelled out and the tramp of hobnails began.

They soon found their marching rhythm, and the songs that so often rang among the men of the legions began, except in this case, the songs were Greek, and completely foreign to the Romans of the first cohort. That did not stop Argus, however, who began to sing out as if to clear his frustrations.

"I went to the brothel,
And what did I find?
Big-breasted women,

And sour wine!"

Maren, Eligius, Garai, and the others laughed and sang out as well, their voice vying with the Greeks behind them.

Lucius laughed. It was just like Argus to sing that one. He was glad his friend's mood seemed to be lightening. He sang a little too, but it was more difficult with the extra weight he carried. The large satchel which was strapped to his back along with his pick-axe, shovel, pots and other items, made finding his marching rhythm more difficult. It worried him. While others wore their covered scuta on their backs, he had to carry his in his left hand to march, while his right held his pilum. If they were attacked and immediate action was required, he would be in trouble.

Lucius knew that he needed to find a way to have his ancestral armour transported safely, but how, he did not know. He had already been chided, but surely there was a way. For the meantime, he marched and focussed on the land about them.

As they headed into Mesopotamia, he breathed deeply of the clean spring air, and admired the scrub and new growth of yellow, white, and purple flowers sprouting at the sides of roadside rocks.

Olive trees shivered in the breeze as the legions marched past, shepherds hurrying their flocks up into the hills, away from the marching ranks.

Clean air did not last for long as the legions began to make their way into the less fertile valleys leading to Zeugma, their first stop. For miles in front and behind, dust clouds rose into the sky as over thirty legions of marching men, auxiliary cavalry, and pack animals stomped on the earth.

They marched, the songs eventually fading out and giving way to grim anticipation of the battles to come. Scouts reported that Roman spies told of a great siege of the Roman allies at Nisibis. The commander of the garrison there, General Laetus, was apparently holding out but requesting immediate reinforcements to lift the siege.

The Parthians were at the gates of Nisibis, and they howled for Roman blood.

Every day, the legions marched for twenty miles over rock, and sand, and mountain passes. Every night, they dug in, the fortifications of camp ditches and palisades sprouting out of the ground like the hearty spring flowers that brought life and colour to the region.

It was thus for many hard days until they eventually reached Zeugma, on the banks of the Euphrates river where the settlements of Seleucia and Apamea straddled the broad river like two embracing lovers.

The sight of the Euphrates was welcome among the legions, though they were destined to spend but one night outside the city of Zeugma.

From their camp, it was possible for Lucius to spot the hillside on which much of the city was built. Among the green terraces of the hills were dotted countless villas, built by rich Greek and Roman merchants who had made their livings there over hundreds of years. The area was famous for the richness not only of its inhabitants, but also for the richness and otherworldly quality of the mosaics created by local and foreign artisans.

Sadly, Lucius and the others would never get the chance to see the beauties of Zeugma. It was only by word of mouth that he heard that the work of that far-flung city was superior to anything in Rome itself.

On that night, as the preferred few banqueted in Zeugma with wealthy merchants and suppliers for the army, Lucius and his friends lay back on the mats, dozing fitfully after the intensity of the first few days. Blisters had finally begun to heal, and more fresh water had been consumed with gratitude.

When he was sure everyone was asleep, Lucius sat up and, carrying his small altar to Apollo, went out of the tent.

The camp was quiet, the only sound along the tent rows being the solid snoring of a few despised legionaries.

Lucius crouched in the sand beside the still-smouldering fire pit, and lit a chunk of the incense he had brought with him from Rome. He placed it in the carved bowl on the top of the altar and raised his hands to the star-packed sky.

"My lord Apollo... I feel the first battle nearing. I am afraid, but I believe that to be normal. I know my training is good and more so, that you will not desert me. God of my ancestors, please guide me in the darkness and chaos of battle. Help me to cut my way through to the light.

Lucius felt cold all of a sudden. A breeze swept down the length of the avenue of tents, making him pull his cloak tighter about his person and turn.

He fell backward in the sand beside the altar and mumbled something incoherent before going to his knees.

"My lord..."

Before him stood Apollo, a magical blue cloak swirling about him like a windswept summer sky. He leaned on his silver bow, and eyes like the swirling heavens stared directly at Lucius.

"Apollo, I honour you," Lucius said, and the god answered.

"Rise, Metellus. None can hear us."

Lucius stood.

"I come to see that you are ready for the battles to come."

"Soon?" Lucius said.

"Yes. Soon you will be tested to your limits, but I want you to fight, for yourself, for your family, for your ancestors who honoured me always with blood upon the field, and glorious victories the praises of which could be sung for a thousand years.

Lucius bowed his head, nodding, understanding. Even the Gods expected greatness of him.

"You must preserve your strength, and rest your mind," Apollo said, his voice echoing in and out of reality as though an eerie song.

Then, Apollo held up his silver bow, a weapon larger than any a human could pick up. He plucked a long-shafted arrow from the quiver at his back and nocked it on the string. The god's muscular arm strained and pulled back, his eyes sighting down the shaft which pointed up into the sky, and loosed.

It shot like a comet into the heavens and descended to hit ground far to the East in the direction which they were headed.

Apollo looked at Lucius then and nodded. "Metellus... The field of your first blood is chosen. Tomorrow march to it and know that I am watching over you." He reached out and touched Lucius' bowed head, sending waves of hot and cold through the young man whose skin began to shake and burn all at once.

"Yes, lord..." Lucius said, bowing again. When he looked up, the air was warm once more and he was alone beside his smouldering offering.

When Lucius awoke in the morning, the others were already awake and eating their breakfast.

"Come on, Lucius!" Alerio said. "You're going to miss your rations, and I suspect that they will be much-needed today.

Lucius rolled onto his knees and remembered the previous night, his mind racing, searching for answers. He packed his things and put them, including the heavy bundle containing his family armour, outside the tent. Once he laid it there, a crow flitted down to it and squawked at him.

"Looks like you have a friend," Antanelis said.

"Let's cook it," Argus joked. "Be nice to have some meat for a change, rather than beans and barley."

Lucius stared at the crow, knowing in his gut that the bird was Apollo's messenger. He wondered why it was sitting atop the family armour and then remembered what the god had said about lightening his load.

The crow darted into the air and sailed down the avenue to rest on one of the supply carts near the command tent, continuing to squawk at Lucius.

"Sir, please," Lucius said to Decimus who was growing more and more impatient with the young equestrian.

"What do you want me to say, Metellus? I told you not to bring that stuff with you. That it would just slow you down. Now, you want me to put it in with the baggage train, something that is expressly forbidden."

"I know, sir. The fault is mine. But it means a lot to me and my family, that armour. It would be a great dishonour to lose it, or be killed because I was too slow to manoeuvre."

"Not my problem," Decimus said.

Lucius stood there, humiliated and unsure what to do next. Then Gallus spoke up.

"Sir, might I make a suggestion?" the optio said.

"What?"

"Well, sir. If Metellus is unable to shoulder the load he should not have brought in the first place, and if he is not willing to let it go, he could always put it in the wagon carrying dispatches and supplies. There is some room there."

"Are you out of your mind, Optio?" Decimus said. "Out of the question!"

"What if I rent the space?" Lucius blurted out. "Uhm, sorry sir. But, if there is already room, and I'm not going to be going to any city to enjoy myself soon, then I could pay for the transport of my extra belongings out of my legionary pay, no? Just until there isn't enough room."

Decimus stared at Gallus and than back to Lucius. "The money goes to who then?"

"Well, I would leave that for you to decide the best course, sir."

The centurion was silent for a moment and then nodded to Gallus. "Fine. Put it in there, and extract a sestercius a week from his pay. I trust that is fine with you, Metellus?"

"Absolutely, sir!" Lucius said, relieved.

"Good. See to it. Now I don't expect any complaining from you in the ranks. Got it?"

"Yes, sir."

Decimus marched off and Gallus turned to Lucius with his hand out.

"Now?"

"A deposit" the optio said flatly.

Lucius fished in his scrip and pulled out the coin. "I'll bring the satchel over shortly. Please make sure it is safely buried, sir."

"It'll be up to the Gods whether you lose the items or not, Metellus. You came to us." He turned then and left Lucius behind to go back and finish preparing for the crossing of the Euphrates later that day.

After a couple of days, the last of Severus' legions marched across the Euphrates, leaving the luxurious comforts of Zeugma behind.

They were now in enemy territory and alae of auxiliary cavalry could been seen in the distance, scouting and providing a perimeter, racing back and forth to the part of the column where the emperor and his main commanders rode to give them details about the enemy's movements.

It ran along the ranks that the Parthians and their allies, the Osroeni, the Adiabeni, and the Arabians were everywhere. They held Edessa, which was located to the north of the line of march and needed to be taken, but the more pressing engagement was the relief of the Roman allied city of Nisibis.

Despatches sent to the invading Roman force from Nisibis' commander, General Laetus, spoke of a city whose walls were near to being breached, but that they would hold out to the last if need be.

Lucius and the others had heard of this General Laetus in passing at times, and he seemed to be a highly capable, well-respected commander.

The emperor wanted to go to Laetus' aid with all speed, and the pace of the march was quickened. At the same time, to protect the army's flank, three legions were sent to march along the mountain range to the north of the main column, in order to protect the Roman flank from enemy forces out of Edessa.

The late spring heat began to take its toll on the men in that dry waste beyond the Euphrates. The land was destitute of water, and the men became weary of the sun and heat that beat down upon them throughout the days.

However, the troops took heart from the presence of the emperor. Most men did not see Septimius Severus, but they knew he was there, riding in the column, surrounded by his Praetorians, leading the army, and conferring with his commanders. All the legates and tribunes of every legion and ala had a specific role to play, and could take confidence in the fact that it was all thought through.

Once Lucius thought he had seen a flash of white and purple ride by during an inspection and knew that it was the emperor atop his white charger, his purple cloak fluttering in the dry, dusty wind.

Septimius Severus, the African emperor from Leptis Magna, had remained an enigma for a long time, but it was said that he was on friendly terms with his troops, and admired as a great Roman. The empress too was with the army, close to her husband at all times.

Lucius had heard the jokes about Julia Domna, the empress, and how heavy her accent was when she spoke Latin. However, such talk was stomped out when the emperor or his advisors were about, for men knew he was a man of retribution, and in such cases, the emperor's own Latin was said to be 'perfect'.

Lucius felt relief as he marched without the added weight of his ancestral armour and weapons upon his back. He had felt like Atlas, the world upon his shoulders, something matched only by the expectations he placed upon his own. For the moment, without that armour, and the legacy of the dragon, he felt that he could run the rest of the way to Nisibis.

They continued to march in the dust and heat. Men sweat, and spat dirt and dust from their parched mouths, each day collapsing after digging in so as to be safe behind moat and stockade. In the mornings they tore it all down, filled the ditches and began again.

Among the ranks of the Parthica legions, the new recruits began to anticipate their first experience of battle. Most were terrified of it, though they did not readily admit it. Then there were some who relished their first engagement and the chance to show their commanders what they were made of.

Then word came one evening that the following day, they would make their first attempt to relieve the siege of Nisibis. That night, in each legion's camp, sacrifices were performed, omens read, and the auguries taken.

All seemed favourable.

In the emperor's camp, the imperial astrologer was busy reading the stars beneath the desert sky, and giving the emperor and empress their horoscopes. After much

162

deliberation and decipherment, it was clear that the heavens were in agreement with their actions. The order was given to form up at dawn to attack the attackers of Nisibis.

It was quiet in the tent that night. While Corvus sang a song of the sea that he missed so much, Lucius thought about how far they had come, all of them.

They were good, hard-working young men, and Lucius was proud to be among them. They had indeed achieved much, but they had not yet fought in the shield wall against an enemy whose only wish was to skewer each and every one of them and to leave their bones to rot on the Mesopotamian earth.

There was comfort in the size of the Roman force, to be sure, but battle was still a realm of the unknown. The young men were still unbloodied. Now the time was there, and the night held the prospect of unease with silent restlessness running among the men sleeping upon the ground.

Before they knew it, the sun was up and the cornu sounding to arms.

Lucius finished a few mouthfuls of boiled beans which they had prepared the night before, drank some water and stood to attention until it was the turn of their contubernium to march out onto the plain.

"III Parthica!" Decimus yelled from the command tent a short distance away, where he stood with Tribune Livius. "Our friends and allies are trapped inside that city to the East, and we're going to help them. Time to show me what you're made of!"

The image of the emperor was hoisted by the imaginifer, then the vexillum with the centaur, and then, the aquila rose high above them, gold and glinting in the morning light.

"Time to prove to your brothers what you Greeks, Macedonians, Thessalians, Thracians, and ROMANS are made of! Now, march, and remember your training, for you will remember this day as it is burned into your minds!"

The primus pilus stood in the centre of the road and raised his vinerod to cheers and acclamations.

"Well done, Centurion," Livius said as he kneed his horse forward and the centuries fell in behind him and the standards of the legion.

Nisibis was a key strategic position that Rome needed. It lay directly on the main route that ran from east to west and vice versa. As an important settlement for trade, it had few equals.

Running through Nisibis was the river Mygdonius. To the South was dry desert plain as far as the eye could see through the clouds of dust. To the North, beyond the plain of rock and scrub, rose the mountain of Nisibis, a high, forty eight mile long ridge that swept up to a plateau overlooking the city.

From their vantage point at the front of the first century, Lucius and the other Romans of the first cohort could see the desert plain come into view with Nisibis in the distant centre, smoking and bubbling from siege, like a festering scab in the desert. It appeared that the besieging Parthians and their allies had begun early, and in earnest, on the walls and gates, hoping to crush them before the legions showed up to surround the city.

The tramp of hobnailed boots on the floor of rock and sand became a constant, rhythmic thrumming as thousands of men marched, flanked by cavalry alae.

As he marched, Lucius felt lighter than he had in a long while, without the weight of the ancestral armour upon his shoulders, a burden that carried so much more weight that its fifty pounds. Now, he felt like a legionary.

Lucius Metellus Anguis hefted the two pila in his right hand and felt the weight of the large rectuangular scutum in his right. His chin strap was tight, the knot rubbing on his skin slightly as he marched, his gladius swaying comfortingly at his left side.

III Parthica had not been involved in any of the skirmishes that had taken place along the line of march with Parthian and Osrohoene scouts. They had become impatient, but that would soon be remedied, as it appeared that III Parthica was heading directly for the enemy lines which seemed to be forming up before the river by the south gates of Nisibis.

The young men were impatient for a taste of battle, and now it seemed the Gods were about to grant their wishes.

It had been the waiting that fed their youth's impatience, the not knowing what to expect in a pitched battle when their lives were on the line. They had been prepared and given great skill through their training, true, but as they marched closer to the conflict, as it became clear the new legions would be among the first to engage the enemy, each of them wondered if his own nerve would hold. Would his knees buckle? Or would Disciplina stand beside them when the shield wall collided with the enemy, and blades of steel stabbed in and out of the thick ranks?

The men of III Parthica knew they had something to prove to the veterans, and to their commanders. To themselves, the evidence of their worth would mean the difference between life and death beneath the Gods' fateful gaze.

The cornu sounded and the legions marched forward in concert, downhill toward the flat plain about the city. It seemed thousands and thousands of enemy cavalry and horse archers buzzed about a great hive that was Nisibis. Another set of cornu sounded from the walls of the city as the liberators were spotted between plumes of black smoke beyond the siege-darkened walls.

At the front of the century, Lucius looked out to see the enemy horses, covered in chain and plate armour that glinted in the dusty light, accented with colourful fabrics. The earth shook with their horses' hooves and they milled and formed up to receive the Roman advance.

Lucius felt his heart beating uncontrollably in his chest, as though it would crack his ribs any moment, and he took some deep breaths, his lips and tongue dry and longing for water. To his left stood Corvus, and to his right, Argus. For that, he was happy. They had trained together, learned to protect the man beside him, anticipate his moves and stay with him to keep the all-important line intact.

Then III, II, and I Parthica advanced toward the line of the enemy, the veteran legions coming up behind them.

"What are they doing?" Corvus said, panic lashing his face. "They're sending us in first?"

"Shut up!" Argus said. "You think they'd waste the veterans on an initial onslaught? This is our test, Corvus!" Argus looked out, trying to control the racing of his own heart, as much as he had convinced himself that he would enjoy this. "Still, it would be nice to know the plan," he said to Lucius as they marched. "How are we supposed to fight if we don't know the strategy?"

"We're not supposed to," Lucius answered grimly. "Just remember your training. Remember Disciplina. Whatever commands are given, we do exactly that, nothing else...nothing else!" Lucius realized his voice had risen and his hand carrying his two pila was slick with sweat.

"Enough chatter!" Gallus called from the end of the row. "Make us proud, III Parthica! Listen for the commands, follow them, and you'll live!"

They continued, closer and closer, until the faces of the enemy were almost visible. Tribune Livius had dropped away to the rear with the legate, and the offensive was now led by Centurion Decimus who marched blatantly, slowly, toward the ranks of enemy horse with his scutum hanging by his side and his gladius still sheathed.

Then it began. A series of loud cracks from the river that ran up into Nisibis, and the dimming of the light coming from the east.

"Testudinem facite!" Decimus commanded, and without thinking Lucius held up his shield in front, and Antanelis' scutum covered his head behind him so that they were protected, the century perfectly encased in a shell of Roman wood and steal.

The sound was deafening as the arrows rained down on them, thousands of shafts embedded in the scuta as they continued to march.

Lucius looked at Argus. He was smiling wildly as though he could not believe it worked. But this was one of the manoeuvres they had drilled at more than most, and it paid off. They continued their advance, repelling three more volleys of arrows with only a few squeals from within their armoured tortoise formation where stray arrows had penetrated a careless gap between shields.

The unmistakable tramp of horses began, and the legionaries began to feel the earth tremble beneath their caligae.

"Prepare to repel cavalry!" Decimus, who yet lived, yelled above the raucous sounds of battle now coming from all directions. The noise got louder and louder, and many of the men had the urge to cover their ears but they held their discipline, waiting for the commands.

"Pila iacite!"

As smooth as could be, the front row hoisted their first pila and launched them, before stepping aside for the second row.

Lucius saw his pilum soar across the ground between him and the charging cavalry to take a man's mount in the leg, laming his horse and sending the warrior head over heals in front of Decimus who dispatched the man with one stab of his gladius.

More and more pila soared over head, laying a wall of broken horses and riders before the Romans, but with each broken charge, the next one came even closer until every man had spent both his pila and Decimus yelled another command.

"Gladii out! Shields up to repel cavalry!"

Lucius heard the slither of his blade as he drew his gladius and crouched with Antatenlis' shield covering his head once again.

A loud groan and crack of wood ran along the line and Lucius heard several cries farther down the line. The vibration tore into his shield hand.

"What the bloody hell was that?" Corvus yelled.

Lucius turned his head to answer Corvus, but in that same instant a cavalry spear bored through the top lip of the man's scutum and the one covering him.

Lucius felt a spray of hot blood fan over his face as he looked to see the spear planted into Corvus' eye socket, the other eye gaping horribly in instant death.

"Hold, Lucius!" he told himself. "Hold the line." He shook his head downward to allow the blood to trickle off and when he looked up, a pair of wild dark eyes was staring at him from behind a probing blade.

Lucius' gladius stabbed out from the side of his scutum and he felt the soft flesh give way to grinding ribs and then a dead weight that threatened to pull his sword from his grasp. But he held on, yelling as he pulled it free to stab again, and again, each time ducking back behind his shield.

Beside him, Argus echoed his movements and together, they stabbed at each enemy form before them. The gap left by Corvus was now filled by Alerio. The line was solid once more.

A flash of red before them showed Decimus to be still alive, tough as ever, his face covered in blood, his armour speckled with offal.

"Form up! We move for the main gate. Left!"

Lucius, Argus, Alerio and the rest of the century stood up and they saw clearly for the first time, the killing field about them.

"We're at the river?" Lucius said out loud, incredulous that they had gone that far, pressed through the enemy cavalry and archers. They were now pressing toward the city gate where a large force of enemy troops fought the Romans in front, and still attacked the gates of the city behind.

They continued, their limbs tired and shaking, trying to take advantage of the cool bloodlust that they each waded through as they stepped over the corpses of horsemen, archers, writhing animals, and some Roman dead, whose red cloaks lay about their bodies like exaggerated pools of blood.

When arrows began to rain down on them from the other side of the river, they wheeled at Decimus' command and formed another testudo.

The rain of arrows stopped suddenly then as, from the east side of the city, one of the legions emerged to slam into the enemy archers and horses who were hitting their flank.

"To the gate!" Decimus yelled and they rose as one and continued to plod on.

Atop the wall, over the main gate, Lucius could see a great crimson crest going back and forth. Its wearer hacked at enemy soldiers who yet saw their opportunity to climb ladders, some of whom had made it to the top of the wall. The man slashed and slew like a fury, his troops about him doing the same all along the walls, their vigour renewed by the sight of Rome's legions come to their aid.

The rhythmic pattern of slaying that Lucius now fell into was terrifying to him, another part of his mind that seemed to watch from afar, from atop the mountain of Nisibis where, for a moment, he thought he spied the godly form of Apollo watching the carnage from his eyrie. Lucius felt heat and light run through his body as exhaustion set in and he renewed his attacks and held the line with Argus, Alerio and the others.

Each row of legionaries moved from back to front to relieve their brothers, and then made to attack again, the sound of the dead and dying ringing louder than any theatre chorus in Rome.

Deafening chaos whirled about them, but their discipline under those conditions helped them to carry the battle and deal death until the remaining enemy turned and fled into the desert to the south, pursued by the auxiliary cavalry.

When they reached the destruction and mounds of bodies that lay before the gates of Nisibis, the order to halt was given and the roar of Rome's legions soared up the walls of the city and into the heavens.

The siege was lifted.

The aftermath of a battle, even one as small as the one Lucius and the others had just taken part in, was filled with nightmare images that have forever haunted the dreams of every man of war.

Forever more would the stench of fear, of sweat, of piss and shit, and the iron scent of blood stick in their noses. The cries of men killing, and of men dying, would always repeat in their minds, a deranged chorus of tragedy beyond reckoning.

The men of III Parthica stood to attention on the bloody plain of rock, sand, clotted blood, and offal as the gates to the city were finally opened and the commanders of the city, led by General Laetus, came out to greet some of the legions' legates, including Octavius Tertullius Varo.

Lucius stood there, beside Alerio and Argus, breathing heavily like all the others, eyes wide open with shock, while the officers greeted and congratulated each other for the work the troops had done. While he stood, swaying a little on his feet, he saw it over and over again, the spear point exploding into Corvus' eye socket, the blood, and then the flashes of death thereafter, mostly dealt by his own blade, beyond the edge of his shield.

Death had come easily to his chosen targets, faceless men who bore down upon him and his brothers with fury and rage. Lucius remembered the whites of their eyes, and the shock in those eyes when his blade dove in and out like a great serpent's bite.

Lucius looked sidelong at Argus who was also covered in congealing blood. The dark head turned to Lucius and nodded, the eyes slightly crazed as the battle fury leached slowly away. They stood on the remnants of the living, swarming with flies, the air accented with the cawing of feeding carrion crows.

"You all right?" Alerio whispered to Lucius. "I never thought it would be like that." He shook his head. "The training saved us. Like we didn't have to think."

It was true. Lucius knew now why they had drilled so intensely, why Decimus was so ruthless with them, so punishing of anything less than perfect.

Disciplina, their training, the motions that had become second nature to them, these were the only reasons they were still standing, breathing, feeling the wind on their faces, able to smell the scene about them.

But also by the Gods' will am I still here, Lucius thought, remembering seeing Apollo on the mountain, his blue cloak whipping around him, the heat and light finding its way to Lucius' aid.

Lucius reached up and scratched his face. It was sticky and his hand came away with thick red strands of Corvus' blood. The look in the man's eyes as he died, the surprise, the instant change from living to dead with a spear shaft ripping through his head, and the hot spray across the face afterward.

Unable to hold it, Lucius bent over and vomited onto the body of a dead archer whose intestines snaked their way loose of his opened body.

"Suck it up, Metellus!" Gallus said, walking over to Lucius. "You did well." He slapped Lucius on the shoulder, but turned when the sound of more vomiting came from down the line and a few rows back. "Don't worry lads, everyone pukes after their first engagement. Just let it out and stand back to attention. You'll be hungry later, I promise you," he laughed.

He actually laughed.

Lucius could not believe it. He had known, in theory, what battle and war meant, but the assemblage of all of war's stimuli was something he had not been prepared for.

When they received the command to sift through the dead to find their own fallen men, their feet never felt so heavy, their bodies so exhausted, as they did then. But they were Romans, they were legionaries, and that meant obeying their orders. If they had to do it while puking, so be it. They would do it.

After a while, a cheer rose from near the gates, and Lucius and the men stood from their gruesome task to see General Laetus striding over the bodies with Legate Tertullius, and Tribune Livius toward Decimus who turned and saluted to his superiors.

Laetus was still dirty from battle, but he went right up to Decimus and grasped the centurion's forearm tightly.

"Primus Pilus, I saw how you fought down here. My thanks to you and to your men."

"Just doing our duty, sir," Decimus answered.

"I know how tough it is to lead green recruits into battle so early on. I saw how well they performed, and I know that they could not have done so without expert training at your hands. I shall speak of this to the emperor when I see him. He will know that the Parthica legions have earned their decorations this day.

"Sir!" Decimus saluted.

As Laetus turned to leave, he scanned the men and as he did so, Lucius saluted him. His eyes rested on the young man standing on a mound of bodies, covered in blood.

Then the general did something unusual. He saluted back. Livius looked from the general to Lucius and leaned in.

"That is our Equestrian legionary, Lucius Metellus Anguis. One of the few Roman recruits we have."

"He was in the front, was he not?" Laetus asked Decimus.

"Yes, sir. Only place for him, sir."

Laetus nodded slowly and turned. "I must clean the blood from my person now, for my audience with Caesar." He began to walk away, followed by his aides when a cry of acclamation rose from the ranks of men on the plain and upon the walls.

"Laetus! Laetus! Laetus!" they yelled as he passed, for he had held the city, a crucial foothold for Rome, against all odds. If there was indeed a hero there that day, it was General Laetus.

Lucius watched the man go and he found himself admiring his manner, the commanding presence he had, and the respect that presence garnered from his peers. His thoughts were broken by Antanelis's question to Decimus.

"Centurion?"

"What is it, soldier?"

"Will the Parthians come back today?" Antanelis asked, all the others around him turning to their centurion.

"Ha! Those were not the Parthians, lad. Those were Osrohenian and Adiabenan troops. Easy."

Lucius felt as though a stone had dropped in his guts, and so did many other men within earshot.

"No," Decimus continued. "We haven't met the Parthians yet, but we will. Don't you worry. We will." Decimus turned to Gallus, gave an order which the optio wrote down on his wax tablet, and then turned to go along the rest of the century to see how the work was progressing, how many new recruits lay dead in the sand.

In their tent that night, on the dry plain to the South, away from the gory ground, and safe within the Roman palisade of III Parthica's camp, Corvus' spot in the tent lay blatantly vacant, like a wound that had not been tended to.

He had been the first of their group to fall, but would he be the last? Lucius wondered if there had been anything he could have done to save Corvus. Had he missed something?

The empty place in their contubernium's tent seemed enormous, drawing each young man's eyes to it in the darkness.

Lucius heard Garai muttering something to himself in a low voice. He presumed it to be a prayer to his chosen god. Perhaps Mars? If it was Mars, then the god had revelled in the day's work. For himself, Lucius closed his eyes and thought of light, of Apollo, and imagined himself in the temple back on the Palatine Hill making his offerings. Eventually, he and the others fell asleep, each man gripping his gladius close as they headed into myriad nightmares of battle and blood, while outside, their comrades' bones yet smouldered on one of the many pyres for Roman dead which they themselves had helped to build from the broken rubble of Nisibis.

Later that night, in the Praetorium of the emperor's camp, surrounded by a legion of his own guard, Septimius Severus sat on his ivory chair and held aloft a golden cup full of wine as he toasted General Laetus before all the commanders of the legions.

"General Laetus, I salute you for your hard-won victory in keeping the city of Nisibis for the Empire. The Gods, the stars themselves, have smiled on you this day, and rewarded your courage and the duty you have carried out with such fervour and steadfastness. General Laetus!"

The emperor swept back his long purple robe and scratched at his thick beard as his gaze fell over the assembly of commanders, each of whom waited his turn to congratulate Laetus.

Beside the emperor, Julia Domna sat quietly perusing scrolls, yet listening to every word that reached her ears. Occasionally, one of the generals would approach her to give greeting, but this was not a night for philosophy, it was a time for war, and talk of strategy and troop dispositions. The empress reached across and touched her husband's hand.

"Sire," she said in a low voice that only he could hear as she leaned toward him, her silk ruffling loudly. "We cannot linger in Nisibis. I have word here," she held up a scroll, one of the dispatches that had come in, "that Edessa is held by the enemy. If we do not take it back, your supply route to the sea risks being cut off."

Septimius Severus winked at his wife, looking at the dark eyes he loved so much. "Two legions are already on their way to Edessa, and more will follow. These Parthians are going to pay for what they have taken from Rome."

The empress leaned back in her chair and nodded. Her husband had been at war for so long, she sometimes forgot how such things came easily to him, and yet, he always took the opportunity to confer with her, and with the stars that dictated their destinies. It was a comfort, but also a certainty that they were such a good pair. The stars had truly matched them well, she knew.

The emperor stood again and stepped down among the generals to the centre of the room where an enormous map of Mesopotamia was spread out. The generals stepped aside for Caesar as he ran his hand up and down the blue lines of the Tigris and Euphrates rivers, his golden wine cup in his other hand.

"We must succeed where Trajan failed," he said. "The Parthians are assembling south of Dura Europus, where we will go after them with all our might. But first, we must crush their allies in the North. Edessa is next. Then we move swiftly to take Seleucia, Babylon, and the Parthian capital of Ctesiphon."

"Sire," Laetus stepped forward, all eyes upon him. "There is one more city that will cause us no end of grief if we do not take it."

"Yes, general?" the emperor said, though by the look on his face, he knew very well which.

"Hatra."

The emperor took a deep breath and drained his cup, placing it on the table and leaning on both his battle-hardened fists. "Yes. It lies there mocking us, in the land between the two rivers, an affront to Rome's might."

There were sounds of agreement. All of them knew previous emperors had failed to take Hatra. Would Severus be the leader to finally do it? It was a staunch supporter of the Parthians, a place where many Parthians lived, dominating the inhospitable terrain of the surrounding desert, too far from either the Euphrates or Tigris.

"We will take Hatra at the opportune moment," the emperor said. "However, first we wipe away any remnant forces of Osrhoenians or Adiabenans who fled the field today or hold sway in Edessa."

The generals nodded, for they all knew the importance of keeping their supply lines back to Antioch safe before committing fully to taking the Parthian capital.

"We have struck our first victory today, gentlemen," Severus said. "And Legate Tertullius, the Parthica legions carried themselves admirably in their first engagement. You are to be congratulated."

"Thank you, Caesar," Tertullius said, bowing.

"The bulk of the army will move west to retake Edessa. However, I have a command for generals Laternus, Candidus, and Laetus." Severus turned to Laetus and the two men either side of him. "I want you to head north, northeast, and southwest of here with each of your legions to clean away the remnant forces or any other Parthian allies that will threaten our advance. Understood?"

"Yes, Caesar," the three generals said all together, bending over the map to whisper where they would direct their legions, and how they could support each other and remain in contact."

"We will remain in Nisibis for three days so that the legions can help rebuild and refortify, but after that we move for Edessa. General Tertullius?"

"Yes, Caesar?"

"I want you to leave I Parthica to garrison Nisibis. We need our veteran legions when we march against the Parthians themselves. Agreed?"

"Absolutely, sire," the legate said, relieved that he could keep Decimus with him on the march to Edessa. The primus pilus was one of his greatest assets.

"Very well, gentlemen," Severus said, moving to take the empress' hand and help her down from the dais. "I will to bed now, but you may stay and finish your wine if you wish."

"Hail, Caesar!" they saluted.

Severus saluted them in return and swept from the tent with the empress, several Praetorians and secretaries following in their wake.

The following day, as commanded, the generals Laetus, Laternus, and Candidus all set off in different directions with their legions to hunt down the enemy allies that had dispersed into the desert or been spotted by the Roman cavalry patrols that swept in great arcs across Mesopotamia.

Those who remained at Nisibis began the gruelling work of rebuilding the fortifications and gates, reparing roads and gutted out buildings that had burned in the long siege of the city.

The citizenry had nearly wept for the departure of General Laetus, the man who had saved them, but they were comforted by the presence of over twenty legions surrounding the city. Trade began once more to flow through Nisibis, and it was as though the city began to breathe once more after a long suffocation.

When the legions finally marched east from Nisibis, it was still with the stink of their burning comrades in their nostrils.

As they left, Lucius looked back over his shoulder to the place where he had experienced his first battle. He wondered how many more he would have. During times of Pax Romana, legionaries went for years without fighting a battle, but in times of war and retribution, the number of enemies one man of Rome's legions could be forced to kill was unmentionable.

You knew it would be like this, Lucius told himself often. *March on, and follow orders.* He did it. So did all the others marching around him.

From the liberation of Nisibis onward, the land between the Tigris and Euphrates rivers became a place of battle and blood, a place where the legions manoeuvred about the Parthians and their allies, trying to push for a final contest.

Edessa was the second city to fall to Severus' forces.

King Abgar of Oshroene was holed up in the city, a staunch Parthian client, and Severus wished to make the king pay dearly for his mislaid loyalty. It was from Edessa that many Oshroenian units swept to attack Roman columns before retreating behind her great walls.

When Rome's legions encamped about Edessa, the city grew silent and still, as if a child holding its breath, hoping the enemy would not be able to find it, or that it had done something inexcusable. The place was completely surrounded.

The truth was that Septimius Severus wished to take Edessa and Oshroene because they had supported his rival for the imperial throne, Pescennius Niger. That bitter conflict would rule many a decision.

The waiting began, as Severus allowed a few days for King Abgar to quake at the sight without his walls. Any strength or might that the king took comfort in was purely illusory.

Every day, grim-faced legionaries stood still around the city, waiting for the chance to have at the walls and the spoils within, but the commanders held them back. Instead, in turns, they paraded and drilled in preparation for larger quarry.

Among the Roman staff was an engineer by the name of Priscus of Bythinia. When Severus called the man to present himself, there were whispers about what it meant. Priscus was a master of siege warfare and expert at the design and creation of siege engines, learned in the designs used by men such as Alexander against ill-fated Tyre and others.

When shipments of wood arrived from the mountains to the North, Priscus and his staff got to work, and after over a week, the army marched out with rolling towers, catapults, and cranes that could reach to the top of Edessa's walls.

One hazy morning, the heat began to beat down early on the legions. When the cornui sounded, Lucius was standing among the men of III Parthica, beside one of the massive catapults, whose great arm was aimed directly at Edessa's west wall.

One breech, and the legions would pour in. The people of Edessa were permitted to watch the silent ranks of legionaries from their walls, the menacing structures created by Priscus of Bythinia standing still amongst the ranks of Romans.

Lucius could not see the imperial command post to the south of the city from his posting on the west, so they just waited as the sun rose, growing hotter and hotter.

"What are they waiting for?" Alerio said as they stood there, Decimus pacing slowly before the men of the first cohort.

"Maybe they're waiting to see if Abgar will capitulate," Lucius said.

As if in answer, the cornicens of every legion began to blast commands on their curved horns and the winches of the siege catapults were pulled back. Then a torrent of boulders and ballista bolts shot in brutal unison at the walls of the city, and Edessa felt Rome tear at her flesh from every side, sending up a chorus of screams and alarms from within the walls.

Twice, three times, four and more, the siege engines drew back and fired, their crews sweating as they loaded, fired, and reloaded over and over again so that the sound of falling rock and crumbling stone could be heard through the dust storm of the siege.

Lucius wondered what it must be like inside the city, the horror they now imagined. He thought of the women and children who must surely be cowering in their homes, the families of those men who now lined the walls in vain hope that Rome would forgive, or simply walk away.

"Rome never walks away," he said to himself.

Lucius was thankful for the command that had been given forbidding any looting or rapine, though many a legionary had complained at that. Despite that, he knew that when they entered the city, they would have to kill rebels, and step over the shattered bodies of those within. Blood would paint the walls and streets either way.

A loud crack and groan to the left and right indicated that two breeches had been made in the city walls and the battering rams began to move forward with the cohorts of Roman troops in those areas. Along the tops of the walls, enemy soldiers could be seen running to the trouble spots to try and slow the Romans' advance. Arrows began to fly at the Romans, and ballista bolts from the siege engines began to cleave the tops of the walls, sending men to their instant deaths through the air beyond.

Then the wall collapsed in a small section immediately before III Parthica.

Decimus yelled, "Forward III Parthica!"

They began to march slowly, steadily toward the narrow crevice in the wall where the stonework had given away. Arrows began to fly toward them.

"Shields!" Decimus yelled and they raised their scuta. "Keep moving!"

They continued, feeling the occasional heavy pelt of arrow shafts on their wooden scuta, or glancing off the sides of their helmets.

Lucius felt alive then, strangely so, as if walking into the face of death took away all inhibitions and fears. He could hear everything, and see every movement about him. He could hear his brothers' breathing down the line and behind, he could see arrows splitting the air, and movement of troops on the other side of the breech they were headed for.

"Almost there!" Argus said, grinning. "Too bad we - "

Lucius' shield shot up to block an arrow that would have crashed into Argus' face. The barbed head shuddered on the face of his scutum and Argus stared at it.

"How did you - "

"Get in there, First Cohort!" Decimus bellowed urging them over the fallen stonework and up into the crack.

The centurion was the first to the breech where he was met by a group of soldiers.

"On your centurion!" yelled Gallus, pointing the brass orb on the end of his hastile toward Decimus.

Lucius ran forward, his scutum over his head to repel against the rocks and arrows that the few men above them were firing down.

The hail stopped suddenly as a ballista bolt tore through two of the men on the wall at once, throwing them down from on high into the city street beyond.

Lucius lowered his scutum and jumped after his centurion who was hacking and cursing at five enemy soldiers in light armour and flowing, multi-coloured cloaks. He drew even with Decimus, and then Argus, and Alerio, Antanelis, Maren, Eligius, Garai and more came through to cut down their oponents.

"You, Eligius, Garai, Antanelis and Maren," Decius ordered. "Get up to the top of the wall with Gallus. Now!" The men jumped to it and found a broken staircase that led up to the ramparts. Gallus signalled to the artillery to stop firing as there were Roman troops within the walls now, and more of the legions pressed forward to tighten the noose on Edessa.

"The rest of you, on me!" Decimus growled and they followed him down a street toward the centre of Edessa as more and more of III Parthica flowed through the wall to follow the centaur vexillum. "Only kill those who attack or oppose us," Decimus ordered. "This city is to be an ally of Rome again."

The streets were confusing after the open desert plain, stifling and dusty. The Romans marched through, their scuta up, gladii out, ready for anything. Two by two they went, in different directions toward the central palace of King Abgar.

Every so often, a screaming trooper, or suicidal local ran at them from an open doorway only to be hacked down quickly and efficiently as they swept along the streets, over rubble and burned or bruised bodies.

Lucius numbed his mind to the sights about him, the sounds of wailing babies hushed vainly by their terrified mothers, young boys who quaked in corners holding shuddering kitchen knives out before them. Up ahead he spotted a red banner and crimson cloaks where some other legionaries were scuffling with some locals in a house.

"Keep moving!" Decimus ordered as they drew even with the dwelling.

Lucius chanced a look inside and saw two men standing over a young woman clutching a baby. They laughed and began to pull at her robes as she screamed and pleaded.

"What are you doing?" Argus said as Lucius broke away and went in. He looked ahead to where Decimus was waiting at an intersection, and then followed Lucius.

"Get back here!" the centurion howled.

Inside Lucius saw to his horror that one of the men had taken the baby roughly from the mother and tossed its screaming form into a corner. The woman yelled and made to get to the baby, but the big legionary stood above her and pulled at her legs.

"Our orders are not to harm innocents!" Lucius said as loud and menacingly as he could. "Leave them alone!"

The big man stopped pulling on the young mother and turned about slowly while his comrade held his gladius at Lucius' back.

When the man turned, Lucius' breath caught at the sight of the pulpy nose and those wicked eyes.

The man he had fought at the legionary recruitment in Rome, Bona, stood there, full recognition of Lucius on his face.

"You?" Lucius said.

"Ha! Surprised to see me, Metellus? You think III Parthica is the only legion?" Without another word Bona's fist flashed out, but Lucius dodged it and kicked out sending him into a wall. Argus and the other man began to struggle too.

Lucius looked at the baby in the corner, its arm badly bent, and then at the terrified girl who scrabbled to her child. The fury rose up in him just as Decimus entered the doorway, rage on his face, and Lucius ran at Bona and kicked him down again. His fist hammered the man's face again, so hard that Bona's helmet came loose.

"Stand down, Metellus!" Decimus yelled, wading in and slamming his vinerod into Lucius' back. For good measure, he laid another across Bona's shoulder to make sure he did not retaliate.

"You four!" Decimus pointed to four men from second century. "Restrain Metellus and Argus! The gods piss on me!" He looked at Bona. "Who the fuck is this?"

"We were just questioning the woman, sir," protested Bona's friend. "Metellus just came in and attacked us."

"Shut up, soldier!" Decimus said. "Don't fucking lie to me."

The man shut up.

"I know what you were doing. All of you, get out in the fucking street and back in the fight! You'll wish you'd died today rather than go through what I've got in mind for breaking orders. Now get out of here!"

Lucius looked at Decimus, trying to make the man understand, but it was useless. The centurion had seen such things a thousand times over in his career, and he would see more. It was the price of war. Women and babies were mere inconveniences.

Lucius moved ahead without another word, though he was aware of Decimus' angry stare the entire time, and of the hatred that followed him from Bona's bloodied face.

"Nice work!" Argus said to Lucius as they came into the main market where several centuries of Romans were already at attention, or holding enemy soldiers at sword point. "We're fucked. You know that, right?"

"I know." Lucius could not shake the image of the young woman and her child, or the thought of what Bona would have done had he not stopped him. He also knew that several hard lashes would be awaiting him when they got back to camp. His hopes of promotion had been shattered in one heated decision and action, and he would regret it always.

"III Parthica to attention!" Decimus ordered as Tribune Livius rode up with Legate Tertullius and several other legionary commanders.

"Problem, Centurion?" the legate asked Decimus.

"Some disciplinary problems on the way in, sir. I'll take care of it later," Decimus said, his ragged brow turning toward Lucius and Argus.

"Very well," Tertullius said, looking a little disappointed. "I thought this went smoothly." He turned away as King Abgar came down to meet the commanders.

The king had long curled black hair and a beard curled in similar fashion. He wore a long tunic of Tyrian purple bordered with gold brocade and was followed by several of his acolytes.

"Emperor Septimius Severus commands the surrender of Edessa, King Abgar," one of the legates said as the king came down the steps.

Just then as Legate Tertullius dismounted and walked to join the other legates before the king, a man came screaming out from an alcove beneath the palace steps with a long curved dagger in his hand. He ran directly toward Tertullius and the other legate, and just as he was about to strike, a legionary slammed into him and together they rolled in the dirt until the man's body shuddered and blood poured out on the last of the white marble steps at the legates' feet.

"Metellus!" Decimus roared, striding forward as Lucius rolled over, blood sprayed across his armour from the assassin he had just killed. Decimus swung hard with his vinerod and Lucius toppled over. He raised his hand again but was halted.

"Centurion, enough!" Tertullius bellowed, his eyes finding those of King Abgar. "Can I assume that you are surrendering the city?"

The king stared at the assassin lying dead in the dust and nodded.

"Yes," King Abgar said. "Tell the Emperor that Edessa is his. Willingly, I give it to him."

"Good," Tertullius said, "taking the golden sceptre from the king and tucking it smartly under his arm. "The emperor will be most glad to hear it."

"I'm disappointed in you, Metellus," Legate Tertullius said, with Tribune Livius, and Centurion Decimus standing to the side. The legate paced behind his table in the Principia of III Parthica's camp. He had just come from the emperor with news of the city's surrender and the last thing he had wanted to deal with was disciplinary action.

"Metellus disobeyed a direct order, sir," Decimus said. "We could have been hacked to bits in the city streets when he left my back exposed."

Lucius knew he had let his centurion down, something the veteran would not easily forget. He stood there in his red tunic, bracae and boots, weaponless, feeling quite naked for it.

"The fault is mine, Legate Commander," Lucius said. "I saw some of our men in direct breech of orders not to harm the populous and..." he cleared his throat, "the men, sir, they threw a young woman's baby to the ground and were attempting to rape her. I thought that-"

"You thought you would disobey orders and leave your centurion's flank exposed in the middle of a fight!" It was Livius this time, a mixture of anger and embarrassment etched on his face. "We need Decimus a lot more than we need you, Metellus."

"And yet..." the legate interrupted, "Metellus here saved my life." Tertullius came around the table and stood before Lucius. He was a tall man, his keen eyes like a hawk's as they studied Lucius. "But we cannot let your disobedience go, Metellus." He turned to Decimus. "Centurion, what is the minimum punishment for disobeying an order?"

"Fifty lashes, sir."

"Fifty? With that many, he'll not be able to fight and we need him in the field. From the reports, he's one of your best."

Lucius glanced at Decimus and knew instantly that the centurion was regretting the praise he had given him in the reports to Livius and Tertullius.

"But Disciplina must be honoured, Legate, at all cost," Decimus stood tall, broad and stubborn, his vinerod across his left forearm beneath the decorations covering his muscular chest.

"Yes," Tertullius agreed. "Of course. I believe the legionary named Bona is being disciplined by his centurion, so you shall do the same to Metellus."

Decimus did not smile. Lucius could see that he had not wanted this at all, that in asking Lucius to follow him into battle, he trusted him implicitly.

Lucius had lost that trust, and it would take a long time to earn it back.

"Three lashes, before all of first cohort," the legate said.

Lucius felt the sweat falling down the back of his neck and beneath his tunic. He knew it would be painful, but he also knew he had asked for it, and that three lashes was far and away better than fifty.

"I want the cohort here in the Principia courtyard in one hour. Livius," he said to the tribune. "Have a post erected in the centre."

"Yes, Legate Commander," Livius said, his eyes meeting Lucius'.

An hour later, with the late afternoon sun angling its way into the sandy courtyard of the Principia, all the men of the first cohort of III Parthica had gathered as ordered to witness the punishment of one of the few Roman troops amongst them.

Stories had gone around about Lucius, and now many looked on eagerly to see what would happen to the man named after dragons. Some sniggered, others looked concerned,

191

mulling over the intended thought that if it could happen to Lucius Metellus Anguis, it could happen to anybody.

Lucius was walked out to the middle of the courtyard by Gallus. He was bare-chested, wearing only caligae and breeches. By the entrance to the Principia tent stood Livius, Tertullius, and the man whom Lucius recognized as General Laetus, no doubt returned from his hunt of the enemy to report to the emperor.

In the front row of legionaries stood Argus, Alerio, Eligius, Garai, Maren, and Antanelis. The friends all stared at Lucius, unable to do anything but watch as he was made to face the thick post that stuck out of the ground. Argus looked at Lucius as if to say he would rush out and help him if needed, but Lucius shook his head very slightly.

"We stand here this evening," Centurion Decimus began to say in his parade ground voice, "to honour Disciplina, for she is our salvation and shield. She is why we continue to live, why we are victorious against our enemies. Today, in the city, Lucius Metellus Anguis disobeyed a direct order. He thought he was doing the 'right' thing, but he was mistaken. Never disobey. NEVER! Or you too shall feel the iron fist of Mars across your head and back..

Decimus nodded to Gallus who stood on the opposite side of the post from Lucius, took both of his hands, and leaned back so that Lucius' back was exposed tightly to Decimus behind. Gallus held Lucius' gaze, his eyes hard.

Don't cry out, Lucius thought as his heart began to race. *Apollo give me strength, Don't let me cry out!*

Without warning the first lash of the whip came, ferocious and biting, so quick and shocking that Lucius could not have uttered a word had he wanted to. He felt his body begin to shake, but he held Gallus' gaze, his jaw tight, his breath ragged through his nose.

The second lash came harder than the first, and Lucius came close to yelling, but stopped himself. He could feel the huge welts rising already on the muscles of his back, the skin splitting on the second lash. Decimus was not holding back.

When the third one came, the lash whistled through the air and Lucius closed his eyes tight, his head against the post, his eyes watering they were shut so tightly.

"Three!" Decimus yelled. "Punishment administered, Legate Commander," Decimus saluted to the legate, and then proceeded to roll up the lash.

"Metellus," Gallus whispered. "It's done, lad. Bravely done." The optio loosened his grip and Lucius fell to one knee, but not onto the ground. He gripped the post and pulled himself up, his breath ragged and shaking. He forced himself to stand, his head up, even as the blood trickled down his back. When he turned, he saw all the men staring at him, some nodding in approval, some terrified, some others who did not like him, happy and smirking.

Lucius turned to his legate, tribune, and centurion who also stared at him, along with General Laetus, the latter standing still with his arms crossed. When Lucius saluted them, the shocked looks on their faces were enough for him. He had handled it well, but it was not something that he wanted to undergo again.

"Lucius Metellus Anguis has been given the punishment due to him," the legate said out loud, stepping out onto the sand before Lucius to address the cohort. "This same day however, he also saved my life from an assassin's blade. This act too carries recognition, though it is far more honourable. I present to Lucius Metellus Anguis, this armilla for his quick thinking and the saving of a Roman citizen's life. Metellus?"

Tertullius held out the iron bracelet to Lucius whose shocked look made him smile. He put it around Lucius' wrist, and the men cheered, all except Decimus and Livius.

"Dismissed!" Tertullius said, and the men began to filter out of the Principia courtyard, leaving Lucius standing there. "Thank you, Metellus," Tertullius said, before turning and walking inside with Tribune Livius.

"You handled yourself well," Decimus said from behind Lucius.

Lucius turned and nodded. "Sir. It won't happen again."

"See that it doesn't, Metellus. I'd rather whip Parthians than my best troops. But that doesn't mean I won't hesitate to do it again. Got it?"

"Yes, sir." Lucius nodded and saluted.

"Good. Now get yourself to the medicus. I want those lashes to heal so you can wear a lorica."

"Yes, sir."

Decimus turned and left the courtyard leaving Lucius standing by himself next to the post, droplets of his blood on the sand at his feet. He looked down at the armilla, but was unable to smile, despite receiving his first decoration.

"You did well, Metellus."

Lucius looked up to see General Laetus standing before him, nodding his approval. It took him a moment to recognize the man he had seen hacking away at the enemy on the ramparts of Nisibis.

"Sir." Lucius stood to attention but winced a little.

"At ease, Metellus, at ease," the general said. "Are you all right?"

"Yes, sir," Lucius answered. His eyes slowly turned to the general.

"I don't want anything. I just happened to be here to admire your courage. I heard what you did in the town. A tough lesson in disciplina, no?"

"Yes, sir. Quite."

"Here, drink this." General Laetus held out the clay cup he was holding.

Lucius accepted the watered wine reluctantly, but was grateful for it. His hand shook as he brought it to his lips. He took a long sip, and then handed it back to the general.

"Lucky for Tertullius that you were there when King Abgar came down those steps. The legate won't forget this."

"I still got the lash, didn't I?" Lucius said.

"Yes. But you deserved that, and it could have been much worse." Laetus walked about the post where Lucius had been whipped and ran his hand up it. "Victory and punishment often go hand-in-hand on the great field of Mars."

"Then perhaps I should strive for mediocrity," Lucius said under his breath.

Laetus laughed. "I don't know if a Metellus is capable of that! I know that I'm not either."

"Not such a bad thing, sir, to be deservedly lauded as the saviour of Nisibis, is it?"

General Laetus said nothing for a few moments, rubbing his chin in thought before speaking again.

"When I became a general, I carried with me all the arrogance of my class, that sense of entitlement and the thought that nothing, no one, could touch me. After months on the front line with Parthia, and then locked behind the walls of Nisibis, fighting for our lives, I realized that yes, I do have certain gifts that set me apart, but in the end, I am no different or more deserving than the mothers and babes, the old men and young boys in the streets I was set to defend."

Lucius looked at the man, thought of the odd words that escaped him then. *Why is he telling me all this?* he thought.

"We all have our role to play on this great bloody stage, Metellus. And you don't get second chances."

"What are you saying, sir?"

"Stay true to yourself, Metellus. No matter the cause, for in the Afterlife, all that you will have left is the person you were in life."

"I think I understand, sir." Lucius wanted to move, he could feel the blood drying and cracking on his back and it stung every time he moved.

"I'll let you go. The medicus will have an ointment for those wounds. They always do. Gods know, I've had my share."

"You, sir? But you're a hero?"

General Laetus gave Lucius a pitying look. *I remember being that naive. So long ago...*

"Some would call me that, yes. But I am just a mortal man. I have no divine lineage, no drop of godlike blood in my veins." General Laetus looked up at the sky then, the sun slashing it red with its late rays. "I have one piece of advice for you, dragon of the Metelli. No matter how many victories you carry, no matter how lauded you are in the tent rows or the Forum itself, no matter how blessed by the Gods you are, remember that the closer to power you stand, the more the risk of getting burned. Your life is yours to honour, but it is dust to others. Remember that."

"Yes, sir. I will."

"Gnaeus?" Legate Tertullius stuck his head out of the tent. "Good. I'm glad you are still here. Come, have some more wine with me before you go back to barracks."

"I'm coming, Gaius," Laetus answered, smiling as he turned to Lucius.

"You're off to a good start, Metellus. The trick is to keep going. It's a dangerous world for *good* men. But, for some of us, that is all we can and will be. And that must suffice, no?"

Lucius said nothing. He nodded to the general and turned to limp back onto the Via Principalis to find the medicus and go back to the tent where his friends were waiting for him.

IX

Casus Ctesiphonis

'The Fall of Ctesiphon'

With the subjugation of Edessa, the cranes, catapults, and siege towers were dismantled, the legions made ready to continue their campaign in the scorching summer sun.

If the toll taken on the legions by their initial confrontations at Nisibis and Edessa had been small, relatively speaking, they now suffered beneath the relentless hammering of Sol's light from above. High summer in the land between the two rivers was unrelenting.

As the legions marched south from Edessa, men fell not to Parthian arrows or the thrust of kontos lances, but rather from heat, dehydration and the exhaustion of a desert march. The legions needed to stick to the rivers as long as possible, and so it was decided that a fleet would be constructed to sail almost half the army down the Euphrates while the majority followed on land either side of the river.

The campaigning season was moving along at a quick pace, and Severus and his advisors wanted to take the Parthian capital of Ctesiphon before the end of the year. That meant that Hatra would have to wait behind its high, round walls.

It did not mean, however, that Hatra would escape the Romans altogether. The city was isolated in the middle of the most brutal part of the Mesopotamian desert, and with three legions keeping a distant perimeter about it, there was little chance of the citizenry escaping.

So, Septimius Severus, convinced that the stars had aligned themselves to his cause, decided that the timing was perfect for taking Seleucia, Babylon, and the capital of Ctesiphon.

If Lucius and the rest of his contubernium hoped they would be assigned to the ships sailing down the Euphrates, they were disappointed in the end. III Parthica was not to enjoy a leisurely cruise up the river, but rather, a march on the east side of the Euphrates, their flank exposed to enemy territory and the biting raids of Parthian horse archers who swept in upon them with speed one moment and were gone the next.

The wounds on Lucius' back had finally begun to heal after a few weeks on the march, not without a great deal of discomfort, and copious amounts of the medicus' ointment.

After his punishment, Lucius had sat silent before the cooking fire of their tent. The others did not disturb him, for they had come to know the look of that silent stare that he bore more often now. The words of General Laetus had not ceased to ring in his mind over, and over again. He fought hard to curb his rage, anger, and embarrassment, though some of the others encouraged him to let it out.

Shockingly, King Abgar had been allowed to retain his seat at Edessa as client king of the Roman Empire. This chaffed at Lucius' mind almost more than Lucius' steel lorica upon his back.

He stared after the ships that sailed the Euphrates, ships that transported the legates, the empress and the emperor. He wondered at the discussions the elite had, the thoughts and words over a cup of wine that decided the fate of so many thousands of men so easily.

"This is what we signed up for, wasn't it?" Alerio said to Lucius one evening as they stood guard duty along the palisade facing the desert. "We can't really complain, can we?"

"No. We can't." Lucius gripped the shaft of his pilum and pounded the iron end into the sand and rock at his feet. "I don't know what the Gods' plan is."

"You're not supposed to. That's the whole point. We live, we fight, hopefully someday we'll find a woman each to love."

"You sound like my sister now."

"From what you've told me of her, Lucius, that's not a bad thing. I just hope that we're the same men after this war."

"I suspect that none of us will be the same, Alerio. But what my old tutor used to say was that 'war and conflict change every man, but only a few are made better by it.'"

"Just like a Greek philosopher to say such a thing. Not much hope in it, is there?"

Lucius laughed. "Not much. But it is there. It's always there."

They stared out at the night, grateful for the fullness of the moon which allowed them to see farther than usual. They were easy targets where they stood on the ramparts, no matter how high their position or the wooden stakes that protected them above the deep ditches.

The next day they arrived at Dura Europos, that mighty fortress built by Alexander's successors, and now occupied by Rome. If there was a haven in that remote part of the Empire, it was the sprawling fortress that stood ninety or more meters above the flow of the Euphrates. The armies could resupply, regroup, and plan for the final onslaught of Seleucia, Babylon, and Ctesiphon.

The fortress came into view as the river narrowed, and dust settled to reveal sandstone walls with intermittent towers where Roman troops lined the walls to watch the legions' approach. Horns rang from the city walls and voices were raised as the imperial ship came to port along with the Praetorian Guard.

Lucius, Argus, and the others had heard of the baths and temples of the city, the markets and brothels. They secretly hoped that they would be allowed to enter the city for even a few hours.

However, it seemed doubtful, especially after Decimus told them not to get too comfortable, that the year was wearing on and they still had the Parthian capital to take. He also indicated that those men who were adherents of Mithras would be permitted to worship when Decimus, their Pater in the order, went into the city to make an offering to the Lord of Light and Truth.

Of all of them in the contubernium, only Antanelis went with Decimus, and when he returned, he was unable to speak of what had happened. All followers of Mithras were sworn to secrecy, but the younger man did say that it was a thrill to worship in the land where Mithras once walked.

On their second day outside the walls of Dura Europos, the men of III Parthica were given leave in turns to bathe in the river below their camp. It was not a proper bath house, but it did feel good to wash the dust and dirt from their pores and everywhere else the sand got stuck.

As Lucius stood waist-deep in the water, looking up at the fortress, he wondered what it must be like for the troops of III Scythica and XVI Flavia who garrisoned Dura Europos. How many peoples from across the Empire and without did those men come into contact with? How many merchants, traders, families and more passed through this outpost? How many walked beneath the great arch of the Palmyrene Gate to Palmyra itself, or to the Middle Sea beyond?

He began to realize just how big the world was, the impact that the Empire had on it and the millions of people who lived within the titanic reach of its borders.

After three days, the command was given to march on Seleucia, and so the fleet set out, flanked by the legions, all of which had been moved to the east side of the river to sweep south across the dusty desert to the lusher lands which the Persians and Parthians had laid claim to for so very long.

As they marched, each soldier could not help but look around him and take pride in the sea of crimson crests, cloaks, and standards of the legions. Golden aquilaea glinted in the intense sunlight as they pressed on, a force that not even Alexander had mustered.

Lucius thought back to his learning about Alexander and took comfort in the thought that perhaps he was marching in the conqueror's footsteps as they headed for Babylon. He wondered what it would look like, how it would feel, to walk through the great Ishtar Gate, to see the Hanging Gardens and more.

Alexander had favoured Babylon. There must have been a reason for it.

The legions expected a fight as they approached Seleucia, but none came. The Parthians that led the legions on only offered short skirmishes to their Roman guests. It was said that the emperor was frustrated and eager for engagement. Most everyone was.

Seleucia stood on the west bank of the River Tigris, just across the swift water from Ctesiphon, where the Parthian fires burned brightly. The city built by Alexander's general, Seleucus, was but an abandoned shell of empty villas, temples, and unguarded gates. The Parthians had abandoned it, and some time before it seemed, their spies and scouts having kept them well-informed of the Roman advance. But for the desert city of Hatra, Rome now controlled most of the lands between the Tigris and Euphrates.

From the west bank of the Tigris and the ghost of Seleucia, the Romans could see that bridges had been burned by the Parthians to slow their advance on the capital. However, that did not stop Severus from heading straight to Babylon while three legions kept the enemy holed up in Ctesiphon with a garrison across the river in Seleucia.

The land was more lush as the legions marched south to Babylon, fed by the life-giving rivers and the irrigation channels that had made crops abundant for ages.

III Parthica was among the legions that marched on Babylon. The air was stiffling, and more humid than in the desert stretches to the North. The men sweat, and drank, and sweat some more as they marched, ready for a fight.

When night fell, the guards were doubled on every legionary camp's defences and gates, with shifts shortened to allow every man some measure of sleep before the inevitable engagement the next day.

Lucius sat at the fire before their tent, finishing some food after one of his shifts on guard duty. He had been unable to sleep that night and decided to re-read a portion of Arrian's work that had haunted him since he first read it. He thought of the victory at Gaugamela that Alexander had won over the Persians, against incredible odds, and the king's subsequent entry into Babylon.

Not far from the city, which he took the precaution of approaching in battle order, he was met by the people of the place who with their priests and magistrates came flocking out to bring him various gifts and to offer to put the city, with the citadel and all its treasures, into his hands. He marched in accordingly, and instructed the people to restore the temples which had been destroyed by Xerxes, in particular the temple of Bel, the god held by the Babylonians in greatest awe.

What must it have felt like to enter that famed and ancient city at the head of an army, horns blaring, the people chanting his name, his troops' loyalty unquestioned?

The thought sent a chill down Lucius' spine, and he wondered if on the morrow they would experience such a thing. He doubted it, but if they survived he did hope to be a part of something magnificent and memorable, a victory that no Roman had enjoyed to that point in time.

"You should be sleeping, Metellus," Decimus' voice came out of the darkness as he emerged into the circle of the fire's light. "I need you fresh in the line tomorrow."

The centurion's face was hard, emotionless, but not hateful as Lucius had seen it in the streets of Edessa.

"I'll be fresh, sir," Lucius said formally, standing up with the scroll hanging by his side.

"Some men whore before a battle, or drink themselves into oblivion so that they don't have to think on the following day. You read."

"Yes, sir. It inspires me."

"Tales of Alexander again?"

"Yes, sir."

"Humph. Man left the golden age a long time ago, Metellus. The days of gods walking among and leading men are long gone."

Lucius turned quickly to face Decimus. "But, sir... the emperor is a god."

Decimus looked doubtfully on the young man. "Some say. But what would the Gods say? I pray to Mars, and to Mithras. We honour the cult of the emperor and carry the imagines before us in battle, yes. But a god?" Decimus crossed his arms over his thick chest. He looked tired. "Don't be shocked. You're an educated man, Metellus. You know as well as I that the emperor, though a man of military greatness and strategy, is just a man. He coughs, and spits, and limps like any other. But he is no Alexander."

"Why do you fight then, sir?"

Decimus actually looked confused by the question. "Why?" He sat down and motioned Lucius to do the same. "In

Alexander's day, men fought for the man. They followed the god. Today, it's not like that. Not often anyway. I fight for Rome, Metellus. I'm a Roman, just like you. I want to make this empire the greatest ever, greater than Alexander's. If I can be a small part of that, so much the better. But, Gods help me, I do love the fighting too. It's simpler with a gladius in your hand, fighting for your life. I hate politics, and frankly, I don't know how men like Laetus toe the line in both worlds. He's a warrior born and bred, despite his Patrician upbringing, but he's also a savvy politician."

"And you have no wish for politics, sir?"

"Pah! Gods no! Mark me, fighting men are safer on the battlefield than in the Forum or the Curia. Out here, you can trust the man at your back," he paused, hit by the irony of what he was saying.

It made Lucius feel ashamed for a moment, and though he did not regret helping that poor girl and her baby, he did regret betraying the man before him.

"As I was saying, you can trust your brothers-in-arms, but on the Senate floor, you could be shaking hands with your enemy and get stabbed in the back by your best friend." Decimus touched the pommel of his gladius and looked at Lucius.

"It won't happen again, sir," Lucius said frankly, holding the centurion's gaze.

Rather than harsh words, Decimus nodded, and extended his hand to the young man before him.

Lucius took the thick forearm and gripped it. No words were needed. He valued the respect of this man more than his own father's, and now he had reclaimed it.

"Get some sleep, Metellus. You may not be tired tonight, but tomorrow, when we're fighting our way through the hot streets of Babylon, you'll wish you had done."

No fighting was needed.

As the legions approached the sprawling walls of Babylon from the North, the scouts returned to inform the emperor that the Parthians had deserted the city.

"The cowards!" Severus roared as he gazed toward the ancient polis. "They've abandoned Babylon and given it up without a fight!"

"Sire," said General Laetus, who had rejoined the marching army with his legion. "They're mustering their entire force at Ctesiphon. That will be where we'll be tested."

Severus looked annoyed, but they all knew that was the truth of it. The Parthian heavy cavalry had stayed out of the skirmishing until now. The Romans knew they would be hard-put to take the Parthian capital.

"The sun is low in the West now," the emperor said out loud. "Let us march into Babylon as Alexander once did, and camp without its mighty walls."

The cornui sounded and the legions began to march forward with the Euphrates on their right. Seven legions were sent around the eastern edge of the city to make camp and scout the terrain, while the rest moved with caution into the city, including III Parthica.

As they approached Babylon along the road that ran through the fields surrounding the city, Lucius gazed ahead at the walls that stretched away on either side. They were massive, and it appeared that the walls were as big as Diodorus had told him, wide enough for two chariots to pass side by side. Directly ahead, he could see the great ziggurat of Babylon rising into the sky, its stepped sides as a staircase for titans or gods. Nearby were the famed Hanging Gardens, built by King Nebuchadnezzar for his Median queen. They were suspended above the city still, full, leafy and labyrinthine.

The tramp of thousands of hobnails, and the wail of horns and horses set flocks of resident birds to flight as they approached the Ishtar gate of the city.

"Look at that..." Alerio mumbled beside Lucius as they came onto the bridge over the canal, flanked by giant stone lions which were, in turn, dwarfed by the massive gate of blue enamel. "Never thought I'd see this."

"Me neither," Lucius answered. He closed his eyes for a moment and imagined Alexander's army marching through as the crowd cheered, palm fronds waved, and flower petals were thrown at their feet.

However, the Romans had not fought to take this city. It was abandoned, and upon closer inspection, the blue tiles were dirty and cracked, the golden images of gods and beasts faded.

In the streets of the city, those who had been too scared or reluctant to follow their Parthian masters to Ctesiphon huddled in doorways, clutching their children fearfully, their pets, their sole possessions, as the Romans passed them by. Few fires burned in the many temples that dotted the city, the altars of Ishtar, Adad, Marduk, and Belit-Nina, of Samas, Ninurta, Ninmah, Nabu-Sha-Hare, and Ishara all bereft of fresh offerings. All that remained were the mouldering remains of past gifts to the Gods, left unattended as if the hopes of Babylon's people had long since gone.

Lucius felt sadder the further they marched through the city's countless squares and streets. The people were as sad and worn as the great monuments upon closer inspection. The great ziggurat was crumbling, scrub sprouting from between its massive blocks, and the Hanging Gardens were no longer rich and colourful, but thick and overgrown, choked by parasitic vines and long neglect.

"Not much, is it?" Argus said as they stood to attention in the middle of the great avenue running alongside Etemenanki.

Lucius did not answer, but he knew Argus had a point as his eyes reached across the faded glory of Babylon.

That evening, once the city was secure, every inch of it checked by the men of the legions, the empress arrived. Shortly thereafter, centuries were assigned to clean all of the major temples of the city.

There were some grumblings among the troops that they did not want to honour the temples of such foreign-sounding gods, but the empress and emperor were adamant that they be honoured. The Parthians had neglected them, and so Rome would honour them in thanks for the victory they hoped for over their long-time enemies.

In the morning, as the legions marched out of the Marduk gate and north, back to Seleucia and Ctesiphon, the smoke of fragrant offerings flowed once more among the cedar rafters and out of the doors of every temple in Babylon.

A single legion was left to garrison the city with strict orders not to harm those who had remained to rely on Rome's mercy.

As they marched in the quickly intensifying heat of mid-morning, Lucius hoped that men like Bona had not been left behind as part of the garrison.

When the army arrived at Seleucia to rejoin the three legions that waited on the west bank of the Tigris, the sight that met them on the other side of the water, before the walls of Ctesiphon, took each man's breath away.

It seemed that the Parthian force had tripled in size since they had last been there, for the earth shook with the thunder of thousands of Parthian cataphracts. The dust they created sent up a cloud so vast that Vesuvius itself could have been hidden within it.

The legions were ordered to make camp so that they sprawled along the west side of the Tigris as far as they eye could see. Along the shoreline, the Roman fleet had docked and unloaded the siege equipment and artillery, all of which were now pointing toward the masses of Parthian troops and their allies.

Lucius and the others had never seen anything like it, such a mustering of military might on both sides. No one had seen such a thing.

As III Parthica made camp, they could see Severus and his generals riding along the edge of the Tigris to observe the Parthian dispositions and to try to gain a glimpse of the walls of Ctesiphon beyond. The latter, however, proved impossible due to all the dust that rose into the sky.

It was unknown when they would strike, but some time later, after the camp was fully prepared, word went round that the emperor had consulted with his astrologer who told him that it was not a propitious time to begin the battle, when the sun had already graced the sky for a large part of the day. Sunrise was when the Gods wanted Severus to attack.

Some of the generals had tried to discourage this, as the sun would be full in their men's faces at sunrise. The emperor's decision stood however, and a war council, to which Decimus had been commanded, was called that evening.

"I wish I could hear what they're saying in that council," Antanelis said as the seven of them ate around the fire before their tent. "I'd like to know what I'm walking into."

"In a word, 'Hades'," Maren said darkly from across the fire. "You saw what's on the other side. We don't have near enough cavalry to face them down."

"As long as our ranks hold," Lucius said, "we can take them. It'll be hard, but we've got the numbers."

"I don't know, Lucius," Alerio said, shaking his head. "The other battles were probably nothing compared to what we're going to face tomorrow."

Lucius looked around the fire at each of his friends and finally saw the fear eating away at them, even as the tramp of thousands of horses' hooves shook the surface of the Tigris half a mile away. Even Argus stared into the fire without saying a word, not meeting anyone's gaze. Lucius could only guess at what he was thinking.

"I'm going to bed," Lucius stood.

"How can you sleep?" Garai said, rubbing his hair roughly. "I won't manage a few minutes. Those horses are so loud on the other side."

"That's what the enemy likely wants," Lucius answered. "So don't give it to them. Sleep as best you can. We're spared from guard duty tonight, so take advantage of that." Lucius looked at each of them a moment, smiled thinly and went inside the musty leather tent.

He unhooked his gladius and pugio and put them on the ground beside his tent roll. His lorica was laying on the ground beside, oiled and ready for the morrow. Beside where he lay his head stood the little statue of Olympian Apollo. Lucius knelt before the image of the god who protected him and his family, and closed his eyes, trying to block out the bickering of his friends outside the tent flaps.

"Far Shooting Apollo... Tomorrow will be our ultimate test in battle, courage, strength, and stamina. And yet I feel that so much more relies on this battle, and the role I play in it. Help me to sustain my courage in the fray. Let me not shrink from a fight, nor fall victim to fear. I... I am afraid, but let me control it, beat it in my heart and mind. Guide me in battle tomorrow, Apollo. Help me to honour my family and you. You have been with me for so long, guided me, aided me in my darkest times. Please do not desert me when the ballista bolts fly and the cavalry charges. I honour you, Apollo, and I thank you for your guidance and protection in the dark."

Lucius sat up and lay back on his mat, closing his eyes and trying to empty his racing mind of all thought and sound.

The sun broke the eastern horizon with an orange brilliance that belied the dread of the day before them. Few men had slept, and the Parthians had clambered all through the night in an attempt to keep the Romans from sleep the night before.

The cohorts of III Parthica had all gathered for inspection by Legate Tertullius, the tribunes, including Livius and Decimus, and the remainder of III Parthica's centurionate. After inspection, the men had been marched out onto the field along the Tigris, two and three legions deep with cavalry on the flanks and interspersed throughout.

Boulders and ballista bolts were set at intervals beside the siege equipment, their crews at the ready; scorpions, onagers, ballistae were all ready to rain down on the enemy in order to give the Roman troops a chance to claim a beachhead on the other side of the river.

The Tigris' current was swift, and Lucius wondered how they were planning to cross until he saw where six wide pontoon bridges had been constructed by the engineers, their final barges waiting to be put in place before the attack. He realized the barges must have been ferried up river during the night.

The night before, the entire camp had been abuzz with the sound of preparations for battle - the hammering of smiths, carpenters chopping, the bark of centurions ensuring the legions knew their orders.

The centaur vexillum of III Parthica swayed loftily in the heat at the front of the legion, beside the imagines of the emperor and of course the golden aquila. Tribune Livius sat atop his horse, having just arrived to converse with Decimus and the other centurions.

Lucius could only just hear what was said from his position at the front, but it seemed that III Parthica would be one of the last legions across the water. The veteran legions were going to follow the auxiliaries over the bridges to establish a foothold on the side.

The rest of their conversation was drowned out as the siege equipment began firing across the river.

"Here we go!" Lucius said to Argus who clenched his scutum and two pila intently.

No one else spoke. They only watched as the auxiliary cohorts marched across behind the engineers who were hastily fastening the final barges to the end of the bridge while the artillery gave them some breathing room.

Dust clouds rose up as boulders and ballista bolts slammed into the foremost Parthian ranks, scattering them to left and right.

However, the rain of arrows began and several Romans fell to Parthian shafts, their screams silenced as they fell into the Tigris' watery embrace.

Lucius turned to look at the centre of the Roman lines and saw the mass of Praetorian banners where the emperor sat atop a white horse with his generals, watching the drama unfold. Runners were going back and forth to the legionary tribunes with orders from their legates and then the second phase of the attack began.

One, two, three, and then the rest of the pontoon bridges were across, allowing the auxiliaries to move forward and take the brunt of the initial Parthian onslaught. The range of the siege engines was adjusted and the Roman forces began to

spread in a red swathe on the grass and sand on the othe
of the Tigris, choked by brown dust.

A few men behind Lucius vomited, their anticipation
getting the better of them as the screams of auxiliaries reached
their ears. Glints of Parthian armour flashed in and out of their
line of sight, and cornui bellowed the commands for more
legions to press forward with groups of allied archers at their
backs as they went. All the while, artillery flew over their
heads keeping the full Parthian force at bay, but falling just
short of them.

Two centuries at a time were crossing over each bridge,
those who went first under the greatest threat. They needed to
hold their ground on the other side and give time to their
fellows behind them to muster at their backs.

The omens had been good in every camp that morning,
and it seemed to the men that the Gods might indeed keep their
promises.

"First century! III Parthica!" Decimus' voice suddenly rang
out, echoed by the cornu. "Forward!"

Lucius' feet began to move forward of their own volition,
the hot sand sifting between his toes in his caligae. Then they
stepped onto the nearest pontoon bridge and it swayed beneath
their feet.

Blood spattered several of the boards of the bridge and
Decimus had to kick several corpses out of the way as they
went.

"Shields up!" the centurion yelled and they all lifted their
scuta just as Parthian shafts came down on them. "Forward!"
he yelled again when the hail stopped and the Roman artillery
fired again.

Lucius' knees felt week beneath him but they held him up. His eyes stung as the sweat and dirt poured down his face. They charged the final few feet across the undulating structure, Decimus' yelling ringing in their ears.

The Romans were formed up in a massive chequered formation and III Parthica joined them mid-way through the ranks.

Lucius had never imagined chaos like that which they now witnessed, and he fully realized the importance of the man next to him, the importance of the shield wall.

"Pila iacite!" Decimus yelled, and the men responded in the direction of the thunder of hooves. Horses screamed and riders cursed above a sound of muffled mail and breaking bones.

Throw pilum, scutum up.

Throw pilum, scutum up.

They pressed forward now, stepping over the bodies of slain Parthian men and horse, and writhing Romans who tried dragging themselves back to the rear.

Soon the river was far behind them and, looking up, Lucius realized they were in the middle of a swirling dust cloud of Parthian cataphracts and horse archers in a maelstrom of war.

The Parthian kontos did its work on that day, and the archers harried the Roman flanks, firing their backward 'Parthian shots' as they fled for another run.

"Form testudo!" Decimus yelled and the order was relayed up the ranks so that they could press forward into the Parthian ranks while arrows rained down on them. Their cover fire had stopped, the Romans now within the engines' range. Now the men manning the artillery began to move the engines across the bridges, behind the emperor and the Praetorians who began to cut their way into the fray.

Within the testudo however, Lucius and the others sweat and puked, the danger from heat and dizziness too much to bear now as the arrows continued to come without relent. One arrow pierced Lucius' scutum and sliced the side of his hand. The pain that this caused woke him from the daze of the heat beneath the testudo. He looked around and saw Alerio and Argus still there. He could hear Decimus yelling between sword thrusts at passing Parthians, urging them to break testudo and press forward.

They were in deep now, and never had Lucius heard such urgency in his centurion's voice.

Lucius lowered his scutum and raised his head slowly from behind the upper edge of it to take stock of the scene about them.

The ground was strewn with bodies of both man and beast. Battles raged on both the Roman flanks, signs of weakening showing on the left.

"Decimus, we need to reinforce the left flank!" Livius was yelling at Decimus. "Go now with half the legion!"

"Yes, sir!" Decimus turned to look at first century, his eyes meeting Lucius'. "Let's go!" he said and began to cut to the north where the sound of clashing steel and screams came from.

Lucius' legs were moving and he felt a surge of strength in his limbs. He had gained control of his senses, and was back in the world about him, strangely alive. He marched in the front rank of the first cohort, his eyes on Decimus' red cloak and crested helmet, his gladius' point protruding from the edge of his scutum.

Several hundred Parthian cataphracts had hacked their way into the centre of the legions from the left flank and were inflicting heavy casualties, stabbing downwards onto the heads of Roman troops.

It seemed to Lucius and his friends that the earth was exploding with blood as weapons punctured and cut through men.

"On me!" Decimus yelled, and they followed, for he was the only one near enough whose orders could be heard. The sounds of the emperor's cornicens could no longer be deciphered amidst the crash of battle and blinding dust in which they fought.

Arrows tore into them and Lucius felt his skin rip in more than one spot, but he was able to keep going, his scutum close to his face and body, his person packed tight with his brothers.

Then a group of cataphracts managed to slice their way through the Roman ranks and were suddenly bearing down on the centuries of III Parthica.

Apollo, protect me, Lucius thought as the fully armoured Parthians bore down on them, blood and Roman offal dangling from their long black beards and their horses' armoured trappings. He saw a long kontos coming directly for him, and bulbous iron clubs swinging down to crush the heads of other Romans as they came his way.

Life went still, and the blood pounded in Lucius' ears with a deafening rush. He felt the adrenaline flowing within his limbs, making them lighter, quicker. His body moved faster than his mind, instinct and training taking over. If anything could save them, it would be the Gods, and Disciplina.

Lucius thrust his gladius as riders went by, their spear thrusts deflected off of their shield wall, the horses shying from the protruding teeth of their gladii. They passed as if a momentary earthquake had risen in the bowels of the earth beneath them, causing some of the men to look down as if waiting for the earth to open up.

Then it happened. In front of first cohort, Decimus lunged to retrieve the fallen vexillum, its shaft still gripped by the severed hand of the screaming vexillarius. The centurion turned to toss the shaft to Gallus farther down the line and in doing so, exposed his right side to three stray Parthian horsemen.

One horse rode into Decimus' shoulder and turned him wildly, his gladius biting out like a viper to the beast's flank. He spun, a vicious gash across his face and before he could catch his balance in the chaos, another rider bored his kontos through the centurion's right side so that he stood there confused and angry, gripping at the shaft and cursing the enemy.

"To the centurion!" Lucius yelled and they pushed forward faster, even as a third horseman planted another shaft into Decimus' shoulder in a splash of gore from the neck.

"Arrrrggg!" Decimus roared, holding both shafts, so that the riders struggled with him.

"No!" Lucius broke rank first to get to Decimus and ran for the first rider who broke away from the centurion and came at him with his iron club, his face snarling.

"Lucius!" Alerio yelled, trying to get to him as he tripped over the piled bodies.

As the rider closed on Lucius, the latter raised the pommel of his gladius and smashed it into the chest of the rider, bringing the man down with a crash.

The man regained his feet quickly and came with a broken spear shaft at Lucius, one which he had just pulled out of a Roman. His face was covered with chain mail which hung from the brim of his conical helmet and Lucius felt as though he was fighting a ghost.

The Parthian swung and stabbed at him with the spear, as Lucius parried and blocked with his gladius and scutum. The spear shaft kept Lucius at a greater distance but he managed to spin toward his opponent narrowly missing the Parthian's spearhead.

Lucius crashed into him knocking him over again, drew his sword back and stabbed at the eyes, lodging the blade firmly in his opponent's head. Lucius fell to his knees trying to pull his blade free and chanced to look up to where Decimus lay writhing, Argus kneeling over him.

Argus? Lucius thought but before he could call out to his friend, he was knocked back by a heavy blow to his shoulder as another Parthian clubbed him as he rode by. "Ahh!"

"Lucius!" Antanelis' form charged over Lucius as he gazed up into the brown and blue sky, a sound of metal on metal echoing around him.

"Form up!" Gallus yelled, his voice gravelly and vengeful. "Now!"

Lucius felt himself pulled up and saw Alerio.

"You all right?"

Lucius nodded. "Yes, I think so."

They were brought to by the sound of horns in the distance, and as they tried to form up again, they could see the Parthians making another charge at the weakened left flank. To their relief, one of the Thracian cavalry cohorts had come round the back of the line to meet the Parthians and both forces collided all about the Roman infantry.

Then it seemed the path had opened up ahead of them, for the wavering walls of Ctesiphon shimmered in the heat, within sight.

"Forward troops! Form up and move on, to Ctesiphon!"

Lucius looked up and saw Septimius Severus atop his white horse, in gleaming armour with a gold and purple cloak flying in the dusty wind. The emperor, surrounded by his Praetorians, surveyed the ground around them, encouraging them as he prepared to move forward with his personal guard and generals.

Lucius looked about at the few men he recognized, Alerio, Antanelis, Argus, Garai, Eligius, Maren and a few more. They locked shields and pressed on, urged by Gallus.

Lucius yelled out. "Form up and press on!"

The others looked at him oddly but then followed, their minds needing a voice to give order to the chaos about them.

Then they wheeled round as Parthian war cries shrieked behind them. Antanelis stepped out first, his gladius and scutum up to meet the horseman facing him.

"Repel horse!" Gallus yelled from somewhere down the line.

They were trying to get at the emperor from behind, having slipped through.

One threw his club so that it took Antanelis in the side of the head and spun him, and Lucius dove forward quickly to grab hold of a fallen spear to launch it at the horseman who was following up his throw with a long, straight blade aimed at Antanelis' neck.

The horse screamed as the spear planted itself in its breastbone and it toppled forward toward Antanelis, throwing the rider into the air to slam into Antanelis' face and take him to the ground.

Lucius retrieved his gladius and set upon the horsemen with the others, trying to keep Antanelis from being trampled. Amid the screams and sounds of clanging metal, they managed to unhorse a few more riders, knocking them to the ground beneath their horses' hooves, to be crushed or despatched by gladii.

An inner demon grabbed hold of Lucius and he jumped onto one of the stray horses and set into another group of Parthians who were harassing Gallus and another small group of men.

Lucius could hear Argus and the others yelling after him, but he rode on, kicking at the flanks of the massive beast as it galloped over the bodies of the fallen, fearless, charging into more of the oncoming enemy around Gallus and the vexillum with the centaur upon it.

The enemy horse reared and their riders stabbed down at the Romans, their points putting out the life of one, then another.

Lucius lunged from the top of his animal into the two Parthians hacking away at Gallus and the others, knocking them to the ground to fall with a crushing impact. Behind him came Argus, Alerio and Maren whose gladii struck out to claim the lives of the two Parthians and allowed Lucius time to find his feet.

Lucius lungs heaved and burned, the taste of blood all over his mouth.

"Metellus!" Tribune Livius suddenly appeared before them on his horse. "Where's Decimus?"

"Dead...sir..."

Livius stared about and saw the broken but still fighting legions moving on to Ctesiphon. "Damn!" The tribune looked at the group of them and to Gallus who was collecting some of the remnants of III Parthica together. There were only about thirty men left from the first century of III Parthica on the left flank.

"All right, Metellus. You're optio for the moment, and Gallus is centurion. Start making your way toward the walls but keep a lookout for Parthians at our backs. Stay in formation with the other three centuries over there with Gallus, and intercept any enemies. Understood?"

"Yes, sir!" Lucius saluted. *Have I just been given temporary command?* he thought as Livius rode off to see what was left of III Parthica and the other tribunes.

Lucius formed up the men that were left in first century, and went over to where Gallus was standing over Decimus' hacked body.

"The tribune said we need to move toward the city, Optio."

"Hmm," Gallus said absently, staring down at the hacked and bloody form of his centurion, his friend. "I'm not leaving him here like this."

"But...sir, the tribune."

"He was a primus pilus, Metellus. I'm not leaving him here to be eaten by dogs and carrion birds."

Lucius felt for the man. It was a grisly sight. Decimus' chest had been torn open by the Parthian lances, but his neck had also been slashed. He remembered something then, and stood up, the bile in his throat, to see Argus at the front of the formed-up men, staring at him.

"Sir, the tribune made me temporary optio. You're centurion now, but if you order it so, I can lead two centuries to the walls while you stay here with Centurion Decimus."

Gallus looked up, quick and angry, his eyes studying Lucius for a few moments. "You got your command, then, didn't you?"

"No, sir. Just temporary. I didn't want it like this." Lucius meant it too. He remembered the night at Babylon when Decimus had sat down with him. He was a good man, as good as a primus pilus could allow himself to be. "I would like to honour him later with you, sir," Lucius said.

Cornui started to give the command for pursuit and the clash of battle and charge of cavalry rang out from before the walls of the city.

Gallus looked up and shook his head. "Very well. Go! Take the men and do what is ordered. I'll stay here and protect the dead."

"Yes, sir!" Lucius saluted and ran over to the others. "Two centuries, on me! We make for Ctesiphon!"

"You in command now?" Argus said as Lucius passed.

Lucius did not answer. He could not at that time, the ugly slash across Decimus' throat flashing in his mind.

"Form up!" he yelled, and led the way to Ctesiphon.

There was no more fighting that day. They all stood there, numb, at attention before the walls of the Parthian capital. The sights and smells of battle, the sensations, the death that surrounded them, now had its chance to sink in, and many were forced to face their feelings of anger and regret, fear and elation. Many of their brothers lay dead on the sands between the city and the banks of the Tigris.

Lucius looked down and noticed the caked and clotted blood that covered his armour, arms, hands and legs. He felt like retching, but managed to save the urge and swallow his disgust.

Others behind him, however, could not do the same and he heard several men purging themselves of the appalling, bone-chilling feelings that accompanied a real taste of battle beneath the Gods' scrutinous gaze. Mars himself would have revelled at the sight of the offal-strewn earth and the mingling of heat, flies, and bleeding flesh that surrounded them.

In fact, Lucius at one point walked forward, believing he saw a tall, armoured figure, dark and foreboding, walking the battlefield and smiling, a massive spear in his hand. The young Roman looked around to see if anyone else saw what he was seeing, but none seemed to.

He shook his head. He was tired. He had survived again, bloodied and scarred, and was happy to be alive. In a way, he was grateful to the Gods for putting him through the ordeal.

His reverie was broken by Argus.

"If we stand out here, the veterans are going to get all the spoils from the city and we'll be left with nothing!"

Lucius turned, his face angry. "Don't break ranks!"

Argus stood there for a moment, staring. "Don't order me, Lucius."

"You're setting a bad example. I've been given command for now. Back in line!" Lucius yelled, surprised that Argus actually obeyed the command. He turned away from the line of his staring men, his friends, and spotted riders coming their way. In the background, a rush of fire and splintering of wood could be heard from several of the city's gates.

"Who's in command?" the rider demanded.

"I am!" Lucius said.

"New orders. The city has fallen. All units are to move into the city and finish the job."

"Finish the job?" Lucius repeated.

"Are you deaf, soldier?" the rider said. "Sack the city and kill all the inhabitants."

"On whose orders?" Lucius asked.

"The emperor, you idiot! Now get your men in there!"

When the rider sped off to find the next group of legionaries, Lucius turned to the two centuries behind him. He did not want to give that command, but he could see the eagerness in their eyes, a look he had not seen in them until that moment.

He caught Alerio's eye where he stood holding up Antanelis, whose face was a mess of caked blood about the whites of his bright eyes.

"You heard him!" Lucius said aloud. "To the city!"

The men broke rank, forgetting all discipline and ran for the shattered gates of Ctesiphon, passing beneath fanning flames that were spreading amidst the screams of the population inside.

Argus stood a moment watching Lucius, and, without saying anything, began to jog toward the city, smiling as he went.

"You should go with them, Lucius," Alerio said. "Antanelis and I will stay here and check for survivors along with Gallus over there." He pointed to where the centurion stood with one century, scanning the bodies that littered the clotted sand of the plain.

"I'll be back. I want to make sure they don't get out of hand."

"Just be careful," Alerio said. "They're not themselves right now."

Lucius nodded, hoisted his scutum, and began to run toward the city.

That night, Lucius' view of the Empire, the legions, and of the genus humanum was struck hard and fast by the realities of war. They had won the day, and the emperor had a great victory, but it was not over.

When Septimius Severus' legions took Ctesiphon, and while the emperor and his staff dined in the Praetorium of the main camp, the legions were allowed to plunder the city and slay the people within. Those that were not slain, about a hundred thousand, were sold into slavery.

Lucius soon realized that the discipline that had set them apart, that had saved their lives, was all but forgotten as utter chaos took hold of the Roman conquerors. He walked the streets of the city, dazed, confused, and disgusted at the sights that met his eyes around every corner.

Homes and holy shrines of the great Parthian Empire were burned to ashes. Riches were looted and civilians were hacked to pieces, burned alive, or tortured. The Parthian cavalry had fled north, to Hatra, leaving the populace to fend for itself beneath the Romans' rage.

Around many corners, Lucius found women being raped by one or several soldiers whose arrogance and total disregard for life had turned them into animals.

He searched for men from his cohort, but as night fell, the soot-darkened faces of every man with a Roman uniform began to look the same. It seemed everyone carried a bundle of loot, and raped whomever he felt like.

Lucius' head spun from the smoke, the disgust, the smells of death and burning blood. When he thought he caught sight of Eligius and Garai's blonde hair sticking out beneath their helmets, he ran after them.

When he came around a corner, there he found the two of them along with Argus and Maren, tearing at the clothes of a couple of sisters whose bodies displayed the nail scratches of the crazed men.

"Stop it!" Lucius roared, grabbing Maren and throwing him back, away from the one girl.

Maren rose quickly, a fist flying toward Lucius' head, but Lucius was ready with a block of his forearm and locked his other around the soldier's neck.

"What's wrong with you? Just take the loot and go. They're just young girls! Argus!" Lucius yelled as his friend continued to pull at the other sister whose arms lashed out as she screeched and cursed in Parthian. Lucius hammered Maren on the head so that he fell and then flew at Argus. "Please, stop this!"

It was the pleading in Lucius' voice that made Argus stop. He had rarely heard that. He liked it.

"Leave us!" Argus said to Eligius and Garai, who both picked up Maren and went out into the main street. "Let's have some fun with them, eh? You know you want to, Lucius."

"No I don't! What's wrong with you?" Lucius pushed him hard so that he fell. "I saw what you did to Decimus! You killed him!"

"He was already dead. Anyway, what do you know? You're not the one he's humiliated over and over. He deserved it!" Argus spat, drawing his gladius.

"Put that away," Lucius said.

"You don't order me around, you hear me?" Argus stood up, tall, rolling his shoulders. "We were given free reign in the city, and I'm going to follow orders."

"Why did you kill Decimus?"

"I hated him. He thought he was better than all of us."

"He was a good man."

"You're stupid. He whips you, and you think he's a good man. Well let me tell you something. How many cities do you think he went through over the years, doing exactly what I'm doing now? Keep your high ideals to yourself, Lucius. No one cares!"

Without another word, Argus' blade whipped out and took one of the sisters across the neck so that her head fell sideways, hanging by only a few tendons.

The girl's sister screamed and screamed, pushing Lucius' hands away as he tried to help her, to pull her away from the horrors beside her.

When he backed off, Argus was gone. Lucius rushed out into the street sidestepping legionaries carrying bundles of riches, jugs of wine, and wailing women. He ran down the street and after about fifty yards he felt himself knocked off his feet to crash through a blue wooden door that was hanging off its hinges.

"Hey, Bona! Look what I brought you!"

Lucius shook his head and scanned the room. His scutum was out in the street and his gladius on the floor by the door. Two men stood over him, blocking the door, and behind him, along the wall, was Bona.

Lucius stood quickly and backed away, keeping the three men at a distance, his mind racing. Bona was leaning over something, someone, her legs spread wide beneath his form, his bracae down about his ankles.

"Funny how we keep running into each other like this, pretty boy," Bona snarled. "Let me finish." He turned away from Lucius and continued pumping.

Lucius went to lunge for him, but the two men at the door grabbed him and pulled him back. He could hear Bona laughing as he took the young girl. He could feel the rage building to unimagined heights inside of him.

Gods, help me kill them!

Lucius' head shot backward and took one man in the nose so hard that he fell back into the street only to be trampled by passing legionaries who didn't even notice the brother beneath their feet.

As Bona groaned, Lucius struggled with the other man, feeling his fingers groping for Lucius' neck, the room growing hazy as his body threatened to pass out.

Both men were laughing and even as the light of the fires began to fade, Lucius remembered his pugio, drew it, and stabbed wildly at the man's face, plunging the blade deep into his eye socket.

Air rushed into his lungs and just as he tried to regain his feet, he was pinned to the floor, Bona's half naked form on top of him.

"Now I'm going to fuck you, pretty boy!" he laughed.

Lucius struggled, but Bona's knee was in the small of his back, his weight pinning him as hands pulled at his helmet roughly, the chin strap cutting into Lucius' skin.

"I bet you're nice and tight, Metellus, eh?"

Lucius struggled, unable to get any words out. His legs flailed and he felt something at his foot - the pommel of his gladius which he had dropped.

Bona shifted his weight momentarily to try and pin Lucius better, his laughter heard even above the screams outside, and that's when Lucius heaved up with his arms and kicked out a leg, throwing the man off balance. He immediately followed it up with a forearm to the side of Bona's head and dove for his gladius a few feet away.

As soon as his hand closed around the handle of his sword, Lucius swung up and slashed Bona'a sword hand clean off even as it was coming down to hack at him.

The man screamed and raged, spittle flying from his mouth as he ran half-naked at Lucius.

Lucius kicked up, the anger in him boiling over, sending Bona back against the wall. It was as if Lucius wanted to make Bona pay for everything that was going on in Ctesiphon at that moment.

"Ahhh!" Lucius roared as he lunged in one great stride and his gladius stabbed straight into Bona's throat, only stopped by the impact on the mud wall behind. Lucius spat in the death-wide eyes of Bona's hateful face and wrenched his gladius clear, letting the body fall to the floor and kicking it a few times, screaming.

The girl! he remembered and jumped over the other man's body to kneel beside Bona's young victim.

"It's ok... You're safe now..." Lucius whispered, his voice shaking as he brushed aside her wet hair to see her face where she was huddled, her body scratched, bruised, and bloodied. "No one's going to hurt you again-"

Her face, the dark brown eyes. They were lifeless. Lucius stumbled back, realizing that Bona had killed the girl before he had taken her.

Lucius stood, his legs shaking as he backed away from the body and vomited on the floor, tears of rage stinging his eyes. He wondered why the Gods would allow such a thing, and even as the thought came to him, he knew he was indeed being naive.

"Metellus?" came a commanding voice from the doorway.

Lucius turned to see General Laetus standing there, flanked by several of his guards.

The general looked about the room at the dead forms of Bona and the other legionary, and then at the girl, and the pool of Lucius' vomit on the floor among sherds of broken pottery.

"Leave us!" Laetus commanded his men who remained in the street, their swords drawn. "Metellus, what's happened?"

Lucius stood up, his body aching as he did so, but he stood to attention and croaked a reply, his throat hoarse from the smoke and screaming.

"General... I came into the city to find my men. My tribune made me temporary optio when our centurion was killed," he explained. "I found these men in here raping this young... this girl..." Lucius caught his breath. "I tried to stop them but they set upon me. I...I killed two of them, sir."

General Laetus looked at the bodies and then again at the girl. He took in the half-naked form of Bona and nodded. "There's nothing you could have done, Metellus."

"They had killed the girl before they..." Lucius closed his eyes, and gripped his gladius and sheathed it. Then he went to the other fallen man and pulled his pugio out of his eye socket, wiping it on his cloak. "They gave me no choice, sir."

Lucius was scared. He knew the emperor had commanded the sack of the city, and that included everything and everyone within in. The punishment for killing fellow Romans was death.

"Stop, Metellus. I know you're a man of quality," Laetus said, his hand on Lucius' shoulder. "I knew it the first time I spoke to you. These men," he looked at Bona and the other, "were animals. I don't need to know more."

"Sir?"

"Get out of the city, Metellus. You don't want to be a part of this any more than I do. Gods know I hate the Parthians for all that I suffered at their hands at Nisibis over the years, but this..." he waved his hands as if indicating the whole city. "This is barbarism."

"Thank you, sir." Lucius tried not to look at the girl's body on the floor. "I should go find more of my men and make sure they are not out of line."

"You won't stop them," Laetus said frankly. "Get out of the city and wait for the storm to pass."

"What will you do?"

"I'll inform the emperor of the situation within the city, and try to bring my own troops under control. The Parthians may yet come back at us while we gorge ourselves on the bones of this city."

"Yes, sir. What about them?" Lucius looked at the floor.

"Victims of the sacking of a city. Killed by Parthians within the walls. No more. Understood? You weren't here."

"Sir."

"Go now," Laetus said, nodding to his men in the street to let Lucius pass.

Lucius stumbled blindly through the city, his sword and scutum ready as he went. The horrors of that night were something he had never even imagined he would see. The murder of women and children, and of older men, the burning of mud-brick homes that collapsed on the inhabitants who had locked themselves within only to burn screaming with their little ones.

Painted columns and shrines burned and peeled and turned to dust as Roman troops howled, and drank, and raped, and stuffed their bags with loot, and their bellies with food.

Eventually, Lucius made his way out of the city gates. He had not found any more of his men, nor had he seen Argus again. He could not bear it anymore. Night had fallen around the burning city.

As he stepped out onto the plain beyond the walls where wild dogs tore at the bodies of the dead in roving packs, he spotted two lone soldiers standing still and at attention. Lucius walked over to where Alerio and Antanelis were. They had not moved the entire time.

They spotted Lucius coming toward them, and as he got closer, he could spot their looks of disgust and outrage.

Antanelis's face was covered in dry blood, but Lucius could see the traces of tears streaming down the young man's face as he stood watching and listening to what was happening.

Lucius came to a stop, and stood beside them.

"Lucius, thank you for saving my life out there," Antanelis said.

"We saved each other's lives out there. Every one of us. You fought like lions. Both of you."

"You kept us together, Lucius," Alerio said. "I wonder if the others realize what's happened." He looked disappointed.

"Where are Argus and the others?" Antanelis asked.

"They're 'finishing the job'," Lucius said, his head hanging down now. Suddenly he was extremely tired. He knew that some crucial differences between the three of them who stood there, and all the others were severely highlighted that day.

Unable to help the people of Ctesiphon, Lucius, Alerio, and Antanelis watched the flames lick the sky as they must have done when Persepolis had been burned by the drunken

Greek army so long ago. As Ctesiphon smouldered, the three friends held a sort of vigil to the day's fallen warriors before the crimson and orange glow of the giant, flaming pyre that was the capital of Parthia.

X

Hatrae Muris

'The Walls of Hatra'

A.D. 199

After the destruction of Ctesiphon, most of Severus' legions regrouped and marched north to winter quarters in Nisibis. The legions had been split, some following the line of the Tigris, others the Euphrates, with fleets following both along each artery.

However, the Parthians were not yet fully defeated. At the emperor's war council, held outside the smouldering walls of the Parthian capital, the legion commanders were all in agreement with the emperor that the Parthians still posed a threat to Roman gains and supply lines. The surviving Parthian units from Ctesiphon were still out there in the desert, but more importantly, there was the problem of Hatra, which lay in the middle of Mesopotamia.

Hatra, it was decided, would have to be dealt with in the Spring, for it had become a refuge for those Parthians who had fled the fallen cities in the wake of Rome's victories. It was located in the middle of an inhospitable desert, the only water fit to drink within its own walls. A siege would take careful planning.

In the meantime, legions were stationed at Edessa, Dura Europus, Seleucia, Babylon, and Ctesiphon, with the majority of the force based at Nisibis, including III Parthica.

In the spring, war would come again.

Ctesiphon changed Lucius. It had changed all of them.

Men whom Lucius had thought of as brothers, he could barely look at without feeling rage creep upon him for all the atrocities they had carried out. Much of it, he knew, was rumour, or inflated gossip, but far too much was not. He felt apart from the men of the legions then, and he hated it.

From the beginning, Lucius had enjoyed the camaraderie of his fellow legionaries, the drinking, the gaming, even the occasional visits to the vici outside the camps where prostitutes had set up to serve the army.

All of that was soured now.

He was glad of Alerio and Antanelis' company, for they had become close friends. He still interacted with his other tent-mates, of course, especially Argus, but it felt as though there were always an accusing shadow in the background. He woke with nightmares of the dead girl beneath Bona, or dreams of his own execution for killing Roman soldiers.

General Laetus had remained true to his word and had not said a thing about what had happened at Ctesiphon with Bona and his friends. Lucius was grateful for that, at least, and could honestly say he felt no guilt about taking those men's lives. *They deserved it,* he told himself. *They would've killed me first, if I hadn't killed them.*

He had told Argus about the incident as they were drinking alone late one night, and his foster brother's answer had not really surprised him.

"Fuckers deserved it, Lucius. You did the right thing. I only wish I were there to help you."

The irony of this was not lost on Lucius. Had Argus not been raping and looting his way through the city, he would have been there to help. As it was, Lucius left it alone. He had helped the sisters Argus and Maren had been attacking, but there was no way that he could have helped every woman and girl in Ctesiphon.

"I took care of it," Lucius answered as Argus played with his pugio and finished his wine.

"Have you written your family?" Argus asked.

"No, I haven't."

"You going to?"

"I should..." Lucius said, thinking that he really should write to Alene, but somehow, he felt ashamed to do so, after all that he had seen.

Argus stood.

"Where are you going?"

"To find Maren. There are a couple of nubian girls in the camp that he wanted to try out tonight. We're off duty tomorrow, right? A little less sleep won't hurt."

"I guess. Have fun," Lucius said, turning to stare at the firelight in front of their tent as Argus left without another word.

That was the extent of their conversations. A few short questions and answers, nothing of depth as they might once have spoken.

Lucius realized that war did that to men. It stripped them of their ideals, and brought baser thoughts to the fore - food, water, survival, marching, fighting, killing, and dying. There was no room for history or philosophy. Lucius tried to think of Alene's favourite poems by Ovid, but he could not muster his thoughts, interrupted as they were by the sounds of the camp, of hammering and gaming, of cornui, and sharpening stones upon blades.

In a few days, they would reach Nisibis and life would become routine again.

When Nisibis came into view to the West, flashes of Lucius' first battle came to mind in a torrent. He remembered the chaos, the speed with which things happened. He remembered the sight of General Laetus fighting atop the walls of the city, and wondered how the general must be feeling returning there.

The men found it hard to believe that the battle had been less than a year ago, for it seemed an age since they had freed the city of the Parthian allies' siege.

There were a few skirmishes with Parthians on the march north, but they were overcome by the Roman forces. With the cessation of fighting as the cold winds swept down from the North, off of the mountains onto Nisibis and the plains to the South, the need for drills came back into effect.

Gallus was centurion and commanded in Decimus' place. He had not been the same either since the death of his friend. His anger was always up, and he swung his vinerod with ease onto their backs for the smallest of infractions.

Lucius was glad that he had not taken it to Argus' back yet, for he feared what the outcome might be, tormented as he was by the sight of Argus over their former centurion's body.

He had vowed not to say anything, for that would have meant Argus' life, and he did not want to be responsible for that loss.

So, the legions set to drills and training, road works across Mesopotamia and Ohsroene, patrols, and guard duty upon the walls of city and camp. They guided supply chains along the road from Antioch to Edessa, and on to Nisibis, and protected traders who came to Roman-held territory to do business in good faith with the men of the legions.

When Janus saw the new year underway, there was a great celebration in Nisibis. A banquet and games were to be held outside of the walls to celebrate the announcement that Septimius Severus had named his son, Caracalla, as 'Augustus', and the second son, Geta, as 'Caesar'.

The troops of all legions stationed at Nisibis were treated to wine and fresh meat, roasted on great fires outside the walls of every legion's camp. Contests were held the following day, involving sprints, javelin, boxing, and wrestling.

Many of the legions took part in the games, enjoying the momentary lull in campaigning, but III Parthica was not among them.

The Parthians continued hostilities throughout the winter, harassing Roman patrols at every chance when they went too far beyond the walls of Nisibis and Edessa, or too close to the mountain ranges to the North. Some of the engagements were brutal, the Parthians closing in quickly on horseback, firing volleys of arrows quickly into the Roman ranks, and then turning tail to retreat, sometimes luring the Romans into an oncoming charge of cataphracts.

The legionary medici were kept busy.

It was while on patrol east of Nisibis, along the caravan road near the Tigris, that two cohorts of III Parthica were hit by a surprise attack just as they were digging in for the night.

"Attack!" Gallus yelled, giving the order to the cornicen to sound the alarm as two forces of heavy Parthian cavalry came at them from north and south at the same time, swinging inland to attack the Roman flanks before circling back.

"Form testudo!" Lucius and the men around him snapped to, grabbing their scuta and pila if they could get to them in time, and forming the only defensive formation that could withstand the Parthian charge.

All twelve centuries began to form up, but some of the men were already tumbling headlong into the ditches they had been in the middle of digging.

In the red light of the setting sun, some of the centuries ploughed into the Parthian horse as they passed, surprising the hardy beasts enough to get their riders thrown or off-balance. Other riders fell down the soft embankment of the Tigris and into the rushing waters to drown beneath the weight of their full-body chain and plate armour.

When the testudo of a century from third cohort fell apart, the Parthian's rode in for the kill, to hack at them among the disarray.

"To them!" Gallus called, rushing into the fray. "On me!"

Lucius and the others shifted their trajectory and moved to help their brothers at the double. Maces and war hammers came down on them like iron on an anvil and the impact upon their thick wooden scuta was so fierce that it threatened to splinter their bones.

"Where's Gallus?" Lucius yelled.

"Over there!" Argus said, pointing quickly with his pilum to where the centurion stood beneath the flailing hooves of a giant warhorse, his gladius stabbing up at the Parthian rider.

"To the centurion!" Lucius yelled and they shifted again, heading straight for Gallus.

A moment later, the testudo broke, and arrows hammered into them, ricocheting off the scuta at odd angles. Lucius lunged to push Gallus out of the way but was knocked aside by another horse as it backed away from Roman steel. He fell face down beside Gallus who lay prone, his face and skull crushed by the iron-shod hooves of the Parthian warhorse.

Lucius rolled away quickly and ran to the other side of the rearing horse to jump up and grapple with the rider whom he stabbed in the ribs with his gladius, having worked the pointed blade between the links and pushed as if opening a stubborn walnut. He threw the rider down and scanned about, his red cloak whipping in the breeze.

The view he had from atop the horse gave him incredible perspective, and from there he charged at another rider, parrying the long kontos lance as he bore down on him, and slammed his gladius beneath the rider's chin.

"Form testudo!" he yelled at the men of their century, some of whom stared at him in confusion.

"Lucius!" Alerio yelled as a Parthian rider darted toward him with his kontos reaching out for Lucius' death.

The rider spun then, apparently for no reason, and the horse slammed into the side of Lucius' horse. On the ground, Lucius could see Argus holding the lance shaft, wrenching it free from the rider's grip and driving the point of his gladius into the rider's eyes.

The Parthian horses all about the camp were failing as the Romans were able to form up and counter-attack, and soon, the survivors were gone, as quickly as shades in the night.

All that was left were the moans of the wounded legionaries, and the frenzied breathing of the Romans as they gasped for air.

Lucius watched the Parthians ride away in the distance until he was sure they would not come back. When he dismounted, he walked over to Argus and put his arm about him, both of them unable to speak right away.

"Tha...Thank you," Lucius managed to say. "You saved me there, Argus."

"You're fucking crazy jumping on that fucking horse, you know? You're not a cavalry officer! What happened to staying together, keeping formation and disciplina?"

Lucius smiled, a little dizzy from the blood loss of cuts he had sustained. "Sometimes, the rules are meant to be broken. Fight an unexpected attack with an unexpected counter attack."

Argus said nothing, but stood to attention then as a few of the centurions from the other centuries approached.

"Gallus is dead?" said one burly centurion whose cheek had been torn open by a spiked mace.

"Yes, sir." Lucius nodded to where Gallus lay, his face a bloody pulp.

"By Hades," another centurion said. "They came out of nowhere."

The first centurion turned to Lucius. "We've lost a lot of men. I need you to assume responsibility for your century until we get back to Nisibis. You and your men see to finishing the ditches on the south side of the camp, while we clear the dead Parthians and horses."

"Why me, sir?" Lucius asked.

"You kept your head when your centurion was killed. I saw it. Besides, it's only temporary. I'll inform the tribune Livius of your actions though. Good idea pushing the whoresons into the river."

"Thank you, sir." Lucius watched the centurions go, and turned to his friends. "Let's finish the ditches before they come back."

The others agreed and did as he asked without any questions. With the shock of the attack, they were grateful that someone had taken charge again.

Tired, his limbs aching, Argus picked up his gladius, cleaned the blade on the cloak of a dead Parthian, and picked up his pick-axe. He watched Lucius go along the lines of their century, directing groups of men as he went. *Bloody sheep,* he thought, watching the men, Romans and Greeks, set immediately to what Lucius ordered.

"You going to help us?" Garai said from the bottom of the half-finished vallum, as he heaved a shovel-full of rocky dirt onto the growing rampart. "Come on!"

"Shut it!" Argus said as he slammed his pick into the ground and pried at it. The blood from the battle was still fresh upon their limbs as they dug and the other units collected the dead and wounded.

They all knew the Parthians could return at any moment, and so they did not complain, just dug, and heaved.

At the far end of the southern ditch, Argus could see Lucius digging too, laughing nervously with some of the men around him as they worked.

Three days later, they were back at III Parthica's camp outside the walls of Nisibis. It was morning, and the dawn sky was filled with red and purple light suffused by distant clouds that dotted the skies above the desert to the south.

Spring was nearing, and so was the renewal of all-out campaigning. The men had drilled and fought skirmishes for months, not without some losses, and they were ready to finish things with the Parthians. Some however, wondered if it would ever be fully finished, General Laetus among them.

The general was never far from the emperor and his council, and he was respected throughout the camps, often lauded above the legions' own legates. It was often whispered, however, that General Laetus and the emperor rarely saw eye-to-eye on the coming campaign, mainly the taking of the last Parthian stronghold - Hatra.

Losses in the frequent skirmishes throughout Mesopotamia over the winter had resulted in the need to replace important positions in the legions, particularly positions of command.

III Parthica had not escaped unscathed and many members of the centurionate had fallen, including Decimus, and then Gallus. As a result, in the Principia of III Parthica's camp, those centuries that had experienced heavy losses were now gathered before Legate Tertullius, and the tribunes, including Livius.

"Soldiers of Rome!" the legate said aloud so that all could hear him. He stood there, resplendent in full ceremonial armour, the sash about his cuirass, and his crested helmet wavering in the breeze. "Throughout this campaign, III Parthica has proved itself most worthy to be counted among the emperor's legions. You are no longer green recruits, but veterans of this war. You have each been bloodied, and killed the enemies of Rome. You have upheld Disciplina."

Tertullius walked back and forth a couple of times before continuing.

"We've lost many good fighters, many good centurions, optios, and others. And we will lose more, make no mistake. But Rome needs strong leaders, and so today I am announcing those among you who are to rise in the ranks, those among you who have proved themselves in this conflict." Tertullius paused and looked around, his eyes meeting every man in the front rank, and then a few rows back.

Lucius stood at the end of the front row, not entirely convinced that Tertullius believed what he said, but understanding the need to say it.

"The army has changed. War has changed," Tertullius continued, "and so the course a man might take to rise in the ranks of the legions has changed. That is the world we live in, and the emperor is keen for positive change, even if it may be unorthodox."

Some of the men exchanged confused looks, wondering where the legate was going with this.

"Today I am announcing who among you will become optios, and who will be joining the centurionate. Listen well, and honour those men whom I mention, as they will be your guiding force in the coming months."

Tertullius turned to Livius and the other five tribunes who stood to attention in their own polished armour and crisp crimson cloaks.

They began with those present from the sixth cohort and moved down the line. The names that were announced were met with scattered applause and playful jeers. The men laughed and accepted their new commissions. Over and over, heroism and cool thinking were rewarded with advancement, but also more responsibility. Hastiles were handed out to those who assumed the role of optio within each century that needed one, and ceremonial vinerods and phalerae were given to the new centurions, those men who would wear the chain mail and harness rather than the lorica of the average trooper.

"I didn't realize so many had been lost," Alerio said to Argus as they stood at attention. "Think Lucius will get it?"

Argus did not answer. If he was truthful with himself, he hoped not. He believed that any of them deserved the opportunity to rise through the ranks, that their century, above all others, had proved itself in battle.

"Lucius Metellus Anguis! Step forward," Tribune Livius said out loud when it came time for him to speak.

Lucius, who had been lost in thought about the letter he felt he should still write to his sister, looked up quickly at the mention of his name. He could hear Argus breathing heavily beside him as he stepped forward on the sand, before all the men gathered there in the Principia.

"Metellus!" Legate Tertullius said. "After so many battles and skirmishes, the sack of Ctesiphon, and this latest attack on the banks of the Tigris, Tribune Livius and several centurions have come forward with commendations for your courage, skill, quick thinking and discipline at all times."

"Sir." Lucius nodded, feeling the heat rising up his neck as he stood there with all eyes upon him, many, he was sure, not so friendly as he would have liked.

"In particular," Tertullius said, "General Laetus, came forward with a strong recommendation that you be given the opportunity at command, and be made primus pilus of III Parthica."

Lucius felt the air go out of his lungs. *Primus Pilus!* He felt dizzy, but forced himself to step forward to take the thick vinerod from Tertullius, and accept Tribune Livius' forearm. He held the heavy wooden staff in his left hand, and saluted the legate and tribunes, who saluted back.

"You honour me, sir," Lucius almost whispered.

"It will not be an easy task, Metellus. I won't kid you. Use a heavy hand, and keep them in line. We have a tough battle ahead of us."

"Yes, sir." Lucius saluted again, turned, and went back to stand at the end of the line, out front, feeling his friends' eyes on him as he passed.

"Now, men of III Parthica!" the legate said out loud, stepping forward before them. "We go back to the battlefield soon. Continue your training, and get some rest while you can. For in two weeks, we march on Hatra!"

"Maintaining discipline? Ha! Can you believe it?" Argus laughed as they sat all together in their contubernium tent, watching Lucius pack up his things to take to his new quarters. "What about the whipping you got?"

"Ease up, Argus," Alerio said. "Lucius slipped up one time, and hasn't since. They've overlooked that for all the rest of his actions."

"And a lot of centurions have died in recent months. Got to replace them with someone, don't they?" Eligius added.

"Come now, Brother," Garai said, tying back his long blonde hair. "Any one of us could have been made centurion. Lucius has the family name, is all."

Lucius looked sidelong at Garai. His fists clenching around the satchel he was holding. He stood and stared at all of them, lastly at Argus.

"Look," he said. "I've worked hard. We all have, yes. And yes, I've wanted to rise through the ranks, and yes, I messed up in Edessa. A wrong I've tried to make right. But I like to think that I've done more right than wrong in the ranks, that Disciplina has not deserted me. I know some of you are pissed, but it would be great if I had your support in this. We've been through so much and -"

"Come off it, Lucius. It's your family name. Old as it is, it looks good on the rolls of the centurionate," Maren said, leaning back.

"My family name doesn't take me as far as you think, Maren." Lucius picked up his tent roll, flung the packed satchel over his shoulder and went to the door. "It would be nice if you all continue to set an example in the ranks. I know I'm young to be a centurion, let alone Primus Pilus, but if we can keep the discipline up, then it bodes well for all of us."

"That's fine, Lucius. We won't break ranks and run. Doesn't mean we won't sack Hatra when its walls crumble either." Argus stood and followed Lucius out into the sunlight and wind.

"What's wrong, Argus?" Lucius said, turning on him in the middle of the road when they were alone. "I thought you'd be happy for me. The Gods have favoured me in this. Isn't that a good thing?"

"For you, yeah. But it isn't the Gods. Maren's right. You're a Metellus, and that gives you an advantage."

"You don't know what your talking about," Lucius shook his head, staring down the tent rows to where his new quarters were. "Look, just help me out in this. I'll make sure you get recognition."

"Oh you will, eh?" Argus' face contorted. "Fuck recognition, Lucius. And fuck your help. I'll help because I'm a good soldier, not for you. Got it?"

Lucius stared at him. *What's got into him?* he wondered.

"I've got to go to a briefing on the campaign. Come by my quarters later and we can talk some more about this. All right?"

Argus shook his head and went back into the tent without answering.

Lucius stood there for a few moments and then turned to walk to his new quarters at the end of the tent rows for first century.

He entered the newly emptied tent and allowed his eyes to adjust to the darkness of the interior.

It was an older leather campaign tent, Gallus' previous one having been replaced by this one. Small blotches of sunlight dotted the sand floor of the tent where various holes in the leather allowed light to sneak in. It was in rough shape, but it was his, and it was big compared to the eight-man tent he had shared with the others.

In the centre of the tent was a folding campaign table with stools. On top of it was the large sack that he had not seen in some time. He walked over to it and unlaced the ties to reveal his ancestral armour.

Immediately, the material fell away to reveal the black cuirass with the dragon upon it, wings outspread and jaws agape with fury. He ran his fingers along the silver outline of the image and closed his eyes.

I can't wear this yet. Not yet... he told himself, his ancestors whom he could feel watching him. *Apollo, guide me in this...*

Lucius took out the family gladius and pugio which he had packed in the large satchel and unrolled them from their linen coverings.

"But I can used these," he said, smiling as he unsheathed the gladius and held it up in one of the stray rays of light. The images of pegasus stood out on the hilt, as did the eagle on the pommel. How many Metelli had held that blade, he did not know, but it looked as strong and pure as ever.

Realizing he was indeed going to be late, Lucius looked at the stand beside the cot that was to be his. On the stand was a set of centurion's chain mail, and the leather phalerae that were a part of his new kit. On top of the stand was his own helmet to which the armourers had affixed the horizontal crimson crest of his new rank.

Lucius quickly laid his things down on his cot, took the satchel from the table, hid it behind the cot, and began to put on his new uniform.

"Need some help?"

Lucius looked up to see General Laetus standing there in the doorway to his tent, the wind pulling at his cloak.

"Sir? Ah, I'm fine. Just used to a lorica. This chain mail is a little harder to put on."

Laetus laughed. "The trick is to bend over, put your arms in, and then swing upward so that it falls down over you."

Lucius tried, and after wriggling a bit, got it on.

"That's it. Don't worry, you'll be doing it in your sleep after a while. Mail is actually pretty comfortable, more so than a lorica."

Lucius put on the harness and looked up.

"Good. I thought I'd come by and get you for the briefing. Tertullius wants me here too, as our legions will be working in tandem."

"In the attack on Hatra?"

"What else?" Laetus smiled. "Come, let's go before my fellow legate gets himself worked up. Don't forget those, Metellus," Laetus said, pointing to the vinerod on the table, and the helmet which he had placed on the bed.

Lucius grabbed the two items and followed the general outside toward the Principia of the camp.

"So," Laetus said as they walked. "How do you like your new post?"

"I have to say, I was surprised," Lucius said, feeling awkward as men saluted him and the general as they passed. "I should thank you for your recommendation, sir. Legate Tertullius said you put in a good word for me."

"You deserved it, Metellus. And not for your family name."

Lucius looked up and the general smiled.

"Trust me, I know what it's like to be promoted above others. The men will feel differently toward you now. They will try to find reasons why you were promoted above them, even if those reasons are completely unfounded."

"Why then, sir?"

"You're a good soldier with good leadership qualities. Rare qualities. You keep your head, you're fierce in battle, but you have compassion and a will to understand the enemy beyond the killing and rapine. To my mind at least, those are reason enough for you to be promoted. You don't belong in the ranks."

"I have a feeling it will be a lonelier existence though."

"Yes. I won't lie to you. But you have the power to influence your men for the better, to lead them and guide their actions. We need that if we are to remain civilized, don't we?"

"My tutor would have agreed with you, sir."

"So did mine, long ago... Here we are." They stopped outside the Principia and the guards let them through. They crossed the courtyard and went into the large central tent where several officers were gathered for the briefing.

"Settle down, gentlemen! Settle down!" the legate said out loud. "Now... Hatra..."

Lucius stood there feeling his age acutely. He wasn't sure if he was the youngest man there. III Parthica was a young legion, and he one of the few Romans below the rank of tribune.

He also felt awkward in his new uniform, the weight of the mail even more than his lorica. His vinerod felt strange in his hand, and the horizontal crest that now sat atop his helmet made it difficult to tuck under his arm.

This has all happened so fast... he was thinking when the legate's voice echoed over the room.

"Primus Pilus?"

Lucius realized the legate was talking to him, and snapped to attention. "Yes, sir?"

"Come to the front, Metellus."

Lucius gently pushed his way through the crowd to the front where the generals and tribunes were gathered around the broad table.

"First century is going to be crucial in the initial onslaught of Hatra," he said to Tribune Livius whom Lucius stood beside. "The outer walls are going to be tough to breech, but the inner curtain wall will be tougher. The Hatrans man both walls." He pointed to a smaller map of the city that showed two great circular walls, one within the other, with the city and temples in the middle. "Between the walls, they have crops, grazing, and scattered wells. But, if there is cavalry within the walls, they can form up and charge us once we're in. We'll have to move quickly to breech the inner curtain wall."

"Which part of the walls has III Parthica been ordered to take once inside the first wall, Legate?" General Laetus asked. "I'm to bring my legion against the west gate."

"We're to take the southern gate and the two towers flanking it," Tertullius said. "The artillery is going to try and pin down the troops manning the five towers concentrated on the southwest. Those troops will be used to bolster the areas that are breeched, so we will need to move quickly."

"Sir," Lucius found himself speaking up. "Pardon me, sir -"

"Don't stand on ceremony here, Metellus. Speak you mind."

"Yes, sir. I would like to concentrate on drilling the men with the covered battering rams before we march. Seems to me that if we aren't quick about taking advantage of the breeches we make, we'll be dead before the first man sets foot inside the walls. Can we procure a couple of rams?"

"I was getting to that, Metellus. But yes, you have my thinking exactly. Continue with regular drills, especially for when we get inside the city, but focus more on testudo formations and battering ram techniques."

The officers nodded, and murmured as they crowded around to look at the map more closely.

Lucius could feel the sweat running down his back in rivulets as he gazed about at his fellow centurions. He kept forgetting that he was the senior centurion in the room, and that there was a lot of expectation upon his shoulders. Some resentment as well.

"One more thing!" Tertullius said above the voices. Everyone quieted. "Water will be essential. From reports, there is no water that is fit to drink outside the walls of Hatra for over seventy miles in any direction. So, we need as many amphora of water as we can carry. Extra carts will be used so the column of march will be longer than usual."

"Sir?" one of the junior tribunes spoke up. "The emperor has sent several of the legions to garrison the cities we've taken and hunt down some Parthian remnants. Do we know how many legions we'll have to take Hatra?"

"We'll have close to twenty-five legions, Cassius." There was laughter from some of the centurions, and a couple of the tribunes. "A hundred and twenty-five thousand men, plus cavalry alae and other auxiliaries."

Several of the officers nodded and smiled, but Lucius did not. He could see the looks on General Laetus and Legate Tertullius' faces, and they were not comforting.

"Sir, permission to enter!"

Lucius looked up from the wax tablet he was writing on to see Alerio standing in the entrance of his tent.

"Come in, Alerio," Lucius smiled. "I could use a break. I'm just going over the accounts that Graecus gave me," Lucius pointed to the pile of wax tablets that his newly-assigned optio had given him to review.

"Graecus?" Alerio said. "What's he like then?"

"One of the Athenian recruits. You know, the one that asked Decimus if he could read?"

"Oh, him! The one who felt Decimus' vinerod on his first day? Yes, I remember. How is he?"

"He's fine. Eager. Though if I'd been allowed to choose my own optio, I would have chosen you."

"Well," Alerio waved it off. "I'm fine where I am. Besides, someone needs to keep an eye on Antanelis. He's not one to think before charging into a situation."

"I guess not."

"How did the briefing go?" Alerio asked. "Feel strange?"

"Of course. Too strange. I'm senior centurion, but I feel like a child with too much responsibility."

"You'll get used to it. If anyone can do it, you can. There's no one in the legion who's Roman and has the skill and presence to be Primus Pilus."

"Tell that to Argus."

"Don't mind them, Lucius. Least of all, Argus. The man's devoted to you, even though he shits all over you."

"That's comforting." Lucius thought for a moment. "I suppose I've been rubbing things in a bit. Still, I have my orders directly from Livius and the legate now, so I can't disappoint."

"Just try not to hit Argus with that vinerod," Alerio laughed darkly. "I don't think he could handle it."

For the next two weeks, III Parthica drilled and practiced the siege techniques that were indicated in the briefing. They drilled from morning until evening, in the cold wind and dusty air, until their limbs ached and they dropped at the end of each day.

Some of the men grumbled that Lucius was trying to show the tribune and legate that he was worthy of his new position in III Parthica by pushing his men harder than all the other centurions.

Lucius knew of the rumours, but thought it best to accept that. Part of him suspected that was true, for every time he undertook to carry out a command, or give an order himself, he thought of how he had let down Decimus in the streets of Edessa. In fact, he often beat himself with the shame of that memory and the subsequent lashing he had received before his brothers. When he drilled his men in the use of the covered battering ram, the quick formation of a testudo, and the infiltration of narrow enemy streets, he pushed all of them, including himself, more than he would have thought possible.

When the legions finally set out from Nisibis, Lucius felt that he had sufficiently prepared his men. He felt proud to march beneath the centaur banner of his legion.

With a legion of Praetorians at the centre of the line of march, Septimius Severus' army swept southward in a great swathe across Mesopotamia to converge on Hatra, the last Parthian stronghold to stand out against Rome.

The late spring weather was already dry, and the heat at midday bordering on unbearable for the Roman troops. They sweat in their wool tunicae, beneath their lorica and helmets, as they dug in around the desert city, preparing to set Hatra ablaze.

The imperial camp stood out from the rest with the emperor's great tent at the centre, topped by a golden eagle. Smoke from the imperial altars was a constant sight, snaking its way into the sky at all times. It was said among the troops that the empress, Julia Domna, saw to it that the priests, augurs, and astrologers were constantly seeking the Gods' favour in this last assault.

As if in challenge to the Romans, smoke from the great Temple of Bel, at the centre of Hatra rose constantly into the sky above the city, blanketing it and her people in a protective cloud.

Severus waited several days to see if the Hatrans would send emissaries, or stage an attack themselves, but that did not happen. They sat still, patient, waiting for Rome to make her move.

Lucius, his new optio, Graecus, Alerio and Argus stood at the top of a dune one morning looking toward the south gate of

Hatra, the point where III Parthica had been ordered to assault when the time came.

The walls were titanic, stretching in a great circle at the centre of the Mesopotamian plain. Towers dotted the walls like spikes, and along the tops, one could see the glint of sunlight upon Parthian armour. Everywhere one looked, small figures of men walked casually along the walls, watching the Romans, mocking them and challenging them.

"How in Hades are we going to take that?" Argus said.

"Easy soldier," Graecus said. "If we follow the plan, we'll take it."

Argus glanced sideways at the Greek optio and rolled his eyes.

Graecus had taken to his position as optio with fervour, taking copious amounts of notes on the wax tablets that hung at his waist. He also seemed to enjoy ordering the men around.

I'll soon break him of that, Argus thought to himself.

"It won't be easy to take," Lucius acknowledged. "The plan is to hit them hard with artillery first. If there are several breeches around the city at once, they won't be able to defend each one."

"Well, we've got them completely surrounded," Alerio said. "We just have to see how strong the masonry is."

Lucius looked at the sky and back at the walls. "The artillery assault is going to start in about three hours." Lucius turned to Graecus. "Optio, I want you to check with the camp prefect to make sure every century has their rations of water, a guard on each one."

"Is that necessary, sir?" Graecus said, his long black curls sticking to the sides of his face. "Might that not cause distrust among the ranks?"

"Yes. But it's more important to have enough water. Once the siege is under way, we may not be able to send detachments to get more. It's seventy miles to the closest water source outside of Hatra."

"Very good, sir. I'll see to it."

"Do so now, please." Lucius nodded and Graecus saluted.

"Yes, Centurion." He went away to carry out the orders.

"What an obedient little twat, you've got there," Argus said.

"Easy now. He's your superior. Besides, he knows to obey commands, and he's very detailed in his notes. I don't have nearly as many administrative tasks to catch up on since he started."

Argus crossed his arms and shook his head as he stared at Lucius, Alerio continuing to gaze out at Hatra's walls.

"Administrative tasks? Detailed notes? Whatever happened to fighting the enemy, to standing beside your brothers in the century's shield wall? You know what you sound like, Lucius?"

"A primus pilus with a lot of responsibility. Responsibility which was given to me by the legate, I might add." Lucius slapped his thigh with his vinerod. "I don't want to go over this every time you hear me give an order, Argus. Just do what's asked of you, all right?"

"You're unbelievable," Argus spat and stormed off, sand churning up behind him as he went.

Lucius watched him go. He was tired of the constant fight to defend his promotion, something which he had been honest about wanting since he enlisted with the legions. He had told Argus, his father, everyone, that he wanted to climb the ranks on his own merit and nothing else.

Alerio came and stood beside Lucius and they turned to look at the walls of III Parthica's camp and the tent rows within.

"So many men... The legions surround Hatra."

"Yes, they do," Lucius said.

"What happens if we don't take the city?"

Lucius did not speak for a moment and then remembered the legate talking about the emperor's determination to take Hatra, to succeed where other Romans like Trajan had failed.

"I don't think that's an option, really."

"But if -"

"Then the Gods are not on our side in this!" Lucius said quickly. He breathed deeply. He felt responsibility for this assault, and yet he knew the absurdity of the thought. There were hundreds of thousands of men on the plain, and every one of them was ready to lift his sword for Rome. The Gods had to be with them.

That night, even as the sounds of catapult, ballista, and onager slammed in the background, battering the walls of Hatra, Lucius returned to his tent and went to his knees before the small altar where the statue of Olympian Apollo stood before him.

He neither thought nor spoke for a few minutes, enjoying the quiet and solitude of his tent, the smoke of the incense swirling about him. He gazed at the image of Apollo, his great muscular arm outstretched, and closed his eyes.

"Far-Shooting Apollo... I know my offerings have been infrequent. I am sorry. This burden of command... I did not expect it so soon."

Lucius swayed on his knees, his greaves digging into the packed sand. A cool breeze crept in under the walls of his tent and the lamps hanging from the ceiling swayed, papyrus scrolls on the table at the centre of the tent fluttering beneath the small stones that weighed them down.

Lucius had started a letter to Alene, but had not finished it, his mind wandering to the long list of duties he had, the orders to be dished out to his optio, the quartermaster, the camp prefect and more, the reports he had to collect from the other centurions and in turn pass on to the legate. The list was endless.

Then there was the waiting, half of each century ready at any time, standing by in case a section of Hatra's walls fell, providing Rome with a way into the city to flood its streets and begin drowning it in blood.

Lucius sighed. "Lord, I have an ill feeling about this siege. I don't know why. I-"

Lucius whipped around to look into the corner of the tent behind him and thought for a moment that he had seen a shining man standing in the corner. There was a flash of light and he covered his eyes, still upon his knees.

"My lord Apollo?"

Yes, came the voice, strong, calm, and commanding. *You must be ready to fight, Metellus... But do not think this will be quick. Stay your course, stay by your men... Act from your heart, and you may live through this...*

"My lord? May?" Lucius stood up and looked about the tent, feeling the hairs on the back of his neck tingling. "I will... My lord?" Lucius stood there beside the central table and reached up to stop the swaying lamp that hung low from the ceiling over his papers. His hands shook and he felt cold. Behind his lids, he could still see the glare of Apollo's outline, he was sure of it.

"I will stay upon the path. I swear. I will be guided by you."

Again the sound of the artillery came into his thoughts and distant thumps and cracks could be heard, but no cries of success. Only silence, and the fall of boulder and bolt upon the stubborn walls of Hatra.

The following day, the sun revealed the walls of the city still standing, with not a breech to be had.

Lucius stood with a group of officers around Legate Tertullius who had just returned from the emperor's war council. They all stared out at the south gates to see the pock marks of their assault in the sand before the walls, as if the boulders had bounced off without causing the least bit of damage.

"Unbelievable!" Tertullius said out loud. A night of bombardment, and look, nothing to show for it. It's the same all around the circuit wall. All commanders report little damage. These walls must have a weakness. They're not god-built!"

It was the first time Lucius had seen Tertullius on edge, and he wondered if the legate suspected that the siege would go on for a long time.

Already the desert heat was getting to the men who were on constant standby, ready to attack.

"I want smaller rations of water given out to the men," the legate said to his officers. At this rate, we'll run out before we can get more."

Lucius wondered what it was like inside the walls of Hatra. What did the people hear? Were they afraid? Were the streets rank with the anticipation of what the Romans would do to them once they broke down their high walls and raged through their streets?

"We can't have the men standing here, catatonic while we wait for the walls to fall down," Tertullius said. "I want shifts at drills to keep the cohorts limber and ready for a fight. Primus Pilus?"

Lucius turned to the legate. "Yes, sir?"

"You lead the first groups in drills, Don't tire them out too much, just enough to keep them in shape. Got it?"

"Yes, sir," Lucius answered. "First cohort will lead the way."

"Good. Now, gentlemen, we wait. I'm going to the Praetorium to finish some work. Send for me if there is any sign that the walls are weakening."

"Yes, sir!" they all said and saluted. When the legate and tribunes returned to the Principia and Praetorium, Lucius and the other centurions stood watching and waiting as dust rose high into the sky and nothing happened.

They waited a long time. Days, weeks, and eventually months passed and still the walls of Hatra stood.

Men began to wonder if the walls were indeed built by the Gods themselves, as at Troy, the walls of which had only been breeched by trickery in the end.

The Hatrans were not idle either. Their numbers were such that they could man their great circular walls with enough archers to keep the Romans in check.

It took the Roman commanders no small amount of work to keep their men in line, impatient as they were to close with the enemy. Supplies were running low, and there were reports of Parthian attacks farther afield on the edges of some of the Roman garrison settlements, the enemy fleeing before there could be any engagement.

It was at an imperial war council, Lucius' first, that the military command were told of the next step.

The emperor stood on the short dais in the middle of his Principia in the Praetorian camp, his eyes washing over the assembled generals, tribunes, first centurions, prefects and engineers.

Lucius stood there, taller than most of his fellows, but by far one of the youngest. The decorations upon the men surrounding him told him that this was a warlike company. Some of the men spoke with him, others ignored him, and still others looked down their Patrician noses at him. The empress and her entourage were not present at this meeting, for this was a council of war.

"The campaigning season is nearing its end," the emperor began, holding his arms out so that his gold and purple cloak hung down in folds from his wrists to graze the floor. He coughed for a moment, and then continued, his face stern, thoughtful.

"I've spoken with our head siege engineer, Priscus," he nodded to the Bythinian Greek standing to the left of the dais, "and we feel that it may be possible for the siege engines to reach the inner walls of Hatra if we move them closer to the outer walls."

There were instant mutterings, mostly of doubt, but the emperor put up his hands for quiet, nodding his head in understanding.

"I am well aware of the risks. The Hatrans are not incapable with their little bows. Yes, General Laetus?"

Maecius Laetus stepped up before the dais and made to speak.

"My imperator, even if we could attack the inner walls from without, what good would it do us if we are still held at bay beyond the outer wall?"

There was agreement from the assembled veterans, but Severus smiled.

"I agree, General. If the outer walls are not breeched, then we cannot hope to get at the inner walls. However, if we get closer, we can fire their crops that lie between the walls. We can poison the river that runs within, and thus their water supply. More importantly, we may divert them slightly from the outer wall to see to the fires within, and then, General, we will make our assault on the outer walls, harder than ever."

The room was silent, and General Laetus rubbed his chin as he looked at the map of the city that had been laid out on the massive campaign table before the emperor.

Lucius wondered at the plan, and he thought it stank of desperation, but he would never have said so. The emperor had a lot of experience in warfare, and had been one of the most successful military commanders in recent years. With the Roman numbers at Severus' disposal, Lucius thought that it might just work.

"Tomorrow, gentlemen," the emperor said, "we move closer, and pour all manner of fire and death upon the people of Hatra so that the roofs of their very dwellings bury them!"

There were still cheers and excited talk as Lucius exited the tent with Tertullius, Livius, and the other tribunes of III Parthica.

"He's too impatient," Livius whispered to Tertullius as they went down the Via Decumana of the Praetorian camp.

"Keep quiet!" Tertullius hissed. "We follow our orders, just as the men will." The legate turned to Lucius who was walking in step behind him. "Metellus, we'll need a century with each of the siege engines in our charge. See to it, and give the men instructions to stay close. When the Hatrans leave the walls, our own assault will begin in earnest."

"Don't you mean, 'if' they leave the walls, sir?" Lucius said.

The legate stopped and turned to face Lucius, the others waiting around them.

"Of course. But I want every legionary ready to puncture those damned walls as soon as the opportunity presents itself. Understood?"

"Yes, sir." Lucius said no more.

"They'll riddle us with arrows badly, sir," Livius said. "As soon as we're close, they'll fire."

"We'll form testudos. Are you not up to this, Tribune?" Tertullius was in Livius' face, but the tribune stood his ground.

"Of course I am, sir. We all are. We just don't know what's beyond those walls, do we?"

"Eternal glory is what's behind those walls, Tribune. Glory favours the bold. Isn't that what the poet said?"

"Yes, sir."

"Good. Now, all of you. Get to your cohorts and prepare the men. This is going to start first thing in the morning while the Hatrans are still wiping the sleep from their eyes."

With that, Tertullius stormed off through the gates of III Parthica's camp and made his way to his Praetorium, his aides rushing behind him to keep up.

Livius watched him go and then turned to his first centurion. "Metellus, I'd keep my opinions close if I were you. This siege has gone on long enough, and it won't do to tear down the emperor's plan in front of anyone, as much as we would like to."

"Understood, sir." Lucius scanned the tent rows and saw all the men cooking, sharpening blades, and dicing with their pay. "I'll see to the men and get the message round to the other centurions."

"When this starts tomorrow, we need to all be out on the field."

"Yes, sir." Lucius saluted, turned, and walked away toward the barracks where the first century was stationed.

When the sun rose the following day, it was as though new siege engines had sprouted out of the very ground. The walls of Hatra were surrounded, massive boulders piled high around the onagers and ballistas, as were bolts about the scorpions.

Great clay jars of naptha were also piled two high near each of the onagers. The smell was strong and stuck in the nostrils of all the men as they watched and waited for the signal to begin moving the engines closer to the walls and begin the bombardment.

Lucius stood there at the front, watching Roman archers and Cretan slingers get themselves into position. There was an unsettling hush all along the nimbus of war that had formed around Hatra, and then the command from each officer to his soldiers.

"Iacite!"

All the Roman artillery fired at once, an initial volley before moving closer under the covering fire from archers and slingers in the areas around the gates.

"Forward!" Lucius yelled to the men under his command to help the artillery groups push their siege engines closer. "Shields up!" he yelled, as Hatran archers appeared once more atop the walls and fired into the Roman ranks.

There were a few screams about him, but Lucius was relieved to hear the hard knocks of arrowheads upon scuta.

"Forward!" he yelled once more as their covering fire streaked into the sky to clap heads and pierce bodies on the walls.

"This doesn't seem right, Centurion!" Graecus yelled as he marched forward beside Lucius. "They could rain a few more volleys down on us."

Lucius thought about it a moment and agreed. The Hatrans had more men than this, unless they were manning other portions of the walls.

"Come on! Let's pick up the pace!" Lucius yelled. "Forward! Iacite!" a boulder from the onager nearest him crushed a part of the crenelations atop the wall to the left of the gate they were headed toward. "What's our range now?" Lucius called back to the men manning the artillery.

"Well past the outer wall, sir!" one man said as he heaved on the torsion to pull the onager's arm back again. "We need to advance one more time!"

"Right," Lucius gazed at the walls, an arrow whizzing by his face, its fletching grazing his cheek guard. "Shields up!"

Another volley of Hatran arrows slammed into them and then the Romans fired back.

"Forward!" Lucius roared, leaning into the engine's body and rolling it forward in concert with the others all down the line. "Bring up the naptha!"

Men ran back to pick up a jar each of the naptha, their course erratic so as not to get hit by the Hatran arrows. Soon after, each siege engine had pots of the black, flammable liquid piled about it.

"Load!" Lucius said. "Cover fire... Light them up... Iacite!"

Several balls of flaming pots soared into the sky well above the walls to land on the other side.

Lucius waited for the screams, but he could not hear anything for all the noise along the Roman ranks. He stared about a moment, waiting for another volley from the defenders, but they did not come.

"Something's wrong!" Alerio said out loud, as he and Antanelis, hoisted another pot onto the pile.

"Shields!" Lucius suddenly yelled. "Take cover!"

At the top of the walls, there appeared a long line of Hatrans with tiny flaming pots on the ends of long ropes which they swung in a circular fashion about their heads. Then their archers appeared and fired, sending the Romans behind their shields.

"Get away from the siege engines!" Lucius yelled, pushing his men away even as the flaming pots were launched from the top of Hatra's walls to soar over the ranks and crack on the jars of naptha piled about the engines.

There was a rush of hot air and then explosions of fire and heat punctuated by horrifying screams as men burned and rolled on the ground only to continue burning.

"No!" Lucius yelled, as he ripped his cloak from his shoulders and tried to smother the flames that were melting the flesh beneath the armour of the man nearest him.

More arrows came out of the sky like Stymphalian birds to take his men in the sides, the legs, hands and face.

He gazed along the lines and saw that the other legionary units were pulling back from the walls, fire and smoke engulfing everything everywhere.

"Fall back!" Lucius cried out as he faced the walls, waiting for the last survivor, Argus, to get up from where he had been thrown in the explosion. "Argus, get up!"

Argus did not move.

Lucius ran to him, his scutum held high as arrows rained down and pots of naptha exploded feet away from him, pocking the sandy earth.

"Argus, talk to me!" Lucius said, shaking him.

Argus' eyes suddenly rolled to life as his consciousness returned. "What happened?"

"Hurry up. We're dead if we stay here!" Lucius hoisted him to his feet and an arrow tore a line in his calf muscle. "Ahh!" He picked up the scutum and gave it to Argus. "Can you hold this?"

"I think so," he said, wincing.

"Good." With that, Lucius hoisted Argus over his shoulder and began to run back to the Roman line which had fallen back. "Shield our backs!" Lucius said as he scampered among the detritus of the attack. His legs and lungs burned, for Argus was a heavy man, but they reached the lines and Lucius collapsed.

Hatran arrows pounded into the ground just before them, unable to reach any farther.

Lucius could have lain there but he forced himself to his feet. "Medicus!" he called one of the Greeks in his century. "Take care of the wounded, starting with him!" he pointed at Argus. "Graecus? Where's the tribune?"

"He's dead, Lucius," Alerio said. "Graecus burned back there."

"Ahh! Alerio, you're optio for now. Rally the men and form details to help the wounded."

"Yes, sir!" Alerio snapped a salute with a bleeding arm and gathered some men.

"There's the tribune!" Antanelis said, pointing as Livius came charging up.

"Metellus! What's your status?" Livius said, reigning his horse in hard.

273

"Sir," Lucius saluted. "The Hatrans hit us with fire and set the naptha alight. We've got heavy casualties, sir."

"It's the same all along the line. Almost all the siege engines have been fired by naptha pots and flaming arrows. The siege is done for the day. New orders are to rescue survivors from the field and move to a safe distance."

"Already underway, sir," Lucius said.

"Good. I'll check on the other centuries. Keep a watch for a charge from the gates!" he said as he rode away.

Lucius turned to watch him go, his eyes straying to the black plumes of smoke that rose all around the outside of Hatra's walls.

"Gods, help us," Lucius muttered as he bent to check on Argus.

Not only was the siege done for the day, but for the season. As the Roman siege engines still smouldered on the plain outside of Hatra, the legions moved out, their casualties heavy, the men tired, thirsty, angry, and on the verge of mutiny.

They left many dead beneath the walls of that desert city, and the emperor marched his armies away with great reluctance, even as the defenders laughed and chided them from their high walls.

It was said that the emperor swore to tear the city down, and to ravage the population that had defied and taunted him, and insulted Rome.

As the legions began the march north to winter quarters in Nisibis, the imperial party, surrounded by Praetorians, remained behind for a short time, staring at the walls of Hatra.

The men later found out that the emperor and empress were taking auguries before those walls, to complement the readings of the stars the previous night.

It seemed the Gods were in concert. Severus would return to Hatra in the spring.

However, word of this decision was not spread among the exhausted men of the legions. Severus knew how to nurture their loyalty, and rest and reward was one way to do that.

Priscus of Bythinia and his team of labourers and engineers were put to work right away once they reached Nisibis. New, bigger, and better siege engines were to be constructed, and teams were sent immediately into the mountains north of Nisibis to cut timber.

There was so much building that during the winter months, the sound of chopping and hammering were as common as the cold winter wind and the centurions' call during daily drills.

The world seemed to shrink to Lucius as he went about his daily routines of inspection and drills, the overseeing of building projects such as roads, and holding council with the tribunes and legate commander of III Parthica.

One night, as the officers sat together, finishing the wine that Tertullius had pulled out for them, a special treat for Saturnalia, General Laetus came into the tent shaking his head and cursing.

"Damn it all to Hades!" Laetus said, throwing down his cloak and accepting a cup of wine from Tertullius' slave.

The air was thick and warm inside the tent, but when Laetus entered, a cold stab of air penetrated the space and the officers awoke from their wine-warmth.

"What is it, my friend?" Tertullius said, rising to greet the general.

Laetus looked about the room and nodded to the tribunes and Lucius before turning to Tertullius.

"He's waiting to attack the Hatrans. Two more months of waiting."

"We never fight in winter," the legate said.

"No, but this gives the Hatrans an advantage. As we sit here, celebrating and drinking, licking our wounds, the Hatrans are repairing and reinforcing their mighty walls. And more Parthian troops are flocking to their city to boost the garrison's numbers."

"If we head out in the winter, we could be taken by a surprise storm, and the water sources could be frozen. The emperor does not need a mutiny on his hands, Maecius." Tertullius walked around the tent, his tribunes' eyes following him. "We're all tired of this war, but even though Ctesiphon has fallen, Hatra remains, yet a crown of victory upon the Parthians' brow. Rome would loose face if it were to run."

"I'm not saying we should run. Trust me, I never run," Laetus spat, the edge of his voice emphasizing the last word.

"I know... I know," said Tertullius. "I never said you did run."

Tertullius calmed and sat down on a stool beside Lucius.

"I see you survived the naptha attack. Good. It would be a shame to lose a soldier like you to something so stupid."

"The Hatrans played it well I'd say, sir," Lucius said, the echoes of his burning men's cries screeching in his ears.

"How many men did you lose?"

"Too many. But isn't that the way of Mars?"

"Perhaps, yes." Laetus sipped his wine and looked at the rest of the tribunes. "What do you all think? For discussion's sake? Should we attack the Hatrans now, or wait until the spring? Livius, what say you?"

Livius cleared his throat and spoke. "It is the emperor's decision, General."

"Do you have no thoughts of your own?"

"I think the men need to be allowed to rest, to be fresh for the fight in the spring."

"Do you think I had the chance to rest, or my men for that matter, when this gods-forsaken patch of land we sit outside of was surrounded by Parthian troops, while men within the walls beat each other, and young mothers ate the flesh of their family dogs or cats so that they could feed their own babies? Trust me, there were a few winters without rest."

"Maecius, please," Tertullius said, wrapping his crimson cloak about his shoulders. Firelight glinted off the golden embroidery of his tunic cuff as he raised his cup to his lips. "The men are near to mutiny. To push them now would be to unleash furies upon ourselves. See reason and stop this talk. It's bordering on treasonous."

"My men love me, Tertullius. Do you know why?"

"Because you bring them home alive."

"Because I never give up. Failure and retreat are never an option."

"I hope you're not accusing me of cowardice, my friend."

Lucius, Livius and the tribunes looked at each other and back at the two generals.

"No. Of course not. I'm just saying that is why they love me. Why others do."

"Like Alexander," Lucius said, more to himself, but it was heard.

"Excuse me, Metellus?"

"Forgive me, sir. I just said 'like Alexander'."

"Explain."

"Well, from my studies, Alexander's army followed him through impossible feats. They conquered the world. And I don't think they would have done so if Alexander had not been one of them, suffered with them, but also led them. He certainly never gave up."

"We are past the time of these Greek heroes you always speak of, Centurion," the legate said. "Besides, most men, as heroic as our men are, fight for pay. And the emperor pays them well. They also love him."

"But how far will that love carry him?" Laetus said.

"I think you had better leave, Laetus, and keep this talk to yourself."

Tertullius stepped forward and indicated the tent flaps with his arm.

Laetus nodded solemnly and stood. "I understand. Forgive me for abusing your hospitality. I'm an old soldier, Tertullius." Maecius Laetus swept from the tent as swiftly as he had entered it, and left the camp of III Parthica with a guard of his own men who had been waiting outside in the frigid air.

"He grows impatient," Livius said as Tertullius sat back down.

"He's been to Hades and back," Tertullius said. "He's a man of action, and it has been action that has seen him keep himself and his men alive for so long. Nisibis would be a burning pile of rubble and ashe were it not for Laetus." The legate rubbed his eyes and sighed deeply, Livius nodding to the others that they should leave.

"We thank you for your hospitality, Legate Commander," Livius said as the other tribunes went out followed by Lucius.

"I'll see you in the morning for drills, Tribune."

"Good night then, sir."

"Good night."

Lucius was waiting outside for Livius when he came out.

"What was all that about, sir?" Lucius asked as they fell into step together along the Via Principalis.

"It's about ending this bloody war with Parthia, and about laying groundwork for a new Pax Romana."

"So, do you agree with General Laetus?"

Livius stopped and turned to Lucius. "Keep your voice down, Metellus. The Praetorians have spies everywhere. You need to be careful. I see how Laetus seems to have adopted you. He would have you as his protege. But, my counsel is to keep a safe distance. If he continues to speak like this, he'll be brought up on charges."

"But he's the most popular general among the men of several legions," Lucius said.

"Exactly. Popularity among the men is a very dangerous thing. You may want your men to love and admire you, for yes, they will follow you anywhere. But what if others perceive that the place to which they would follow you could threaten imperial power? You know how the emperor came to power, and why the civil war was fought."

Lucius nodded. Severus' rivals had the support of their own legions, many of them, and thought they should hold the reigns of imperial power. He knew the emperor would be on the lookout for such things again. How could he not?

"Then you know why Laetus should keep his opinion to himself. He knows the Parthians and their tactics better than anyone, he knows their politics. But he has forgotten the politics of Rome. He's been out here too long."

"But you think his strategy is solid?" Lucius' voice was just barely a whisper.

Livius nodded. "But that doesn't mean it should be carried out. The emperor is our chief commander, and we follow his orders. It doesn't matter what rank you are, Metellus. If you remember just one fact of army politics, remember that."

It was Lucius' turn to nod. He felt a cold chill run down his spine now. He had grown close to Laetus, he had enjoyed the indirect acclamation of Laetus' troops as he had walked through the camps with the general on occasion. He needed to stop that.

"You'd better get some sleep, Metellus. The night will be a cold one and we have heavy drills on the morrow."

"The men won't thank me for what I have planned, I assure you," Lucius said.

"Good. Better to breed good soldiers out of your routines, than men who will love you. Good night."

Lucius saluted his tribune and watched him disappear into his large command tent farther down the road.

He looked up at the stars in the cold sky above the desert and felt a sense of dread niggling at the back of his consciousness. The evening had taken an odd turn.

A week later, when the cornui sounded among the legionary camps surrounding Nisibis, the men of the legions began to prepare for yet another day of drills and siege engine work.

As he roused his men and marched first century out of the camp after inspection, Lucius noticed that one of the legions had already begun drilling in full formation to the south. Dust already rose into the pink morning sky as the troops wheeled and formed testudo, launched their pila and jogged in their full kit.

"They're up early," Alerio said, standing next to Lucius and holding the long hastile staff, a mark of his recent promotion optio.

"It's Laetus' legion," Lucius said. He looked around and saw that no other legions had begun drills yet. Then his eyes fell on a group of Praetorian guards who watched Laetus' legions perform their manoeuvres with perfect precision.

"The men seem to love General Laetus," Alerio said. "No offence, but I don't think our men would get up as early for you."

Lucius laughed. "I think you're right. Then again, I don't know that I would expect them to."

The Praetorians who had been watching and listening to the cheering of the troops for Laetus, after he'd led them in an excellent round of drills, now turned and rode back to the imperial camp.

"Come on," Lucius said. "Let's get to work."

Later that day, rumours were going around the officers that the troops were still restless and on the verge of mutiny. A meeting of officers was called toward midday, and Lucius was commanded to attend.

When he entered Tertullius' Principa, the legate beckoned them all to sit down and set four guards at the entrance.

"We've been informed that there are many men who are of the opinion that the army should march for Hatra as soon as possible. Some ring-leaders, mainly from General Laetus' legion have been urging their fellows to march on Hatra so that they can all go home." Tertullius paused.

"I hope that none of you has heard such talk."

They all shook their heads and looked him.

"Good. However, it is not the case in some of the other legions."

Lucius thought the legate looked tired. His hair seemed to have greyed in the last weeks, and Lucius wondered if politics was not beginning to take its toll on the legate.

"Let me just say this," Tertullius continued. "If you hear of any such talk in your ranks, I want it curbed or stomped out completely. Do you understand?"

"Yes, Legate Commander," Livius said for all of them.

"Good...good..."

The men looked at each other as the legate read a dispatch that had only just been thrust into his hands by one of the guards at the mouth of the tent.

"What?" Tertullius flushed crimson, his eyes opening as if to reassess what he had just read.

"What is it, Legate?" Livius asked.

Tertullius motioned for his slave to put his cloak over his shoulders and bring his gladius, which the menial did quickly and efficiently.

"Dismissed," the legate barked. "Back to your units. I need to go to the imperial camp."

"Do you require an escort, sir?" Livius asked.

"No." The legate strode through the group of them and into the courtyard where his horse was waiting, held by one of the legionaries.

Around the inside of the Principia, everyone looked at each other. The tribunes exchanged wary looks and Lucius stared out into the dying orange light of the courtyard.

"You heard the legate," Livius said. "Back to your units. Keep alert. I don't like this."

General Maecius Laetus, the hero of Nisibis, was taken into custody that night.

He had been invited to the emperor's Praetorium for a council of all the generals where, once all were assembled, the charges of treason and inciting mutiny were laid before him.

Laetus tried to reason with the emperor, it was said, but Severus would have none of it.

"The stars are against you, General Laetus," Severus pronounced. "You have been encouraging my legions to move against my wishes. That cannot be tolerated."

"I have done much for Rome in these lands, sire," Laetus had said, as the sound of clashing steel and the cries of dying men and starving children filled the well of his memories. "More than any man here."

"And the empire no longer requires your service," Severus said coldly. "The sentence is death. At sunrise tomorrow."

Weeks later, Livius related to Lucius what he heard had happened after that. Once the pronouncement of death had been given, Legate Commander Tertullius, Laetus' friend, was ordered to bind Laetus and escort him to a cell within the Praetorian camp where he was to be held until dawn.

Laetus' troops came close to rioting and it took being surrounded by three legions, and the execution of the ringleaders, to stop the madness. If that was not enough, the display of Laetus' crucified body before the Praetorian camp deterred any other would-be mutineers.

After the execution of Laetus, Lucius found himself in his tent with Alerio wondering at the swift turn in fortunes of the man.

"I just don't get it, Alerio. One second, Laetus is a hero, a saviour of this campaign, and the next, he's hanging from a cross for all to see."

"I wouldn't talk about it anymore, Lucius," Alerio said. "Just watch yourself. Laetus had taken an interest in you. Now's not the time to put a foot wrong."

"I know. What I don't know is how the legate commander was able to take his friend and carry out the execution, well, order it anyway."

"We all take orders, Lucius. No matter how high one climbs. There is always someone to whom we must yield and obey. For us, it's the officers, for emperors, it's the Gods themselves."

"I don't know if the Gods are happy with this. Time will tell."

A few weeks later, the legions were marching south again over the sand-covered world, to Hatra.

More siege engines than ever followed the armies of Rome to stand before the desert city where smoke from their great temples yet rose in massive plumes of black, grey and purple into the spring sky above.

Scouts and detachments of every legion were ordered to make a circuit of the walls to look for any weak points, or to try and draw the enemy out from behind the walls.

But no weaknesses were spotted. If anything, the walls had been reinforced over the winter months. The Hatrans squatted within and made not a sound as the wind whipped around the men of the legions who stood on their doorstep.

The emperor's camp was set up facing the western gate of Hatra, and the smoke of imperial offerings began to fume into the sky shortly after that.

A great timber tribunal was set up for the imperial family and councillors of the emperor who would watch the siege play out once all legions were in place.

Once more, III Parthica was encamped facing the southern gate of the outer wall, the engines of Priscus of Bythinia set up early to begin the bombardment.

When the pounding began, the legions were ready, and waiting.

There was a ferocity to the second attack on Hatra that the first siege had lacked. Rome did not easily forgive ongoing defiance.

Stockpiles of rock and boulder stood with every legion, fodder for the artillery troops who would rain it all down on the defenders. The bombardment went on day and night, and the clepsydra that counted down the hours in the imperial Praetorium continued to measure time.

The Hatrans fired back, however, just as the Romans began to waver from the constant thrust of battle against the walls. The resistance was fierce and just as the legions began to taste success, they were pushed back.

"Shields!" Lucius yelled from the front of his line, as he dropped to one knee beneath the massive ballista bolts that cut through the air above his head. He turned around quickly to see four of his men impaled and pinned to the ground as they crashed into their ranks.

"They've got double-bolted ballistas, Centurion!" Argus yelled as he stumbled toward Lucius, blood and gore from the men who had just fallen spattered over his lorica.

"Get back in line, Argus!" Lucius yelled, peering up at the walls where the Hatrans above the gate seemed to be reloading. "Archers!" he yelled back, Alerio echoing the order to the rear. "Argus, I need to you to hold things together in that line. After that just now, the men are in danger of breaking and running."

"We can't stop those ballista bolts, Lucius!"

"Just do it!" Lucius' face was sweaty and red, and he shoved Argus into action, busy as he was staring at the gore on his chest. "Archers, on me!" Lucius yelled as the Syrian auxiliaries came running up. "Take out the men on that ballista! Now!"

Lucius ran with seven archers following him. They were on him, he could hear their chain mail shuffling as it hung from the back of their pointed helmets. He glanced back. They looked scared, but they were still on him, picking their way past the bodies of dead Romans.

"They're reloading," he said urgently. "Ready to fire.... Now!"

The bowstrings snapped behind Lucius' head and seven shafts sped toward the ballista atop the gatehouse. One Hatran fell back, a shaft in his face, but the other was only grazed and pulled the lever on his ballista.

"Shields!" Lucius yelled back as the two bolts zipped overhead. He heard the cries of the men behind him and prayed that none of his friends had been hit. "Gods! How do we get past this? Fire! Fire!" he yelled, and the archers loosed again and pinned the other ballista operator in the shoulders so that he fell from the walls.

"Bring in the battering ram!" Lucius yelled and several of the III Parthica troops began pushing the covered ram toward the gate, even as more archers joined the defenders on the wall.

Lucius felt a cut across his right shoulder as an arrow sliced past him, then he saw two of his own archers go down with shafts in their throats. They gasped for air, panic in their eyes as they stared widely at him.

"More archers!"

The rest of the Syrians came running up with the battering ram, firing as they walked, giving the ram time to reach the walls.

Lucius began to feel hope. "Almost there!" he yelled. "Keep moving!" he urged the grunting legionaries on, setting his own body to pushing the ram from behind. he felt his muscles strain and added his voice to the yelling. "We've got it! Alerio, keep firing!"

Farther back, Alerio had the archers covering the walls in a hail of arrows.

"Now!" Lucius heaved the ram back with the Greeks of his legion and felt the shock as the ram slammed into the great wood and bronze gates. "Again!"

They rammed, and pulled back, again and again and the blessed sound of splintering finally cracked the air.

"Again!" he yelled.

"Centurion!" Alerio's voice rushed through the dust to Lucius. "Get out of there!'

Lucius turned, confused and looked up to see a pot of steaming naptha being tipped over the lip of the gate.

"Fall back! Fall back!" Lucius grabbed the two men closest to him and dove out of the way. The rush and sound of sizzling behind him licked at his feet with unspeakable heat as he scrambled away, but it was the screams of his men as their flesh melted that would haunt him, their frenzied flopping about as the naptha was lit from above and the ram went up in flames, a pyre for the men who had pushed it to the walls.

"Centurion!" Antanelis called rushing out from the line to grab Lucius under the arms and pull him back while two men helped the other troops who had escaped the flames.

"AHHHH!" Lucius turned to the walls and cursed. "We'll burn your city to the ground!" he yelled, ripping his helmet from his head so that the hot breeze wafted around him.

"Centurion!"

Lucius turned to see Tribune Livius rein in behind him. He saluted and approached the tribune.

"What happened?" Livius asked.

"I had the gate breeched, sir!" Lucius said, his eyes wild. "We almost had them."

"Rest now, Centurion," Livius urged. "I've just had a report that there is a breech on the north side of the walls. Look!" Livius pointed to the walls where several Hatrans were leaving and rushing away. "They're going to reinforce the north gate. Fourth Scythica is moving into the breech. That'll give us a chance at this gate. When the flames die down, bring in the next ram and get yourselves through. You hear me?"

"Yes, sir!" Lucius said.

"Water over here!" Livius ordered, taking the laddle from the slave and handing it to Lucius. "We're almost in, Metellus," he said as Lucius drank greedily, as if he had never tasted water before. Livius drank too and then spun his horse. "Get ready!" he called back over his shoulder.

Lucius took some deep breaths before giving any more orders. He could still hear himself yelling, feel the heat of the naptha and the voices of more dying men.

"Form up, out of range. Get the next battering ram over here and ready to move!"

"Yes, sir!" the men answered and jumped into action.

They could not hear the fighting on the other side of the city but they could see Hatrans rushing about the walls.

Lucius wondered how much ground they would have to cover to get to the second curtain wall, once they got through. Then he realized the rams would be too slow in getting there as well.

"Alerio!"

"Yes, Centurion!" Alerio came up and saluted. He had taken to calling Lucius by his rank as was proper in front of the troops.

"Find out which of the Thessalians and Macedonians have mountaineering skills, and equip them with grappling hooks and rope. We may need them once we're on the other side."

"Yes, sir!" Alerio saluted and ran back to check among the men. He returned a short time later with a group of ten men who had shed their scuta and pila in favour of ropes, hooks, gladii and pugii.

"Stay close to me," Lucius told them. When the order comes to breech the walls again, the first of us through will rush across the space between walls and find a weak spot to climb. Got it?"

"What about that double ballista?" Alerio asked. "It's decimating us."

Lucius looked up at the top of the gate where the deadly weapon was being reloaded by a new crew.

"Have the Syrians come up with naptha and fire arrows. We're going to set that thing alight."

It was nearing dusk when the flames from the burning ram died down, and the ballista atop the walls blazed with fresh fire, sending a thick plume of smoke up into the sky.

"Push!" Lucius yelled as the men heaved against the second battering ram, willing it to the walls before reinforcements came to pin them down once again.

Shortly before, Livius had come with word from the attack on the west gate. The ballistas there were larger and more powerful, so much so that they had almost reached the emperor's tribunal, narrowly missing the imperial party but crashing into Caesar's personal bodyguard which had been forming a ring around the emperor, empress and their advisors.

Lucius thought on this devastation as he strained against the battering ram housing, the big wooden wheels bumping along over rock and charred bodies until they picked up more speed. He worried over whether or not they would meet one of those double ballistas on the other side of the gate.

Too late to turn back now! he told himself as they rushed the gate.

"Lean into it, men! Push!!!!"

The battering ram slammed into the blackened gate and the men inside the housing felt the impact in their guts and bones. It took a moment for them to realize that the gate was splintering.

"Heave!" Lucius yelled. "Optio!" he called back to Alerio. "Have the rest of the century form up behind us, we go in together!"

"Yes, sir!"

"Again!" Lucius yelled, pulling back on the arms protruding from the sides of the ram. "Now!" The door cracked and groaned, and with another three thrusts of the ram, it caved. "Axes!" Lucius yelled for men standing by with axes to clear a bigger hole so that troops could pass through.

The sound of chopping seemed unbearably loud in the darkening light, and Lucius feared that it would bring the Parthians down on their heads. As the gap opened up, he hoisted a scutum, grabbed a pilum and strode through the gate first, his men following him.

It was dark on the other side of the outer wall. The distant sounds of battle could be heard, but they seemed oddly muted now by the stretches of burnt crops, irrigation channels, and grasses that lay before them, leading to the inner curtain wall of Hatra.

Something whizzed by Lucius and stuck in the sand to his left. He turned quickly, shield up, just in time to meet two Hatrans running at him with swords raised above their heads.

"Ahh!" Lucius lunged forward to slam his scutum into them before the killing arc of their weapons came down. Then a pilum soared out of the dark from behind him to pin one and then the second. The Romans were now formed up behind Lucius.

"Behind you!" Lucius yelled as a large group of Hatrans charged out of the darkness at the Romans.

Lucius' men spun with skill and met the charge on their scuta. With pila flying overhead, their gladii were unsheathed and the killing came at close quarters.

Lucius strained his ears to see if he could detect the sound of cavalry, but there did not seem to be any. He gazed north west to the distant west gate and could see heavy fighting going on there, fire raging and men screaming in the darkness.

After first century finished the last of their adversaries just within the gate, Lucius sent some men to sweep the guard tower and hold it.

"Send word to Tribune Livius that we've taken the gatehouse but can't hold it for long," he told one of his runners. "The rest of the legion can come through with the battering ram. I'm taking first century across the fields to assess the guard on the inner gate."

292

"Yes, Centurion," the man saluted and disappeared back through the maw of the cracked gate.

Lucius stared north along the road that led from the south gate to the city. It cut like the outline of a dark python, curving away until it ended at the well-lit inner walls of Hatra.

"Centurion, what now?" Alerio asked as he stood beside Lucius, the men formed up again behind them.

"Where are my climbers?" Lucius called.

"Here, sir!" the group of men came and stood to the side, thick ropes and grappling hooks wound about their torsos.

"Good. Stay close. We'll distract them at the gates while you ascend the walls away from the light. Try to take the gate house."

"Yes, sir."

Lucius turned to Alerio. "Now we need to find the chink in Hatra's armour." He looked back at the line of men. In the front rank of first century he could see Argus, Antanelis, Eligius, Garai, Maren and others. They were men he could trust in a fight, and he knew he would not prefer anyone else to be there. He nodded to them all, raised his pilum, and set off across the dark fields.

The sound of prayers and wailing became more distinct as III Parthica approached the high walls where the grim faces of Hatran and Parthian defenders stared down on the charred fields.

Lucius held up his hand and crouched, the men coming to a halt with him.

"How many?" Alerio asked.

"Looks like about fifty men above this gate with more along the walls. Look." He pointed. "You can see the pointed helmets near each of the torches."

"Maybe there are more in the dark?"

"No doubt," Lucius answered, straining his eyes to see. He was sweating profusely, and could taste naught but sweat and dust in his mouth. "They're watching the battering ram coming up behind us."

The two of them looked up at the defenders to see them pointing behind them as the ram was being pushed across up the road to the gate.

"You!" Lucius hissed at one of the climbers. "I want you to take your men across the field and come at the wall about one hundred yards to the right of the gate. As soon as we engage the men at the gates, you start climbing and then make your way to the gatehouse. If you can manage it, open the gate. Understood?"

"Yes, Centurion. We'll do our best," said a burly Thessalian.

"Good. Go now." Lucius watched them disappear into the darkness and then turned to Alerio. "Have the archers approach quietly and line up within bowshot of the gates, on either side of the road. As the ram approaches I want them to start firing."

There was a sudden explosion to the west and Lucius looked to see fire shooting into the sky.

"Must be one of the naptha reserves going up," Alerio said.

"Hopefully it's theirs and not ours. The ram's approaching now. Go get ready."

"May the Gods get us through this, Lucius," Alerio whispered.

"All of us," Lucius said. "Go now."

Alerio went to the archers and got them into position, then he returned to the legionaries.

Lucius divided them on either side of the road to allow the ram to be pushed through. He could see the archers lining up on the top of the walls as he fell in behind the ram with the rest of the troops.

There were more screams from within the city, so much so that the men of III Parthica wondered if the city had already fallen on the other side.

"Archers fire!" Lucius gave the command and the archers sprang up from their crouches to shower the defenders with pointed barbs, bringing several down over the wall to land with sickening thuds on the ground.

Arrows were fired back and a few Romans fell too, but the ram pressed on, faster, gaining momentum on the road that led to the gate, and then an impact that sent Lucius and the rest to the ground.

"Fire!" Alerio yelled, and Lucius looked up to see torches and what could only be pots of naptha being hoisted onto the wall.

"Shoot them!" Lucius called back to the archers, and the sound of snapping bowstrings cut the air, followed by a scream, a crash, and then an explosion of fire on top of the gatehouse.

Liquid fire leached down the walls between the battlements, making the god-made walls of Hatra look like they bled fire in the night.

There was a clang of metal atop the walls and several more defenders came crashing down, one through the roof of the ram housing.

"Heave!" Lucius yelled again. "Hit hard, before they regroup."

The ram slammed into the door once, twice, and then a third time before there were calls in Greek on the other side.

"They're trying to open the gate!" Alerio yelled above the raucous battle that seemed to be closing all around the walls of Hatra as the rest of the legions poured into the various gaps in the outer curtain.

They stopped the ram and the gate shuddered, slightly dislodged, but it eventually began to swing inward.

Lucius slipped through and then Antanelis and the others.

They were brought up short by a row of men and boys lined un on the road before them, the road leading to the centre of the city and the great temple of Bel.

The legionaries lined up before them, their blades pointed at the Hatrans' throats.

It was hard to see their faces, but Lucius could certainly smell their fear in that street. He could hear women weeping in the homes lining the way, and chanting from the various temples about them.

"What are we waiting for?" Lucius heard Argus say, only to be hushed by Alerio.

Lucius stood still for a moment, unable to speak or move, and the men began to look at each other.

"Centurion?" Alerio ventured, but Lucius did not answer.

Beyond the rows of shuddering Hatrans, their skin slick with sweat in the firelight, Lucius felt a cold stab of guilt run down his back. He could see something beyond the people, something tall, and bright as starlight. He stepped forward, entranced, blinded by the silver light that he saw shining in the street beyond, blocking the way to the great temple at the heart of the city.

Do not press on, Metellus... a voice said in Lucius' head. *This is not worthy of you. The Parthians are finished, but this place is sacred and cannot be touched without experiencing the Gods' wroth.*

Apollo? Lucius thought, shaking his head. *How can I stop this, Lord?*

You must. Do you remember Ctesiphon?

Lucius closed his eyes. Of course he remembered. He would never forget, the cries of dying men and women, boys and girls, babies whose skulls were cracked in the streets, on the paving slabs and against the columns of the temples of their gods.

I shall do it, Lord... Lucius thought, bowing and turning back to his men who were crowded into the full width of the street.

He was about to speak when a cornu sounded outside the walls, and then another, and another. Then, from the gate entrance came Livius and the legate Tertullius atop their mounts.

"Hold, III Parthica!" Tertullius commanded. "Hold! Stand down, men of the legions!"

Lucius turned back to see the street was empty beyond, the god having gone back to his heavenly eyrie. When he looked at the Hatrans, they were backing away slowly, heading toward the voices that were shouting behind them.

"Metellus!" Livius said, coming up. "What happened?"

"We were getting ready to...to... Well, sir, we had just made it through the gate when the cornui sounded. What's happened?"

"The west gate and north gates have also fallen," Livius said. We've been ordered to pull back outside the inner curtain wall."

"Why?"

"The emperor has given the Hatrans twenty-four hours to capitulate and accept Roman rule."

Lucius nodded, trying to understand after the intensity of the last two days.

"It's well done, Metellus," the legate slapped Lucius on the shoulder and then turned to lead the way. "We're to stand at attention outside the walls, until the Hatrans give us their decision. Otherwise..."

"Understood, sir," Lucius said, saluting and ordering his men out of the city's inner walls. He turned back to see a young boy standing in a doorway, watching them as they slowly left his city, his street, and his family home alone.

But Lucius was still haunted by the vision of Apollo, and the mention of the horrors at Ctesiphon.

In his head, he heard Apollo speaking of *the temples of many gods and goddesses that must remain standing at all costs...*

The night was long, and the men had trouble bringing themselves back down from their battle frenzy. Fights had broken out among the ranks and Lucius and the other centurions of III Parthica had been forced to slam their vinerods on more than a few backs.

"Are you managing to keep them in line, Metellus?" Livius said as Lucius entered the tribune's tent.

"Yes, sir. I think such an abrupt end to the fighting, and just as they were about to enter the city, has been difficult for them."

"No doubt. They've waited months for this, and stories of Hatra's riches have run rampant among the rank and file." Livius stood and paced the tent. He looked tired, drawn, as they all did.

"Do you think the Hatrans will accept the emperor's terms?" Lucius asked, removing his helmet and wiping his brow.

"I don't know. They'd be fools if they didn't. But these people are of a stubborn nature. Who knows? It would be easier for us if they did. We've lost a lot of men to the fires in this assault."

Lucius thought his patrician tribune seemed to have had enough. Politics was more to Livius' liking, not the cavalry charge, or the smell of battlefield blood and charred flesh.

"There's something I should say, sir... I mean..." Lucius found himself fidgeting with his helmet like a nervous recruit, but the words had already come out of his mouth. "I saw something in the streets of Hatra, sir."

"What?" Livius looked up from his wine cup.

"Well, it's difficult to explain.You might think me mad, but... What if the Gods don't want us to sack Hatra?"

"Why would you say such a thing, Metellus? Mars is obviously on our side, Jupiter too. The city is about to break for us, as much as a nuisance as it's been, they'll give in in the end. What did you see?"

"Well, sir..." Lucius took a deep breath. Apollo had spoken to him, and he had a chance to save those families he had seen defending the city. They had not been Parthian warriors, but rather Hatran citizens defending their home, a city renown for its many temples, not least of which was the great temple of Baal. Lucius looked up and met his tribune's eyes.

"When we were about to charge the people in the street, I saw... I saw... a god appeared in the street, tall and shining in the darkness."

"What?" Livius stood up, his eyes looking differently at Lucius now, not unlike the eyes of his own father that day long ago on the Palatine Hill, a look of trepidation, fear, and a little disdain. "What god?"

Should I say? Or now? Apollo, I would not betray you...

"It was a god. Which, I am not sure, but he seemed to say not to sack the city. That it is sacred to the Gods and that to press on would anger them."

Livius put his hands over his face and breathed deeply, sighing on his last breath.

"You've put me in an awful situation, Metellus. If I dismiss your claim to have seen a god, which I'm inclined to do, and something goes wrong, then I'm to blame. If I take this to the legate, who then takes it to Caesar, then we're all going to end up in chains, or worse, executed for cowardice. Let alone them thinking we're all mad."

Livius paced some more, kicking the sand of his tent floor.

"Are you sure this wasn't your exhaustion from battle? Maybe you thought you heard something? Even I could hear that incessant wailing from the temples."

"There was wailing, and prayers, sir, but that was not what I saw or heard."

"You're sticking to that, are you?" Livius seemed disappointed, but Lucius knew that the Gods' will was more important. He would accept whatever fate Apollo had for him.

"I am, sir."

"Very well. I'll speak to the legate about this. I think he knows the emperor's astrologer. Perhaps he can speak with him."

"Thank you, sir."

"But not a word of what you think you saw to any of the men, not even Argus, Alerio or Antanelis. Understood?"

"Yes, sir."

"Good. Now, go prepare. If the Hatrans don't take the offer, we'll be back at those walls before their morning offerings are burning again.

Lucius stepped out onto the Via Principalis and took a deep breath of the cool pre-dawn air.

He knew he had just put his career on the line, and that it was quite possible that Livius and Tertullius might never trust him again. They might even demote him. But he also knew he had no choice.

Back in his tent, he drank some of his ration and washed his face in the basin of sandy water that he had been reusing for some days. If the siege went on, they would be running out of water again.

Kneeling down in front of the statue of Apollo, Lucius closed his eyes and prayed that he had done the right thing. *I will always trust in you, my Lord. Guide me as always.*

The next day, twenty four hours after the cessation of fighting, the legions assembled in battle order around Hatra, filling the fields between the outer and inner curtain walls. Legionary banners fluttered in the breeze and golden aquileae glinted in the desert sun.

Before the main west gates of Hatra, the emperor and his advisors, surrounded by a legion of Praetorians, sat waiting for the Hatrans' answer.

The siege engines were lined up again, facing the walls, and were now closer to the inner temple complex of the city.

When the cornui rang along the Roman lines, Septimius Severus stood on a newly erected tribunal facing the west gate of Hatra, surrounded by myriad banners fluttering in the morning breeze.

All the troops nearby could see Severus, clad in purple and gold over his military cuirass. Caesar waited, with his young son and the empress on either side of him, waiting, as if he were a judge about to carry out a sentence.

When the chorus of cornui ended, and Rome waited for a response from the Hatrans, there was a flurry of activity atop the tall gatehouse. After a few moments there was a great snap as four ballista bolts launched from the walls to crash into the the ranks of the X Fretensis legion.

Septimius Severus bellowed in anger from his seat and the siege began once again. The legions marched toward the walls beneath the fire of their artillery, battering rams rolling toward the gates which the Hatrans had secretly repaired and reinforced during the night in stealthy determination.

When Lucius heard the call to attack, he hung his head and took a breath.

Forgive me, my lord... he thought. I tried.

"Ballista, iacite!" Lucius gave the order to the artillery with his century and the firing began again on the south gate where only the night before he had broken through to look the Hatrans in the eyes.

The screams and the prayers within the city walls began anew as Rome's legions, led by the III Gallica, X Fretensis, IV Scythica, and VI Ferrata, began to claw at the stubborn stone and wood of the city.

The siege upon Hatra's inner walls went on for another twenty bloody, failed days. Temples and homes within the city burned around the desperate populace. Outside the walls, Romans fell time and again as they tried to scale or batter the walls, only to be burned alive by the seemingly inexhaustible supply of naptha the city possessed.

Both sides suffered in the heat of the desert summer, and the troops grew closer to mutiny than ever. Men were desperate, and desertion became more and more of a problem as those tired of futile fighting decided to brave the journey west to the sea on their own rather than fight beneath the unbreakable walls of Hatra one day longer.

Still the smoke of offerings from the great temples, especially of Baal, at the heart of the city rose into the sky, constant and unwavering.

Lucius stood, leaning against the inside of the outer wall, gazing at the plumes of smoke rising from Hatra after a particularly gruelling assault upon the walls in which he had broken a rib, and several of his men, including Alerio and Argus, had been taken from the field with serious injuries.

He breathed in and out, his mind dazed and rattled, his men laying all about him, resting while other legions took up the tragic pursuit.

"The emperor is mad, Lucius," Antanelis whispered to him as he came to lean beside him. "Why are we doing this? It's obvious the Gods don't want this city to be taken, don't you think?"

"It doesn't matter what I think, Antanelis, or what you think. We follow orders."

"I know, but this is madness. How many more men are we going to execute for desertion? This is the last stronghold, and there aren't even many Parthians inside the walls!"

"Quiet," Lucius said, his eyes going to the approaching form of Tribune Livius.

Men lying on the ground rose hurriedly to salute their tribune as he passed, and Lucius stepped forward, his helmet beneath his arm, his face black and sweaty.

"Sir!" Lucius saluted.

"Leave us," Livius said to Antanelis and the other men about them. When they were alone, he turned to Lucius. "That was not an easy attack, Metellus. I know you tried."

"Yes, sir. They won't give up, the Hatrans that is." He looked at his tribune who would not meet his eye for a few moments.

Livius looked tired and unshaved, His once-flawless and clean cuirass and cloak were now dirty and torn, the hems of his broad-striped tunic stained with blood and ash.

"Sir, did you tell the legate about what I reported in the streets of the city nearly a month ago?"

Livius looked up and his hand reached out to grab Lucius leather harness. "Careful, Metellus! I risked a lot telling them that. And yes, of course I said it!"

Lucius did not remove the tribune's hands, but continued to stare at the man. He had grown in confidence and strength and had come into his own as first centurion of the legion. He and his men were no longer green recruits to be cowed by anyone, though they still respected the order of things and Disciplina above all.

"Truth is, Metellus..." Livius let go and leaned against the wall with Lucius. "The emperor knew some time ago, after the legate passed on what I learned from you, though he didn't mention your name specifically. I said that some of the men saw what you saw..."

"So what was the hold-up? They thought we were mad, sir?"

"No. The emperor found out from the legate, but the empress did not know."

"The empress?" Lucius said, confused.

"Yes, she apparently saw the import of what you told me, and the imperial astrologer confirmed it. Her father was high priest of Baal in Antioch for some years."

"So what does this mean?" Lucius asked, his voice cut off by the loud sounding of cornui around the walls of Hatra.

305

Livius looked up and his eyes closed, water dripping down his dirty face as he lifted his head to the sky.

Lucius could not tell whether it was tears or sweat upon Livius' face. "Sir? Tribune?"

"It means, Lucius Metellus Anguis, man spoken to by the Gods...that we are abandoning the siege of Hatra. The war is over."

Part III

Alexandria

A.D. 199

XI

Urbs Alexandri

'The City of Alexander'

The provinces of Mesopotamia and Osrhoene were now annexed and garrisoned with veterans of the Parthian campaign. The lands between the Tigris and Euphrates rivers were now bristling with Roman swords, left behind by Emperor Septimius Severus, conqueror of Parthia.

As the emperor's legions marched south-west to Caesaraea, the memory of Hatra began to fade in the minds of every general, officer, and soldier. Though some whispered that Hatra was a defeat to be swept away, others claimed the Gods had been pleased. It was a small consolation that with Hatra surrounded, anyone, Parthian, Hatran, or others who might try getting in or out of the city, would not get far.

Inside the city, the Gods protected the Hatrans, but outside of those circular walls was the land of men, and of battle.

In Caesaraea, the emperor stopped for a month to tend to affairs of state, but more so to ensure that his power and presence were secure. Gaius Fulvius Plautianus, the emperor's kinsman from Leptis Magna, and Praetorian Prefect, had sent word from Rome that all was well, despite the usual Republican grumblings in the Senate.

Septimius Severus trusted his kinsman well, and so focussed on the task of winning back the troops he had almost lost to mutiny and desperation. He raised the pay for troops of all ranks, and offered promotions wherever he wished, ignoring much of the usual military cursus.

It seemed to work, and word from the officers of the legions was that the men were happy and healing, content to bide their time in drills, light patrols, and gambling by the sea. The furnace of the desert was forgotten except for in the nightmares that racked their slumber at night.

"Well look who's come to pay us a visit!" Argus said from where he scrubbed a blackened pot beside the contubernium's tent. "Salute!" he stood and snapped a salute to Lucius, dripping with the sarcasm Lucius had learned to ignore when they were among close friends.

"Good to see you too, Argus," Lucius answered, as he sat down next to Alerio on a dried out log before their tent.

"What news, Centurion?" Eligius asked as he took a blade to the beard that sprouted from his face.

"We're leaving in a week," Lucius said, drinking from a cup of water that Antanelis handed him. "South."

"Where?" Maren asked.

"Alexandria."

The men did not speak at first, but then they burst out laughing joyously.

"Oh ho! Lucius, that's the first good news you've brought us in a long time!" Argus slapped him on the back and sat down beside him.

"I guess you've heard they have a lot of whores and taverns there?" Lucius said.

"Some of the older veterans have told us they have a lot of everything there!" Garai exclaimed, raising his hands in mock prayer to the heavens.

Lucius laughed, realizing that with the burden of his command, and all of the duties it entailed, he had missed some lighthearted talk.

"Patrols and drills won't stop over the winter," he warned, "but you'll all have frequent chances to go into the city."

"Didn't Diodorus tell you a lot about Alexandria, Lucius?" Argus recalled, rubbing his chin.

"He did," Lucius replied, enjoying Argus' good humour.

"What did he say?" Antanelis asked.

"Well, it's about as big as Rome, but cleaner, richer. It was designed by Alexander himself, and the Pharos towers over it, seen from fifty miles out to sea. It's the busiest port in the Empire, so we should be able to find anything we want."

"Come on, Lucius. I heard you say more than that before," Argus said. "Tell us the good stuff, not history!"

"The Alexandrians are a lot less conservative than us Romans. Anything goes in that city, apparently. Their parties are legendary, filled with men, women, boys, girls, eunuchs and more."

Lucius realized the thought of all those crazy symposia did not really appeal to him, but from the look on his friends' faces, he had struck a chord.

"If you show the tribune that you are working just as hard as during the campaign, I'm sure I can swing us some extra time in the city now and again."

"Oh, don't worry," Garai said. "For some sweet Alexandrian cunny, right now we'd build an iron road all the way to Hades and back!"

They all laughed.

"I thought you preferred hairy Alexandrian balls!" joked his brother.

"Well, I prefer cunny, but if hairy balls is all they've got on offer, that'd have to do," Garai roared. "I'm tired of my hands!"

"All right, all right," Lucius said, standing up. "Well, work hard, obey orders," he raised his eyebrow, "and I'm sure you'll have your fill of both, plus some things you haven't seen before."

Garai looked perplexed, and the others laughed at him again.

Lucius smiled and turned to go back to his tent, their laughter behind him uplifting and welcome.

Perhaps things are changing for the better? he thought.

Aegyptus was, in truth, an ancient land that had mesmerized Lucius from a young age. As they marched along the coast, he revisited those lessons in which Diodorus had told him all about the glorious city of Alexander.

Even before the legions set foot in the province of Aegyptus, Lucius' imagination had run wild, so eager was he to see the wonders of that land with his own eyes - the giant temples to strange exotic gods, the colossal monuments that reached to the heavens, the Nile, and the desert to the west that had been created when Phaethon's chariot had scorched the earth.

The sun was beginning to dip when Lucius saw the Nile delta for the first time, glittering in the distance, and beyond it, the beacon of the Pharos, the great lighthouse of Alexandria which guided ships from all over the world into the harbour of the city.

As the legions approached from the East, ferrying themselves across the waters to the other side, Lucius' eyes stayed on the Pharos. He recalled Diodoros' lessons precisely, how the city was built by Alexander, but the lighthouse was completed by Ptolemy II, the son of Alexander's general. The Pharos itself was composed of three levels - a square base, an octagonal second story, and finally, a round tower at the summit which contained the blazing beacon fire that was reflected out into the world by a massive bronze mirror.

It was just one of the things that Lucius wanted to see desperately. The other was Alexander's tomb, which was said to lie along the Canopic Way, the main thoroughfare of Alexandria.

Aegyptus had been one of the final realms to be annexed by Rome, making it the Empire's primary source of grain until the rise of the African provinces. In its day, Alexandria had been a thriving, cosmopolitan city displaying great wealth, beautiful buildings, and a harbour in which every ship was fully laden. It had been a centre of learning for centuries, and contained a magnificent library. Unfortunately, when Gaius Julius Caesar had come to the country, the library ended up burning in a fire that started during a siege. Only a portion of the collection remained, but even this was larger than anything in Rome. It pained Lucius to think of it.

Lucius remembered from his lessons that the city was Greek in style, and had been erected on the seaside in a grid formation, the plan designed by Alexander himself, with the streets intersecting at right angles. The Canopic Way was unusually wide, flanked by splendid monuments, temples, and colonnaded villas built in marble, white limestone, and red granite. Down the centre of the street, stretching from the Canopian Gate on the east side of the city, to the Moon Gate on the west side, there were numerous pools of fresh water that were constantly fed by underground canals running from the neighbouring Lake Mareotis to the south. Most of the buildings had private access to these subterranean canals.

When Rome's forces arrived outside the city, the Alexandrians came out to greet him with much ceremony. As the emperor and empress were welcomed by the city magistrates, the legions were ordered to make camp on the north end of the Eleusis Plain, beyond the east gate, and beside the sea.

Lucius could feel the anticipation in his men, not least because it required him to push them harder to finish the simplest of tasks. He understood, he was distracted himself. He too wanted to explore the city, but they had work to do as well - many requests for road work from the legions had been submitted by the city officials when they found out the emperor was coming with such a large force.

"But don't worry," Lucius told his men after inspection on their first morning waking up with the sound of crashing waves and a gentle salt-sea breeze beneath their tent flaps. "We're going to be given leave in shifts to go into Alexandria and experience it for ourselves."

The men cheered and slapped each other on the backs, each one of them forming an image of the activities he preferred, activities which, if Lucius was honest, he probably did not want to know about. But he knew that after such a long campaign, the sights, smells, and life of a bustling, rich metropolis were gifts from the Gods.

"You're to go into the city, out of uniform, unarmed," Lucius told them. "Punishment for disregarding this order will carry serious consequences. You'll go three contubernia at a time, understood?"

"Yes, sir!" some of the men shouted.

"I don't know how long we'll be in Alexandria, but it should be for some time. So don't harass the locals and bring down a load of complaints on our heads."

The men cheered again. It had been a long time since Lucius had seen them smile so much.

The merchants of Alexandria rubbed their hands at Rome's approach, the tabernae doubled or tripled their stocks of wine and beer, and every brothel, large and small, from the Draco River to the Grove of Nemesis had its array of women, girls, men, and boys, washed and oiled in preparation.

It was common knowledge that the men of the legions had had little chance to spend their hard-earned denarii, and there were plenty of Alexandrians who were prepared to relieve them of the weight.

During their second week outside the walls of the city, III Parthica's turn to go into the city finally came. It seemed an eternity to Lucius and the others since he had told them about going into the city. They were a junior legion, so naturally it fell to them to go as one of the last.

"All the whores will be dirty again," Argus groaned to Maren as they stood in their plain tunics outside of the camp, waiting for Lucius who was taking care of some last-minute items.

"Here he is," Alerio said as Lucius came out of the main gate wearing a light crimson cloak and white linen tunic.

"Ready!" Lucius said, clapping his hands.

"Finally!" Argus said. "I mean, lead on, Primus Pilus, to the pleasures of Alexandria."

Lucius laughed. "Let's go then!"

He led his three contubernia among the rows of camps until they passed the Temple of Ceres and Proserpina, just outside the Canopian Gate. At the gate, he showed his papers to the guards, including a few Praetorians who had been posted there. The men waved them through.

Immediately, when they reached the other side of the gate, there was a rush of cheering and roars. To their right, the walls of Alexandria's hippodrome rose out of the sand and paving slabs. Its alcoves were full of vendors plying their wares, and whores doing the same thing.

"Bloody hell!" Maren laughed, pointing at a legionary thrusting himself into one of the whores in plain view of everyone. "Slow down, brother! We're here for a while!" he yelled, howling with laughter along with some of the others in the century.

"This looks like my kind of place!" Argus clapped his hands and stared at the rows of women lined up along a wall beside the hippodrome. "Anyone for the chariot races?" he laughed, veering off. "Centurion, I'm off!" Argus called over his shoulder.

Lucius waved him away and kept walking. "Idiot," he said to Alerio. "Those whores will be dirty and quadruple the price."

"Aye. I'm afraid you're right," Alerio answered. "He'll get crabs for his tourist-priced cunny."

"As long as he can still march and fight, I guess." Lucius said. He looked back and they had already lost most of the men of the three contubernia. "Don't let me hold you both back if you want to find some fun," Lucius said.

"Oh, I do," said Antanelis, but I think my afternoon would be spent with someone cleaner. Someone told me the Via Corpriae has some decent brothels. I'll walk with you as far as-"

He stopped speaking as they stepped onto the main stretch of the Canopic Way to take in the sense-tickling atmosphere of Alexandria's most famous street.

The city greeted them and pulled them into its welcoming arms.

It was evident from the outset that Alexandria was the centre of the world for merchants from every corner of the Empire and beyond. It was at the crossroads of the Empire, Africa, and Asia, and everything from grain, oils, and papyrus, to poisons, spices, incense, ivory, and precious gems passed through merchants' stalls or were loaded onto ships that awaited their cargoes in one of the massive harbours.

Alongside haggling merchants and shopkeepers mingled wealthy citizens who shopped with their slaves, conversed on the steps of the numerous temples, or simply lounged outside

316

high-priced inns along the road. It seemed to Lucius that thousands of ornate litters milled about the bustling streets, back and forth, their colourful silk trappings fluttering in the warm sea breeze that was channeled down through the streets that met the sea at ninety degrees.

Groups of anywhere from four to eight slaves carried the luxurious, strongly-scented, transports on their shoulders, the higher the better the view for the occupant within. Many of the litter-bearers appeared to be either gladiators or bodyguards, armed and, as a result of their professions, very strongly built. Other carriers were tall, slender Nubian slaves from the south, whose stature put their owners above the crowds where everyone could see them. These litter bearers plodded about in a smooth rhythmic dance up and down the golden streets, the weight of tiny perfumed mistresses, or fat oily merchants upon their glistening backs.

Lucius, Antanelis, and Alerio walked about in a mixed state of awe and excitement at the new world around them. Alexandria was a playground for the rich and pleasure-seeking people of the world. They strolled around the streets going into various shops where weapons of every nation seemed to be for sale. Some were recent, shoddily made copies of Roman and Parthian arms, but others, such as the numerous swords, were expertly crafted with intricate inlays, carvings, and gems set in either gold, silver, or bronze. Antanelis bought a Scythian-made blade which he wore proudly at his side, making sure the sun shone off of it at all times.

"Just make sure you put it away soon," Lucius told him, not wanting to disparage his purchase. "We're not supposed to be carrying weapons."

"Just a tourist trinket, sir," Antanelis said, winking.

Lucius didn't tell him that he had his own pugio concealed within his tunic. Since the day he had been made centurion, he had not let it out of his sight.

The three friends ate a large meal at a taberna along the Canopic Way before Antanelis told them he was leaving for the brothels.

"My friends," he said, smiling broadly, sweat glistening on his scarred brow. "The Via Corpiae beckons, I think. How about you both join me? I see a lot of nice looking women around." He sighed. "Might be we'll find our own personal Venus in that street."

"Not me, Antanelis," Lucius said. "There are some things I want to see first."

"Haven't we seen so much already? What about a bronze-skinned beauty to massage the knots from your muscles? Com'on, Lucius!"

Lucius thought about it for a few moments. The thought was appealing. He had not been with a woman in a long time, but he felt compelled to get to know the city first, before laying down with it.

"You go ahead. Enjoy. I'll see you back at the Canopic Gate in a few hours."

"Suit yourself," Antanelis said. "Alerio? How about it?"

"Sorry, Lucius," Alerio said, "but I feel like I'm carrying two melons between my legs. Finding a dark beauty to help me with that is something I can't turn away from."

Lucius laughed. "Ok, you two whoremongers," he joked. "Go, get fucked, and then you can get some culture!"

"I rather thought we were!" Antanelis said. "I'm getting to know the locals!"

The two men went south down the Via Argeus and Lucius stood there watching them, a smile on his face, and a hint of jealousy in his heart.

He continued his walk, tall among the milling people on the Canopic Way. He could feel eyes on him, and cursed himself a little for looking so very Roman. He made his way past the temples of Saturn and of Isis Plusia on his right, and from there he could see the tall outlines of the imperial palace built by Hadrian, looking onto the sea from above the seats of the terraced theatre and obelisks.

From the number of Praetorians along those streets, he figured that the emperor and empress were in that residence. One of the Praetorians nodded to him, and Lucius nodded back before walking further along until he came to the Library of Alexandria which looked out over the agora.

The columns of the library rose up above the street at the top of some broad steps. It was a temple-like structure, a place to honour the works of men, as much as the Gods or Muses.

If ever you get to Alexandria, young Lucius, you must go to the library and see its wonders, Diodoros used to say to him.

Lucius remembered his old tutor speaking to him about this wondrous place which held, it was said, every written work created by men. Since the fire that occurred during the siege when Caesar was defending Alexandria, the scholars of the great library had gone back out into the world to attempt to gather copies of those famous works they had lost. Of course, no one knew if they had succeeded or not. In fact, many of the scholars never returned from Bactria and beyond.

Still, there were indeed wonders to be seen and read within those hallowed walls, and Lucius promised himself he would come back. He also remembered Diodoros mentioning his old friend Aelius Galenus, and that if ever Lucius made it to Alexandria, he should ask after Galenus, who was, Diodoros swore, drawn to the great library like a moth to flame.

Time enough for that later, Lucius told himself as he pushed on through the crowd and into the agora to his right.

Beneath the shade of monstrous palm trees that swayed to and fro in the sea's breeze, there were hundreds of traders selling everything from chickens and rabbits to elephants and lions. The noise was almost as loud as the roars from the hippodrome.

Men gathered in bunches, haggling over the price of this peacock, or that giraffe. It was a sight that Lucius had not seen before. So many exotic animals from every corner of the earth, herded together in pens or cages, waiting to be sold to provide entertainment in the amphitheatres, or to adorn the tables and pleasure gardens of the rich whose villas lined the canal of Alexandria all the way to the Nile Delta.

In one corner of the market there was a large crowd of men gathered in a circle beside which was a merchant standing on a platform, taking bids for whatever it was that was within the large pen. As he made his way over, pushing through the tightly-packed bodies, Lucius noticed that he was in the middle of a horse auction. In the large, round enclosure there were a couple dozen Arabian horses.

Lucius' breath caught in his chest. They were beautiful, the most spirited, and strong-looking horses he had ever seen. They were mostly pure white, or rich black, though there were some dappled mounts. Lucius stared at the beasts in awe for a time, thinking what it would be like to lead cavalry in battle, just as Alexander did. The sense of speed and power would be overwhelming, and hugely effective. He thought back on the Parthian cavalry charges that had so terrified his men only months before in the attack on Ctesiphon.

"You like them?" asked an old man beside him, in Greek.

"They must be as fast as the winds," Lucius said.

"You are officer?"

"Yes, but not with a horse."

"Hmm. Too sad. They are wonderful, loyal animals," the man said, shaking his head and eyeing Lucius' pouch at his belt.

Lucius nodded politely and went away, his fist holding onto his pouch.

As he walked away, he knew he would be back, many times.

For now, he walked along the sea wall until he came to the heptastadion that led across the bay between the two harbours, to the island of Pharos where the lighthouse of Alexandria rose up into the sky.

The breeze was fresh, reviving, as if sent by the Gods themselves. It whipped in warm waves about him, as he approached the fort on the other side, and the temple of Isis Phariae. On the shore near the temple, Lucius found a spot where he could look out up at the lighthouse and the city of Alexandria where it lay stretched out along the shore.

He breathed deeply of the salt sea air, enjoying the rhythm of the waves as they crashed mutely in the distance on the other side of Pharos island.

"I finally made it, Diodoros," Lucius said. "Apollo has guided me here at last."

It seemed to Lucius that every man he led into the city that day returned lighter, ridiculous smiles spanning their red faces.

"Gods, what a city!" Argus said, hugging Lucius when he saw him. "You have to come with us next time."

"So, it was good?" Lucius said, knowing the answer.

"Was it good, boys?" Argus said to the group.

"Yes, sir!" they all roared.

Antanelis and Alerio were the last to arrive at the meeting place near the hippodrome.

"This lateness won't be tolerated, Optio!" Lucius said, unable to hold back the smile that cracked his face. "What's the meaning of this?"

"Sir," Alerio answered, "I had to rescue legionary Antanelis here from an overly-attentive whore."

There were catcalls from the rest of the legionaries behind Lucius.

"Don't call her that!" Antanelis said, puffing out his chest and bumping Alerio playfully.

"I think he's in love, sir," Alerio said, still looking at Lucius, and smiling himself.

"Is this true, legionary Antanelis?"

"Yes, sir. It's true. A beautiful barbarian woman from Germania, with corn-gold hair and the body of a goddess." He pretended to faint and Alerio caught him and slapped him across the face.

"Good you survived the German invasion, trooper," Lucius said. "I guess whenever we're looking for you, that's where we'll start."

"Yes, sir!" Antanelis said loudly and at attention.

Lucius chuckled along with all the others. "All right then. Enough joking. We'll be back in the city soon enough. For now, you have duties first thing in the morning, so we need to get back to camp."

There was a collective sigh of disappointment, but Lucius ignored it and strode to the front of the column as they filed out of the Canopian Gate, across the Eleusis Plain and back to III Parthica's camp.

The legions settled into an Alexandrian routine after several weeks, and though it took much cajoling and whacks with the centurions' vinerods, the troops eventually settled, having found an outlet for their passions for gaming and circuses, women and boys, in the streets and establishments of this most cosmopolitan of cities in the Empire.

The legions were put to work, and new roads began to stretch in every direction across Aegyptus from Alexandria. City walls were reinforced, and new canals were dug or deepened.

With the emperor in residence, the city's harbours were at full capacity and the main agora and other markets were bursting at the seams with choice goods from around the world.

The troops also continued to drill through the winter months and into the spring and summer. They were still a long way from home and there was talk of activity to the south, though nothing ever materialized.

Lucius had taken to walking the streets of Alexandria in his off-duty time, marvelling at the ornate temples of Serapis, and Isis, Bendis and others. He had not lost his tourist's curiosity and enjoyed the new discoveries around every corner. However, he spent most of his time alone, as his friends wished only to frequent the brothels.

At the beginning of his forays into the city, he made his way directly to the tomb of Alexander the Great, which he had been hoping to see for a long time. Diodoros had, of course, told him all about it, and he wished to go and make an offering at the tomb of the young Greek king who had inspired his early years.

"Think about it, Argus," Lucius told his friend. "Alexander was just about our age when he delivered his first crushing defeats on the Persians. He built an empire bigger than Rome's, and which was the envy of Caesar himself. And he's buried right here!"

"Come off it, Lucius," Argus said, yawning. "You can't honestly say you prefer to see some dead king rather than dip your spear in some soft, warm Alexandrian cunny."

"I've already done that, and it was nice, Argus, but there's more to life than fornicating with whores."

"Not as I see it. These have been the best weeks of my life!" Argus said. "I'd be happy staying here in Aegyptus. Who needs Rome?"

"Rome is home, Argus. Don't you want to go back there some day?"

"No. I don't."

"Well, I do. So, I'm going to go and see what I can while we're here. I'll see you later at *The Barge* on the Canopic Way, all right?"

"Yes," Argus said. "I'll have the drinks waiting for you!" He slapped Lucius on the back. "Go on, enjoy your history lesson with the dead."

Lucius smiled half-heartedly and turned to leave, his red cloak wrapped about his white tunic with the thin purple stripe on the hems. He made his way among the camps along the familiar path of his choosing and into the Sema quarter of the city, along the Canopic Way where Alexander's tomb was located.

He had waited to visit the tomb until he had a good amount of time in which to do so. His heart raced as he approached the building, its pediment higher than all the buildings around it, the gilded image of Alexander atop his famous horse, Bucephalus, leaping out of the pediment supported by eight Corinthian columns made of white Parian marble.

Lucius carried with him an ornate Parthian dagger which he had taken from the body of a warrior who had nearly killed him as an offering to the spirit of Alexander. He had carefully cleaned and wrapped it in white linen, and carried it ceremoniously in both hands.

Gods, thank you for bringing me here... Lucius thought as he began mounting the steps, imagining the body of the conqueror inside, lying in silent state for hundreds of years thanks to the skill of the Egyptian embalmers.

The Alexandrians had taken care of their pharaoh, preserved his remains and built a house suited to holding them.

Lucius looked up at the great golden doors and proceeded.

"Hold there!" a harsh voice cut into his reverie. "No admittance!"

Lucius stopped dead and looked up to see four Praetorians standing before the doors which, he had not noticed, were locked shut with a chain.

"Good day, brothers," Lucius said collegially. "I was hoping to visit the tomb today while I'm off duty."

"Tomb's closed, soldier," the optio among them said, the orb of his hastile staff reflecting the blinding sunlight onto his face so that his green eyes seemed pale and translucent.

"What? Why? This can't be? I heard that the emperor visited the tomb with the empress and their son. How can it be closed?"

"The emperor ordered it closed yesterday before sailing up the Nile."

"Why?" Lucius could not believe it.

"It's not for us to question, soldier," the man said. "You should know that by now."

"I'm Primus Pilus of III Parthica legion, Lucius Metellus Anguis, and I'm no mere soldier."

"You hear that, boys? Junior here is a fucking primus pilus of that legion of Greek virgins," the optio laughed, then moved closer to Lucius, his voice more menacing. "Look here then, pussy foot. You may be a centurion, but we take our orders direct from the emperor himself, so why don't you shove off and let us get on with our conversation?"

Lucius looked at the four of them, then the chain on the doors to the mausoleum, and knew there was no way he was getting inside.

He tried to ignore the laughter at his back as he walked back down the steps and disappeared into the crowds heading to the public gardens and the theatre. He stopped and sat on the ledge of one of the public fountains and looked out to the sea, beyond the Macedonian acropolis.

It drove him mad, the thought that once he left Alexandria, he would probably never return there. He remembered Diodorus telling him that oftentimes, when one was in need of an answer, the best thing was to sit and watch the world go by. Lucius did just that, as he watched women in glittering jewels and rustling fabrics parade by with their slaves following them. He watched off-duty troopers swerve their way down the streets, and the rich merchants avoiding them as if their mere proximity would reduce their vast wealth.

"Fucking bastards!" Lucius suddenly burst out, causing many people's heads to turn in surprise. Lucius bent over and put his head in his hands. The sweat on his head felt cold all of a sudden as a cool breeze whipped around him. The sounds of the city were all too loud then, and he began to think of home, of Rome, or of the peace of the Metellus family estate in Etruria.

Is this all there is to this city? he wondered. *Stinking crowds of people selling trinkets, whores, and hawkers, and bum-boys in alleyways?*

"You all right, Lucius?"

Lucius looked up and saw Argus standing above him.

"What are you doing here?" Lucius asked.

"Well, I came after you to see the tomb, but when I saw it was closed by Severus, I came looking for you. You can't just sit here and turn purple in the face."

Lucius stood in front of Argus and looked him in the eyes.

Argus stared back and smiled. "Can't leave you alone among all these Gypos, can I?"

"I'm glad you came back," Lucius said, slapping Argus playfully across the head. "So, early drinking?"

"Better. I met one of the guys from third century. Seems his Greek dad does some kind of business in Alexandria, supplying oil to the brothels. Anyway, he told me that there is this place along the Fluvius Novus that puts on the best orgies."

"Come on, Argus -"

"No, wait!" Argus pressed. This is supposed to be a key establishment. High quality, and clean. And only by invitation."

"So, we can't go then, can we?"

"Well, we are, you see? The guy from third century said he could get us in."

"I don't know. We've got drills and some building duty tomorrow around the temple beyond the Eleusinian complex."

"Come on, Lucius. You really could use a good screw with one of the local girls. Word is, they'll let you do anything."

"Great," Lucius mocked, wondering what kind of disease he might pick up at this event.

"Fine then. I tried. You boring shit! Next time I won't -"

"All right, I'll come!" Lucius barked. "Lead the way. I've got nothing better to do."

"That's my boy!" Argus laughed as he led him past the temple of Saturn. "You're in for a night of wine and women and whatever else you want!'

Lucius let himself be led away, Argus pushing through the crowds as they went, past the dicosterium and down the Via Argeus until the came to the line of the Fluvius Novus, the canal of Alexandria.

Small groups of men, and some heterai, walked along the water, already tipsy from their drinking, making their way to various villas that lay along the water, sprawling, gaudy, and decorated, waiting to welcome their guests inside, between the fiery torches flanking their doorways.

Large bodyguards stood by everywhere, checking names and invitations to some of the parties.

Argus looked for the house with a Sphinx above the door. "There it is!" he said, pointing and leading Lucius that way, the coins in his leather pouch jingling as they went to join a small queue of other legionaries and merchants.

The bodyguards, two massive eunuchs, checked people's names and nodded some of them through. Others were pushed to the side when it was discovered that they were not supposed to be there. One legionary tried pushing his way into the house, but was knocked unconscious with one blow from a guard, his body laid down along the wall to the left of the door.

As Argus approached the two guards, he spoke up. "Centurion Lucius Metellus Anguis, and I am Argus. We've been invited."

"By whom?" one of the men said in Greek.

"It's all right, Nuba," said a man from inside the doors. "I invited them." A legionary in a plain tunic approached the door waving Lucius and Argus through. "Glad you could make it!"

"Us too!" Argus said. "Who else is here?"

"I found Maren and Eligius earlier," the man said. "They're inside now, along with Garai."

"Good. Thanks," Argus said, pushing past the man who watched them pass and blend in with the crowd. "Now this is living!" Argus said as he stopped in the atrium and stared out at the party.

The air was think with the smell of incense, sweat, and roasted meats. Men and women's laughter echoed off walls on which were frescoes of forest scenes which including Nyads and Dryads being pursued and abused by Satyrs who strutted around with engorged phalluses.

"What did I tell you?" Argus elbowed Lucius.

Lucius' eyes scanned the atrium which led onto a peristyle garden dense with foliage. A splash of water could be heard in several areas, and everywhere he looked, Lucius spotted a head, a back, a pair of breasts, or thrusting hips as pairs or groups of people coupled in the hidden, and not so hidden, recesses of the expansive villa.

A slave approached Lucius and Argus and placed laurel crowns upon their heads, while another offered them cups of honey-coloured wine. Argus drained his cup right away and took another.

"Right then! Where to start?" He licked his lips and looked around the room for anyone who was alone, or anyone he knew. "Let's move through to the farther rooms," he said pressing on.

Lucius followed slowly, his eyes ranging over the people in coitus. One women winked at him as he passed her and her partner whose head was between her legs, with yet another thrusting into him.

Lucius carried on. He had never seen such things in Rome. He could feel the wine, his second cup now, leaching into his veins, numbing him. Then again, it could have been the thick smoke of whatever incense they were burning in great braziers set throughout the house. He wondered where the host was, but then again, he realized that this was probably not a dwelling where anyone of consequence lived. This was a business, lived in only by the slaves and whores who worked the rooms. Even the Great Lupanar of Pompeii would have paled next to this.

Flute girls pranced by him, their legs kicking up, their bodies barely covered by the loose chitons which they wore. One ran her hand along his arm as she passed and beckoned him along.

She was pretty, he had to admit, about his age perhaps. He hoped she had not been with anyone yet that night, for he did not relish catching anything like many of his men whose duties had been hindered until he had slapped them across the backs with his vinerod.

"Hail, Centurion Metellus!" a voice suddenly called from the back of the garden.

Lucius looked to see Maren with two girls on him, his face flushed and excited, his black hair wet and oily. Lucius nodded and continued on after the flute girl. His heart raced as his feet shuffled across the mosaic floor, its swirling geometric patterns swimming before his eyes. He passed into a second garden, this one even bigger than the last. The sound of the flutes drew him in, soft and punctuated by excited bursts of energy. Orange flames from more braziers danced on the frescoed walls, lighting images of gods and goddesses making love on green slopes beneath high-columned temples.

The music suddenly stopped and a hand grabbled Lucius' arm. Instinctively, his hand went to the concealed dagger beneath his tunic, but he froze when the wide brown eyes stared up at him, flirting, and yet a little fearful.

"Forgive me," he said, letting his hand fall away as the flute girl pulled him into a secluded spot beneath a full jasmine bush.

"This is a night for relaxing, Roman," she said, a smile spreading across her tanned face. Her hands moved up and down his torso, as if she were getting the lay of the land before going on campaign.

Lucius looked at her, small as she was, like a forest nymph, or a deer, delicate, with soft, straight black hair, small shoulders, and tiny pert breasts. He felt himself stirring quickly and she looked up at him, smiling again, yet not so innocently.

"I heard someone say you are a first centurion," she said. "Is your spear ready?"

Lucius wanted to laugh, but he could not. He was enjoying looking at her, touching her unabashedly as she placed his hands on her breasts, buttocks, and pubus.

The girl moaned as she moved over his body, her tongue flicking in and out at his sensitive spots, his clothes falling away unnoticed. She smelled of clove, and the scent entered into his senses with ease. She was behind him, stroking him slowly, softly.

Lucius groaned and then turned quickly to pick her up off the ground and kiss her breasts and her soft mouth. In the background he heard a giggle, but he did not look, so enjoyable was the encounter. Then he felt a second pair of arms wrap about him from behind, and a tongue licking at his back.

"Save some for me, little nymph," said a slightly older girl's voice.

Lucius let the first girl down and looked to see a Nubian woman, her body sleek and oiled, glistening beautifully in the firelight.

"Don't worry, I won't hurt you, soldier," she smiled, her full lips pressing against his mouth with welcome intensity.

Together, the two pulled Lucius down on a wide bench that was there, taking turns kissing his mouth and other parts of his body, then each other while he stroked and caressed and explored their private places, making them groan, and smile, and giggle.

Lucius did not know how long he was there, but after a while, all three of them were moving in erotic concert, reaching a crescendo of pleasure until the unimaginable release.

Lucius lay there with the two of them, sweaty and breathing heavily, the cool night air from the open roof wafting downward to prickle their skin.

"How long must we wait for you?" the younger one said to Lucius, kissing him on the mouth and neck.

"We must do that again," said the Nubian, her hands rubbing him, ascertaining his willingness. "Seems like it could be soon," she said to her friend.

Lucius smiled. "Oh, daughters of Venus, I wish I'd met you sooner," he said, laughing and feeling lighter of heart than he had in a long while.

"There you are!" A harsh voice broke into their private space and Lucius looked up to see Argus standing there with Garai behind him. "Lucius, you can't keep them all for yourself, you greedy bastard!" Argus laughed and pulled his tunic from his body.

"There are plenty more, Argus. Leave me alone."

"It's not you I want, but that little one. She winked at me as she passed with her pipe, and I've been looking for her. Is she nice and wet now?" He reached out a dirty hand to grab the girl's arm and pulled her away from Lucius.

The latter stood up quickly, one hand still on the girl. He was naked, but it did not stop him. "Get your hands off her, Argus. You're drunk."

"Of course I'm drunk, moron. You're supposed to be." And with that, he pushed Lucius back into the jasmine bush so that Lucius and the Nubian fell into the thicket, the branches tearing at their naked bodies. Then Argus turned the young girl around and inserted himself from behind.

The girl cried out and the sound shattered Lucius' sanity. He extricated himself from the jasmine bush and rushed Argus.

The girl fell aside, onto her hands and knees.

"Get out of here!" Lucius raged, but Argus swung first and landed a blow across Lucius' jaw.

Lucius reeled but came back, catching Argus' leg as he was kicking, and then kneed him in the groin.

Argus fell to the ground in agony.

"You going to try something now, Garai?" Lucius said, his eyes wild, his voice full of venom. "Why couldn't you just leave me alone?"

Lucius bent to help the young girl up, but she pulled away.

"Forgive me," he said, but she and the Nubian did not reply. They gathered their clothing and slipped past Lucius and the other two.

"Fuck you, Lucius," Argus said, getting to his feet.

"It's your own fault. Just find your own way. Leave me to mine."

"I think you should leave, Centurion," said another voice from the entrance to the little alcove. A thickset, bald man flanked by two eunuchs stood there staring at the scene. "I invited legionary Argus here, and he brought you as a guest. But with you, it seems chaos reigns."

"I'm his centurion," Lucius said. "He's insubordinate."

"This isn't the army. This is my business. Now, get out before I have you thrown out," the man said.

Lucius, feeling humiliated and full of rage, looked from the man to Argus, and Garai. Without saying anything he gathered his clothes, slipped his tunic over his head, tied on his cingulum, and walked past them.

One of the eunuchs reached out to grab the dagger away from Lucius.

"Try and take my pugio away and I'll fucking drive it through your skull," Lucius said, pushing past him.

"Let him go," said the man. "And you, Argus, you might want to wait a little longer before taking one of the girls."

"Fuck you too," Argus said.

The man nodded and one of the eunuchs kicked him across the face so that he fell unconscious on his side.

"You want to try something too?" the man said to Garai.

"No."

"Good. Now get your friend out of my establishment."

The man walked away with one of the eunuchs while the other remained behind to ensure that Argus and Garai did not stay.

It was early when Lucius stepped out of his tent the following morning. The camp was barely stirring. He had not been able to sleep for all the anger that had infiltrated him the previous night. It had taken a long time for him to calm himself and take stock of the situation.

I'm an officer...and first centurion! I should be able to discipline myself better, he chided himself. He was upset at Argus' presumption, yes, but he was even more angry with himself for losing control. He realized that anyone could have been in that house of whores, someone with ill intent toward the Romans who had flooded into the city like a Nile deluge.

They were just whores, he told himself. *Used to pleasing men. It was nothing...*

When he pulled back the tent flap and stepped outside, the sky was filled with clouds and a damp breeze was blowing in off the sea. They would sweat that day, he knew. He had plans for drills.

Lucius marched down the dusty street, looking at the tents of his century, listening to the groans as men roused each other after their night of carousal. A few stumbled out as Lucius passed and gave him wary salutes.

He cut an imposing figure with his increasingly more decorated harness across his chest, the slap of his pteruges, and the swaying of his horizontal horsehair crest atop his helmet.

"Get up, First Century!" he barked. "Drills in half an hour! Piss, eat, and get dressed. Now!" Lucius commanded, a distant cornu backing him up over the whole camp.

Lucius arrived at the last tent of their century to see Argus, Maren, Eligius, Garai and Antanelis sitting out front, cooking oats over the fire.

"Finally, some troops that are ready," Lucius said.

"Morning, sir!" Antanelis said, saluting.

The others did not do so as enthusiastically.

Lucius ignored it for the moment. He had something else on his mind. "Argus, can I speak with you?"

Argus looked up from his wooden bowl, nodded, and stood up, giving the bowl to Maren.

The two of them walked a short distance away from the others in silence before Lucius spoke.

"I'm sorry about last night," Lucius said. "I was wrong to get angry. They were whores, and you had brought me there when you didn't have to."

They stopped walking and stared at each other.

"I thought a good fuck would lighten you up a bit," Argus said, crossing his arms over the front of his newly polished lorica. "Guess I was wrong."

"It did," Lucius protested. "I just... I just wanted to relax there a bit more with those girls, that's all. We weren't done." Lucius shook his head, thinking how ridiculous he must look saying that in his centurion's uniform. "Look, I said I was sorry and I meant it. I'm sorry I hit you."

"Don't do it again," Argus warned, and Lucius could tell he meant business.

"Did you stay long afterward?"

"No. Those two fucking big eunuchs kicked us out before I could get any action, thanks to you. And my balls still hurt like Hades, sadly no thanks to the whores."

"I'm sorry," Lucius said again. "Really."

"Fine. But I'm going whoring alone next time, all right?"

"I don't blame you. I'm sure there are lots of other orgies in the city where you can get in. That one likely isn't the only one now, is it?"

"No. There are a few more." Argus smiled.

"So, we're fine then?" Lucius held out his hand.

Argus looked at it, and after a few seconds, gripped Lucius forearm. "Yeah, we're fine."

"Good." Lucius breathed deeply, feeling better than he had all night. "I have to go and check in at the principia. Tell Alerio that I'll meet you and the men on the parade ground soon."

"I will," Argus said, saluting.

Lucius nodded, smiled, and then turned to go back toward the principia.

As Lucius walked away, Argus spat at his back.

He did not notice Antanelis watching him.

XII

Domi Cognitionis

'The Houses of Knowledge'

The men of III Parthica worked hard over the coming weeks, filling their days with building projects, private escort duty for the Roman elite, and guard duty at various points around Alexandria's walls.

There had been whispers of remnant Parthian forces massing near the border with Arabia, but no confirmation, no engagement by troops who were sent on patrols in that direction.

Most of all, the men drilled. They were veterans now, their green days of the past far behind them. Now, each man of III Parthica was at one with his scutum, pilum, and gladius - every muscle knew its motion and speed so that as a unit, each body, each contubernium, each century, each cohort, moved in perfect concert with the others.

Lucius was proud of his men, and he rewarded those who excelled, pushed those who seemed not to care. He never thought he would be such a harsh task master, but he discovered that to lead such a deadly killing machine as was formed by the men of the legions, disciplina could only come of a strong hand.

However, Lucius Metellus Anguis, the centurion, was isolated from his men, his friends. With more and more administrative work building up, he found himself spending more nights alone in his tent with a cup of wine and the smoke from his offerings to Apollo swirling about him.

Several times he thought to sit down and write to his father to tell him of his promotions, his successes, but again and again he turned from the task of putting stylus to wax or papyrus.

On some nights, when the men were on leave in the city, he had thought to go in search of the flute girl, but always decided against it. Alexandria both intoxicated and repulsed him.

Lucius had grown used to the gaudy sophistication of Alexandria, the statues of foreign gods that peeked out at him from hidden places, and the strange language that flowed out of their temples. It was exotic. However, he was exotic too, and he hated the looks of interest that his uniform drew from the locals. No matter the presence of so many thousands of Roman troops outside the city walls, the inhabitants of Alexandria vastly outnumbered them.

He felt his distance from Rome, from home, more acutely than ever. But there was one place where he believed he could feel at home - the library.

It was as if in the library he could still feel the shade of Diodorus standing beside him, urging him to learn, to improve, to better himself, encouraging him in the ways that his father should have done, but never managed to.

Lucius stood up and began to pick his way to the library where he knew they must have some sort of plans for the layout of the mausoleum of Alexander so that he could at least visualize it.

Why did the emperor have to close it? he wondered.

When he arrived, the doors were open and he walked in through a soaring atrium where the noise of the street was suddenly silenced, the heat reduced. In the rounded space were statues of the great Greek philosophers and scientists whose works no doubt graced the shelves of that sacred place of knowledge and the Muses. The faces of Socrates, Plato, and Aristotle stared down on him beside Euclid, Pythagoras, Euripides and others.

It was overwhelming, so far removed from the world of war and military regimen that Lucius simply stood there, mute as men passed by him.

"Can I help you?"

Lucius turned to see a tall, lanky young man wearing a ruffled white Ionic chiton. His head was closely shorn and he carried an armful of scrolls, clutching them to him cautiously.

"Oh, ah, yes. I'm with the III Parthica legion stationed outside the city, and -"

"Do you wish to research something in the library?" the man asked, clearly wishing he had not stopped.

"Ah, no. Not today. I'm looking for someone."

"Who?"

"Aelius Galenus. My former tutor, Diodorus of -"

"Why didn't you say so?" the man said, cutting Lucius off a second time. "Follow me." With that, the young man sped off down a column-lined corridor flanked by rooms that were filled, floor to ceiling, with scrolls kept in pigeon holes.

At the end of the corridor, they passed through a large marble courtyard where groups of men stood about in discussion to the tune of a splashing fountain beneath tall palm trees that swayed in the hot breeze.

"Galenus is in that auditorium there," the man said, pointing straight ahead at a door that led into a circular room with terraced seating on either side.

"My thanks," Lucius said, but the man was already off in another direction clutching his precious scrolls.

Lucius straightened his tunic, pushed back his cloak and went through the door. Inside several students seemed to be leaning in toward a central table at which a white-haired man stood peering down, doing something with his hands.

Nobody noticed Lucius who approached cautiously, detecting an odd odour in the air. One of the students at the back of the circle turned to look at Lucius, but then turned back to look at the teacher.

Lucius knew he was running short on time, that the others would be waiting for him. He was reluctant to disturb the session, but being berated for not setting an example for his men was a worse prospect.

"Ahem..." he cleared his throat. "Please forgive my interruption, but I'm seeking Aelius Galenus. I was told to come in here to see him."

The voice that had been muttering in the background stopped suddenly and the crowd of students parted down the middle to reveal the old man at their centre, hunched over something dark on the large marble table.

"There is a Roman in the room today, gentlemen," the old man said. "What interest have you in Aelius Galenus?"

"To speak with him," Lucius answered. "My own tutor, Diodorus of Athens, told me that I should find him if ever I came to Alexandria."

"Diodorus?" the old man stood up straight and peered at Lucius with squinting eyes. "So, the legions have come with a learned man among them?"

"Uhm..." Lucius did not know what to say. "Are you Aelius Galenus, sir?"

"Yes. Who are you then? Name and rank, soldier?" the man said, some of the students tittering a little.

"Lucius Metellus Anguis, Primus Pilus of the III Parthica Legion."

"Very good. Now, come and help me with something, Lucius Metellus Anguis."

Lucius stepped forward slowly until he was almost beside Galenus. He stopped when he saw what was on the table.

On the marble table, a monkey of some sort lay splayed with its four limbs stretched to each corner. Its chest cavity was open and peeled back to reveal its organs, which Galenus prodded methodically with a bronze surgical instrument.

"Well don't just sit there gawping, Centurion. Come and help me. As a student of Diodorus' you will be able to help me. Here, hold this with your fingers."

Galenus pulled one of the flaps of skin back tightly and directed Lucius to pinch it to hold it back. "Good. Now, you see? The veins run throughout the body, connecting the organs and muscles. To what purpose?" Galenus looked about the faces of the young men. Then one raised his hand.

"Sir, to circulate blood to all parts of the body?"

Some of the students laughed, but Galenus shushed them. "Quite right, Milos. The veins run everywhere in the body. If you cut an animal or person anywhere, they will bleed, some places more profusely than others, but still, they will bleed."

He took his scalpel and slit across one of the larger veins running along the inside thigh of the hairy beast and blood immediately began to trickle out.

Lucius felt the bile rising at the back of his throat. He tried to push it back, swallow it, but could not get over the sight of the animal. A moment later, he was running for the door behind which he purged his guts in dismay.

"Hmm," Galenus said, smiling. "I am ever fascinated by the fact that a soldier can hold his lunch on the battle field, even with the most gruesome of cuts, gashes and other injuries all about him, but then when he sees a simple dissection, he is incapable of holding back his bile. Fascinating."

Lucius stood up, wiping his mouth with his hand and looking mortified. Before he could apologize or leave the room altogether, Galenus was dismissing his class.

"Next week, we shall discuss my theory of how the brain moves the rest of the body."

As the last of the students filed out of the room, Lucius walked over to where Galenus now sat on the front row of seating, smiling at Lucius.

"Forgive me, Centurion. I can get a little moody when my work is disturbed. I take it Diodorus never covered dissection with you?"

"No, he didn't. We talked more of philosophy than of science, sir."

"Please. Call me Galenus. I may have been physician to Caesars and more, but we are all human, and I am no more privileged to walk this earth than any other man."

"Doesn't that depend on the man?" Lucius answered.

"Ah. Now there's a question, and a much longer discussion." Galenus smiled. "I miss my old friend Diodorus." His smile faded but returned when he looked up from the floor, his helpers beginning to clean up the remains of the monkey. "Come. Let us feed our physical bodies with some date wine, whilst we look out at the sea and you tell me about your time in Alexandria thus far."

With that, Galenus stood and walked out into courtyard and up a set of stairs that led to a large terrace facing north and covered by great white linen sheets. Lucius marvelled at how quickly the old man went up the stairs and struggled to think back on what Diodorus had told him of Galenus.

"I was sad to hear of Diodorus' death," was the first thing Galenus said once they were sat down, each with a green glass goblet filled with date wine. "I think I was back home in Pergamon at the time, seeing family."

"It seems an age since he died," Lucius said, staring out at the brilliance of the sea. The white sheets above snapped in the breeze and giant, potted palms whisked in a corner of the verandah. "It's beautiful here," Lucius said.

Galenus looked askance at the young centurion beside him. "Do you mean this city, or the spot in which we find ourselves at this moment?"

"Oh, ah, this spot. Don't get me wrong, I like Alexandria, well, parts of it anyway. I just miss Rome."

"Rome?" Galenus said. "You miss Rome? I suppose you would. You are Roman, and your family is there. I know your father, by his views against imperialism, that is."

"I am nothing like my father, sir," Lucius said,

Galenus looked keenly at Lucius. Though the man was old, he was as keen an intellect as Lucius had ever met. "You speak plainly before I ask anything, young Metellus. That tells me, you have other things on your mind."

"Forgive me." Lucius sat up straight and turned toward his host. "The peace of this spot has dulled my wits, maybe."

"Or rather being a centurion in a strange land?"

"Perhaps."

"I have lived in Rome," Galenus said. "I do not miss it. Rome is for Stoics, like your father, like my former patient Marcus Aurelius. Oh yes," he added when he saw Lucius' look. "I have seen behind the curtains of imperial power, young Lucius. I've healed and tried to reason with Marcus Aurelius, Lucius Verus, Commodus, our Leptis Magnan, Septimius Severus, and now his son Caracalla who visited me the other day with an ailment. I have had the privilege of their company and the insight into their thoughts. It's amazing when a man is naked, being inspected by his physician, the things he will tell you!"

Galenus laughed and eyed Lucius who spotted the playful glint in the old man's eyes.

"Worry not, young Metellus. You can relax here in the library away from the madness that overtakes the young in the streets of this wily mistress, Alexandria. Diodorus always spoke highly of you in his conversations with me, and in his letters, you were always the pupil he spoke of with the most pride."

Lucius smiled sadly. Being with Galenus brought home the gap left by Diodorus' death.

"I know you already, I feel," Galenus said, raising his glass. "But the young man of awareness, faith, and many gifts, by nature and the Gods, has experienced new things since his beloved tutor departed this world. Hasn't he?"

"Yes," Lucius answered.

"War makes animals of us all," Galenus said shaking his head. "For the last couple of years, I've been hearing of the emperor's campaign against the Parthians, of the fall of Edessa, Seleucia, Babylon, Ctesiphon, and Hatra."

Lucius closed his eyes a moment and Galenus noticed his balled up fist.

"I see the memories are still wet with blood, as a fresh wound to a sensitive area of the body takes time to heal."

Lucius did not answer. He had not expected this intellectual assault. Diodorus had always been more sensitive and gentle in his approaches to difficult subjects, but Galenus, perhaps because of his old age, seemed to see no need in delaying getting to his point.

"Be at ease, young Lucius. Diodorus' shade is pleased, I'm sure, that you are here. Here, in these houses of knowledge, as I like to call the rooms of the library, you can take the time to heal through knowledge and wisdom, for as long as you are posted to Alexandria. Agreed?"

"Thank you," Lucius said, a genuine, relieved smile spanning his face.

"I see that pleases you. Excellent. Only one thing."

"Yes?"

"You must agree not to attend my anatomy class again. A vomiting centurion will be too much of a distraction for my students."

347

"I wholeheartedly agree," Lucius laughed and they drank some more.

Lucius returned to the library every chance he got, but more often than not, duty required him to take up the work of the legions, work which, he told himself, he had longed for over the years.

When the emperor and empress returned to Alexandria from their Nile cruise into Upper Egypt, the troops were once again on edge, guard duties doubled throughout the city.

The tomb of Alexander remained closed by order of Severus as well. The emperor had not announced his reasons, though some said it was because he wished to remain alone with the body of the great conqueror, in quiet contemplation of the latter's deeds as well as his own.

As summer began, and the heat rose in the city streets, Septimius Severus addressed a massive crowd in the agora, outlining his plans to create a series of city councils to assure the smooth workings of the city and its services.

"Alexandria, with Rome," Severus said, "remains a beating heart of the Empire, and we must nurture it, care for it. We must have trusted men who are beyond corruption, to lead these councils in the name of the people."

The crowd clapped, though many did not realize the implications of this. Was it better organization, or a series of small cliques to be run by tyrannical administrators in the name of Rome?

"Our genus humanun, of the Empire, will thrive, will never want for safety, for food, for trade, or indeed favour from the

Gods. For we are strong, and fierce, and we have defeated our enemies in the hopes of securing all of those things."

This the throngs understood and they began to chant the name of Severus so that it reverberated louder than the crashing waves beyond the harbour.

"The city of Alexander shall thrive for a thousand more years!"

Lucius, where he stood guard in a line of men at the back of the forum, leaned over to whisper to Alerio and Antanelis.

"He's learned how to make a speech, I think. Look how the Alexandrians love him."

"I know," Alerio said. "They were so disgruntled at his closing of their hero's tomb, and now they sing his praises."

"The promise of peace and prosperity goes a long way to securing the mob's favour," Maren said from Lucius' other side.

"Too right," Argus added on Maren's other side.

The crowds began to disperse and Lucius walked up and down the line of his men.

"Right! You're off duty for the rest of the day!" Lucius said out loud. "Back to camp to stow your kit, and then the hours are yours to do with as you please."

Several of the men cheered and began lining up to make their way back to camp.

"Alerio, will you lead them on?" Lucius said. "I've got to go somewhere."

"The library again?" Alerio asked. "Why not join us this time? We've found a cleaner brothel where the whores aren't sick, and they clean throughout the day. Nice, quiet cubicula."

"No thanks."

Alerio nodded, and turned to go, shaking his head as he fell in step with the others, the orb of his hastile staff bobbing up and down among their heads.

Lucius looked about the agora and watched the crowd dispersing. He removed his helmet and tucked it under his left arm. He looked up at the limestone outline of the library, at the flapping white awnings on the verandah where he could see Galenus leaning on the railing looking down at the square as he spoke with another.

When he looked again, the agora's centre was empty once more with everyone having moved to the fringes to haggle at the market stalls that had opened that day. There were the usual colourful arrays of spices, dried fish, pottery, and animals.

A crowd gathered around one of the animal paddocks at the far north-east corner of the agora, and Lucius approached to see what was going on. As he came closer, he heard the loud neighing of one of the animals, spirited and high-strung.

Four men attempted to harness a pure black stallion with very little success. The beast reared, and kicked, and spun, but it did not seem angry. It seemed to be enjoying the dance in a way, and Lucius was captivated by the animal.

He pushed his way to the front so that he was leaning against the fencing, and simply stared. A few people turned to look at the Roman who had just joined them, but Lucius ignored them, his fist clamped around his purse.

"You optio?" said a man in flowing white robes on the other side of the fence.

Lucius pried his eyes away from the animal and shook his head. "Centurion," he answered. "Where is that animal from?"

"Arabia," the man said. "But it is a wild horse. Only fitting for an accomplished rider and warrior."

Lucius gazed across the paddock to where a group of what appeared to be auxiliary cavalrymen were looking at the horse, and a few others that were tied to the interior of the fence for showing. A man who appeared to be the leader of the group was looking into a purse of his own, trying to figure out how much he had, before shaking his head. When he had decided he did not want to spend the money, he looked up and his eyes caught Lucius'.

A chill went up Lucius' spine as the man looked at him, then back to his fellows.

"They big shits, them," said the trader. "Alexandrian cavalry ala who think they know everything." The man spat. "Cheap too." He looked back at Lucius. "You can ride?"

"Yes," Lucius replied, thinking of the rides he would take long ago on their estate in Etruria. "But never on such an animal."

"Some centurions ride with the army, no?"

"Some," Lucius replied. "I march with my men."

"Oh. Too bad then."

"How much is he, out of curiosity?" Lucius asked, dreading the answer.

"Five thousand denarii."

"Five?" Lucius' eyes popped wide. *What am I thinking?* Lucius thought. *I don't even need a horse.*

"My thanks," Lucius said, turning to go, but the man pulled on his tunic sleeve.

"This horse is very young, like you, if I may say. Give him some time to mature, and he'll be a mount to rival Bucephalas himself!"

Lucius smiled. "Thank you, friend. But I've no need." Lucius nodded his thanks and cut across the agora toward the library, the sounds of the market fading away behind him.

It was cool and quiet inside the hallowed halls of the library, a relief from the sweltering streets. Lucius nodded to a couple of the men he had come to know in passing during his visits, Serapion of Antioch, and Origen Adamantius, a known Christian who was in the city during the emperor's time there.

Lucius went up a flight of marble stairs at the back of the main atrium until he reached the second floor, and made his way to the verandah where he had seen Galenus.

"Ah, there you are, young Metellus!" Galenus said as Lucius came out of the darkness and into the bright Egyptian sunlight. "How was the emperor's address? I could not hear his words from here, though I could tell that the people were pleased."

"Our emperor is a rousing speaker, Galenus. He addressed the people as he addresses us in the camp. Rousing as ever." In truth, Lucius had almost forgotten what the emperor had said, so smitten was he with continued thoughts of the horse he had just seen. "It is not really for me to say. You would know more of Caesar than I do, having been his personal physician."

Galenus looked at Lucius as he poured out some wine and brought the cups over, his old hands as steady as ever.

"I gave a class today which you would have liked," Galenus said, seeming to ignore Lucius' statement. "You know by now that I am a Platonist to some extent?"

"Yes. I thought as much, from what I can remember. I know you are no Stoic."

"Mind your tongue, lad," Galenus coughed, his eyes chiding, despite the smile. "We've covered that. Today I taught my pupils about the effects of Psyche on the brain and the body. I also spoke of the soul and its constituent parts."

"Parts of the soul?" Lucius should have known he would be drawn into philosophy again.

"Yes. The soul of a man consists of three parts: the Rational, which resides in the brain and perceives the world around us; the Spiritual, which resides in the heart and contains our passions, and the potential dangers that accompany those passions; and lastly, the Appetitive part of the soul which lives in the liver and is more animalistic in nature, determines our natural urges, and want for pleasures."

"Diodorus covered this with me to some extent but not fully. It was not long before he died."

"I thought as much. So, let me ask you this, Lucius. We are in the city of Alexander, the greatest city the world has ever known, yes?"

"All right, for argument's sake," Lucius said, knowing that would rankle a little.

"Keep Rome out of this for a moment," Galenus continued. "Alexandria is the personification of its progenitor. It is very rational, the heart of scholarship and science, of knowledge and of thought." Galenus waved his hand about, indicating the library. "It is also highly spiritual. In Alexandria there is a tradition of worship to the Gods that goes back thousands and thousands of years. There are temples to every god in this city, and they are all respected and sacrosanct. Faith, despite the passions it arouses, is thriving here in Alexandria."

"And it certainly is appetitive in nature," Lucius said, unable to hold back.

"As you know very well by now, given your outings with the troops. Alexandria is a city of pleasures, and it caters to the pleasures of every kind of person, for better or worse. I myself enjoyed indulging my appetitive side overly much in my youth when I first came to this city."

Lucius looked at Galenus and saw a whimsical light cross his features for a moment before the scientist returned.

"But Alexandria is balanced between all three natures of the soul. As was Alexander. Some may gainsay me on that point, but to those people, I would say this: We are all capable, and have done things we regret, including Alexander, but what is to be scrutinized is the good we have done, the kind of world we've left behind, however big or small that world may be."

Galenus stood and paced a little in the shade of the awning. "Alexander had a grand vision, and though he went to extremes to achieve his dreams, the product of those dreams, Alexandria, and what it stands for, is like a perfectly balanced soul."

Lucius stood up, quiet, to stand beside the old man as they both gazed out to see the Pharos on the island across the harbour.

"Even for me, the expression of this thought is trying. I find it easier to explain the anatomy of a pig, the uses of herbs and medicines, or the effect the brain has on the body. But, explaining the perfectly balanced soul of one of the greatest men to have ever lived is, well, humbling. And trust me, I am not easily humbled, young Lucius."

Lucius smiled. This was a side of Galenus that reminded him more of Diodorous than anything he had seen to date.

"Yes," Galenus said, smiling knowingly.

"What?"

"I know what you are thinking. And the answer is yes, Diodorus is the one who succeeded in explaining this to me."

Lucius nodded and wiped the sweat from his brow.

"You said I knew our emperor better than you. Ask yourself, how balanced a soul he might have."

"I couldn't begin to know, Galenus."

"No. Of course. Nor would you presume. We are not the god Anubis, weighing the souls of the departed against that heavenly feather," he said, smiling. "Our emperor is a very spiritual soul, with a rational streak that sets him to eliminating the perceived enemies around him. There was a civil war to that end."

Lucius looked around cautiously.

"Worry not. I've spoken with Severus on this matter. He is very candid and more philosophical than you might think. And I am very old, and don't mind risking a bit of frankness with a student of knowledge." Galenus began walking again, this time into the library and down another corridor. "We all have our own paths, and the nobility of that path, the outcomes that arise from the choices made along that path, are very telling. How balanced are our choices through the prism of our souls? What kind of people do we trust? How do we treat our fellow human beings? Are people made better for being around us? Alexander certainly inspired others around him, and he continues to do so. Now, ask yourself, as you pray to all-knowing Apollo, what do you bring to the world about you?"

Lucius stopped and stared at the old man who reached out to steady the young Roman's shaking hands.

"It is no easy thing to think on. But better to do so when you are young, than in the winter of your life." He pulled Lucius along into a large, quiet room in which a few people were gathered around a woman dressed in a flame-coloured stola sitting at a white marble table. A veil hung loosely from the top of her head, revealing dark hair that was set in waves, like the sand of a beach when the tide has gone out. She was reading out loud to the others, but Lucius could not understand the language. The men about her, evidently scholars of the library, seemed rapt by her words. When she finished, Galenus spoke.

"My Empress," Galenus said, bowing.

The woman looked up and Lucius could feel the heat rising up his neck. *The empress!* he screamed inside, unprepared for the meeting.

"Galenus, my old friend," the empress smiled and rose in a rustle of silk from her seat to go to the old man.

Lucius bowed as she approached, his helmet stuck tightly beneath his left arm, his right over his chest as it clutched his vinerod.

"My lady," Galenus smiled and bowed his head again as she took his hand. "Forgive the disturbance of your Aramaic readings to my colleagues."

"Not at all. We were just finishing," the empress said, looking back at the group who immediately began to gather up their scrolls and wax tablets, each bowing in turn to the empress as they left the reading room. "I always enjoy our discussions, Galenus, so it is no upset to see you."

"We have been having our own discussion, my lady."

"Oh? About what?" her eyes turned on Lucius. "Rise."

"My Empress..." Lucius said.

"And you are?"

"Lucius Metellus Anguis, Primus Pilus, III Parthica Legion."

"Ah, yes. One of our new legions. And you have distinguished yourselves admirably from what I have heard."

"We have done our best, my Empress."

"We were just discussing the soul, and its three respective parts, as they relate to Alexander, the founder of this glorious city of knowledge."

"Ah yes," the empress' face lit up, and she became beautiful, despite her relatively plain looks. "The rational, spiritual, and appetitive parts," she said.

"Yes. Young Lucius has studied Alexander for some time. His old tutor, Diodorus of Athens, was a friend and colleague of mine."

"I remember a discussion I had with Diodorus, long ago," Julia Domna said. "A kinder man, I've never met."

"Young Lucius has been hoping to pay his respects at the tomb of Alexander, but..." Galenus' voice trailed off.

"But," the empress continued, "my husband has closed it to all outsiders. Yes, the locals are not happy about our blocking access to their god."

She stopped and looked at Lucius for a moment. Her dark eyes bored into him, as if she were some strange eastern sphinx, assessing his worth.

"I was hoping to go myself," Galenus said. "I've not been in some time."

The empress smiled. "It is closed to outsiders, but we, I have a feeling, are students of the houses of knowledge, and so the remains of Alexander would be safe under our observance. Do you agree?"

"Emphatically, my lady." Galenus bowed again.

"Let us go, then," the empress said. "Do you have the time, Centurion?"

"Yes, Empress. I have no further duties this day."

"And you prefer to come to the library rather than whore and gamble with your brothers-in-arms?"

"That is so, my Empress."

"Let us go, then."

Julia Domna set off at a slow pace so that Galenus could keep up with her and they could converse the whole way. Lucius tried not to listen, but part of the conversation about the emperor's health reached his ears, though he pretended not to notice. They were followed by one of the empress' ladies-in-waiting, as well as two guards who appeared to be Syrian, as she was. Trusted men.

When they reached the lower levels of the library, the guards opened a large bronze door that led onto a torch-lit tunnel that lay beneath street level. The tunnel was clean, and bright, and their footsteps echoed the length of it.

Lucius did not know how far they had travelled, but before long they were passing through another door that opened onto some polished, green marble steps that led up to a large room with a cedar roof high above them. Lucius looked up as they mounted the stairs and he could see the glint of gilded Argead stars, the symbols of Alexander's home, painted on the rafters.

They came onto the large floor, their breathing soft and still as each, the empress, the scholar, and the warrior stared at the brilliant marble and alabaster sarcophagus in the middle of the room.

Lucius stopped dead in his tracks to stare at the body that was visible through the thin veil of the alabaster that allowed visitors to see Alexander the Great.

Lucius thought he could hear the sound of charging horses, and of men yelling in battle, the clang of swords and the rush of fire. Indeed, around the sides of the sarcophagus were carved scenes of the battles fought by Alexander and his army on their journey from Greece to India, tales of the fall of the Persian Empire.

Torches flickered all around the walls, and incense fumed up from four massive, bronze tripods, the sort that Lucius imagined would have been fought over by Hercules and Apollo themselves at Delphi.

"Come closer, young Lucius..." Galenus whispered, motioning for Lucius to approach.

Lucius felt his heart leap, his hands shaking as he gazed upon Alexander, his face peaceful and preserved by the great skill of the Egyptian embalmers.

Alexander was short, but the body seemed stocky, covered as it was in white and purple robes, decorated with rosettes, eagles, and stars of purest gold. He was buried with a crown that appeared to be Persian in design, as well as the crook and flail of an Egyptian pharaoh.

"It is when we gaze upon such as this that we realize how fragile we are," the empress said. "He was, arguably, one of the greatest men in history, a god as many believed."

"And yet, here he lies..." Galenus added.

"What do you glean from this, Centurion?" the empress asked.

"I am overawed," Lucius said. "I've waited to see this for so long."

"Only to look upon the hollow remains?" she challenged.

"No, my Empress. As my initial shock wears away, I feel sad and inspired all at once. To be able to believe in the possibilities he believed in, to achieve them!" Lucius voice had risen and he toned it down at the echo. "Forgive me. Being here makes me question my own beliefs and dreams, the goals of my life."

Galenus and the empress stood staring at Lucius, slight smiles on their faces. Finally, the empress spoke.

"I don't know that I've ever come across a philosopher centurion who believes in dreams and destiny before."

"I do believe, Lucius Metellus Anguis," said Galenus, "that Alexander and his city have spoken to your Psyche in a most unique way."

Lucius looked up at both of them and then back at Alexander the Great, lying in state for all time, revered and cared for, whether anyone outside or in worshiped him or not. Even the Gods themselves could not ignore him.

After the empress, Galenus, and Lucius had made their offerings at the altar facing the sarcophagus, they descended the green marble steps once more, the closure of the bronze doors echoing along the corridor behind them.

Lucius knew he would not be the same after that.

XIII

Concubina

'The Hetaira'

After a year in Alexandria, Lucius began to settle into a new kind of life, one nurtured by the strength and skill he developed at all times in himself and his men, and also by the constant influx of knowledge that came from his visits to the library of Alexandria and his interactions with Galenus and his fellow scholars.

Lucius had no illusions about being a scholar himself, though he was on occasion able to get the better of some men in an argument; there are times, he found, when life experience counts for far more than isolated reading. Diodorus had taught him that since he was a young boy during their forays into the Forum Romanum back home.

III Parthica spent most of its time patrolling the surrounding areas of the Nile Delta, training, parading, and in their spare time, enjoying the pleasures of Alexandrian life, or proximity to it.

Many of the men who had amassed savings over the campaigning months in Parthia now found themselves at a loss, having gambled or whored their funds away. Many came to Lucius with requests to tap into their burial club deposits, but Lucius forbade it, earning him not a few angry looks. There was no way he would break with protocol just because the men had grown cocky during a time of relative quiet on the front.

There were still whispers of Parthians, and so the patrols went out daily, rotated among the legions each of which sent three centuries out each time, accompanied by an ala of cavalry.

Lucius met with Galenus less frequently now. The emperor's health demanded much of his time, and though Severus was still relatively strong, he wanted his physician close-to-hand at all times.

It was during Lucius' leisure time, when he was not able to go to the library, and sat by himself in his tent, that he realized he had become unbalanced by war and routine. Every day he made his offerings to Apollo without fail, his prayers rising up to the heavens with the smoke of his offerings as he waited for a sign, some direction.

Apollo was silent at this time. He did not appear to the young Metellus who began to wonder whether or not he had imagined those times when the god had appeared to him.

Reading scrolls had been fulfilling, but Lucius could only take in so much after a day of drilling, patrol duty, or overseeing the men on some road-building project or other duty.

Lucius thought back to his conversation with Galenus about the spirit and its three aspects, and realized that his appetitive side had been neglected.

He hated to admit it, especially when he differed so much with Argus on such things as whoring and pleasure. Still, in Alexandria, during a trip to the public baths where men and women bathed together, it was hard not to think of a soft body next to him, or of being inside one. His thoughts often drifted back to the two girls at that orgy when they had first arrived in the city, but Lucius did not want something like that confrontation anymore than the bad cases of crabs that led many of his men to try and shirk their duties.

He missed some measure of tenderness in his life, he realized, but was unsure if that was even something he could find in a city that was always on the make for a quick denarius.

He had been invited to several luxurious parties by some locals who wanted to display their Roman connections to their friends and clients, and at these he met more than one lady who was willing to forget herself. But those evenings always left him feeling empty rather than satisfied.

Women. Leisure time had left more room for thought of them. In later years, Lucius often felt as though he had grown up in Alexandria, that he had become aware of the mystery of women, and the spell that can be cast upon a man when he gives in to his passions. Until then, he had only experienced certain aspects of life - war, bloodshed, death, and knowledge. Sex and intimacy with a woman skilled in more than the spreading of her legs was something he had not known prior to his second year in Alexandria.

Lucius did not want to indulge in the forceful taking of women that Argus seemed to enjoy. There was a regular circuit of orgies that catered to the troops, and Argus, Eligius, and Garai loved to go to each of them.

They were little more than indoor slave markets.

Lucius realized that if he wanted to enjoy the company of a proper woman, he would need to spend more of his money. After all, were beauty and skill not worth it?

After leaving several of Argus' pleasure evenings early, and out of disappointment, Lucius decided to go elsewhere. This led him to Barbarus, a man whose name he had heard spoken of by several rich, discerning citizens.

Barbarus catered to a higher level of taste.

After finding out who he was, and where he could find him, Lucius sought him out.

Barbarus' domus, was not some shabby tenement in a seedy district of the city, but rather a rich, unassuming villa on the banks of the Draco River. It had a colonnaded portico surrounded by lush gardens with pillars of pink and white marble lining the courtyard. A gentle trickle of water from several fountains made for a peaceful, idyllic surrounding bettered only by the inner rooms of the library.

Lucius was led into the garden where he sat down on a couch opposite Barbarus. This was the first time they met.

Barbarus was a middle-aged man, of medium build with a dark complexion. He was not the usual, sleazy man of business who sold pleasure slaves or prostitutes. He was well-spoken, educated, and polite. In all, a man of good behaviour from a good family.

"Things are more lax in Alexandria compared with Rome," Barbaras said, leaning back and sipping his wine after the preliminaries were dispensed with.

"I figured that out for myself, five minutes after entering the city," Lucius said, laughing a little.

"You are Roman, and it is a shock. You have an old family name too, so I'm guessing that you are from a quite conservative upbringing?"

"Yes. That is true."

365

"What sort of woman are you interested in seeing?" Barbarus asked after a few more minutes of talk about the city. "Keep in mind that I run a long-term business. My women are not holes to be breached once and then tossed away." He looked disgusted, as if things had happened to his girls that he would rather not speak of.

"I understand. Of course!" Lucius sat up, abashed by the insinuation. "I would like someone to spend time with. The duties of a centurion in camp are many, and they are intense. I would like to forget the real world for a time when I can. I guess a woman that is beautiful, exotic, and skilled, but not averse to conversation. Someone who..."

Before Lucius could finish, Barbarus was speaking. "I know. A hetaira, skilled in the arts of love, of poetry, of manners and more. I see."

"See what?"

"I know which girl you will like. She is perfect. Venus on earth."

Lucius laughed uncomfortably at the situation in which he found himself describing his desires to a Alexandrian man who was nearly of an age with his father.

"I know exactly the woman for you, Lucius Metellus Anguis." Barbarus turned and said one word to his slave, "Medea."

The slave went into another room and returned with a piece of papyrus on which was a seal and some directions.

"She has a villa to herself, just up the Fluvius Novus, near to the temple beyond the Hypogea south of the Eleusinian plain."

"That is the side the legions are camped on," Lucius said, worried.

"Do not fret, Centurion. It is well hidden. The villas along there belong only to quiet, wealthy Alexandrians and are well guarded. Be at her place tonight. She will be waiting for you."

"And...how much will this cost?" Lucius asked.

"She will decide that."

When night came, Lucius made his way out of the camp to the south west, toward the bend in the Fluvius Novus of Alexandria, the canal that ran from the city to the Nile itself. Once he crossed the open space of the Eleusinian plain, the gardens and walls of the villas along the canal came into view. His senses were alert in the gathering darkness, but the scent of jasmine and rustle of palms overhead soothed him somewhat.

What am I doing? he asked himself, his hand on the pugio beneath his cloak.

Medea. He had to admit that the name unnerved him slightly as he made his way down the quiet path leading up to her villa that night. He squinted at the piece of papyrus on which the slave had scrawled the directions, and looked down the path again before moving farther.

Thoughts of the Ancient Greek sorceress filled his head, and her betrayal of the hero Jason, but he tried to dismiss them. His palms were sweaty and he felt awkward. He had made a second trip to the baths that day, just to wash the day's dirt from his pores and ensure that he did not smell of the streets.

The villa was surrounded by tall palms and jasmine bushes that let loose their pungent fragrance in the moonlit air. A torch burned at the entrance to the house where a tall, muscular slave stood guard.

Lucius had dressed in his formal toga that evening, and covered himself with his black cloak. As he approached, the slave simply nodded, evidently expecting him, and opened the door for Lucius to enter.

Inside, another slave conducted Lucius through frescoed hallways lined with statues of gods whose knowing faces were lit by the dancing light of several braziers along the way.

He was led into a secluded garden that was floored with intricate mosaics of nymphs and satyrs. Water flowed throughout the garden, falling over several terraced ledges in imitation of a waterfall. From a great tripod opposite Lucius rose the smoke from some exotic, eastern incense, swirling about the courtyard in a seductively elusive dance among the barrage of foliage and flowers.

Lucius was given a cup of wine by a young girl who appeared from an anteroom and who disappeared with as much stealth. It was nectar, and helped to ease his nerves.

Why am I so nervous?

He shook his head, and sat himself on one of the large couches that were arranged in the centre of the garden. He breathed deeply to calm himself and chase away the apprehension. It was balmy in the courtyard, the floor still warm from the Egyptian daylight that had beat down on it hours before.

There was rustling from behind one of the palms. Lucius turned.

Medea. She stepped into the firelight with a warm smile, and bowed slightly. "You must be Lucius Metellus Anguis," she said.

Lucius nodded, his throat dry as he croaked out an "I'm pleased to meet you... Medea?"

"Yes." Her voice was soft. "Welcome to my home."

Lucius bowed his head in return, trying to stand straight and look into her stunning eyes.

She was one of the most stunningly beautiful women he had ever seen. Medea seemed to be nearly thirty years of age, but in truth might have been a lot less. Her confidence and manner certainly gave her an air of more experience than a girl of twenty.

She was tall, slender, as shown from her light stola, with dark olive skin that shone in the light. Her deep brown eyes looked out to him from behind long curls of rich black hair that caressed her exposed shoulders.

Lucius came to his senses quickly as she moved toward him, offering her hand. He reached out and kissed the soft skin. "I am honoured, lady Medea." he managed to say. "You have a beautiful home."

She smiled, and Lucius had the sense that she saw right through his insecurities. "Thank you. Please sit so we can talk and get to know one another."

Lucius moved over to the couch to which she pointed.

She wore a long, silvery-white stola that hugged her shapely body enough to arouse curiosity without exposing too much. Around her supple neck hung a simple, but beautiful, necklace of lapis lazuli, and around her upper arm she wore a brilliant gold armlet in the shape of an Egyptian asp.

Medea clapped her hands twice and several young women dressed in shimmering silk chitons came into the courtyard with platters of exotic fruits, flat breads, and pitchers of honeyed wine. After pouring some of the wine for Lucius and their mistress, the girls departed quietly.

"I want you to think of this place as your sanctuary. This is your realm away from war and duty. Here, you will not be disturbed. You can lower your defences with me."

Lucius sighed, and he felt a wave of relief wash over him.

"I see this thought pleases you?" Medea asked.

"I'd not thought how much my duties had been weighing down on me, until just this moment. I feel like I've been fighting for an age, and yet, a soldier is what I always wanted to be."

"Sometimes, our biggest dreams can be our greatest burdens." She moved beside him, and Lucius' eyes locked onto hers. "Please, eat something and try some more of my wine. We have made it especially. It is supposed to be good for the senses."

Lucius sipped the wine again, and ate a bit of fig dipped in crushed cloves and honey.

"Tell me about yourself, Lucius Metellus Anguis, about your life in general, about Rome. You do come from Rome, do you not?"

"Yes," Lucius answered, and proceeded to tell her of his life in Rome, his family, and his break with his father. It all poured out of him, words to the ear of this stranger who focussed only upon him, who knew how to listen, how to empathize.

It was liberating.

Lucius felt at ease with Medea, and she seemed to be happy and comfortable with him, opening up in conversation that seemed suitable only for her closest of friends.

As they sat there, the smell of her sweetly scented skin mixed with the smoke of the incense, creating a wondrous, trance-like state that seemed to blanket Lucius in a sort of euphoria of its own. He reclined on the couch, at peace, the courtyard lit by the light of the moon, stars sparkling overhead.

When the conversation slowed, and Lucius was more relaxed than he had been in years, Medea rose and moved to the centre of the courtyard, her eyes never leaving his. In the background, rose a faint music from a distant room on the other side of the villa. As the two were left alone, Medea moved about in a captivatingly slow dance, her arms, her hips, her legs and torso moving slowly, seductively, to the sound of distant cymbals, and flutes, a light drum, and the flutter of a sistrum.

Lucius felt like he should have fallen asleep, but quite the opposite occurred. His senses tingled, as sharp as could be, enrapt by the mysteries of womanhood. Without even touching Lucius, Medea had all of his attention, so much so that he was helpless to do anything but remain where he was, still, his heart pounding in his chest.

Then, as she swayed back and forth to the lulling music, she shed her stola, slowly, to reveal the full extent of her beauty, every shape and line, every perfectly placed curve.

Lucius thought to himself that she would tempt the mightiest of gods, and thus he, as a mere mortal, was helpless.

Nothing was rushed, though a part of him wished it so. He was teased and tantalized, her hands caressing his face, and then his neck, before working with ease to unwrap the complicated folds of his toga.

Lucius' chest was bare and he felt the cool night breeze prickle his warm skin. He sighed, resigned to give in and allow her to do whatever she wished. If she had pulled a dagger on him, he would not have flinched, but instead she poured scented oils over his young, muscular torso, hardened by war and worry, and began to massage away any aches and pains that he had as she hummed softly to the now faint music.

After a long while, she led Lucius away, both of them completely naked, to a room decorated with gold and blue trim around walls painted with serene forests. In the middle of the room was a large bed with bronze legs in the shape of pillars, and a mattress stuffed with the softest down. A tripod blazed at each corner of the room, and in the scented air of that fire-lit room, the goddess Venus revealed all to Lucius, holding him close to her breast for the whole of the night.

As Medea straddled Lucius, he moaned and looked up at her, their eyes locked as she pressed his hands to her swaying hips, and he felt the warmth of her pubus on his body.

All worldly cares melted into oblivion.

Thereafter, with that measure of tenderness returned, Lucius felt lighter and happier. Not even the good-natured ribbing about his secret whore by Argus and the others upset him.

Lucius moved easily now from the the field of Mars, to the library, and to the arms of his hetaira with delight.

He saw her as often as he could, and every time he showed up at her door, she was waiting in the atrium with food and wine, poetry and song, conversation, and new aspects of the many faces of Venus to be revealed.

Medea introduced Lucius to a world that he had been ignorant of, and he was forever grateful to her. In fact, he returned to her over and over, not only as a lover, but as a friend to whom he could express his deepest secrets and longings. As they lay sweaty and entwined, he spoke and she listened and asked questions, of his youth, his travels and battles, of Rome and what he hoped for the future.

He never had an answer to the latter. He had stopped thinking that far.

"I would carry on like this, with you, forever if possible," he said one day.

Her eyes alighted at that, almost imperceptibly, but not as much as the sad smile that marred her thoughtful lips.

Lucius did not pursue things, realizing that perhaps her life was not her own, successful as she was.

He never asked about her other clients, or about her relationship with Barbarus. It was enough for him to know that she was happy to see him, and seemed to delight in his company as much as he delighted in hers.

"You do know she's a whore, right Lucius?" Alerio said one day as they shared some wine in Lucius' campaign tent by the light of a flickering bronze oil lamp. "I mean, you must be paying quite a lot of your salary to be with her?"

Lucius sipped his wine slowly, his mind on Medea, her face, her smile, her soft skin, and her long limbs.

"She hasn't charged me yet. And I haven't asked."

"What?" Alerio set his cup down. "Listen Lucius. I know she makes you feel like a god, and helps you to forget the shit you have to deal with sometimes, but honestly, you'd better find out how much you owe before you get a huge bill slapped on you and a couple of sweaty fucking eunuchs show up at your tent to collect. I've heard stories about this Barbarus character. And it wasn't anything good."

"It just wouldn't feel right, Alerio. I would be insulting her. She's not some common lupa out of Ostia."

"Oh, I get it, I really do. She sounds like she's of a quality that most grunts wouldn't be able to even conjur in their seedy minds. But Lucius, she's a slave. No matter how many eastern silks are draped over her body, or exotic oils glisten on her skin, she's still a slave, and you're a Roman centurion who may not be posted here forever."

"I know, I know!" Lucius said loudly, waving his hand quickly as if to chase away the unpleasant thoughts of reality which he knew he must face at some point in time."

"Remember why you joined the army? It wasn't to travel the world and whore like Argus, as much as he's having fun doing that. You joined to prove yourself, to prove to your father that you could do for the Metelli what he could not. You always used to talk of disciplina and duty, and how your dedication to both would help you raise your family name out of the ashes."

"I know, Alerio. I've said all of those things. I remember. It's just that...I don't know... somehow, all of that is not a complete picture of where I want to go in life."

"Where *do* you want to go?"

"I don't know. What about you?"

"Well, I know that the army's the place for me, but I also know that I'd like to meet a nice girl someday, someone clean and kind to have a family with. Maybe on a farm? Something like that."

"Hmph! You know better than me."

"Just try and reign yourself in a bit with this woman. Be careful is all."

"I will. Now, Optio Kasen, you're late for your guard duties."

Alerio put down his cup and stood, chuckling. "Always pulling rank on me, eh? We'll see, Centurion!" Alerio saluted and left the tent laughing to himself as he went.

As often as Lucius wanted to return to Medea and the peace of her garden sanctuary, daily duties of the legions always managed to push their way into paradise.

A couple of weeks later, after a particularly hot patrol, and series of military exercises just beyond the Nile Delta, Lucius lay once more beside Medea in the garden. They were alone, and lay there panting and sweaty after a particularly passionate reunion.

Lucius lay back looking up at the stars, his eyes closing and opening again, one of Medea's long legs resting on him as she lay on her side. Her fingers ran in lines up and down his torso, making tracks in their mingles sweat, and her head nuzzled into his neck.

"Seems you missed me," she said softly, feeling Lucius' arm tighten around her.

"I always miss you. Every time I'm away from you, I miss you." He looked down at her, and she stared up. "You're so beautiful and kind... I never thought to feel this way. Ever..."

"Me neither," she whispered, so low that Lucius almost didn't understand what she had said.

"Some days, I wish we could run away from all of this. Just be us, and nothing else, make love, and talk, and laugh."

Medea was silent. She could feel her heart beat pick up and tried to calm it, her eyes closed.

"Maybe we could?" she said.

Lucius' hand stopped stroking the side of her breast. "What?"

"I've fallen for you, Lucius Metellus Anguis. Much as I've tried to keep my head about me, Aphrodite has weaved a spell within me that I cannot escape."

Lucius sat up, his eyes wide with something between awe, fear, and joy. "I, ah... I don't know what to say." He kissed her on the mouth and held her face in his hands, kissed her again, slowly.

When he pulled away, Medea was staring into his eyes, searching for something. "I'm not that much older than you. I can still have children. I am healthy and strong. I would be a good..."

"Good what?" Lucius asked.

"I would be good to you. In all things. We could indeed leave all of this, Lucius. We could."

Lucius stroked her long hair down over her shoulders and along the line of her back to the top of her thigh. Then he stopped, his smile fading slightly.

"What is it?" she asked.

Lucius took his hands off her and turned to sit on the edge of the bed, his muscular shoulders hunched now as he stared at the mosaic floor of the courtyard.

How many men have sat here? he thought. *Richer, more powerful men have been with her.* He rubbed his hair and and felt her approach from behind, her breasts against his back, her legs entwining about him like wild grape vines around a solid column. *Yes, she's picked me...*

Lucius shook his head a little, his conversation with Alerio coming back to him. His friend had heard something about Barbarus. He had warned him.

"What's wrong, Lucius. Speak to me," Medea said into his ear, her voice shaking a little.

"My family... I, I couldn't just disappear, forget about them. I owe it to my family to rise in the army, to prove that I can do what I set out to do." He thought of the dragon armour that he had not yet worn, which lay in a dusty trunk in a corner of his tent. *Anguis...* the name wavered in his mind, a reminder in the voice of Apollo.

Lucius turned and knelt before her, his knees on the mosaic, and he noticed the shock on her face, the minute hint of disgust and disappointment.

"Your family?" she said. "The family you said doesn't understand you? The family you needed to get away from? The family you don't even write to to let them know you are alive?" Medea's legs unwrapped themselves from Lucius and she stared at him. "You would put your family's happiness above your own?"

"It's not that easy, Medea... I feel like... I don't know...like the Gods have a destiny in mind for me. Ever since I was young I knew... To turn my back on that would -"

"What? Eagles and omens? I'm talking about the possibility of a life of peace and love, far from the worries of war and death. Aren't you tired of seeing blood?"

"Mars always finds his soldiers," Lucius said stubbornly. "One can not escape the Gods' will."

Medea reached out and held Lucius's face with her hands. They trembled slightly, and Lucius realized that he had never seen her so vulnerable.

"I love you, Lucius. I love you. From the moment you walked into my villa, I knew the Gods had sent you for a reason."

Lucius leaned forward and wrapped his arms about her. He could feel her heart beating against his chest, her ribs beneath the soft, olive skin expanding with excitement and emotion. But within himself, he was not sure what he felt. There was so much uncertainty.

"What about Barbarus?" Lucius said. "He owns you. I can't just take you away."

Medea became instantly rigid and pulled back slowly. "I control my own destiny. Not Barbarus."

"I know. I know." Lucius reached out to touch her cheek, but she turned her head. When she turned back to him, her eyes were full of fire and passion of a different sort.

"I haven't even paid Barbarus for our time together," he said.

Something in the way she looked at him changed in that instant. Mingled looks of hurt and something approaching hatred flashed behind her dark, pooling eyes.

"Get out!" she hissed.

"But Medea... I love being with you. I didn't mean -"

"Get out of my home. Now!"

Lucius shook his head. The sudden change was overwhelming and confusing. *What just happened?*

Before Lucius knew it, Medea was standing and padding naked across the courtyard to her private rooms, and one of the girls appeared with Lucius' clothes in her hands.

"I don't know what's happened?" Lucius said to the girl who did not respond or even look at him. "Please tell your mistress I'm sorry. I care for her deeply."

The girl left before he finished, dropping his clothing on the bed beside him.

He suddenly felt his nakedness, the shame acute and embarrassing. When he was dressed, he stood in the middle of the courtyard, looking around, looking for her.

Medea did not appear.

The stars above, brilliant and silvery, felt mocking.

"Rrm!" a voice cleared at the far end of the garden where the eunuch stood with his arms crossed, waiting to escort Lucius out of the house.

Lucius nodded and followed slowly, looking back over his shoulder in the hopes that he would see her, that she would come running back and throw her arms about him.

When they reached the atrium, Lucius turned to the eunuch.

"Tell her I'm sorry," he said when he stepped beyond the threshold.

The door slammed behind him, and the iron bolt slid home with a loud crack.

XIV

Subversio Paradisi

'The Destruction of Paradise'

A.D. 201

It had been almost two years since the legions had come to Alexandria. The walls of Hatra seemed like a distant memory, and the smoke of Ctesiphon had long since fluttered away on the breeze.

Lucius tried to forget Medea, but he could not. He tried to return to her villa to see her, but he was always refused entry. Part of him cursed himself for being so weak, for neglecting duty, at least in his heart, but the void left by the tenderness she had given him seemed to be growing.

And yet, he knew what she had proposed, as idyllic as that sort of life might have been, was just not realistic. He knew he could not have it both ways.

One night when he was lying in bed after a long day of leading drills for the legion, Lucius was staring at the statue of Apollo on the altar beside his bed. He watched the smoke of his offering swirling around the god by the light of the oil lamp that flickered in the breeze that seeped beneath the tent wall.

His eyes closed and opened slowly, exhaustion beginning to overtake him when he thought he saw the statue move, point at him.

Lucius blinked but could not move, his lids still heavy with exhaustion.

You must seize the opportunities that will lead you to your destiny... a voice said in his mind.

It sounded like lyre strings, then like a chant, and a song. Then a command.

Metellusssss.... Harken to me. Your ancestors watch you...and I watch you. Step forward, young dragon. Stand out among the eagles of Rome...

The howl of the cornu woke Lucius up. There was a mumbling sound and Lucius looked up to see Alerio shaking him, Argus standing beside him. They were both dressed in full uniform.

"Wake up, Lucius!" Alerio said.

"Are you drunk?" Argus said. "Lucius! The men are fucking kitted out and marching to the Principia for an emergency assembly. Wake up!"

"What?" Lucius' eyes shot open and he swung his legs quickly over the edge of his cot, his head nearly hitting Alerio across the face. "What's happened?"

Alerio stepped back and Argus tossed Lucius his pteruges.

"The call to arms sounded a short time ago, with orders to assemble before the legate," Alerio said. "Come on, we'll help you."

Lucius stood up and put on his tunic, and pteruges. He took his boots from beside the bed and began lacing them up, before allowing Argus to put his chain-mail on and begin tying it up.

"Why can't you drink like this when we're together," Argus said. "You'd be a lot more fun if you did."

"I wasn't drunk," Lucius said as he raised his arms to allow Alerio to hang the phalerae over his chest, followed by his gladius and pugio. "I just overslept."

"Well, it won't do to have the primus pilus lashed before the legion," Alerio said. "Let's go!" he fastened Lucius' crimson cloak over his shoulders, handed him his helmet and vinerod, and they marched out into the daylight, Lucius chewing a hunk of stale bread he snatched off the table as they went.

When they arrived at the open space before the Principia, the last of the men of III Parthica were falling in.

Lucius arrived just in time to stand at the front before the legate began to speak. Lucius could see Livius staring at him.

A wind was up, and Lucius could feel it tearing at the crest of his helmet. Dust and sand whipped around the Principia, biting at the bare parts of his calves, but if felt good, reviving. He tried desperately to shake the cobwebs from his mind.

Seize the opportunities that will lead you to your destiny... he remembered the voice.

"We've received reports that a massive force of Parthians is gathering with intent on the border of Palaestina," Legate Tertullius said loudly. "II Traiana returned last night with heavy casualties from their own routine patrol with the report."

The men began to mumble at this, and Lucius turned to stare them all down, his vinerod slapping his hands. "Quiet in the ranks!" he barked, before turning back to allow the legate to continue.

"A swift, decisive action is needed, and I thought III Parthica would be well-suited to this. You've been drilling well, but there is no substitute for real combat. We may be leaving Alexandria soon to go back to the fronts on the Empire's borders, but first we need to finish the Parthians once and for all. Men of III Parthica, are you ready to fight for Rome?"

"Yes, sir!" the voices of the troops rumbled and shook the air, and Lucius felt a chill run up his spine.

"First!" Tertullius said, his hands raised for quiet. "The terrain is difficult. It won't be easy. Only one legion at a time can move into the area." Tertullius eyed the ranks of soldiers. "The are reports of Parthian cataphracts in this force. Many of them."

The air was silent then, only the sound of a few hungover sniffles could be heard, the clearing of some men's throats as some stared at the sand and not at their commander.

"Who will lead the van?"

"I will, Legate Commander!"

Lucius found himself standing out in front of the legate and tribunes, before the whole legion. He stood stiff, at attention, his eyes staring directly at his commander.

Tertullius nodded, obviously proud and relieved that someone had come forward so quickly. III Parthica did not disappoint.

"Very good, Lucius Metellus Anguis!" the legate said out loud.

"Might I lead the men of First Cohort from the front, sir?" Tribune Livius said, stepping forward to stand before Lucius.

Tertullius looked taken aback by this. He had thought to have the tribunes with him at the rear command position, but he nodded his assent. "Very good. Very good!" he said loudly for all to hear. "We leave in one hour!"

The men cheered and Lucius nodded to Livius.

"I'll meet you at the east gate, Metellus."

"Yes, sir," Lucius saluted and turned to see his century standing there waiting for his instructions. "First Century!" he barked. "Get your kit together! We meet at the east gate in ten minutes!"

The men saluted and turned to go about their business.

Alerio, Argus, Antanelis, Eligius, Garai and Maren all waited for Lucius who approached them when the rest of the men had gone.

"Looks like we're in for a fight," Lucius said. "You ready?"

"You doubt it?" Argus said, smiling, the others chuckling good-naturedly.

"Never," Lucius said, before leading them all out of the Principia.

The winds were up the whole of the march, the sand that enveloped the Nile Delta spinning out of control and hampering the marching legion's view.

III Parthica was at the front of the column, with Lucius and Tribune Livius in the van with the vexillarius holding the standard, the imaginifer with the emperor's image, and aquilifer carrying the legion's golden eagle.

The line of various legions ran all the way back to Alexandria, a long, thin, red line of war with Lucius and Livius at the head.

Squinting, Lucius could spot the distant rocky hills of Palaestina, a brown haze of sand before them. They continued to march, and Lucius looked up at Livius to see the tribune fidgeting with his reins. His mount was edgy too, no doubt attuned to his rider's state of mind.

"We can handle this, sir!" Lucius said.

Livius looked down from his horse. "I know, Centurion. I just don't like this sand. We can't see a bloody thing."

"The scouts will be returning soon, sir. They'll give us warning, then we can reap the Parthians like Egyptian wheat."

"Glad to see you up for the fight, Centurion," Livius said. "Hold!" he said suddenly. "I see the scouts. They're coming up quickly." Livius held his hand up and the cornicen sounded the note to halt, the other centurions echoing the order."

Lucius stepped forward to stand beside Livius' horse. Out of the dusty air, three riders in red cloaks sped directly toward them.

"Why are they waving their arms like that?" Livius said.

Just then, one of the riders was pitched over his horse's head with a long arrow shaft protruding from his back.

"Shields up!" Lucius yelled, raising his scutum to stop an arrow plunging into Livius' chest.

The tribune's horse reared as the other two scouts fell from their horses, their backs, and their horses riddled with shafts.

"Testudinem facite!" Livius yelled as he drew his golden spatha from his side and spurred forward, wild and panicked.

"First Century! On the tribune!" Lucius yelled, holding up his scutum and leading the men forward in their tortoise formations into the hail storm of Parthian arrows.

385

The sounds of the whiz and crash of arrows upon their shields was deafening as the Parthian horse archers did their worst. Men cried out as barbed arrows shredded their calves and pinned their feet, the occasional one cutting its way into the testudo formation.

Lucius walked crouched behind is scutum, his helmet's crest askew from the glancing arrows that the Parthians aimed at him.

Far-Shooting Apollo, make me impervious to their arrows. Make them miss me... he prayed as more of his men cried out behind him.

His eyes searched for Livius in the maelstrom of dust kicked up by wind and whirling horses ahead of them. With the tribune in front, he could not order the pila thrown, which was the only way to slow down the horse archers.

Then he heard it, a clang of swords pitched above the violent neighing of a horse. Directly ahead, Lucius could see the figure of the tribune, his red cloak whipping in the wind as he whirled, hacking away at the passing archers who seemed to be teasing him, putting the arrows where they would not kill the man.

"Forward!" Lucius yelled. "First rank, pila ready!" He plunged forward toward Livius, the latter swaying on top of his saddle with several shafts sticking out of him. Lucius spotted the dead Parthians at his horse's feet, but it did not look good.

Lucius felt a rage fill him up. He hefted his own pilum, which he had decided to take this time, and began to run toward the tribune. With a great bellowing cry, Lucius launched the pilum so that it soared directly for the group around Livius. The spear shaft took two Parthians together, their linen armour easy prey for the iron tip.

The two riders fell in a heap, and Livius stared at Lucius, his face exhausted, tears of pain running down his sweaty face.

Lucius yelled. "Pila iacite!" to the men coming up behind him.

The pila of the first rank launched and the rest of the horse archers swarming Livius either fell or turned quickly to regroup farther away as was their tactic.

Lucius ran toward Livius. He could hear the other centuries coming up behind them, the beautiful sound of their cornui, and the harsh orders of the other centurions.

"Tribune!" Lucius said, his hand steadying the wounded horse. "You need to get to a medicus at the back of the line right away. You're losing a lot of blood, sir!"

Livius nodded. He was exhausted. "I won't argue with that, Centurion. My thanks for coming for -" Livius was suddenly clawing wildly at his throat and neck now.

Lucius felt a spray of hot blood across his face, and wiped his eyes to see. He looked up and caught Livius just as he fell onto him, a black Parthian arrow going through his neck, in one side and out the other.

Livius struggled, his eyes wide as he choked to death in Lucius' arms.

"Medicus!" Lucius yelled. "Alerio! Four men to carry the tribune back!" He looked down at Livius again when he felt the struggling stop.

Livius' eyes were wide, but the life had gone out of them.

As if the god of war laughed now, the ground began to shake, more and more with each second. A chorus of hooves, and jingling chain mail against plate armour simmered beneath the pounding, and Lucius knew, every man behind him knew, that the Parthians were coming back. But it was not the archers this time.

"Arrgggg!" Lucius stood up, in front of Livius' body, hoisted his scutum with a shaking hand, and stared ahead. "Prepare to repel cavalry!" he yelled, trusting for all he could in the drills they had practiced again and again, hoping that Disciplina would not desert them.

He felt his legs wobble on the shaking earth and then, "Pila iacite!" he yelled out, before throwing one of his own and crouching behind his scutum just as the first cataphracts came into view.

He could hear the song of hundreds of pila soaring overhead, could feel the strength of the men at his back, right on him, there to challenge Death alongside him.

Horses screamed as the first wave of Roman javelins scythed them down, finding chinks in the armour of both horse and rider.

But the Parthian cataphracts were not easily turned, sweeping around First Century and flowing along the flanks of the other centuries like raging waters rushing around a boulder.

"Ten men to stay around the tribune's body!" Lucius called back. "The rest, on me! Tight formations! Forward!" Lucius yelled as he rose and began picking his way over fallen horses, his gladius slashing down at still-living Parthian riders.

The cornui sounded and Lucius could hear the rumble of their own cavalry on the wings engaging the Parthians.

Forward, Lucius, he told himself. *Keep going forward,* he thought as the command to advance echoed from far behind them.

Ahead he spotted something glinting in the pale light and he gasped.

A group of three Parthian riders held aloft one of Rome's aquila standards, taunting the advancing Romans.

Lucius knew it was III Parthica's eagle, and felt shame at the sight of it in enemy hands.

It was as if a fury took hold of him. He looked back at his men as the rumble of hooves started in front of them once more, and he knew they saw it too.

"First Century! To our eagle!" and without another word, they rushed the Parthians.

Lucius' legs carried him over the bloody sand and litter of bodies into the teeth of those fourteen-foot kontos lances. He screamed revenge and felt he could not put a foot, or hand, thrust or parry wrong. His scutum checked the first kontos which he got under. The second he grabbed with his hand and pulled so hard that the armoured rider came crashing down.

As the third Parthian cataphract turned to ride off with the eagle, Lucius drew his gladius and jumped onto the horse's back. He grappled violently with the rider, who head-butted Lucius with his helmet.

Lucius held on, his breath rapid as he struggled to prize the aquila's shaft away from the man's iron grip, until the horse reared and they both fell to the ground.

All around the fighting pair, other Parthians attempted to ride in and skewer the Roman centurion trying to take back the eagle, but Argus, Alerio, Antanelis and the others formed an impenetrable wood and iron ring around them, their gladii and pila cutting down any approaching riders who sought to take the legion's eagle away.

As Lucius fought the massive Parthian, the other's spiked cudgel whipped out taking Lucius in the chest, tearing away some of the steel rings of his mail armour.

Lucius grabbed his pugio and let it fly at the man's face when he swung around again, and the Parthian screamed as it took him across the eyes. Lucius dove in with his gladius then, driving the blade up and under the helmet to push it into his enemy's skull as he yelled.

All about Lucius, it seemed a storm of screams and fury raged. The iron tang of blood, and shit, and piss of dying men rose up in his nostrils. He felt dizzy and sick, but he fought it down, forced himself to scan the area.

Then he felt the shaft of the aquila in his grip and felt the battle joy run through his body. With the eagle in one hand and his bloody gladius in the other, Lucius raised his arms and yelled.

His men, who were all blood-soaked and wild, but still holding position around the eagle cried out with him.

The sound to advance on the retreating Parthians sounded then, and the crunch of Roman hobnails from the other arriving legions now drowned out the rumble of the Parthian cavalry.

"Forward III Parthica!" Lucius yelled, and holding the aquila, he plunged forward into the storm of battle to finish the job.

III Parthica lost all of its centurions that day, except Lucius.

Word spread quickly that Lucius Metellus Anguis had saved the legion's aquila, saved them from disgrace. Though the legion had taken the heaviest losses to the Parthian cataphracts, they were not humiliated in the eyes of their brothers, or the Gods.

As III Parthica regrouped, three more legions carried on to pursue the enemy survivors until the commanders were sure the threat was eliminated. Those legions met with little resistance.

When Commander Tertullius rode up with some of the other generals, Lucius and the survivors of his century were standing guard around the body of Tribune Livius. Lucius still held III Parthica's aquila in his cut and bloody hands.

Tertullius looked down at him and took in the shattered armour, and the flowing wounds of Lucius and his men where they stood on the clotted sand.

"Hail, men of III Parthica!" he said as he dismounted and saluted them.

The other tribunes fell in behind their commander and looked down in horror at their colleague who lay there with a shaft through his savaged neck.

"Metellus," Tertullius said softly as he put both his hands on Lucius' shoulders and stared into his exhausted eyes.

It took Lucius a moment to register his commander's voice and face. "Sir!" he snapped out of his daze, his grip still tight around the aquila.

"I know what you did, Metellus," Tertullius said, shaking his head in disbelief. "Good work, lad. Good work."

Lucius met his commander's eyes and nodded, but did not say anything.

"Good work, all of you!" the legate said to the men around Lucius. "III Parthica should be proud this day!"

The men of the legion cheered, their voices rising up to heavens so that the Gods themselves could hear.

Lucius did not join in the shouting, but among the chanting, he could hear his own name being called out by many of the men. "Metellus! Metellus! Metellus!"

In his mind, he could hear another name being whispered from some far-off place... *Anguis... Anguis... Anguis...*

A week later, III Parthica was back in Alexandria, the men of its ranks finally given the respect they had earned as they walked along the streets between the other legionary camps.

They had been given a week's furlough to recover from the battle and many of the men had gone into Alexandria to drown their sorrows at the loss of so many friends, or sing songs of victory for having survived. Every man celebrated in his own way.

Lucius was sitting alone in his tent on a day when the sun shone brightly without. He had tried reading some of his scrolls to distract his wandering mind, but he could not focus. It was not the tightness of the numerous bandages that hampered his thoughts, but rather Medea.

Though he tried not to think of her, she came into his mind. He thought, frustratingly, of what she was doing at that moment, who she might be with. The tortuous thoughts laid waste to him as he sat there in his tent with a cup of wine and a scroll of Caesar's memoir of Gaul.

Lucius whipped the scroll across the room so that it hit the leather tent wall with a thump and fell into the sand.

"What did she expect?" he said out loud, inwardly cursing his inability to understand her.

He needed to see her, he knew. Else he would go mad. He tried to remember her smiling, her dark, happy eyes, her face straining with pleasure, but all he could conjure was her face contorted with anger on the day she had told him to leave.

He knew she was a hetaira, but...

"I'm being stupid," he chided himself.

"Centurion Metellus?"

Lucius whipped around to see a Praetorian messenger standing in the entrance of his tent.

"Yes?" Lucius answered, looking up at the massive soldier.

"You are commanded to report to the imperial palace near the harbour in one hour."

"Why? For what?"

"The emperor wishes to see you. That is all you need to know."

'The emperor?' Lucius' mind raced. "The emperor?"

"That's what I said," the man answered, his expression haughty. "I suggest you come in full uniform."

"I... I will," Lucius said. "Yes, of course."

"Good. I'll meet you at the east entrance to the palace, at the end of the via Corpiae. Don't be late."

"I won't," Lucius said, as the man turned and walked out without another word.

Lucius leaned on the table for a moment, gathering his thoughts. What had happened? He raced through the possibilities in his mind. *Did Barbarus complain about his lack of payment to imperial authorities?* Lucius knew the man

393

was well-connected with the upper echelons of Alexandria. *Maybe my men are in trouble in the city?*

He busied himself in gathering the new chain-mail that he had acquired, and other items, his pteruges, cloak, the iron brooch to fasten it. His wounds made it hard to arm himself, and he thought about going out to find someone to help him, but decided against it.

"What are you doing?" Argus' voice said from the doorway.

Lucius turned in surprise. "I thought you were in town with Maren, Eligius and Garai?" Lucius said. "The whores too busy right now?" he laughed.

"No," Argus said, walking in. "I've had my turn."

"No drinking then?"

"Yes. Later."

"So?"

"I came check on you, you crazy son-of-a-bitch."

Lucius stopped what he was doing and looked up.

Argus continued. "I can't believe what you did out there...in the battle."

"We all pulled our weight, Argus. You too."

"Yeah, well..." Argus seemed awkward. "I... You led us, kept us together, even though we were at the front. I was talking with some of the survivors from the other centuries, and they said that their centurions panicked when the cataphracts charged them."

"That's why they're all dead," Lucius said, standing up, his eyes closed against the throbbing in his wounds.

"Well... we're not, Lucius. And I think that's thanks to you."

Lucius looked at his long-time friend and nodded. He knew how hard it was for Argus to spit those words out. He did not need to answer, just nod and smile, acknowledge the sentiment.

Argus nodded and sat down on a stool at the table, pouring a cup of wine for himself. "So what are you doing?" He nodded toward the uniform Lucius was laying out.

"A Praetorian messenger just came to summon me to the palace in one hour."

"What? Why?"

"The emperor wants to see me."

Argus' eyes were wide. "Severus? Why do you think?"

"I don't know. But I could use some help getting dressed."

"Why didn't you say so!" Argus stood up and began helping Lucius with his chain mail, and pteruges, his greaves and the phalarae which he fastened over Lucius' chest. The latter had more decorations on it now than when they had started out.

After a few minutes, Argus stood there with his arms crossed.

Lucius checked to make sure they had not forgotten anything. "Gladius, pugio...vinerood..."

"Helmet!" Argus grabbed the helmet with the new crest off of the stand and handed it to Lucius.

Lucius put it on over his head and fastened the strap.

"How do I look?"

"Like the legion's best fucking centurion!" Argus said.

"The legion's only centurion for now," Lucius added.

"Do you want me to come with you? I can get kitted out quickly."

"Best not. The order was just for me." Lucius paused for a moment, his eyes going to the statue of Apollo for a second. "If anything goes wrong... If I don't come back for some reason... Can you tell Alene that I'm sorry I didn't write more. That I love her and miss her."

"Don't talk like that. You'll see her again and tell her yourself."

"Right... Just, well in case I don't -"

"Fine. All right."

"Thanks."

"You'd better get going. The streets will be packed after the races in the hippodrome. I'll walk with you."

"Back to your favourite ladies?" Lucius laughed as they walked outside.

"Where else?" Argus said, slapping Lucius on the back as the two of them walked out of the camp toward the city.

It had been several years since Lucius left Rome with the emperor's legions, and not once had he met his imperator, or even seen him up close.

Now, he was on his way to a private audience with the most powerful man in the world. He was nervous and sweating beneath his armour, but he knew that he had to be the dutiful, strong centurion that he had come to be.

When he arrived at the palace steps he was met by the Praetorian who had come to his tent with the summons.

The man looked Lucius up and down and nodded. "Better," he said. "Follow me."

As they walked, there were Praetorians everywhere. They had been hand-picked from the emperor's own legions when he won the civil war, to replace the treacherous Praetorians who had been in power before. The previous Praetorians had auctioned the Empire to the highest bidder, and had grown too powerful for their own good. Now the emperor had men that he could trust surrounding him.

Lucius wondered if they were different from the previous men of the Guard.

He was led through corridor after corridor until they came to a large set of cedar doors.

"Leave your weapons here, Centurion," his escort said.

Lucius felt a prickle of dread at this, but knew he had no choice. He unsheathed his pugio and gladius and handed them to one of the guards flanking the big doors.

The messenger nodded to the other two guards who turned to open the doors.

"Go in," the man said.

Lucius moved forward, his eyes scanning for anything amiss.

The room was ringed with gigantic Corinthian columns, and appeared to be empty. At the far end of the pink and green marble floor was a large seat or throne made of gold, above which was an eagle with outspread wings.

No one was there, and Lucius turned in a panic, his eyes raking the walls and each alcove for signs of movement.

Apollo, guide me...

A door near the throne opened then on the far right, and in came Emperor Septimius Severus. He was dressed in a flowing purple cloak under which he wore a gold and black cuirass emblazoned with a seated Jupiter beneath a noble eagle.

"Hail Caesar!" Lucius said, snapping his best salute, and then bowing low, his heart racing.

"Rise and approach, Centurion Metellus," the emperor said, his voice hoarse from one of his coughing fits.

A slave and a secretary followed close behind, the one pouring wine into two cups, and the other sitting on a nearby stool with his stylus poised above a wax tablet.

Lucius stood straight and approached the throne slowly.

Severus was older than he had expected, taller too. The full, curling beard seemed to hide his mouth so that it was hard to see if he was pleased or angry. His brow was creased a lot from the pressures of the Empire, and of incessant thought and strategizing. He limped a little, but Lucius could see that he was a soldier at heart, that the armour and sword he wore were a part of him, and not just decorations of power. Lucius could tell that though he had had health problems, the emperor was still muscular in his older age.

"Be at ease, Lucius Metellus Anguis. I too am a soldier." Through dark eyes, he gazed down at Lucius as he played with the curls of his dark beard with one hand. "I have heard a great deal about you for some time, especially of late." He put up his hand. "Oh, all good. Do not worry yourself. Come closer."

Lucius moved closer, standing as straight as he could manage atop his buckling knees.

"You are a formidable young man, Metellus. Legate Tertullius was right, and Tribune Livius spoke true of you." The emperor rubbed his forehead and sniffed. "I am very sorry for his loss. He was a good soldier, a tribune with much promise in the Senate."

"He was a good leader, sire. Much admired," Lucius said inclining his head, trying to shake the image of Livius with a Parthian shaft through his neck, choking on his own blood as it flooded down his throat.

The emperor stared at Lucius, the latter not knowing where to look, away or directly at Caesar.

"I'm told you retrieved his body from the field. That you tried to save him from a group of Parthian cataphracts?"

"I tried, sire, but I'm afraid my efforts to save him fell short. I am sorry."

"And you did so on foot?" Severus continued.

"Y...yes, sire."

"I can see that you are humble, Centurion Metellus. The Gods love humility, but they also favour the bold." Severus stood up, using his strong arms to compensate for the work his legs found more difficult. He descended the three steps from the throne and walked over to a table that was laden with scrolls and wax tablets, maps and other dispatches.

"Tertullius has told me about you, Metellus, how well you command men, how you always keep your head in battle, and maintain discipline. Those are attributes that I like to see in my officers." Severus held his head up higher as he looked Lucius up and down, his bearded chin jutting out slightly. "Let me get right to the point. I had chosen Tribune Livius to undertake a crucial patrol for me across the African provinces to the West."

Lucius stood to attention, his ears cocked, his mind surprised at the direction the conversation was taking.

"My spies have informed me of plots against us in Cyrene, Africa Proconsularis, my home province, and in Numidia. These plots need to be stamped out immediately." Severus paced a bit more, his hands behind his back as he looked up, seeming to stare past the ceiling to the stars beyond.

"Unfortunately, Livius is no longer with us." He paused briefly as if recollecting the young tribune, and smiled slightly. "He, and your legate, had spoken to me of promoting you. I have heard what you did on the field of battle the other day, and I believe you were the only surviving centurion of III Parthica's first cohort for a reason. You're just the sort of man I need to command in the legions. As you know, I've been making many changes to the legions, new assignments and troop dispositions." The emperor stopped pacing and stood directly before Lucius who found it hard to keep his head up in Severus' presence.

"This mission I had set for Livius would not be misplaced, I think, if I were to put it in your charge?"

Lucius could not speak for a moment, was unsure if he had heard correctly. *Listen, Lucius! Speak up!* he told himself.

"You honour me, sire. I don't know what to say to such generosity." Lucius bowed low.

"Do you accept the sensitive assignment, Metellus?"

Lucius looked up, and for an instant, he thought he spied a tall figure in the sunlight beyond the throne, where a balcony looked onto the sea.

"Yes, Caesar. I am honoured beyond words." Lucius stood tall now, his heart racing inside his shuddering rib cage. *Can this really be happening?*

"Good. From what Legate Tertullius says, you're perfect for this undertaking. It may sound easy patrolling across peaceful provinces, but be warned, where there is quiet, Mars always sits in the shadows, waiting to rear his head when least expected."

Lucius nodded. "I understand, sire."

"So, Lucius Metellus Anguis..." Severus motioned to his secretary who handed him a scroll with the imperial seal on it. "You are now Tribunus Angusticlavius of the Imperial Legions." He handed Lucius his new commission which had already been drawn up.

"I don't know how you feel about the cursus honorem, or what your plans might be, but I suspect that this will please your father, Senator Metellus. I'm sure he wants you to pursue politics, does he not?"

"Sire, my father and I rarely see eye-to-eye. I had thought to make a career in the army."

"Then that will please me, Metellus," Severus smiled amiably. "I want good men in higher positions, not sycophants whose only wish is to get to the Senate, or milk a province dry for their own ends. Times are changing. Only the stars and the Gods know what is in store."

"Yes, sire. I won't let you down." Lucius bowed again.

"You'll need trusted men. I want you to form a cohort of the best and most trusted men you know. You are free to assign six centurions of your own choosing, provided Legate Tertullius agrees with the selection. Also you will be assigned an ala of auxiliary cavalry. They'll be sent to you in your camp the morning you leave. Do you have any questions, Tribune?"

"Yes, sire. If we should uncover a plot, how would you like me to deal with it?"

"If possible, deal with it through the normal legal avenues, that is if they are Roman traitors. If they are not within the

401

Empire's purview, defeat them on the field. The first option is preferable. Those are my home provinces, and I don't want them soured against me. If you need to, seek the help of the local governors, magistrates, or prefects. Here is a letter giving you my permission to use whatever means you deem necessary."

Severus' secretary handed the Lucius another scroll with a seal on it.

"This isn't an easy assignment, Metellus. Stay alert, and be ready for anything. Once you reach Numidia, you will be absorbed into the III Augustan legion at Lambaesis." He smiled at Lucius, almost like a father, and went back up the stairs to sit on the throne. "Oh, and by the way, you should buy yourself a horse for the patrol. You're a tribune now. It's hot as Hades out there, trust me, and you don't want to trudge through the sands with ordinary troops. That's a centurion's job." He laughed playfully. "You leave in a week. Good luck, Tribune Metellus."

"Thank you, sire. Ave Caesar!" Lucius saluted, spun on his heel, and went out of the great room and the emperor's presence. Once he had collected his weapons from the guards, and been escorted out of the palace, he stood in the middle of the Canopic way and stared up at the sky, feeling the sunlight on his face and smiling at the wave of relief that washed over him.

Thank you, Apollo. Thank you...

That night, Lucius paced in his tent, waiting for them to arrive. His mind had been spinning since he met with the emperor, his mind constantly challenging the reality of his new situation.

All my hard work has paid off, he told himself. *Apollo has guided me this far, and now I must prove myself worthy.*

A large chunk of incense smouldered on the altar beside the statue of Apollo. Lucius stopped pacing to stare at the image of his family's patron god.

He wondered for a moment how his friends would receive the news he was about to give them. Would it give rise to more jealousy, especially in Argus, with whom he was tired of fighting. He looked at the pitcher of wine and seven clay cups that sat on the table beside a map of the North African provinces. He had purchased a jug of Chian wine from the city, but forced himself to wait for the others. He would drink after he told them.

The laughter outside of the tent reached his ears and he crossed his arms as he stared at the entrance.

"Finally!" Lucius said loudly. "I've been waiting."

"Centurion!" Antanelis laughed and saluted as the others came in after him, each saluting with varying degrees of respect.

"Come in, all of you. Take a seat around the table." Lucius reached out to stop Maren's hand as it went to the wine jug. "Not yet, Maren. Business first."

"Well... This must be serious then?" Maren said, standing back slowly, his blue eyes looking to Argus and then back to Lucius.

"It is. I have news," Lucius said, when Argus finally sat on one of the stools.

"So? What is it? They sending us back into Parthia? Another road need building?" Argus said. "Wait! The emperor wants us to erect a giant granite cock along the Nile!"

They all laughed, except Lucius.

"None of those, Argus. Though the latter might be your monument to the whores of Alexandria," Lucius chuckled.

"Yeah," Antanelis laughed. "It could say, 'Argus was here'."

"All right," Lucius continued.

"What did the emperor say today, Lucius?" Argus asked. He knew Lucius had returned safely, but Lucius had refused to tell him what happened before now. "You seemed pretty happy earlier. You going to tell us finally?"

"Yes. The emperor has promoted me to Tribunus Angusticlavius."

There was a moment of dead silence.

"An Equestrian tribune?" Alerio said, finally speaking. "Really, Lucius?"

"Yes."

"In III Parthica?" Antanelis asked, his face serious now.

"No."

"So you're leaving," Argus said flatly.

"What in Hades is going to happen to the rest of us?" Garai said, Eligius putting his hand on his shoulder to quiet his brother.

"I've been given command of my own cohort of four hundred and eighty men, plus an ala of one hundred and twenty cavalry."

"That's a lot of men. You've been wanting this for a long time, Lucius. Congratulations!" Alerio said, though Lucius could see the disappointment in his face, the looks of the others.

"There's more," Lucius said, reaching out to pour the wine slowly, careful not to spill a drop.

"Don't tell me some fucker from Rome is going to be commanding us now!" Argus said.

"No. I don't care what happens to III Parthica now."

"How can you say that, Lucius? After all we've been through, all we've lost. What about us?" Antanelis stood up quickly now, his face red with anger and frustration.

"Sit down, Antanelis," Lucius said, laying his hand on the younger man's shoulder before continuing to pour the wine and hand out the cups himself.

"I'm to pick the men of my own cohort," Lucius said. "All of them."

"They'll let you do that?" Argus asked.

"Yes." Lucius raised his cup to all of them. "So, may the Gods smile on us and this toast. "Lucius spilled some wine on the sand to the Gods before telling them. "To you six, the centurions of the new cohort assigned to the III Augustan legion."

They all looked at each other, confused for a few moments before the smiles began to spread across each of their faces.

Lucius watched them keenly, and noticed that Argus was the only one who did not smile.

"Centurions? All of us?" Eligius said, looking at his brother, then back at Lucius.

"Yes. To all of you!" Lucius said tipping his cup and feeling the rich wine pour down his throat.

"Woohoo!" Antanelis yelled. "This is great news! My parents won't believe it!"

"We've been given a special patrol duty across the African provinces from Aegyptus all the way to the legionary base at Lambaesis, here." Lucius pointed at the map to show them how far they had to travel. "You're not to talk about this to anyone, but we're supposed to hunt down some nomads who are working in the area against Rome. It's going to be dangerous, and we won't know who we can trust. "But this mission is ours, and if we do well, it could lead to great things for all of us."

All the men stared at the map and the banter began, questions about the distance and terrain, the nature of the nomads, their fighting skills, the make-up of the III Augustan legion in Numidia etcetera.

Only Argus stayed out of the conversation, and it made Lucius sad to see him silent at this news.

Argus drained his cup and put it on the table, some drops splattering on the map. He walked slowly around the table until he stood right in Lucius' face.

"You're fucking unbelievable," he said before wrapping his arms around Lucius and hugging him tightly. "You said you would rise, and you did, my friend. I... I can't wait to see the look on your pater's face when he hears this news."

"I don't care what he thinks," Lucius said, though he was unconvinced that was true. He smiled at Argus who held him at arm's length.

"Thanks for not leaving us behind, Lucius."

"I never will."

Before the group of friends left his tent, Lucius made sure to give them all their commission papers which had been drawn up that afternoon. They talked a bit of what troops they would take with them from III Parthica, but that there was a need for more from the other legions.

Lucius told them he would discuss it with Tertullius in the days ahead, after they gave him a list of the men each of them wanted in their individual centuries.

They were momentous days, those prior to the mission setting out. The very next day after he told his friends the good news, Lucius thought it best to take the emperor's advice, and made his way to the agora where the horse traders were located.

The black stallion was still there.

Lucius supposed that the beast had been too wild or too pricey for anyone to purchase him, but the stallion seemed to call to Lucius who had not stopped thinking about him since that first day he had seen him.

As Lucius approached the fence, the stallion was tied alone on the other side of the paddock, isolated from the other mounts.

When the trader saw Lucius looking at the stallion, he approached.

"You're back? It's been a long time, Centurion," the man said. "He is still for sale, too wild for a weak rider. Sadly, your rank does not permit you, as you pointed out to me."

"It's Tribune now," Lucius corrected.

"Really?" the trader said, his eyebrows peaking above his beady eyes. "You will be needing a mount then, I think."

"Yes. But I only have so much."

"That obstacle is only as big as we make it, Tribune."

"I would like to meet him," Lucius said. "If I may?"

The trader nodded. "You may, but I am not responsible for your broken neck, Tribune. What say you look at my other stock over here?" he said, pointing to the horses tied together on the nearer side of the paddock.

"No. I want to meet that one," Lucius said, hopping down onto the sand within the paddock and walking along the side of the railing until he was close to the black stallion. "There, there... I won't hurt you," Lucius said softly. He could see a crowd gathering out of the corner of his eye, some of them placing bets. On what, he did not want to know.

The stallion was much taller up close than Lucius realized. Its coat was deep black, and its mane long and wild. The animal tried to turn to see Lucius as he approached from the rear, but its head was tied and so could not be turned all the way.

"Bad idea, Tribune!" the horse trader called, just as one of the stallion's hind legs kicked out, narrowly missing Lucius' chest. Laughter ensued around the paddock.

"Idiot!" Lucius cursed himself. He moved to the side of the animal, wanting to reach out and run his hand along the muscular body, but refrained, instead walking directly to the railing to which the stallion was tied, and leaning on it, a few feet from the horse, out of biting range.

Lucius chanced a glance at the animal, and his eyes met the big glossy black orbs set in a strong, proud head. He smiled.

"You know, you remind me of another horse," Lucius said conversationally. "Bucephelas...you know? Alexander's horse."

The stallion continued to stare at Lucius, its ears perked toward him.

Lucius continued, moving a little closer along the railing. "The story goes that a mean horse trader came to northern Greece with a herd of horses he had taken from far away. Now, Bucephelas was the strongest and wisest of these horses, but he was also the most proud, and the trader was constantly trying to break him."

Lucius could feel the hot breath of the horse upon his turned neck, not yet facing the animal head-on.

"He couldn't break Bucephelas. One day, Alexander showed up at the trader's paddock where his father, King Philip, had decided that no one could ride the horse. 'Buy me this horse, father!' Alexander said. The king, being keen to show Alexander a lesson to harden him to life, decided to buy it for him if he could ride it." Lucius smiled, and chuckled, the stallion nudging him slightly.

"Now, people warned King Philip that he was going to kill the royal heir, but the king persisted in his challenge and let his son step into the paddock - one not unlike this one." Lucius turned to look behind them where a massive crowd had gathered. Then he turned to the rope that tied the horse to the railing and began to slowly untie the knot. People gasped, but he ignored them as he continued untying and telling his story to the black stallion that loomed over him like a shadow.

"Alexander walked up to Bucephelas and noticed that the horse was afraid of his shadow, as brave and powerful as he was. So Alexander helped him by turning him toward the sun and making the shadow disappear. He spoke to him, much as we are speaking, and then mounted Bucephelas and rode him across the Macedonian plain."

The knot came free and the stallion reared above Lucius, shaking his thick neck and mane, the eyes always keeping Lucius in sight.

But Lucius stood his ground, even though every muscle in him wanted to retreat.

Lucius turned his back on the animal, speaking softly, and leaned on the fence again. "Bucephelas and Alexander rode to the ends of the earth together for many years after that. They protected each other to the very end..." Lucius turned when he felt the heavy nudge at his back again to see the velvety black muzzle in his face.

"I'm no Alexander," Lucius said, but I think we would make a good pair riding across the Empire. What do you say?" Lucius reached up and stroked the strong neck, the solid cheek and forehead. "Will you let me ride you? Of course you'll need a name, and I wouldn't think of giving you Bucephelas'. Something older maybe?" Lucius looked at the ground. "How about... Pegasus?"

Onlookers were becoming impatient now, jostling at the railings and haranguing the man and horse.

"First rule of battle," Lucius said smiling, "don't get distracted in the fray. Stay focussed and you'll stay alive." He moved to the side of the animal, taking in the state of his legs and hooves, the flex of the back. It did not seem like the stallion had ever been ridden. "Pegasus..." Lucius repeated, and the stallion turned its head to look back at him. "Do you like it?"

The big black eyes looked at Lucius for a moment and then the head swung forward slowly, the body perfectly still.

When Lucius gripped the mane with his left hand and put his right over the back, the big muscles tightened and flexed, but the stallion did not move.

"I'm getting up now," Lucius warned, before swinging up with all his might until his right leg was hanging safely over the other side. The stallion raised his big head, and Lucius reached to grab the ropes hanging in front. "Let's do a couple of laps together," he said before nudging with his legs and leading the head around the perimeter of the paddock.

The stallion went into a quick, proud trot, catching Lucius unawares and throwing him off balance on the big back.

Lucius held on however, and tried to straighten his back as the two of them went around the paddock, a feeling of elation washing through both of them then.

At one point, his eyes were drawn to the face of a white-robed man in the crowd, dark and bearded, staring intently at him. It set Lucius on edge for a moment, but then as he sped past and lost sight of the man's face, he moved on.

Lucius laughed joyfully, not at the frustrated looks of the men who lost bets and were now handing drachmae and sestercii to their neighbours, nor at the horse trader whose mouth hung open as he watched to two go round and round. He laughed for the feeling of freedom and power it gave him to sit atop such a magnificent beast. It felt as if he was on air and he wondered if Perseus himself had felt such elation the first time he sat atop Pegasus in ages past as they soared into the skies.

411

After a few minutes, Lucius reigned in the stallion before the horse trader and dismounted, his hands holding the reins firmly in his grip.

"I'll take him!" Lucius said. "How much?"

"Same as before, Tribune. The price is five thousand denarii."

"Two thousand!" Lucius countered.

"I am a serious businessman, Tribune. you insult me in front of all these people."

Just then, the horse snapped at the trader, the latter jumping back and hitting the railing hard behind him.

"You see? Wild, he is!" the trader yelled, pulling up his tunic and showing bite marks on the sides of his torso. "Look what he did?" he said to the crowd.

Lucius looked about, confused by the show, but realized the trader did indeed want to get rid of the animal for all the trouble. He would take the price Lucius offered.

Lucius began to walk away. "Your price is too high!" he said over his shoulder as he walked, the horse following Lucius after another nip at the trader.

"All right, all right. Three thousand denarii! To get him out of my sight!"

Lucius stopped in his tracks and felt the stallion at his shoulder. "What do you think, Pegasus? Time to go?"

He felt his shoulder nudged again.

"I'll take him!" Lucius said, turning to see the trader sighing and rubbing his side.

When Lucius returned to III Parthica's camp, he found a place to stable Pegasus with the auxiliary horses, not too far from

412

where his own tent was located. He made sure there was fresh water, grain, and hay for Pegasus, and after a while of talking to him, and brushing him, he bid the stallion farewell for a time.

"I'll be back soon, don't you worry. I'll not leave you alone for long." He closed the bar to the stable and turned to pat Pegasus another time. "Tomorrow I'll get us a nice comfortable harness and saddle, so we'll both feel fine on the march. All right?"

The big eyes stared back at Lucius, as if the animal were trying to weigh up the man, and not the other way around.

Back in his tent, Lucius began sorting through his things, making notes on a wax tablet of any items he wanted before leaving - incense, oil, some wine, and more. His head swam with all that he might have to acquire and do.

He knew he needed to see Galenus one more time before leaving Alexandria. The old man had been nothing but kind, and, in truth, he had reminded Lucius so much of Diodorus that it had been a great comfort to be in his presence, as if Lucius was an idealistic youth once more under the tutelage of a man of infinite kindness and wisdom.

Again however, his thoughts were torn from the corridors of the great library to that villa along the canal of Alexandria, the lush gardens floored with mosaics, and filled with the heady scent of incense and perfume.

"Medea..." he said in a low, longing voice. He knew they had left things ill, and he also knew that leaving her would be the hardest part of leaving Alexandria, if he was truthful with himself.

Lucius pictured her dark hair and smooth, olive skin. Her voice still whispered in his ears and mind, as did the pain in her voice when she had asked him to stay and he had refused. He needed to see her one last time, not to make love or hear comforting words, but rather to offer his apology, to say that his life had been that much better for the tenderness she had given to him freely, from her heart.

Lucius Metellus Anguis sat back for a moment, wondering at his new reality, the turn his path had taken, and the favour the Gods had shown him, despite the harshness of his choices. In that moment, his eyes went to the trunk at the corner of his tent.

He had not opened it for some time, and a thick layer of sand and dust lay upon it. The dragon armour inside, he realized, was his to don now that he had achieved the rank of equestrian tribune.

Lucius looked at the shattered armour he had worn in the last battle and turned back to the trunk. Slowly, he stood and walked over to it, wiped the dust and dirt away to reveal the black leather and bronze studs that held it together.

"Ancestors of the Metelli, might I now wear this armour?" he wondered as the tent flaps slapped in the wind coming off of the sea, cracks of sunlight appearing on the ground around him, let in beneath and through the tears in the tent walls. "Am I worthy?"

His hand reached out to unhinge the clasps, and he lifted the lid to reveal the linen wrappings, and tufts of red horsehair. Lucius knelt in the sand and reached in to take hold of the black helmet with dragons on the cheek pieces. It was lighter than he remembered. He ruffled the tall horsehair crest, dusting it off, and then placed the helmet on his cot.

The greaves were dusty too, the dragons upon them hidden, but when he blew hard across their dark surface, the beasts appeared, as if shaking off soil in which they had lain in wait.

Next came the pugio of ancient design, a blade that still shone with an edge that could cut papyrus even then. The winged horses and head of Jupiter on the pommel appeared and came to life.

Lastly, Lucius stood and lifted the heavy, black, hardened bull's hide cuirass. He held it up, dust flowing in the rays of sunlight that angled their way into the tent. He gasped.

It was magnificent now that he actually looked upon it - the hard leather, carefully shaped like the muscles of a torso, a god, the silver ornamentation around the edges, and in the centre a huge silver dragon.

Lucius stared at it long and hard, his eyes squinting as it seemed to flap its great wings and breathe fire before him. It was so carefully wrought that he thought the artist must have had some magic which he used to breathe life into it, making it more powerful, more terrifying than any Gorgon's head.

Lucius heard a rustle behind him and turned abruptly to the corner from where the sound came, but the corner was empty, but for the altar and statue of Apollo where he had burned so many offerings, and said so many prayers.

When he looked back at the armour he smiled, and thought of Medea again.

"One last visit," he said. "One last farewell." He then took a cloth out of the trunk, a phial of oil, and began to clean the armour slowly, and carefully.

Two hours later, as the sun was setting in the western desert, Lucius walked across the Plain of Eleusis toward the villas along the Fluvius Novus.

He felt awkward in his full armour, unused to the stiffness of it, the hard rub of his pugio and gladius' pommels on the cuirass' solid body.

He also felt strong and powerful, blessed, and he hoped that these feelings would follow him in all that was to come. Of all the tests he could imagine at that moment the one before him held the most terror.

Saying goodbye to Medea was not something he relished or even wanted to do, that is, if she even allowed him entry to her home.

He stopped beside a tall palm tree and took a few deep breaths, straightened the pteruges that dangled from beneath his new armour, and the clean, thin-striped tunic that protruded from beneath the leather flaps of his pteruges.

Memories flooded back as he made his way up the torch-lit path to the villa, and he was suddenly overwhelmed with sadness once more at the thought of leaving her. As he came to the path that led onto the grounds, he stopped and looked ahead, trying to imagine her, a lovely earth-bound goddess in her favourite white stola, sitting on the couch waiting for him at the appointed time beside a table laden with fruit, wine, and lotus flowers.

It seemed an age since he had seen her, his friend, his lover.

The scent of jasmine filled his nostrils and he began to make his way toward the main doors, taking it all in, trying to remember every part of the place.

But something was not right. One of the main doors was open and unguarded. He stopped, his senses alert and on fire then as he tried to hear beyond the rustle of the greenery surrounding him. He approached, his hand on the hilt of his gladius, trying not to make a sound, but he still could not hear anything, not until he stepped through the doorway and into the atrium.

He heard them immediately - two men's voices, and the sound of weeping.

"Those cavalry troops weren't kidding," said one voice, followed by a smack upon flesh. "Nice, juicy pickings in this place."

"Too right," said the other voice. "But we'd best finish up, else some of the whore's customers show up."

"Let them come! We'll take care of them like we've taken care of all of them." There was a sound of shuffling, and a muffled yelp. "Come on, my sweet. Your turn. We've saved the best for last, you see?"

Lucius felt his heart racing in his chest as he slid his gladius slowly out of its sheath, the gleaming blade coming to life in the torch-light as he made his way down the corridor to the garden where the voices were coming from.

He peered around the corner of one of the peristyle columns. His eyes took in the scene that was both horrifying and tragic.

417

Medea was naked and on her knees, her head bowed beneath the sharp blade of a huge, stinking man who licked his lips at her, his grubby hands grabbing at her breasts as his blade dared her to move.

Strewn about the bloody mosaic floor of the courtyard were the limbs and abused bodies of the beautiful young women who had lived with Medea. Standing among the slaughter was another hulking brute, his bloody sword in one hand as he pulled at his loincloth with the other.

Lucius felt rage surge within. This paradise had been invaded by these two men, and he wanted to see them dead, to kill them with his own bare hands, and wring the life out of them.

Medea winced painfully as her hair was yanked back by the second man, the two creatures drooling over her.

In a second, Lucius was out in the open, standing in front of them.

"Let her go!" he said in his most solid, unshakeable voice, though he felt terror in every inch of his person.

The men stared at him in surprise, and then laughed.

Lucius took a step, but immediately the second in the loincloth came at him, hard and fast. His fat bulk sped toward Lucius whose sword swept up from beneath his cloak so that the man impaled himself on the razor-sharp blade, his greasy innards spilling out as Lucius sliced quickly to pull his sword free.

The other man screamed in rage and slammed Medea's head into the ground before coming at Lucius like an angry bull.

Lucius ran at him, wanting only his death, to parry his sword thrust, but he slipped in a pool of blood and fell backward.

The two of them fell over each other, each gasping, trying to find a hold on the other's throat, or an angle to plunge in a blade. Lucius could feel the impact of the other's sword and fist upon his armour as he struggled to gain his feet on the slippery floor. Finally, he got his foothold and attacked again, but the other was faster, managing to land a kick to Lucius' chest that sent him hard into a column and back onto the floor.

Lucius' sword flew from his grasp to crash with a metallic ring on the floor, making Medea scream. The man was on top of Lucius again, groping at his throat. The smell of garlic filled Lucius' nostrils and the man spat in his face. Lucius punched, and the man hit back, the chin strap of Lucius' helmet pulling his neck to one side as he reached with his free hand for the handle of his gladius.

"Time to die, Roman!" the man said, drawing the long dagger from his belt.

The blade came close to Lucius' throat, but he held it off with one hand. He glimpsed death for a moment, and the life he had led thus far, and closed his eyes for a heartbeat...until his hand managed to grasp the pommel of his family's gladius. He gripped it and swung so that it sliced into the back and side of the man on top of him.

The man screamed and lost his grip on Lucius' throat, the latter kicking him off with all his might, blood pouring from the wound he had inflicted. The man clutched at the gaping wound in his side and seemed ready to attack yet again, but Lucius swung his greaved leg up into the man's face so that he

419

crashed sideways into the table, sending fruit, silver platters and wine all over the place.

Lucius coughed, struggled with the straps of his helmet, and took it off. Blood ran all over his chest, face, and hands. He could hear Medea crying to the side, struggling to get up, but his eyes did not leave his opponent. He stepped forward and took the man's oily hair in his gory fist.

Lucius hated him, and stared into those spiteful eyes as he brought his gladius up and sliced across the man's neck, the blood pouring out as quickly as the life left him.

Lucius held him up by the hair for a few moments, his arm shaking for the dead weight of the corpse, and then he let it fall to the mosaic floor.

He felt like vomiting, but held it back, stopped by the sound of Medea's ragged breathing.

She was leaning against one of the couches, her head bleeding profusely, her body battered and bruised.

"It's over," he whispered, barely able to catch his own breath as he tried to pick her up and lead her away from the savaged bodies of the girls he knew she had loved so much.

In an adjacent room, where a brazier burned in a corner, Lucius laid Medea on a couch and covered her with blankets that had been piled in one of the corners. As he covered her, she looked up, her eyes filled with tears, her hand gripping his arm tightly, not wanting to let go.

He wondered how the Gods could allow someone so beautiful and kind to suffer so much.

What has she done to deserve this? he thought, his mind racing with feelings of dread, disgust, sadness, and pity. *I should have come sooner...*

They sat together, silent and bloody, Lucius still gripping his sword in one hand, his other around Medea.

After a while, Lucius found the door slave cowering in the bushes.

"I should kill you now for abandoning your mistress, coward!" Lucius said, his gladius pointed at the man. "Go and get Barbarus if you can manage to pull yourself out of your own piss."

The man nodded wildly and ran out into the night.

Meanwhile, Lucius lit more braziers, and began to wash the blood away from Medea with a sea sponge and water from the Nile that she kept in the domus shrine. As he did so, she looked directly at him for the first time, and there he saw that look of genuine affection that she had once bestowed upon him.

"Thank you, Lucius... I..."

"Don't speak," he said. "Not now. I'm sorry... I..."

"I know. I know..."

She did not, he knew. How could she? He wanted to tell her that she was the one who saved him by showing him what life is really about, how fragile and precious it all really is. But he could not say that, not when he was leaving and would probably never see her again.

There were, of course, men like that everywhere, those who would tear down paradise itself, lay waste to all that was good in the world.

In that moment, Lucius wanted to protect all that was good. He wanted to kill those who were evil, those who brought decay to the world about him. The dead men in the garden were no different than Bona had been.

They sat all night, silent for the most part, Medea falling in and out of terror-sticken grief, and Lucius wide-eyed and awake, watching over her.

When the sound of peacocks rang along the banks of the canal, and morning light poured over the rooftop and into the peristyle garden, Lucius sighed and shifted in his armour, the dragon upon his chest encrusted with blood. He kissed Medea on the forehead, but she did not stir.

"I'm leaving in a few days, and I won't be able to come back," he said in a low voice.

She did not move, and her lids were still shut.

"The emperor has made me a tribune and is sending me to Numidia." He had no idea if she could hear him, but he felt compelled to speak anyway. "I'm... I will always be grateful for our time together. Thank you, Medea..."

From his vantage point, he did not see the tears running down from Medea's bruised eyes, nor the quiver of her lip where it leaned against his forearm guard.

Lucius felt his heart heavy with a tidal wave of emotion as the sounds of Barbarus and his men arriving at the house reached his ears, and he knew that he would have to leave her.

Duty called, and she was not his to take care of any longer.

Medea shifted and sat up, wincing with the pain, but Lucius helped her up, and made sure she was covered.

"What has happened here?" Barbarus appeared in the doorway, his usual calm demeanour broken, his eyes wild and concerned.

"We were attacked by those two men out there," Medea said, her voice struggling for strength, for some measure of control. "Tribune Metellus here came just in time to help me, else I would be joining..." she stifled a cry, "my friends..."

Barbarus turned to Lucius who was looking at Medea now, knowing she had heard every word he had said. "Thank you, Centurion, or, I mean, Tribune. I must say that Alexandria will be a safer place once the legions have left her doorstep. Do you know who those men were?"

"No, Barbarus," Lucius said. "All I know is they're dead." Lucius stared hard at the man.

Barbarus began to back away from the bloody Roman before him. "Well, it's good you came. Let's consider all debts forgiven, for the service you have rendered here... I mean... yes. That's it," he mumbled, going back out into the garden where he began ordering his men to clean the house and send someone to summon the urban guard. He knew this would be bad for business.

When Barbarus was gone, locked away in another part of the villa, Lucius saw Medea to her cubiculum where he waited outside the door. After a few minutes she emerged, wearing a clean stola and covered by a floor-length cloak.

"Let me take you to the door. I need to get out of this place," she said, walking toward the atrium with Lucius beside her.

When they passed out of the front doors and were standing on the path among the sunlit jasmine bushes, Medea turned to Lucius and kissed him softly on the mouth with her bruised and swollen lips. She even managed to smile.

"I'll be fine," she said as he stared at her. "The Gods have different plans for each of us, Lucius."

"I'm sorry for everything."

"Never feel sorry for giving me joy. I have so little of it. I will cherish the memories of our time."

"Will you stay here?" he asked.

"That will be up to Barbarus. I hope not. I can't. Maybe Cyprus... he has other businesses there..." Shook her head slightly, trying to dismiss the thoughts. Her eyes opened again and she looked up at Lucius one last time.

"Go, Lucius Metellus Anguis. May Apollo light your path, and may your destiny be great."

"I won't forget you, Medea," Lucius said.

"Go," she urged. "Please, go now," her voice cracked and she pushed Lucius gently, her hand lingering on the bloody dragon upon his chest.

Lucius nodded, and began to back away, before turning and walking back down that path, his steps heavy. He turned one last time to see her, sunlight highlighting the tears upon her face before she turned and went back inside that house of slaughtered paradise.

XV

In Deserto

'Into the Desert'

Lucius wanted to leave Alexandria right away, unable to bear the sight of it any longer for all that had happened, but the tasks that a tribune had were many and varied, even when he had six centurions to assign things to.

They were set to leave in a few days, but there was still so much to do.

He and his centurions had to finalize the troop dispatches for the new cohort, and get them approved by the legate. Every new trooper had to have equipment that was up to standard and undamaged, with spare parts ordered and loaded onto the wagons and pack horses that would be accompanying them; those animals had to be acquired too.

The quarter masters were hard-put to gather all of the provisions that over five hundred men and numerous beasts would need, from food and grain, to water and wine, tents, pots, pans, a certain amount of coin for pay, mallets, nails, groma for the engineers when they laid out the camp every night, and then the tools for making camp, other than the pick axes that every legionary carried on his back.

"This list is endless!" Lucius finally yelled, just as Alerio walked in under the tent flaps.

"Not going well?" he joked.

"No, everything is falling into place just perfectly. Only, the blacksmiths tell me we won't need nails in the desert, and the rope makers tell me we'll need more than I've ordered. The saddle and harness I've ordered for Pegasus still isn't finished with a couple days to go, and the grain ships from up river haven't arrived, meaning that we may have to take on extra provisions in Cyrene."

"We'll do that anyway, no?" Alero said, unhelpfully.

"Probably." Lucius stood up and poured some wine, a splash hitting the flame of the oil lamp on the table causing it to sizzle momentarily. "What about you? Your century ready?"

"Almost. We have the final lists from each one." Alerio handed Lucius the scroll, and then poured himself a cup too. "It'll be fine. You'll see. You're more capable than you give yourself credit for."

"Only the Gods know that, my friend," Lucius chuckled, downing the last of his wine and putting the clay cup back on the table.

"I know the last week has been...difficult..." Alerio said, looking uneasy.

"Yes," Lucius said without looking up at him. "I need to leave this place."

"Don't be so hasty. We're heading into the desert now - asps, scorpions, and sandstorms."

"And a good many Garamantians if I'm not mistaken."

"Likely." Alerio pat Lucius on the shoulder. "From the looks of things here," he said, pointing at the scattered scrolls and tablets on the table, "you're almost done. If I were you, I'd hit the baths one last time before we leave Alexandria. Who knows when you'll be able to enjoy such luxury next?"

Lucius closed his eyes. "Yes. You're right, of course. You should too."

"I will."

"I also want to visit Galenus one last time. He's been good to me."

"Take tomorrow," Alerio said. "We can cover for you. As long as you've obtained the imperial pass and procurement papers, we'll be fine."

"Thank you," Lucius said. "For now, I think I had better write home."

"Your father?" Alerio asked, surprised.

"No."

"I see. Well, I'll leave you to it, then. Good night, Tribune." Alerio saluted.

"Good night, Centurion," Lucius returned.

"Ha!" Alerio smiled. "I like how that sounds!" he said, before leaving the tent.

When Alerio was gone, Lucius ordered the documents he had been perusing and placed them in a leather envelope. Then, he found a clean sheet of papyrus among the items in his trunks and satchels, a stylus, and some ink, and sat down at the folding campaign table by the light of the lamp, and began to write.

From Tribune Lucius Metellus Anguis
To Alene Metella

Dear Sister,

I know it has been an age since I have written. I am sorry. I am leaving Alexandria and will be in Numidia by the time Janus takes us into the new year.

Alene, we are heading into the unknown...

The following day, after the morning meal and a final check on his century's preparations for the march, Lucius made his way through the streets of Alexandria for a last visit to the baths. His favourite baths were those in the heart of the Rhakotis district of the city, just northeast of the stadium.

He did not linger long, for he wanted to have as much time with Galenus as possible before heading back to III Parthica's camp and getting swept up in the final snags that would inevitably slow their departure from the city.

Nevertheless, Lucius enjoyed the warmth of the tepidarium, and the sweat that the caldarium worked out of him. He took his time with the oil and strigil, cleaning the lines of his arms, torso, and legs. Alerio was right, he knew. It would be a long time before they enjoyed such luxuries.

By the time he was finished with the cold plunge of the frigidarium, Lucius climbed out feeling fresh and alive.

He paid for a long session with one of the skilled massage slaves, and winced as the knots of worry and remorse were pressed and prodded until they disappeared. He flipped a bronze as to the slave and went to get dressed again in the apodyterium.

When he was back outside, the sounds of the city vendors replaced the play and splash of bath water, he made his way up the Via Aspendia to the library where he asked for Aelius Galenus one more time.

He was shown up to the rooftop where Galenus was taking his customary nap beneath an awning of white, Egyptian linen.

"Thank you, Origen," Lucius said to the young philosopher who had shown him up, and who was a colleague of Galenus'.

"Congratulations again, on your promotion, Lucius," the young man said.

Lucius nodded and smiled, then turned to where Galenus was reclining.

"So, Tribune Metellus..." the old man's gravelly voice said out loud, his eyes still closed. "My patient tells me you had an audience with him, that you are an exceptionally promising young man."

"Your patient, Galenus?"

Galenus opened his eyes and looked up at Lucius. "Why, the emperor of course! Who else?"

Lucius laughed. "He spoke of me?"

"We both did," Galenus said, sitting up now and inviting Lucius to sit across from him so that his back was to the sea.

Lucius could see the city of Alexandria spread out in glittering yellow and gold, brown, green, and purple behind Galenus. From atop the library, it looked beautiful.

"Yes, we did. And I told him that your intellect was wasted wandering the desert hunting down bumpkins and barbarians."

Lucius made to speak but words would not emanate from his open mouth.

Galenus laughed, but there was little mirth in his voice. "I see you are torn in your decision."

"Actually, no," Lucius answered defensively. "The promotion is a good one. The mission important."

Galenus raised an eyebrow and stared at Lucius.

"Do you remember the time I explained to my class the connection between the eyes, brain, and spine?"

"Yes," Lucius said, trying not to feel that familiar repulsion he got every time he recollected one of Galenus' classes.

"What did I say about the brain?"

"You said that most physicians dismiss it as useless."

"But?"

"But that the brain is the god of our bodies, and the other parts are kings and servants feeding into it."

"Yes. I'm glad to see some of what I teach has remained with you through the battles and blood." Galenus hung his head for a moment before continuing. "By the way, I am sorry to hear of what happened at Medea's villa, The experience must have been a traumatic one. She was lovely."

"She still is," Lucius said quickly.

"Of course," Galenus said, then shook his head. "At any rate, if the brain is a god, then you must use yours to its fullest, for you have a good one, despite your weak constitution when it comes to dissection."

"Please, Galenus. No more talk of the insides of cadavers."

"I'm speaking of your future now. I have placed an idea before the emperor which he is open to. He, after all, is a man of great learning and wisdom, despite his propensity for war."

"What idea?" Lucius was not sure he was happy about others discussing the path he should take, but these were powerful men, and he but new to the world in comparison.

Diodorus would have told him to listen to what they had to say.

"I would like to offer you a position at the Great Library of Alexandria."

"Me?" Lucius sat up. "Why? What would I do?"

"You would help me with research, and help to catalogue our scrolls of military history."

"You have dozens of men working on that. You don't need me."

"Oh, but I do. You see, you are a man of the world now. You have seen war, seen things that the young men within these hallowed walls cannot even imagine. That experience gives you a valuable perspective. And that perspective will help me to outline my thoughts on my philosophical studies."

"You don't need me for that. I have trouble keeping up with you." Lucius smiled, but the old man across from him did not.

"Oh, don't be foolish, young Lucius. The Gods rob me of things daily. I hide it well, and there is much I recollect, but there are too many instances where my mind grasps for a thought that I know is there, but the mind cannot reach. I'm getting old, as all men do. And so, I want a good man to rely on, someone I trust. And who better than the finest pupil of my long-time friend and colleague, Diodorus?"

Galenus smiled at Lucius, and reached out to pat the younger man's strong, calloused hand.

Lucius smiled back, but he knew he would have to disappoint him, though he did not want to. *Stay in Alexandria? Then I might be able to remain with Medea?* The thought was tempting, and suddenly, all the decisions he had made were turned upside down.

Galenus observed Lucius' indecision. "What kind of life will you lead in a world of war?" he asked. "Is there indeed such a thing as a long-lasting Pax Romana, or is that something more elusive, a fleeting occurrence between periods of bloodshed? If you make your home on the fields of Mars, what might the future hold for you? For the family you must someday want?"

Galenus stood from his chair slowly and walked past Lucius toward the low wall that looked out over the sea. The water was a bright turquoise, a colour of the Gods' creation, beautiful and perfect. Galenus stared at it for a few moments and then spoke again when Lucius came to his side.

"Do you remember when we first met, our discussion of the three parts of the soul?"

"Of course," Lucius said.

"Name them."

"The appetitive part, which resides in the liver and is represented by our natural urges, the animalistic side of our natures as humans, that side which seeks pleasure."

"Good. And?"

"The spiritual side, which resides in the heart, and which is governed by our passions. Thirdly, the rational part of our soul which resides in the brain and governs our perception of the world."

"Exactly." Galenus turned toward Lucius, the warm wind off the sea gently ruffling his clothes. "When we seek guidance, we turn to the Gods, yes?"

"Of course."

"Yet, as we have already discussed, the brain is the god of our person, something given us by the Gods. The rational part of our souls. Our perceptions. Would it not be right to listen to that part of our souls in times of dilemma, rather than the passionate or animalistic sides?"

"I suppose," Lucius said slowly.

"A life in the Great Library may not seem exciting to a young man, but I assure you that with discovery and knowledge comes much pleasure, especially for those with a passion for learning, as I know you possess. We are in the greatest city in the world, are we not? The city built by Alexander himself! This is a place where you can balance the three aspects of your soul while still making a great contribution to the world, to human knowledge and thought." Galenus stopped and caught his breath. He had grown excited at his thoughts and looked piqued. "Can such be said of a life in the imperial legions, or even in the Senate of Rome?"

Lucius looked at the old man before him for a few moments, a man who had made great discoveries, a man who had been the personal physician and confidant to some of Rome's greatest emperors. He was a man who had been a good friend of Lucius' beloved teacher!

Lucius looked at him then, and saw not the great man, but an old man, a man who now felt time slipping away, a man who had had his chance at greatness and did not want the adventure to end. Lucius wondered for whose benefit Galenus wanted him to stay? Lucius', or his own? There were plenty of young scholars who would gladly have helped Galenus as he wanted Lucius to help. Was Lucius' experience beyond the walls of the library, beyond Alexandria, that valuable? He did not think so.

What would Diodorus tell me? Lucius wondered, turning away from Galenus and pacing the terrace that overlooked the sea to one side, and the city of Alexander on the other. The Pharos smoked and gleamed where it stood across the great harbour, a beacon to lead the world to the greatest city on earth.

"Follow my heart," Lucius murmured to himself.

"What was that?" Galenus said, coming closer, his ear cocked that he might hear better.

"I should follow my heart, my friend."

Galenus sighed. "You are Diodorus' student, aren't you?"

Lucius nodded. "I know and understand all that you have said to be true and right."

"But?"

"But...I believe the Gods have another path set out for me, a path that leads west, across the sandy seas to Numidia."

"And what then? When you reach Numidia? More fighting, more women? We have those things here, in Alexandria."

"Yes," Lucius said sadly. "You do. But I have my duty to my men, to my family, and to my ancestors." For a moment, Lucius was back in the corridor at the Metellus domus in Rome, staring at the marble faces of all his ancestors, lined up in judgement. "I have a duty to the emperor, and to Rome. I'm Roman, not Greek. We are a people of Mars."

"And yet you pray to Apollo, a god of art, light, and healing, whose son, Asclepius, was the greatest physician of all time. I think you would be at home in Alexandria...but also

434

in Rome." Galenus smiled sadly. "I had hopes for you here, Lucius Metellus Anguis."

"I know, and I value your faith in me. I wish I had as much in myself."

"You should. I forget that you are so young. Like all heroes, perhaps you are meant to undergo the trials the Gods give you before settling into a life of peace?"

It was Lucius' turn to smile. "What you say rings true. I'm not saying my path won't lead back to Alexandria someday, just that, for now, it runs west."

"If you ever do return to this fair city, be sure to pour a libation of Chian wine upon my tomb, and tell me of your enlightenment."

Lucius was sad to think of such a thing, this great man burned, or buried beneath the sands.

"Do not be sad," Galenus said, his hand on Lucius' shoulder. "We are all dust. What remains is the goodness we have left behind. That is what matters."

Galenus walked over to the wall again and gazed out at the sea once more.

"Since you are leaving tomorrow, there is one more lesson I would give you, young dragon, man of Rome."

"Yes?" Lucius came up to stand beside him again.

"Philotimo."

"I've heard this word before."

"Not just a word. The word to govern all. A way of life! Did Diodorus ever speak of it?"

"Yes, he did." Lucius remembered Diodorus first telling him about it in the Forum Romanum, after a particularly violent storm. "I'd forgotten," he admitted.

435

"In that case, at this very moment in time, for you, I think it worth reviewing. Philotimo is the love of honour. It is one's deep love of family, and country, of one's society and the greater good. Philotimo is about every man's duty to better the state of his city, his world, and the lives of those all around him."

Lucius felt a chill run up his spine at the thought. He remembered now, and repeated the word in his mind. *Philotimo.*

"Philotimo," Galenus repeated as if hearing Lucius' thoughts. "It is about pursuing a life of goodness, and of selflessness. From what you have said to me this day, I know that there is strong philotimo in you, Lucius. Cherish it always, and do not let the ways of the world burn it from your soul."

"You are sounding more like a philosopher than a physician and scientist," Lucius said, smiling at the twinkle in Galenus' eyes.

Galenus laughed. "Almost eight hundred years ago, Thales of Miletus said that 'Philotimo, to the Greek, is like breathing. A Greek is not a Greek without it. He might as well not be alive.' I may be a man of science and thought, but I am also a Greek, and Philotimo is something that runs through every part of my soul."

"I understand. Thank you." Lucius grasped Galenus' hands and squeezed, overcome with inexplicable emotion in that moment.

Galenus looked back at Lucius, his aged eyes watery. "Lucius Metellus Anguis, stay true to the goodness of your nature in the midst of all the chaos and brutality you will face. Do that, and the Gods will indeed favour you."

Lucius bid farewell to Galenus and the numerous scholars at the library with whom he had become acquainted. They all wished him well as he descended the steps onto the Canopic Way. He felt as if he were bidding farewell to Diodorus one last time, but he knew that the choice he had made would have pleased his old mentor.

After stopping at a vendor of offerings on the slopes of mount Copron, Lucius made his way to the small temple of Apollo one last time.

The temple was empty, but for a single priest who acknowledged Lucius before leaving him in peace.

Lucius moved past the three pairs of flaming tripods until he stood before the statue of Apollo, tall and graceful, so expertly painted that he appeared to beckon Lucius over with one hand, his other holding a silver bow.

Lucius placed his bundle of rosemary upon the altar, then poured the olive oil over it, placing the delicate blue glass phial on the marble beside. He knelt and looked up at Apollo through the smoke that wafted from the two bronze tripods either side of the god.

"My Lord, Apollo. Tomorrow I set out with my cohort into the unknown. I do not know what to expect, but I feel it is the correct path." Lucius felt his heart pounding, the blood rushing in his ears. He shut his eyes tightly.

"Please watch over and protect me and my men on the road west. Grant me the skill, wisdom, and knowledge to be a good leader of men that I might honour Rome, my family, and you who have always been there for me. I... I am afraid, Far-Shooting Apollo, but I will face my fears." Lucius opened his eyes and gazed once more upon the visage of his patron god. "Please accept my humble offering and light my way in the darkness."

As the sun rose to the third hour of daylight the following morning, Lucius, Argus, Alerio, Antanelis, Maren, Eligius, and Garai reported to Legate Tertullius in the Principia while their men stood in the courtyard outside, ready to march.

Alerio and the others had been as good as their word the previous day, each having ensured that the individual centuries were well equipped and ready to depart.

Lucius had spent the rest of the night packing the remainder of his things so that the tent could be taken down and his items loaded onto the pack mules and wagons.

Lucius stood before his legate, with his centurions lined up behind him. His black armour was well-oiled, and every piece of silver polished to brilliance. His crimson cloak and fiery horsehair crest bristled as he stood to attention, his hand resting on the golden hilt of his ancestral gladius.

Legate Tertullius stood before them, his slave handing each of the men a cup of wine before he spoke.

"We've had a long road together," he said, the men nodding in agreement. "The Parthian campaign has been the largest campaign I have ever been involved with during my career. As a legate of the imperial legions, I see countless men, rank and file troops, centurions, and tribunes, come and go. I've seen the best and worst of men in my ranks. Those that have fallen short, I have always dealt with severely, some might say too harshly. But those who have fought bravely, with honour and discipline beneath the Gods' fateful gaze, I have always sought to honour and reward."

Tertullius held up his cup to each man, lastly to Lucius. "Gentlemen... Never were promotions more deserved. It has been my honour to command III Parthica with you in its ranks, beneath the sign of the centaur. I salute you!"

Tertullius drank deeply and the others followed, allowing the nectar to pour smoothly down their throats. Then the legate went to each centurion and grasped their forearms in friendship.

Each man thanked the legate and then left to attend to his century, leaving Lucius alone with Tertullius.

"You ready, Metellus?"

"Yes, sir. As ready as I can be," Lucius said honestly.

"Don't show weakness, Metellus. You are the one in command. You are no longer their friend, do you understand? You are young for a tribune, so you will be challenged."

"I understand, sir."

"Also, don't be too trusting of the provincial magistrates and governors. They will smile to your face, but then gladly put a pugio into your back if it suits their purpose. You are the arm of the emperor on this march. Remember that."

Lucius looked back at the legate and nodded. For a moment he wondered if it might be too late to take Galenus up on his offer, but he knew that that was only fear clawing at his breast.

"I'll do my duty for Rome, sir, and I'll always be grateful for the trust you placed in me."

"You're a true soldier, Metellus. The kind the Empire needs more of." He slapped Lucius' armoured shoulder and smiled. "The ancestral armour suits you well," he said kindly. "Now, take command of your men, and may the Gods go with you. Have the auguries been taken for your mission?"

"Yes, sir. Early this morning."

"And?"

"They are favourable."

"Good. Never make a move without the Gods' favour. It could lead to disaster."

The Principia courtyard was filled with sunlight glinting off of the lorica, helmet, and pilum tip of all four hundred and eighty men, lined up in orderly rows.

When Lucius and the legate stepped out into the light, the cornui sounded loud and clear in the morning air, and the men hailed their tribune.

"Ave, Metellus!" they yelled, their right arms saluting, and Lucius returning the salute, a distinct prickle of pride running the length of his body.

Each of the centurions were with their men, and a lone trooper from Alerio's century held Pegasus' reins for Lucius, to the left of where he stood.

The stallion stood tall and proud, and neighed as Lucius came into view, as if he were eager to get moving.

Lucius turned to salute the other tribunes of III Parthica, and then the legate one last time.

Tertullius nodded, and Lucius turned and went over to Pegasus.

He took the reigns from the trooper and spoke softly to the stallion as all eyes watched him. "Ready, Pegasus? Time for our adventure."

Lucius grabbed hold of two of the four saddle horns and pulled himself up to sit snugly in the saddle. He looked down at all of the men in his cohort, Pegasus moving slowly before them.

The wind picked up and pulled at his crimson cloak, dust flying about the courtyard, stinging his eyes slightly. He could already taste the grit of the desert in his mouth, but he did not mind. He knew this was the correct path.

"We have a long march ahead of us, men!" he called out. "But I know each of you is up to the task. You've been specially selected for this mission, and so I expect you to prove yourselves. Keep Disciplina close, and know that you are not alone in anything. We have fought and defeated the Parthians!" Many of the men cheered. "I know we are strong! Romans, Greeks, Syrians or others, we may come from different lands, but we have all been made in the same crucible of war! We are imperial troops!"

"Hail Metellus! Hail!" several of the men called out.

"Will you march with me?" Lucius asked, spinning Pegasus and then making him rear.

"Yes!" the men yelled.

"Then let's move out, and may the Gods bless our mission!"

The cornui sounded again and Lucius walked Pegasus through the middle of the cohort until he was on the via Principalis heading out of III Parthica's camp toward the Canopian gate of Alexandria.

Outside of the fort, the cavalry ala was waiting to join up with the cohort.

441

"Marching orders, sir?" said the gruff cavalry officer leading them.

"Yes, ah..."

"Brutus...sir."

"Cavalry to bring up the rear as we march through the city. Once we are on the road west, equal files of horse to march on the cohort's flanks. Understood?" Lucius looked across at the man who sat easily upon his mount.

"Understood...sir."

"Move out!" Lucius yelled, not paying any more attention to the cavalryman.

The cohort marched across the Eleusis plain, among the camps of the other legions, and Lucius was surprised to see salutes from other troops in the legions as he passed. He saluted back, and smiled at the catcalls that his men received behind him. Some things never changed.

The guards at the canopic gate had been given their orders to allow the force of troops to march through the city, and so when the gates were opened, Lucius rode through to blaring horns and a hundred thousand pairs of curious eyes lining the Canopic way.

They dazzled in the morning light and he wondered if the spirit of Alexander might be watching from the roof of his tomb.

Lucius looked to the monument of the great hero as they passed and saluted, garnering a cheer from the Alexandrian throng. They passed the library and the agora, and pressed on toward the Moon Gate of Alexandria.

As they approached, the massive doors were thrown open to reveal the line of the sea to their right, and the desert stretching off into the distance on their left.

Lucius shielded his eyes as the wind hit them full on and the march began.

When they were clear of the city, the men began their marching songs, settling into the pace that had carried them halfway around the Empire.

As Lucius Metellus Anguis rode at the head of his cohort, Alexandria faded like a distant mirage behind them.

On a distant dune, watching the file of men, horses, and carts plod on into the sand seas, the tall golden figure of Apollo observed them, leaning on his great silver bow, his sky-blue cloak moving slowly about him.

"I'll watch over you," he whispered. "You are not alone..."

The End

Thank you for reading!

Did you enjoy *A Dragon among the Eagles*? Here is what you can do next.

If you enjoyed this adventure with Lucius Metellus Anguis, and if you have a minute to spare, please post a short review on the web page where you purchased the book.

Reviews are a wonderful way for new readers to find this series of books and your help in spreading the word is greatly appreciated.

The story continues in *Children of Apollo*, and *Killing the Hydra*, and the next Eagles and Dragons novel will be coming soon, so be sure to sign-up for e-mail updates at:

http://eaglesanddragonspublishing.com/newsletter-join-the-legions/

Newsletter subscribers get a FREE BOOK, and first access to new releases, special offers, and much more!

Author's Note

A Dragon among the Eagles is not the first book I wrote in the Eagles and Dragons series. That journey began with *Children of Apollo* and *Killing the Hydra*.

However, I always wanted to go back to the events that led to Lucius Metellus Anguis' rise through the ranks of the imperial legions. The Parthian invasion was one of Rome's biggest military campaigns during the principate, and I thought it worthwhile treating these events in detail.

I had written a lot of back story, including the fall of Ctesiphon, and Lucius' time with the hetaira, Medea, in Alexandria. These and other bits and pieces were cut from the first two novels, and so I thought a prequel novel was a fantastic opportunity to explore the early days of Lucius' military career.

I've striven, as always, for historical accuracy, and attention to detail, in order to bring this world to life without overwhelming the reader with a history lesson. It was my tendency, in the early days of my writing career, to pack as much history into the text as possible. Thankfully, my late mentor, the poet Leila Pepper, and some of my fellow authors, helped me to rein in the sometimes overenthusiastic historian in me enough to allow the story to shine through. I'm certainly grateful to the folks mentioned, as well as my brilliant editor, for helping me to put story first.

The reign of Septimius Severus is a dream for an historical novelist. True, there are few primary sources, but the changes that took place during his reign, especially his changes to the army, allowed me to swing my sword and shield a bit more in the battle line, so to speak. Severus allowed for more mobility and promotion among the troops, and this allowed such things as regular troops being promoted to Equestrian positions. Severus knew how to treat his troops, and they returned the favour with loyalty. That is one of the reasons for his success as an emperor.

Septimius Severus and his Syrian empress, Julia Domna, were an impressive couple, both highly intelligent, and careful to honour the Gods. They were also strict believers in astrology, and so this adds another dimension to their characters which we see more of in subsequent books in the Eagles and Dragons series.

The two main sources for this period at the very end of the second century A.D. are Cassius Dio, and Herodian. Though Dio and Herodian both lived through the historical events of the time, Dio is generally seen as the more reliable source. Herodian held minor civil servant positions, and though unbiased in his writing, he would not have been privy to the imperial court the way Dio was as a senator and consul.

I've used Dio as a guide to my timeline for the Parthian campaign and the places where the action took place, including Nisibis, Hatra, and Ctesiphon. Historically, Septimius Severus did indeed march a force of 33 legions into Parthia. That's about 165,000 regular troops, plus Praetorians, and the auxiliary forces attached to every legion.

When reading Cassius Dio's *Historia Romana*, I realized I had to include the Roman general, Laetus. He was, it seems, one of the heroes of the Parthian war, having held Nisibis against the Parthian siege until Severus and his legions arrived. According to Dio, Laetus' troops were extremely loyal to him, but, as we have seen throughout Rome's history, that is not always a good thing. Severus had just come out of a bloody civil war against opposing generals, Pescenius Niger and Clodius Albinus, and so he was unlikely to allow Laetus to gain any more popularity.

General Laetus is a good example of a soldier who rises to heroic heights, but who is brought back down because of the threat he poses to those in power, mainly the emperor. I thought that Lucius' interactions with General Laetus were an excellent education for a young soldier seeking to rise in the ranks.

Where Laetus is a sort of martial and political mentor to Lucius, Aelius Galenus, or Galen, is Lucius' philosophic and intellectual mentor, as well as a link to Lucius' departed tutor, Diodorus, who was a formative influence on the young man growing up in Rome.

Historically, Galenus is one of the most famous physicians and philosophers of the Empire. He personally attended to such men as Lucius Verus, Marcus Aurelius, Commodus, Septimius Severus and Caracalla. An entire book could be written about Galenus' work and discoveries, too much to go into here, but some of the things he was famous for are his advances in scientific disciplines, including anatomy, physiology, pathology, pharmacology, and neurology, as well as philosophy and logic. Galenus' work provided the foundation for physicians through late Antiquity and the Middle Ages, right up to the early modern era. He was an impressive man.

Lucius meets Galenus while the physician is in the winter of his life, and I saw this as way to balance Lucius' youthful vigour and enthusiasm for war. He presents Lucius with an important choice that will determine the course of Lucius' life.

Lucius Metellus Anguis is, of course, a fictional character. However, the Metelli were real, and quite powerful during the days of the Roman Republic. During the principate, one stops hearing about them however, and so I made Lucius a descendant of a mysterious branch of that ancient family, one bearing the cognomen of Anguis. Anguis refers to the ancient worm, the serpent, python, or dragon. It is a primeval beast that is linked to Apollo, Lucius' patron god, and it is another name for the dragon constellation in the night sky, Draco as we know it. It is an ancient symbol of power and prophecy, and something which will guide Lucius in the years ahead.

Being a descendant of an ancient Equestrian family, the normal path for someone like Lucius would likely have been to do a minimum amount of time in the army as an officer, before entering into politics in Rome. That is what Lucius' father wanted for him, but Lucius, being young and idealistic, wanted to do it all on his own, and because of his constant opposition to his father, he decided to start at the bottom. Severus' changes to the army gave me the flexibility to do this.

Writing about an idealistic, young Roman who is marching to war in the East, it was difficult not to draw the parallel with Alexander the Great. Alexander is a titan of history, and I'm sure that many a warrior or general, including Severus himself, who has marched across that part of the world, has thought about him.

For Lucius, Alexander is the ideal commander, and a strong influence on him as a person and warrior. Alexander was indeed bold, and the Gods did favour him, in Lucius' eyes, and so what better place to end the story than in Alexandria.

This was the metropolis of the ancient world, and some believe that Alexander himself designed it. Alexandria had the busiest port, and was a place where learned men from everywhere came to teach and learn from each other, every subject and discipline imaginable. Of course, we know that the great library was burned during the time of Caesar and Cleopatra, but some research has shown that the library continued to exist. I don't doubt that the Alexandrians would not have given up so easily on one of their greatest assets. For this reason, I had no problem including a version of the library in this book, and having both Lucius and Galenus drawn to it.

The tomb of Alexander was another thing. The sources are a bit scattered, but there is mention by Diodorus of Sicily, and Strabo. Originally, Alexander was buried in a gold sarcophagus, but this was melted down by one of the Ptolemies to pay troops, and so, it was supposedly replaced with a sarcophagus of glass. As far as Severus' closing of the tomb upon his arrival in Egypt, this is something that Dio mentions, though the true reasons for the closure are unknown. It was certainly an odd move, especially as this was the most important shrine and tourist attraction of ancient Alexandria.

I took some liberties as far as my description of the tomb, replacing the glass with alabaster. I have aimed for accuracy as far as the location of the tomb on the streets of Alexandria, but the interior appearance and the tunnel from the library are my own inventions, though not out of the realm of possibility.

That's the great thing about historical fiction – you can explore the possibilities of history!

I do hope you enjoyed this book as much as I enjoyed researching and writing it. This is just the beginning of Lucius Metellus Anguis' journey which continues in the next book, *Children of Apollo*.

You can read more about the history of the period in *The World of A Dragon among the Eagles* blog series which can be found on the Eagles and Dragons Publishing website.

As ever, thank you for reading!

Adam Alexander Haviaras
Toronto, April 2016

Glossary

aedes – a temple; sometimes a room

aedituus – a keeper of a temple

aestivus – relating to summer; a summer camp or pasture

agora – Greek word for the central gathering place of a city or settlement

ala – an auxiliary cavalry unit

amita – an aunt

amphitheatre – an oval or round arena where people enjoyed gladiatorial combat and other spectacles

anguis – a dragon, serpent or hydra; also used to refer to the 'Draco' constellation

angusticlavius – 'narrow stripe' on a tunic; Lucius Metellus Anguis is a *tribunus angusticlavius*

apodyterium – the changing room of a bath house

aquila – a legion's eagle standard which was made of gold during the Empire

aquilifer – senior standard bearer in a Roman legion who carried the legion's eagle

ara – an altar

armilla – an arm band that served as a military decoration

as - a bronze coin; 400 asses = 1 gold aureus approx.

atrium – unroofed entrance room of a Roman house, usually containing a pool, or impluvium

augur – a priest who observes natural occurrences to determine if omens are good or bad; a soothsayer

aureus – a Roman gold coin; worth twenty-five silver *denarii*

auriga – a charioteer

ballista – an ancient missile-firing weapon that fired either heavy 'bolts' or rocks

bireme – a galley with two banks of oars on either side

bracae – knee or full-length breeches originally worn by barbarians but adopted by the Romans

caldarium – the 'hot' room of a bath house; from the Latin *calidus*

caligae – military shoes or boots with or without hobnail soles

cardo – a hinge-point or central, north-south thoroughfare in a fort or settlement, the *cardo maximus*

castrum – a Roman fort

cataphract – a heavy cavalryman; both horse and rider were armoured

cena- the principal, afternoon meal of the Romans

centurion – a Roman officer who commanded a century of 80 men; centurions were usually career soldiers

chiton – a long woollen tunic of Greek fashion

chryselephantine – ancient Greek sculptural medium using gold and ivory; used for cult statues

cingulum – a belt or harness

civica – relating to 'civic'; the civic crown was awarded to one who saved a Roman citizen in war

civitas – a settlement or commonwealth; an administrative centre in tribal areas of the Empire

clepsydra – a water clock

cognomen – the surname of a Roman which distinguished the branch of a gens collegia – an association or guild; e.g. *collegium pontificum* means 'college of priests'

colonia – a colony; also used for a farm or estate

consul – an honorary position in the Empire; during the Republic they presided over the Senate

contubernium – a military unit of eight men within a century who shared a tent

contus – a long cavalry spear; sometimes spelled 'kontus'

corbita – a type of large hold merchant ship

cornicen – the horn blower in a legion

cornu – a curved military horn

cornucopia – the horn of plenty

corona – a crown; often used as a military decoration

cubiculum – a bedchamber

cursus honorem - the course of honour; a specific career path for upper class Roman men

curia – the Senate building in the Roman Forum

curule – refers to the chair upon which Roman magistrates would sit (e.g. *curule aedile*)

decumanus – refers to the tenth; the *decumanus maximus* ran east to west in a Roman fort or city

denarius – A Roman silver coin; worth one hundred brass *sestertii*

dignitas – a Roman's worth, honour and reputation

domus – a home or house

draco – a military standard in the shape of a dragon's head first used by Sarmatians and adopted by Rome

draconarius – a military standard bearer who held the draco

duplicarius – trooper with special skills who receives double-pay (ex. an engineer)

eques – a horseman or rider

equites – cavalry; of the order of knights in ancient Rome

fabrica – a workshop

fabula – an untrue or mythical story; a play or drama

familia – a Roman's household, including slaves

fascies – double-headed axes bound in reeds and carried by lictors who followed senior officials

flammeum – a flame-coloured bridal veil

forum – an open square or marketplace; also a place of public business (e.g. the *Forum Romanum*)

fossa – a ditch or trench; a part of defensive earthworks

frigidarium – the 'cold room' of a bath house; a cold plunge pool

funeraticia – from *funereus* for funeral; the *collegia funeraticia* assured all received decent burial

garum – a fish sauce that was very popular in the Roman world

gens humanum – the human race; gens means clan

gladius – a Roman short sword

gorgon – a terrifying visage of a woman with snakes for hair; also known as Medusa

greaves – armoured shin and knee guards worn by high-ranking officers

groma – a surveying instrument; used for accurately marking out towns, marching camps and forts etc.

hasta – a spear or javelin

hastile – a staff with a large orb on one end, carried by an optio

heptastadion – a causeway built to connect Alexandria to the island of Pharos; seven stades long

hetaira – a courtesan; different from a common prostitute, or lupa

horreum – a granary

hydraulis – a water organ

hypocaust – area beneath a floor in a home or bath house that is heated by a furnace

images – standards that bore the image of the emperor and were carried with the legionary standards

imperator – a commander or leader; commander-in-chief

impluvium – the pool in a household atrium that was open to the sky and caught rain water

insula – a block of flats leased to the poor

intervallum – the space between two palisades

itinere – a road or itinerary; the journey

lanista – a gladiator trainer

lemure – a ghost

libellus – a little book or diary

lituus – the curved staff or wand of an augur; also a cavalry trumpet

lorica – body armour; can be made of mail, scales or metal strips; can also refer to a cuirass lupa – a common prostitute; lupa literally means 'she-wolf'

lupanar – a brothel; example is the 'Great Lupanar' of Pompeii

lustratio – a ritual purification, usually involving a sacrifice

manica – handcuffs; also refers to the long sleeves of a tunic

marita – wife

maritus – husband

matertera – a maternal aunt

maximus – meaning great or 'of greatness'

medicus – a doctor; army field doctor

missum – used as a call for mercy by the crowd for a gladiator who had fought bravely

murmillo – a heavily armed gladiator with a helmet, shield and sword

nomen – the *gens* of a family (as opposed to *cognomen* which was the specific branch of a wider *gens*)

nones – the fifth day of every month in the Roman calendar

novendialis – refers to the ninth day

nutrix – a wet-nurse or foster mother

nymphaeum – a pool, fountain or other monument dedicated to the nymphs

officium – an official employment; also a sense of duty or respect onager – a powerful catapult used by the Romans; named after a wild ass because of its kick

optio – the officer beneath a centurion; second-in-command within a century

palaestra – the open space of a gymnasium where wrestling, boxing and other such events were practiced

palliatus – indicating someone clad in a pallium

pancration – a no-holds-barred sport that combined wrestling and boxing

parentalis – of parents or ancestors; (e.g. *Parentalia* was a festival in honour of the dead)

parma – a small, round shield often used by light-armed troops; also referred to as *parmula*

pater – a father

pax – peace; a state of peace as opposed to war

peregrinus – a strange or foreign person or thing

peristylum – a peristyle; a colonnade around a building; can be inside or outside of a building or home

phalerae – decorative medals or discs worn by centurions or other officers on the chest

pilum – a heavy javelin used by Roman legionaries

plebeius – of the plebeian class or the people

pontifex – a Roman high priest

popa – a junior priest or temple servant

primus pilus – the senior centurion of a legion who commanded the first cohort

pronaos – the porch or entrance to a building such as a temple protome – an adornment on a work of art, usually a frontal view of an animal

pteruges – protective leather straps used on armour; often a leather skirt for officers

pugio – a dagger

quadriga – a four-horse chariot

quinqueremis – a ship with five banks of oars

retiarius – a gladiator who fights with a net and trident

rosemarinus – the herb rosemary

rudus – a heavy wooden *gladius* or sword used for practice and to build strength

rusticus – of the country; e.g. a *villa rustica* was a country villa

sacrum – sacred or holy; e.g. the *Via Sacra* or 'sacred way'

salii – the dancing priests of Mars who performed ritual dances in Rome's streets during the Festival of Mars

schola – a place of learning and learned discussion

scutum – the large, rectangular, curved shield of a legionary

secutor – a gladiator armed with a sword and shield; often pitted against a *retiarius*

sestertius – a Roman silver coin worth a quarter *denarius*

sica – a type of dagger

signum – a military standard or banner

signifer – a military standard bearer

sistrum – an ancient instrument or rattle made up of tiny cymbals spatha – an auxiliary trooper's long sword; normally used by cavalry because of its longer reach

spina – the ornamented, central median in stadiums such as the *Circus Maximus* in Rome

stadium – a measure of length approximately 607 feet; also refers to a race course

stibium – *antimony*, which was used for dyeing eyebrows by women in the ancient world

stoa – a columned, public walkway or portico for public use; often used by merchants to sell their wares

stola – a long outer garment worn by Roman women

strigilis – a curved scraper used at the baths to remove oil and grime from the skin

stylus – a bronze or wood 'pen' used to write with ink on papyrus, or on wax tablets

taberna – an inn or tavern

tablinum – an office or work space where documents are stored and business is conducted

tabula – a Roman board game similar to backgammon; also a writing-tablet for keeping records

tepidarium – the 'warm room' of a bath house

tessera – a piece of mosaic paving; a die for playing; also a small wooden plaque

testudo – a tortoise formation created by troops' interlocking shields

thraex – a gladiator in Thracian armour

titulus – a title of honour or honourable designation

torques – also 'torc'; a neck band worn by Celtic peoples and adopted by Rome as a military decoration trepidatio – trepidation, anxiety or alarm

tribunus – a senior officer in an imperial legion; there were six per legion, each commanding a cohort

triclinium – a dining room

trierarchus – the captain of a ship or fleet

tunica – a sleeved garment worn by both men and women

ustrinum – the site of a funeral pyre

vallum – an earthen wall or rampart with a palisade

veterinarius – a veterinary surgeon in the Roman army

vexillarius – a Roman standard bearer who carried the *vexillum* for each unit

vexillum – a standard carried in each unit of the Roman army

vicus – a settlement of civilians living outside a Roman fort

vigiles – Roman firemen; literally 'watchmen'

vinerod – a stick, or short staff, carried by a centurion that gave him the right to strike citizens

vitis – the twisted 'vinerod' of a Roman centurion; a centurion's emblem of office

vittae – a ribbon or band

Acknowledgements

As with every book I write, there are many people who deserve to be thanked. Some of them are aware of the help they have given to me, but there are many who are unaware of the aid or inspiration that they have provided, directly or indirectly.

This is my sixth novel, and I thought it about time to dedicate one to the troops out there in the world, of various countries, who are risking their lives to keep the world safe and civilized. I know that it is often a thankless job, and that it is most often not the soldier's choice to be sent into peril on foreign fields. To those of you whom I have spoken with, or read about, I thank you for the courage you display, and the horrors you have endured. And I would encourage my fellow civilians to not blame our troops for the failure of our politicians, but to honour them and thank them, to try and be aware of what they have endured, not least of which are the trials of PTSD (Post-Traumatic Stress Disorder).

As ever with my novels, great thanks go out to my dear friend Andrew Fenwick of Dundee, a passionate scholar and historical re-enactor who never stops learning. Our long talks over Skype, or glasses of Skinos in Greece have often fueled my creativity, and for that I'm ever grateful.

Every writer of historical fiction needs someone to review their work and words, and my use of Latin is certainly no exception. My gratitude to Costis Diassitis of Athens for his continued revision of my use of this ancient language, and the authenticity he has helped lend my books. If there are any mistakes, they are entirely my own.

As we all know, people do indeed judge a book by its cover. And so thanks must be given to my brilliant cover designer, Laura, at LLPix Photography and Design. She nailed the cover on the first go and added to the excitement that precedes an imminent launch. It's always a pleasure working with her.

I started writing at the same time I fell in love with history, and it is that love of history that I share with my readers. Thank you to all the wonderful Eagles and Dragons Publishing subscribers for your support and the conversations we have around this shared love of history and fiction.

And to those subscribers who willingly go the extra mile and act as Beta readers, your sound input and work has helped to make this book even better.

As ever, I have to thank my children for their constant enthusiasm, and for helping me to keep my hopes and ideals alive. No matter how dark the world gets, you always help me to see the light.

Finally, I must thank my wife, Angelina, for her unwavering faith in my abilities as a storyteller, and for her hard editorial comments that hurt more than a shower of Parthian arrows. This book is as much yours as it is mine, *Matia mou.*

Adam Alexander Haviaras

Toronto, April 2016

About the Author

Adam Alexander Haviaras is a writer and historian who has studied ancient and medieval history and archaeology in Canada and the United Kingdom. He currently resides in Toronto with his wife and children. *A Dragon among the Eagles* is his sixth novel.

Other works by Adam Alexander Haviaras:

The Eagles and Dragons series

A Dragon among the Eagles (Prequel)

Children of Apollo (Book I)

Killing the Hydra (Book II)

Warriors of Epona (Book III – Coming Fall 2016)

The Carpathian Interlude Series

Immortui (Part I)

Lykoi (Part II)

Thanatos (Part III - Coming Fall 2016)

The Mythologia Series

Chariot of the Son

Heart of Fire: A Novel of the Ancient Olympics

Short Stories

The Sea Released

Theoi

Nex (or, The Warrior Named for Death)

Stay Connected

To connect with Adam and learn more about the ancient world visit www.eaglesanddragonspublishing.com

Sign up for the Eagles and Dragons Publishing Newsletter at www.eaglesanddragonspublishing.com/newsletter-join-the-legions/ to receive a FREE BOOK, first access to new releases and posts on ancient history, special offers, and much more!

Readers can also connect with Adam on Twitter @AdamHaviaras and Instagram @ adam_haviaras.

On Facebook you can 'Like' the Eagles and Dragons page to get regular updates on new historical fiction and fantasy from Eagles and Dragons Publishing.

42553432R00292

Made in the USA
San Bernardino, CA
05 December 2016